THE FIRE BELL STRIKES AT MIDNIGHT

SHIRLEY FREITAS

First published in 2024 by Bloodhound Books.

Image of fictional Piñon County by illustrator, Michael Cashmore-Hingley

www.bloodhoundbooks.com

Print ISBN: 978-1-917449-03-8

The fire-bell at midnight disturbs your sleep, but it keeps you from being burned in your bed.

Edmund Burke, March 1771

A wildfire moves by wind and by whim, burns ferociously in one spot, jumps clean over another, resumes its devastation in scattered tracts far out from the original center of the holocaust. And it moves fast.

So it is with our urban areas. Wildfire-like, they consume a bit here, a piece there.

Samuel E. Wood and Alfred E. Heller,
California Going, Going…
(Sacramento, California,
California Tomorrow, 1962)
[at page 9]

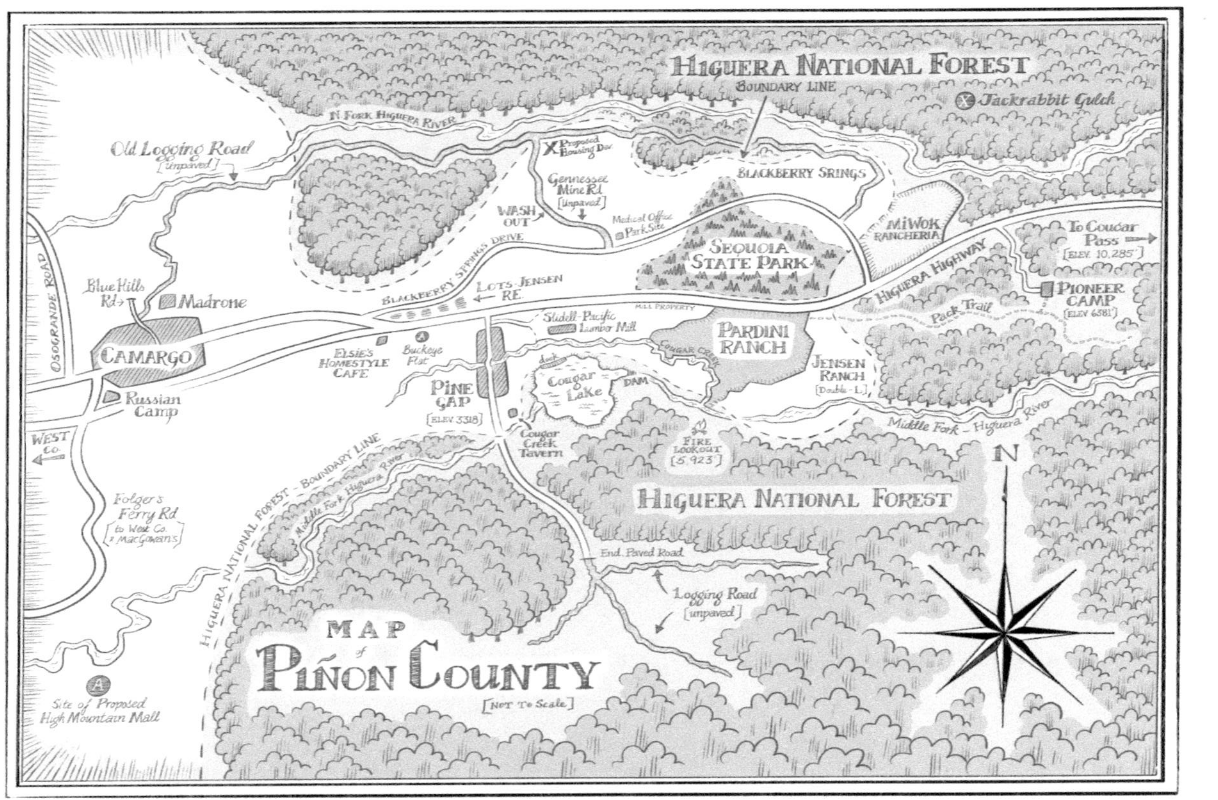

MAP
of
PIÑON COUNTY
[Not To Scale]
HIGUERA NATIONAL FOREST
Boundary Line
Jackrabbit Gulch
Old Logging Road
[unpaved]
El Fork Higuera River
Genessee Mine Rd
[unpaved]
Blackberry Springs
MIWOK RANCHERIA
To Cougar Pass
[Elev 10,285']
PIONEER CAMP
[Elev 6,781']
Blue Hills Rd
Madrone
Proposed Housing Dev.
Washed Out
Marked Office Park Site
SEQUOIA STATE PARK
Higuera Highway
Pack Trail
CAMARGO
Russian Camp
Elsie's Homestyle Café
Blackberry Springs Drive
Lots, Jensen R.E.
Buckeye Flat
Shell Pacific Lumber Mill
PARDINI RANCH
JENSEN RANCH
[Double-L]
Middle Fork Higuera River
HIGUERA NATIONAL FOREST
WEST to
Folger's Ferry Rd
to West Co.
& MacGowans
Site of Proposed
High Mountain Mall
OSOGRANDE ROAD
PINE GAP
[Elev 3,308']
Cougar Creek
Dam
Cougar Lake
Cougar Creek Tavern
FIRE LOOKOUT
[5,923']
End Paved Road
Logging Road
[unpaved]
Middle Fork of the Higuera River — Boundary Line
HIGUERA NATIONAL FOREST
N

Part I

SEPTEMBER 1984

FIRE SEASON

To other parts of the country, autumn brings flaming foliage that is a metaphor; here the flames are real, part of our culture, our literature, our sense of identity.

—Mary McNamara, "When nature's dragons awake,"
Los Angeles Times, Oct. 28, 2003 (page E9)

Chapter One

The first thing Roxanne noticed when her alarm went off Friday morning was that the winds had died; the second, that no wildfire had started. There was no smell of smoke, no sirens in the distance, no low-flying slurry bombers rumbling overhead. For a few moments she stayed in bed, savoring her relief. But duty called.

Thirty minutes later she pinned up her still-damp hair, glanced at her watch, and knocked on the bathroom door. "Carlos, your bus leaves in twelve minutes."

"Did you feed Baba?"

"Yes, he's outside already."

"Don't forget, I got track today." He came out of the bathroom wearing the bland expression he assumed on school days. Her heart constricted. He had never told her that high school was difficult because he was gentle, intellectual, and half-Mexican. He had never complained of being mocked because his poverty was evidenced by his clothes, his shoes, and even his school supplies.

She averted her eyes, not wanting him to see that she knew

he steeled himself every morning. "That's an awfully hot time of day to be running."

"Don't worry. Coach makes us drink a lot of water, and we only run three miles." He took a bowl from the dish drainer and opened the cereal cupboard.

"Well, I'll see you at four, *mijo*."

She took the car keys from the nail, stepped outside, and recoiled involuntarily. Heat from yesterday radiated up from the ground, while overhead the sun cooked up another scorcher from scratch. The door handle of her pickup was already warm.

The narrow streets were filled with aftereffects of the windstorm—pine needles and branches, mostly, but also food wrappers, yard ornaments, and an occasional trash can. The only apparent casualty was the road sign: *"Pine Gap. Pop 1,310. Elev 3,318."* The post had snapped and the sign lay face-down in the ditch.

Just east of town, puffy white columns jetted from the smokestacks, and every so often the ground trembled when a forklift dropped a load of two-by-sixes onto a truck trailer. The houses of people who worked the graveyard shift were quiet, with shades drawn and unretrieved newspapers already yellowing in driveways. The few Pine Gap residents who, like Roxanne, worked somewhere other than the lumber mill were getting ready for their own jobs, and the smells of coffee and bacon mingled with exhaust from idling pickup trucks. Kids of all ages were walking to the school bus stop. In the distance chain saws whined in tandem; dozens of trees must have gone down last night.

One sweeping curve brought her to a stretch of cleared land. It had been like this for three months now, but she still found it jarring. Stripped sugar pine trunks were stacked behind the sign announcing, *'Lots for Sale, Jensen Real Estate.'*

This part of the road used to feel cool and smell pungently of pine and sap. But without a bed of pine needles, the soil had turned to dust; every passing car raised a cloud.

She passed Buckeye Flat. Why it had ever been given that name was a mystery to her; yellow star thistle and poison oak flourished here, but not a single buckeye grew. And none were liable to grow in the future because, as a large sign announced, this was the future site of High Mountain Mall.

Elsie's Homestyle Café was just past Buckeye Flat. The building resembled an old hunting lodge, and according to old-timers it had looked exactly the same fifty years ago, except for the sign, a neon apple pie that blinked alternately with a bright blue 'Open 24 hours.'

Roxanne drove through the nearly full parking lot to the employee spaces. Entering the back door, she suppressed the wave of despair that threatened to engulf her every morning. It wasn't that she hated her job; it was never boring, and most days she felt that her efforts were appreciated. But a job's a job. By the end of her shift, she'd feel like she'd been rode hard and put in the barn wet.

The apron's sashes didn't seem as long as they used to be. Well, no surprise, considering the results of her weekly appointment with the bathroom scales. The real mystery was how in the hell she'd managed to gain two pounds in a week, when the weather had killed her appetite and she'd only eaten two meals a day.

On the other side of the wall, the air conditioner gasped and sputtered as if taking its last breath. Roxanne tensed until it settled back into its usual labored grinding, then walked out into the restaurant. It was seven on the dot. Every one of the twelve tables was occupied and Jill, the teenager who worked from five to eight, looked frazzled. On the jukebox, Tennessee Ernie Ford was another day older and deeper in debt. The cloud from the smoking section had already drifted over the rest of the diner.

Many tables were occupied by mill workers, identifiable—even if she hadn't already known them—by T-shirts so covered with sawdust that they were all a matching shade of beige. The counter seats were mostly the domain of ranchers, distinguished by their weathered skin, Wrangler jeans, and the long-sleeved snap-button shirts they wore year-round, the pockets of which bore round scars from tobacco tins.

She went behind the counter for her order pad, glancing at the blackboard for Wanda's daily words of wisdom, and laughed at today's message: 'Exercise daily. Eat Right. Die Anyway.'

Wanda gestured to the order on the shelf dividing kitchen from dining area. "Grab that, will ya, hon? It's for Seven."

"Got it." Roxanne lined the heavy platters along her arm, and brought them to the gas and electric company workers at Table Seven.

"Hey, Roxanne," Mark said. He was the ex-husband of her best friend, Loretta.

"Bet you boys are having a busy day," she said, sliding platters onto the table.

"Since about three in the morning."

"Oh, man," said the youngest man of the crew. "There's lines down all over the place, and broken limbs hanging off the lines that didn't go down. We lost five poles up highway."

"A lot of power outages?"

"Yeah, but most everyone's back up," Mark replied. "Blackberry Springs was down for the night. We just finished restoring power over there."

"The Rancheria's still out," the youngest man said. "That's where we're headed after breakfast."

Mark caught her eye and grinned. "Twenty houses in

Blackberry Springs. The Rancheria's got fifty houses and a couple businesses. Guess where they sent us first?"

One of the other men gestured to Roxanne that the Hangtown Fry was his. "Yeah, well, money talks, and you know what walks."

"I'll get you guys a refill."

As she went to get the pot, Mark called, "Roxanne, we're drinking Frisco today." So she grabbed the carafe of dark French roast, made from beans Wanda bought from a Bay Area roaster, along with the pot of the almost see-through coffee most customers wanted. She filled the PG&E workers' cups, then wended her way through the restaurant pouring refills and exchanging greetings. Just about every customer was a former classmate, or their parent or offspring.

Despite the poor local economy, the diner was always busy at breakfast. There wouldn't be a slow moment for hours. And whenever the front door opened, a searing blast rushed in, dooming the air conditioner's efforts. Every so often Roxanne ducked into the kitchen for the wet towel she kept in the refrigerator, and held it against her face and the back of her neck. The fry cook cooled himself by thrusting his arms into a bucket of ice, all the way past his elbows. Last week she'd seen him stick his head into the bucket. No wonder; the temperature in the kitchen felt double what it was out of it.

By eight o'clock, when Jill left for school, Roxanne was ready for the pressure of working the tables by herself. She gulped down a glass of ice water, her fourth of the day so far, just as another shift of mill workers arrived. The mill operated on staggered shifts, so that every half hour between seven and nine, another group of workers came in. With only forty-five minutes for their meal break, they needed their food quickly.

She hurried to deliver menus and ice water, and to bring the coffeepot to each newly occupied table, then circled back to take their orders.

At one large table she worked her way around to the sixth man, Jerry, who was still studying the menu like he'd never seen it before instead of seeing it practically every day for ten years. "Well, what I want don't seem to be on the menu," he drawled. "Guess I'll have the meat loaf sandwich. Make it hot, Roxanne. Nice and hot." He handed her the menu but when she took it, he tugged at it. "*Muy caliente,*" he said in an insinuating tone, but let go.

On Roxanne's next trip through the restaurant, she plunked an industrial-sized bottle of Tabasco sauce on their table and kept going.

Another customer came in as Roxanne was wiping down the counter. It was the new woman, the one who lived in Blackberry Springs. She had been coming to Elsie's a couple times a week, though normally a bit later in the morning than this. Roxanne knew only that her name was Arla Stinson and that she was from the Bay Area, was divorced and childless, and had paid $225,000 for her house. That, in a county where the average price of a house was $60,000.

She looked Roxanne's age or a little younger, but it was hard to say for sure; rich women didn't show their age the way normal women did. She had hair so sleek and glossy you'd swear she'd never had a split end in her life. She was petite and trim, with good bone structure and an exquisite complexion; if not conventionally beautiful, she was not far short of it, either.

There was some suspicion among mill workers that she might be a tree-hugger, although Piñon County wasn't a good place to move to if you believed lumber mills ought to be shut down. But so far, Arla hadn't said anything about logging. People's suspicions were based entirely on her being from the Bay Area.

"Morning," Roxanne said as Arla slid onto a stool at the counter. She grabbed the carafe of Frisco—not that she ever referred to it that way to Arla, since most San Franciscans flat out detested that nickname.

"Hi, Roxanne, thanks," Arla replied. "Another hot one already."

"It sure is. But at least the wind's died down."

"Oh, that wind! A big tree blew over."

"No one got hurt?"

Arla shook her head. "The road's blocked and the power was out all night, but they're working on all that now."

The cook called, "Order up!" and Roxanne took the plates over to the mill workers at Table Eleven. They stopped talking when she got within hearing distance. She wondered whether it was her they'd been talking about, or Arla Stinson.

She went back to the counter and took Arla's order. Arla smiled yes to a refill, and opened her newspaper. She probably had no idea that reading the *San Francisco Chronicle* marked her just as surely as what she'd paid for that house did. The *Sacramento Bee* had more local news, as well as all the scores from the previous night's games, which the *Chronicle* didn't because of early printing deadlines for the Piñon County edition. Besides, people just preferred the Sacramento paper, with its unapologetic lack of urbanity.

From the mill workers' table, Jerry called out, "You go jogging this morning, Miz Stinson?"

Arla swiveled in her stool. "Excuse me?"

Roxanne wondered if she realized that this was Jerry's way of saying, *I know who you are. I know your routine even though you just moved here a month ago.* She found herself feeling protective, one woman to another, despite Arla's Currier & Ives image of country life, the kind of romantic image city people often had, which led them to think of a guy like Jerry as a harmless bumpkin.

Another man at Jerry's table called out, "Aren't you afraid you might run into a bear or a lion, jogging up there?"

"Or something worse," one of the men cracked, "a guy like Jerry."

"Not the least bit worried," Arla replied with a smile. "I always bring my pistol."

The men's voices were loud. "Whoa!" "Watch out for this one!" The man who'd made the crack did a double take, and regarded Arla with admiration and unmistakable interest.

When the men left, Arla leaned over and said to Roxanne: "You know, I don't really."

"Don't really what?"

"Carry a pistol. Actually, I hate guns."

Roxanne dumped Arla's dishes into the bin under the counter, bit back a wisecrack, and murmured neutrally.

"Do *you* carry one?"

Roxanne was startled, but she knew Arla didn't mean to be impolite, and winked. "I ain't saying."

Arla laughed. "Sorry. I'm still getting used to…"

"The way things are here?" Roxanne grinned. "It's all right. Can I get you something else? Fresh blackberry pie?"

"You know, I probably shouldn't, but what the heck. *A la mode*, please. I'll just have to run a few extra miles tomorrow."

"I don't know how you can run in this heat." She took the pie from the display case.

"By going very early," Arla replied. "If I don't get out by six-thirty, forget it."

Roxanne was about to ask her opinion of mid-afternoon cross-country practice when two more regular customers arrived: Fred Arledge, the owner of the Cougar Creek Tavern, and Pete Jensen. They always came in after the morning rush, when other people were already at work. Fred kept late hours, running a bar. Pete Jensen owned a cattle ranch and a real estate business. By nine he'd already worked three or four hours on the ranch, which his son ran the rest of the day. Pete kept his own hours at Jensen Real Estate, and left the ten o'clock opening of the office to his secretary.

"Hello, Wanda, Roxanne," Fred called as they went to their favorite table, in the corner by the front window. Pete just nodded, setting his cowboy hat on an empty chair as Roxanne delivered ice water and filled their coffee cups.

She had never liked Pete Jensen. He was a master at ostensibly teasing remarks with a mean undercurrent subtle enough that anyone taking offense could be accused of hyper-sensitivity. Lately, he'd been prone to making crude comments about famous women (Margaret Thatcher, Barbara Walters, and now Geraldine Ferraro), claiming he was only making the sort of jokes women had better get used to if they wanted to compete with men. One recent morning he'd chortled over the female marathon runner who'd staggered over the finish line and been taken away in an ambulance, announcing that it proved a women's marathon had no place in the Olympics. Roxanne hadn't bothered to retort that men sometimes collapsed on playing fields and no one ever said it meant they had no business playing football.

She remembered, as a girl, hearing Pete use words that even before the civil rights movement were considered rude. One time, at a basketball game, he'd exhorted the Camargo High players, "Don't let Sambo get the ball!" He used to call the man who drove the propane truck, a white man who tanned unusually well, 'Blackie.' (Post-sixties these were fighting words, and Pete's use of them was more judicious.) He'd always called her father 'Swede Jim,' never just Jim. True, he'd never said anything to her alluding to her marriage to a Mexican-American and he treated her with the formal civility he used on tourists passing through town, but that worried her more than open antagonism would have.

There had long been rumors about how he treated his wife, although it had been a while since Roxanne had heard anyone talk about that. She saw Laura now and then, and had never seen any bruises on her. She didn't doubt Pete was capable of such brutality, though it was hard to envision even *him* actually hitting a woman as dreamy and placid as Laura. But you never knew what went on behind closed doors.

Roxanne topped up the catsup and mustard dispensers, and eavesdropped on Fred and Pete.

"…lots moving?"

"Once they start building the mall those lots'll sell." Pete stirred his coffee. "Fact is, we all need that mall. It'll bring the construction jobs, then service jobs. Other businesses need it as a draw. It'll be an economic boost for the whole county."

"Won't help me," Fred said gloomily.

The cook put up the order and Roxanne took Fred and Pete their breakfasts. She glanced out the window as a three-quarter-ton GMC pickup, painted purple and gray and bearing the Eagle Development and Construction logo on the door, pulled into the parking lot. That would be Ray coming for his coffee and bearclaw to go. She had them ready for him by the time he came in.

"Thanks, Rox," he said, handing her three dollars.

"You're late today."

"Yeah, it's been a crazy morning." He waved and left hurriedly, the sunlight glinting off his blond hair as he stepped outside.

Arla shook her head like someone coming out of a hallucination. "What did you put in this coffee?"

Roxanne laughed. "That's just Ray."

"Just Ray is just gorgeous."

"He is that."

"I suppose he's married…?"

"Yep. To my best friend's sister."

Arla glanced out the window at Ray getting into his truck. "Is every man in Piñon County married?"

"Nope. Only the ones worth asking about," Roxanne said, and Arla laughed.

"Oh well. I can enjoy the scenery, anyway." Arla took one more glance out the window and sighed. "I'm beginning to think this might be a difficult place for a single woman to live."

"It took you a month to figure that out?" Roxanne said drily.

Chapter Two

Stella leaned her face to the open window as the pickup turned onto the highway and picked up speed. But the wind was hot and provided little relief. Twenty miles later they neared town and she glanced at Joe, who was frowning as he looked at the dashboard gauges. "Is it overheating?" she asked.

"No, but the transmission doesn't feel right. It's shifting itself too soon. Why don't you drive when we come back, and see if you notice anything."

As they reached Camargo the digital temperature sign clicked from 103 to 104. Main Street was packed with cars at noon, but the sidewalks were almost deserted; the few souls braving the outdoors had cameras slung around their necks, and looked miserable. First-time visitors never expected such hot weather in a town at an elevation of over 2,500 feet. Residents, with their western stoicism, downplayed the heat. Tour books written by locals might mention that summers could be 'quite warm.' Planning their journeys from afar, travelers looked forward to the Mediterranean climate of California. After escaping the frigid summer fog of San

Francisco, they stepped from their air-conditioned cars into downtown Camargo and nearly fainted.

Tourism was a distant second to the county's major industry, logging. Other gold rush towns had greater charms than Camargo, and were far easier to get to. Visitors trickled through in summer and all but vanished in winter. Still, they did come, wanting to see where millions of dollars' worth of gold had been mined and hundreds of Westerns filmed.

Years ago stately Victorians stood at both ends of Main Street. They were gone, decimated by a fire at one end and a supermarket at the other. But the one in the center of town remained. She gazed out the open pickup window at the house baking in the high noon-time sun. Two giant valley oaks had once made the house a cool refuge on hot summer days. In 1964, long after she'd moved out, the trees had been cut down preparatory to the house being leveled. Preservationists had won a last-minute reprieve for the house, too late to save the oaks.

The house had been surrounded by a large yard, as all the houses in town once were; for property was not so dear as it was today, and the need for space was perhaps more appreciated. Now other buildings pressed in from either side— and in the back, where her Nonna had grown fruit, vegetables and herbs—was a small parking garage for city employees.

The pickup moved another few feet. The sun beat upon her arm. She slid to the middle of the seat for respite. It seemed that each summer felt progressively hotter and longer than the last, although she could probably thank her hormones for that. But everyone said that summers seemed worse lately. Hot just felt hotter when the land was parched.

For her and Joe, the drought brought more than discomfort.

They had been in the outfitting business for thirteen years.

It had taken five years to finally break even. They had done all right for the next few years. Then the drought struck.

In some respects they were fortunate. Pardini Ranch was blessed with an underground spring, and even now there was no danger of the well running dry. Forest fires were more likely during a drought, of course, but the ranch buildings were in a hollow, safely distant from the forest.

But when the fire danger level was high, the Forest Service prohibited campfires. That caused business to slacken, because no matter how hot the days, nights in the High Sierra were cold. The temperature often dropped into the low thirties, even in summer. For three consecutive years, campfires had been prohibited throughout most of August and September.

Worse, wilderness permits were sometimes canceled altogether. Stella had no quarrel with that; it was a necessary precaution. But it meant they were limited to taking clients on day trips only. Most people wanted to pack in for several days, so with Pardini Ranch unable to accommodate them they went to an outfitter at a different forest, where overnight camping wasn't prohibited.

In addition, last winter had brought a spate of problems. They'd had to replace a septic tank. One of the horses had been seriously ill, resulting in a $2,000 veterinarian bill. They'd had to re-roof both the house and the barn. In debt to suppliers, the IRS, and the Franchise Tax Board, and already paying on the loan they'd taken out to build the guest cabins, they'd gone to the local bank for help. They were able to clear their other debts, and the monthly payment of $1,000 would have been manageable had their business returned to pre-drought levels.

But it didn't. And last month, the day after they found out that one of the propane tanks would have to be repaired, they received a letter announcing a $160 per month increase in their business liability insurance premiums.

Patrick Burnham Insurance had always charged reasonable rates because Joe and Stella had only made a handful of claims over the years, none substantial. He had been profusely apologetic about the increase, explaining that it had been instituted by the company. If he didn't comply, the company might not renew his franchise.

There were few insurance agents in Piñon County, and Stella had spoken to all of them. She'd also spoken to some larger agencies down below. Horseback riding being statistically high-risk, the insurance companies quoted very high rates. Patrick's increased rates were lower than any Stella could find.

At the historic end of Main Street, the sidewalks were wooden, with hitching posts instead of parking meters. When the road divided, the gold rush buildings surrendered to modernity: fast-food emporiums with their spacious parking lots, then the even more voluminous auto dealerships. Joe parked on the far side of Giacometti Motors, away from all the new cars glinting blindingly in the sun. They put the sunshade in the windshield; it wouldn't keep the cab any cooler, but at least they'd be able to touch the steering wheel without getting blisters.

Patrick's one-man business was housed in a tiny office in a Quonset hut at the far end of the car lot. But it had air conditioning. Stella sighed happily as she sank into the proffered chair.

"Now, what did you want to see me about?" Patrick asked when pleasantries had been exchanged.

Joe and Stella exchanged a look, and Joe turned back to the agent. "Patrick, we're going to have to cancel the insurance on our house."

"Aw, Joe. That's awfully risky."

"We don't want to, but we can't afford to keep it up."

"Will it make that much of a difference to cancel the insurance?"

"In and of itself, not so much. We've made a few other changes that'll save us about the same. They add up to a few hundred dollars a month, and right now that makes a big difference."

Patrick grimaced and rubbed his chin. "Joe, if I could have, I would have kept the liability insurance what it was before."

"We know that. You've explained; we understand."

"If you weren't paying that hundred-sixty more a month–"

"It's the drought more than anything," Joe said. "If not for that and a couple of unexpected expenses, the increase wouldn't have been much of a problem."

Patrick was looking through their insurance policy. "What about the barn and stable and the guest cabins?"

"We'll keep the insurance for those," Joe said.

"Good. That's your business, there." Patrick sighed. "I don't like this, I don't mind telling you. You're taking a risk, and after all, this is fire country." They all three glanced out the window at the parched field.

"We don't like it either," Joe said. "But we've got to cut back somewhere."

"All right," Patrick said. "I'll have your policy redrafted and ready for you to sign by Tuesday afternoon, if that's okay?"

Stella smiled. "Patrick, if you wouldn't mind bringing the policy up to the ranch, you could have lunch with us Tuesday."

Patrick grinned broadly. "I was trying to figure out how to invite myself."

AS SHE DROVE the twenty-two miles back up the highway, Stella paid close attention to the sound and feel of the transmission. Joe was right. It would have to be taken to the mechanic. One more expense they could not afford but dare not evade.

She passed the Forest Service sign, *"Prevent Forest Fires! Fire Danger today:"*. Its thermometer-like indicator was at the highest, reddest mark. A half-mile farther, she put on the turn signal to warn the empty logging truck barreling up behind her. When she turned onto the dirt and gravel ranch road, the tension drained from her body at once. As always, she slowed at the rise. From here the center of the ranch spread out below, picturesque and serene.

While Joe rested up before cooking dinner, Stella prepared the cabins for the guests arriving tomorrow morning, then went to the barn to check the supplies. Since the group was small—four guests and Joe—seven horses would make the trip, including two packhorses. As always, Stella had put two extra horses on the special diet, just in case. The alternate jury, she called them. Once in a while, one of the horses came up lame, or wasn't in the proper frame of mind for a pack trip. That proved to be the case today: Mensa was decidedly unsettled, probably because of the high winds last night. But both alternates, Griselda and Decaff, were fine.

Griselda stood patiently while Stella examined her hooves. Griz was the ideal mountain horse. She had good feet, a strong solid body and prominent withers. More important was her temperament: she was quiet, gentle, and reliable, with great stamina and nerves of steel. She wasn't daunted by rushing streams, narrow trails, a coyote crossing the trail, the sudden appearance of mountain bikes, the panic of another horse. She didn't mind being hobbled in a campsite for hours, didn't complain about the special feed, and stoically accepted whatever responsibilities Joe gave her. She never pulled fly masks or blankets off the other horses.

Stella's own horse was the opposite in most respects. Tabasco was her indulgence, because there was no way he could ever go on a pack trip, not even if Stella herself rode him. "Beautiful bad boy," she murmured, stroking his muzzle. Tabasco nibbled at her pocket, hoping for an apple. She saddled him up and led him out of the stable. It would probably be her only chance to ride for the next few days.

Tabasco's hooves kicked up enough dust that Stella had to pull her kerchief up over her mouth and nose as they rode. A few days ago, the national news carried a story about the stunning autumn this year in New England and the likelihood of an early snowstorm next week. No doubt New Englanders weren't happy about raking up copious amounts of leaves and pulling out snow shovels and rock salt, but Stella couldn't help but feel envious. She was always sick of summer by late September, yearning for rain that would not come for another month, if then.

September was especially depressing this year. Ponds that had dried into stagnant mudholes in June were now as desiccated and cracked as a desert floor. Creekbeds were so dry that a scurrying chipmunk could raise a dust cloud. Even the hardy native weeds had not so much dried up as simply disintegrated.

She turned Tabasco south, toward Cougar Creek and the big meadow, parched and brown now. During March and sometimes into April its entire surface was a fragrant carpet of brilliant wildflowers.

She had not been able to shake the slight sense of apprehension for the meadow, a nagging feeling she'd had for three years. That April, unexpectedly heavy rains had produced a lush spring and wildflowers ran riot. At lower elevations, fields were blanketed with gold as far as the eye could see, while wetter areas displayed all shades of pink. Hillsides were covered with orange poppies and purple lupine. One meadow was filled with fiddlenecks, their sticky stems gracefully curved and adorned with small, exquisite gold blossoms. Stella had always been partial to fiddlenecks, the least showy of California's wildflowers.

A few days later, when Joe was in the high country with a group of customers on a quest for golden trout, Stella had taken a party for a day trip. The two men, from the Bay Area, were good-natured and convivial. So, liking them, wanting to share something special with them, she brought them back by way of the wildflower meadow.

"It is beautiful," one of the men remarked, surveying the landscape from horseback. "I can see why you're fond of it."

"How many acres is this field?" the other man asked.

"Oh, probably about fifteen," Stella said. "You see those red flowers by the rocks? That's Higuera paintbrush. This is the only place in the world it grows, this and one other spot in Piñon County."

"Is that right?" murmured the second man.

She imagined telling Joe later, '*Their eyes all but glazed over.*'

"You ever thought of selling this place?" the first man asked.

"You mean the wildflower meadow?"

"The whole spread."

"No, never!" He seemed surprised by her vehemence, and she added, "It's just, you see a pretty meadow, isn't that enough?"

"We're in the real estate business so we're always considering possibilities. It's an occupational hazard," he said, with a disarming smile.

A week later they sent a letter offering $700 an acre for the entire 967 acres of Pardini Ranch. That was before Blackberry Springs was even proposed, much less built; the idea that there would ever be real estate development this high up in the mountains and in so remote an area seemed absurd.

She suspected that the two men had made the offer on the spur of the moment, and probably regretted having made it.

Nevertheless, she and Joe sent a reply at once, turning down the offer.

She turned Tabasco into the national forest and soon heard the Middle Fork. At its shallowest this time of year, the river still rushed furiously along its rocky bed and was ice cold. Tabasco heard the river and perhaps smelled it, too; he nickered softly and picked up his pace.

Chapter Three

Friday passed so slowly that Kit felt trapped in a time warp. Sixth period felt no different today than it had felt yesterday, the day before that, or two weeks ago. The future loomed like a prison sentence. How could she bear this for four whole years?

She stared out the window and thought longingly of Sadie, who was probably anxious to get out, and silently promised: *As soon as I get home we'll go for a ride. We can go up to the fire lookout.*

Finally, the bell clanged. The corridors resounded with slamming lockers, shouts and laughter, Sammy Hagar and Run DMC dueling on boomboxes. Kit shoved her binder into her locker with all the schoolbooks; she had no intention of wasting any of her precious weekend on homework. She flung her nearly empty knapsack over her shoulder and was about to find her sister, but remembered there was a football game tonight. Cindy, a cheerleader, would be at the rally.

Dropping onto the shady grass in front of the gym, which reverberated with stomping and cheering, she took a book from her knapsack. It was a text on equine diseases. She was up to the part about the Chewing Disease.

But even in the shade, the heat was stifling, and it was hard to concentrate. She sighed and lay down, clasped her hands behind her neck, and stared up at the leaves of the sycamore trees. She couldn't keep her eyes open.

"Hey," said a soft male voice. Disoriented for a moment, Kit looked up to see Carlos Tejada looking down at her. She knew him from when they'd both gone to Pioneer Elementary. It had been a year since she had been this close to him, and she was surprised at how good-looking he had become.

"You're not going to the rally?"

"No!"

Carlos smiled. "Me either. I'm going home as soon as my mom gets here; do you want a ride?"

"Yes, that'd be great." Kit scrambled up and they walked to the front of the school. He was a junior, two years ahead of her, though only one year older because he'd skipped fourth grade. He lived over in Pine Gap, the lumber company town. His parents were divorced, and Kit had never seen his father, who was Mexican and from somewhere in the Valley.

She stole another glance at him. He had high cheekbones, as though a lot of his Mexican blood was Indian. His eyes were soft and brown with those long curly eyelashes boys seemed to have more often than girls. She saw peach-fuzz on his cheeks and felt a rush of warmth for him; unlike most boys, he hadn't started shaving just to make it grow in heavier. He had caramel-brown skin and black hair that, being wet, seemed even blacker. He smelled faintly of Ivory soap and store-brand herbal shampoo. Kit remembered that he was on the cross-country track team, so he'd probably just come from practice and a shower.

He must have sensed her eyes on him; he turned toward her. Her face immediately heated up, and she was mortified that he had seen both her gawking at him and her embarrassment at being caught.

But he said only, "We have a pickup. It won't be very comfortable."

"I can ride in the back."

Now Carlos flushed. "I meant, not that there isn't room, just that it doesn't have air conditioning."

"That's okay," she said. "Do you ever drive it?"

"Not yet. I get my learner's permit in two months." They had reached the sidewalk and turned toward the corner. "Next summer I'm going to get a job and save enough to buy my uncle's 1970 Volkswagen Bug."

A few moments later, his mother pulled up. "Mom, I offered a ride to Kit."

"Sure, no problem. Let's move these grocery bags into the back."

"It's okay, we'll get in the back."

"You sure? Maybe Kit would rather sit up here where it's not so windy?"

"No, that's okay, Roxanne," said Kit, and could have bitten her tongue, because she shouldn't have used her first name without asking. But she had never heard anyone call Roxanne 'Mrs. Tejada.' Dad referred to her as 'Swede Jim's daughter' or 'the Sjenstrom girl.' Or by insulting names that Kit quickly shoved from her mind.

To her relief, Roxanne smiled and didn't seem to take offense. "Okay, hop in."

They climbed into the truck bed and both shrieked at the touch of the hot metal. Carlos spread a blanket out and they sat with their backs against the cab. He was so close they were almost touching.

"What do you think of Camargo High so far?" he asked as the pickup joined the slow parade through downtown.

"I thought high school would be better than elementary, but so far it's worse. My classes are boring and the rooms are stuffy." Dare she confess what she hated most? He seemed nice, but what if he was nice only some of the time, or only in order to get her to show her weak points?

Then he said, "And everyone seems either shallow or cliquish, or both."

She looked at him quickly. "Well, yeah."

"That's how I felt, too, my freshman year."

"Not anymore?"

"I still do, but now it doesn't bother me. I just do my own thing and don't worry about what any of them think of me."

Kit knew what some of them thought of Carlos Tejada. She'd heard a few jocks call him 'faggot,' although her impression was that this wasn't because he was suspected of being gay, but because he was not macho.

He went on: "Camargo High is just a place we're stuck for four years. All you can do is get through it and get out. Then you can do what you really want to do."

What do *you* really want to do? she wanted to ask. Instead, she watched downtown Camargo crawling past: the ugly county office building almost right across the street from the elegant Victorian that everyone still called the Minelli House, even though it was now the county museum; the Argonaut, which looked like a bar in a Clint Eastwood Western but was filled with modern sleazy drunks Dirty Harry would've arrested; the big supermarket with its sprawling parking lot, followed by McDonald's, Taco Bell, and KFC. Then they were on the highway and picked up speed, making conversation impossible. Kit's short curly hair held its own against the wind, but Carlos's hair, longish and straight, whipped about his head.

As they whizzed past the Pine Gap turnoff, she noticed a sheriff's cruiser at the stop sign and recognized Dad's cousin Stick behind the wheel. She held her breath for a moment, but it didn't seem like he'd seen her.

Ten minutes later they reached the Double-L Ranch road and the pickup slowed to cross the cattle guard. Roxanne pulled into the turn-around near the house. To Kit's relief, Dad's pickup wasn't there, and neither was PJ's. She climbed out. "Thanks a lot for the ride, Roxanne."

"Sure, anytime." Roxanne smiled.

Suddenly, Kit felt shy around Carlos. He had climbed out of the back of the pickup too, and was about to get into the cab. She felt his soft eyes on her.

"See you around," he said, and his voice rose questioningly.

Kit nodded and walked toward the house. When she dared glance back, he was watching her from the window of the pickup. Safely distant now, she smiled and waved.

She raced upstairs to dump her knapsack and get her hat, kerchief, and gloves. When she ran back downstairs, her father had just come in. He was in the entry hall, going through the mail that Mom had placed where he wanted to find it every day, no matter what time he got home.

He glanced up at Kit, his brow creased with annoyance. "Sounds like a stampede."

"Sorry, Dad."

"What are you doing home, anyway? Isn't there a rally at school?" He paused at one of the envelopes.

"Yeah, but I didn't go. I wanted to come home and take Sadie out. I got a ride home." Immediately, Kit cursed herself for letting that slip out.

Dad stopped going through the mail and looked at her. "A ride? Who from?"

She desperately sought a plausible lie. "That new lady, Arla. She was driving past so I caught a ride with her."

He frowned. "Don't make a habit of that, Squirt."

"Of what?" She was genuinely confused, then it occurred to her that there was something Dad didn't like about the new woman. Probably that she was from the Bay Area.

"Of not going to the rallies. Your sister's the head cheerleader. What you do reflects on her."

The kitchen door swung shut behind him, but didn't close out his voice. "Laura, get me a beer."

Mom's voice was too soft for Kit to hear.

"No, I want it *now*. Do what I tell you."

Kit fled the house. Sadie heard her, and nickered before Kit reached the barn. Kit flung her arms around her horse, breathed in her aroma and laughed as Sadie nibbled at her shoulder with rubbery lips.

They rode all the way to the fire lookout, and proceeded slowly on the steep road up to the tower. When the ground was this dry the pebbles were as slippery as ice, making the trail treacherous even for a sure-footed horse.

The Forest Service no longer manned the lookout, which was on top of a tall, flat-topped mountain that stood by itself. The lookout was so far to the west that Pardini Ranch was now to Kit's east, and from this high up it resembled a model train village with its neat buildings, shade trees, and small pond with horses grazing.

Dad disliked Joe Pardini. He'd never made a secret of that, but lately he'd been more vocal about it. He jeered at the Pardinis' outfitting business and the city slickers who came up to rent Joe's horses and expertise, and called Joe a 'mule-headed dago' for continuing to operate such an unprofitable business.

Kit set off back toward the Double-L, stopping to let Sadie drink at the river. Suddenly Sadie looked up, ears flicking, and a few seconds later a horse and rider approached. It was Stella Pardini, riding a magnificent red quarter horse Kit didn't recognize. "Hi, Kit. How are you? How's Sadie?"

"We're both fine, just hot and thirsty." Kit dismounted and squatted by the river, splashing her face. "Is that a new horse?"

"New since I last saw you. When was that, May? June?"

"June, I think," Kit said. She'd never explained why she no longer visited Joe and Stella, but suspected they knew why. Now she only saw them on the trails occasionally.

"This is my baby." Stella patted the chestnut's neck. "His name's Tabasco."

"He's beautiful," Kit remarked. She broke the carrot in two and held out half on her palm, meanwhile patting and crooning to Tabasco over his good looks and stature. Sadie shook her head and blew; both Kit and Stella laughed and Kit gave Sadie the rest of the carrot, along with a couple of the sugar cubes she always carried in her pocket.

"You heading back?" Stella asked.

Kit nodded and remounted Sadie. They rode side by side.

"You just started freshman year, didn't you?"

"Yeah."

"I'll bet right about now, it seems like you'll be at Camargo High forever."

"Yeah," Kit said, glancing at her quickly.

"Didn't you think us old folks got bored in high school?" asked Stella.

"Uh, well," Kit stammered, and they both laughed. "Were you and Mom in the same class?"

"No, I was in the Class of '53. She was two years ahead of me."

"She lived next door to you, right?"

"Yes, with an empty lot in between."

"Mom said you were best friends," said Kit casually.

Stella smiled and nodded.

Kit wanted to ask the same question she never asked her mother. Instead, she said, "It's weird you were neighbors in town and now here too."

"Well, Piñon County isn't very big."

They rode slowly, talking horses all the way. At the fork, Stella turned west toward her ranch and Kit, east. Kit glanced back and Stella waved and called, "Maybe we can take a ride up toward the pass one of these days?"

"I'd like that," Kit answered. But she knew her father would never let her.

———

BY THE TIME she got home, Kit was late for dinner, which was always served at six-thirty on the dot. Cindy was preparing to drive back to Camargo for the football game; Dad and PJ were filling their plates and Mom sat silently with a pleasant smile. Or maybe a vacant smile, Kit thought, because by now Mom would've had at least one drink.

She tried to sneak up the stairs, but Dad roared, "Kit, get your ass in here!"

"Can't I take a shower first, Dad?"

"Get in here. *Now.*"

When she went into the dining room, her father pointed to her chair. "Laura, fix her a plate."

"I can get it myself, Dad," Kit said, but he ordered: "Sit!" and she did.

A few minutes later Cindy flew through the dining room, grabbing a piece of fried chicken and planting a kiss on Dad's forehead. "See you later."

"I'll be there about seven-thirty," Dad said. "Don't drive too fast, now."

During dinner, Dad and PJ talked ranch business. Kit preferred being left out of their conversation, but resented—irrationally, she knew—not being asked her opinion even on things she knew as much about as they did. Tonight they made plans to spray for flies one more time, since summer was dragging on; but they didn't ask Kit if she had any plans next weekend. They just assumed she was available.

PJ had lived at home all his life, except for a few years when he was in college and then, briefly, married. He seldom dated and often made disparaging remarks about the women in Piñon County. Dad went to Reno for business every month or so, and PJ always went with him. Within the family, the story was that PJ went over the hill to gamble. Kit had guessed the real reason.

She was hungry, as always. When she took a third helping of mashed potatoes and gravy, Dad remarked, "Better learn to curb that appetite, Squirt, or you'll end up weighing two hundred pounds."

"You'll look like junk food eating trailer trash," PJ chimed in. "Like a big fat hillbilly with five kids."

"Every one of 'em with a different father," Dad said.

"You'll have to move to Pine Gap."

"Everyone in Pine Gap isn't like that," Kit retorted.

"Damn near," PJ chortled.

"Not Roxanne Tejada."

PJ's face twitched and he dropped his fork. Dad's eyes flickered over to him. "Talk about a big assed hillbilly, huh, PJ?"

PJ reddened, the small scar on his cheek deepening to purple. "Why'd you mention her?"

"I don't know, PJ, I just thought of her when you—"

"I don't wanna hear about that spic lover!"

"Don't use that word!" Kit returned heatedly.

"I'm in my own goddamned house and I'll say whatever the hell I want! She's nothing but greaser-loving white trash!" PJ stormed from the dining room.

Kit was taken aback by his vehemence. "Geez, what's his problem?"

Dad's eyebrows went up. "PJ has strong feelings about race mixing, Kit; you know that."

"Mexicans are a different nationality, not a different race!" she exclaimed, and even as she said it, she was angry with herself for addressing what wasn't the point, and ignoring what mattered.

"Wrong," Dad said. "Most of 'em are half Indian."

Suddenly, to Kit's surprise, Mom laughed.

Dad glared at her. "What the hell's so funny?"

"We live in a land that was once part of Mexico."

She must be drunker than she looked, Kit thought nervously. Mom rarely spoke during an argument; she'd usually just have another sip and wait it out.

"What the hell does that have to do with anything?" Dad said irritably. "It was a hundred fifty years ago."

"Many pioneer families have Mexican blood," Mom continued, and Kit silently pleaded for her to stop, before he really got mad. "Most of the American gold miners were young and single, and some of them married Mexican women."

"That's right, Dad," Kit said quickly. "We did genealogies in history class last year, and–"

"So that's the kind of crap they've got you kids doing?" Dad curled his lip. "Well, listen, Squirt. Maybe some pioneer families have a wetback in the woodpile, but there's not one in the Jensen family tree. The Jensens are pure European stock. Now, *Laura's* illustrious clan…" He winked at Kit. "You won't be doing genealogies on that bunch."

"Why wouldn't she?" Mom said. Her voice was wavery, as if she was trying to control her anger. "I'm not ashamed that my great-grandmother was a full-blooded Cherokee."

Dad grinned. "That's the Okie side of her family tree. Okies think they're white if they've only got one Indian in the woodpile and no coons."

"Dad, don't," Kit protested.

Dad's grin hardened. "The point is, race mixing rubs most people the wrong way, including your brother."

She declined his invitation to go to the game. After helping

Mom with the dishes, she cleaned tack and swept the stalls, talking to Sadie the whole time. She went to bed after ten o'clock but couldn't sleep. She lay in bed thinking how lonely she was and scorning herself for her self-pity.

I just want a friend, she said to herself. That's all. I want him for a friend.

But she knew it might not be possible. Because it was one thing to be friends with a boy when you were ten, but things were different at fourteen.

She turned her face into the pillow. She couldn't stop thinking about the way his throat had looked with the blue shirt unbuttoned and his black hair lying damp against his skin.

Chapter Four

About to enter the crowded bar, Roxanne paused to orient herself. Cigarette smoke swirled up into the overhead fans, then settled over the patrons like swamp fog. With admiration and a touch of professional envy, Roxanne watched one dexterous cocktail waitress raise her tray at exactly the last moment to avoid a clutch of patrons; swing her hips between an obstacle course of chairs and tables; and sure-footedly skirt puddles of beer and treacherous pools of less savory provenance.

A great cacophony filled the tavern: clinking glasses, the clack of balls on the pool table, twanging guitars and wailing voices from the jukebox, pinball machine bells, the slamming of the cup against the bar in endless games of liar's dice, yells and groans from patrons watching the Giants-Dodgers game.

Aside from the general store-gas station, Cougar Creek Tavern was the only commercial establishment in Pine Gap. Situated south of town, its large sign warned, 'Last beer for fifty miles!' In fact, the road shortly entered the Higuera National Forest, where the pavement ended.

Waiting at the bar to buy a pitcher of draft, she greeted Clay DiMauro, who sat on a stool with a half-full stein in front of him. He wore his work clothes and she reflected that only a Piñon County native could hang out in a lumber town tavern while wearing a Forest Service uniform.

Then someone called out, "Hey, Clay, save another chipmunk habitat today?"

"Not a damned one," Clay replied amiably. "I was too busy building logging roads."

Roxanne chuckled, retrieved her beer and made her way to the rear of the tavern, where Loretta sat at a small table. She looked morose, and told Roxanne the mill had announced another round of layoffs was coming. Loretta was pretty sure she'd be in that one. But she didn't feel like spending Friday night talking about work, and their conversation soon shifted to their kids, then segued to Loretta's sister Terri and her husband. Roxanne was about to tell her how at Elsie's this morning, Arla Stinson had nearly fallen off her stool checking out Ray. But laughter and shouts erupted nearby. She glanced over and saw it was coming from Jerry Frye and his cohorts.

One of the men at Jerry's table was loudly saying: "…and the next thing you know, a Mexican has your job!"

"That's affirmative action," Jerry said, drawling out the words.

People in his vicinity sat silent. Waiting, Roxanne thought, like I am, to see if it ends here.

"If your name's Sanchez or Martinez, boom, you're hired," another man said, snapping his fingers.

Jerry proclaimed loudly, "And why the hell's any Mex need a job at the mill, when there's dishes to wash and lawns to mow!"

The men at his table guffawed.

"Grapes to pick!" Jerry shouted.

Roxanne looked around the tavern. Three MiWok men at the bar had all turned to look at Jerry, deliberately expressionless. At another table, several white mill workers stared at Jerry with open hostility.

"I'll tell you one thing," Jerry yelled above the laughter of his friends, "no beaner has to sleep alone in Pine Gap."

Their whoops sounded hollow against the silence that rolled over the entire tavern. Even the pool players stopped. The only other voices were someone on the TV extolling the feeling of a Toyota and Patsy Cline walking after midnight.

Roxanne felt many eyes upon her and felt too the way a lot of eyes were deliberately not looking at her. She was breathing shallowly.

Then, without warning, Loretta called out: "Why's that, Jerry?"

Through the haze of smoke and alcohol, Jerry squinted in their direction. "Why's what?"

Loretta spoke conversationally. "Why is it no Mexican has to sleep alone in Pine Gap?"

Finally seeming to understand that he had gone too far, Jerry glanced casually around the silent tavern.

"Weird, isn't it?" Loretta continued. "Here *you* are, an eligible white man with a job, but *you* still sleep alone."

The tavern erupted in laughter and catcalls. Jerry's face burned so red it seemed to glow in the dim light.

"Darned affirmative action," drawled a woman from another part of the bar.

Jerry grabbed an empty beer bottle by the neck and stood up so abruptly his chair crashed to the floor behind him. His eyes never left Loretta.

Immediately, he was surrounded by men. One took the bottle away and others began trying to persuade him to mellow out. The noise picked up in the bar again, but Jerry's voice could still be heard calling Loretta, or perhaps women in general, by a very crude word.

"You're the one started it, Jerry," Fred called. "Now take it easy." He spoke with the calm self-assurance of someone reasonably certain that he could deal with whatever arose. Which Roxanne interpreted to mean, he was reasonably certain he had superior firepower.

The three MiWok men were still watching. One of them was grinning.

"What the fuck you looking at, Tonto?" Jerry exclaimed.

"Okay, that's it," Fred said. "You're out of here, Jerry."

Fred, with help from Clay and a few other patrons, escorted Jerry out of the bar. The noise level in the bar rose again and the atmosphere was touched by the giddiness that always came after averted disaster. Roxanne glanced at the clock: bar time was 11:38pm. She had told Carlos she'd be home before midnight. "I gotta go soon. No more beer for me."

Clay stopped at their table to let them know that Jerry wasn't hanging out in the parking lot. "Some people can't drink; it just brings out their inner idiot."

"Yeah," Loretta said, "and in some people, the inner idiot is already pretty near the surface."

"Sit down, Clay," Roxanne said, and filled his stein. "Were you in the forest today?"

He grimaced. "There's way too much dead wood." He took a long gulp of beer. "It wasn't always this bad. You know the Forest Service leases land to ranchers for summer pasturing? Well, up till thirty, forty years ago, the ranchers always set brush fires when they moved the cattle down for the winter, burned off all the dead brush. They don't let them do that anymore. Someone told me they still do it in Mexico, so they don't have the kind of fires we have. We ought to do more control burns."

Remembering one that had jumped out of containment near Tahoe a few years ago, Roxanne said, "Not in this weather."

"No," he agreed. "The winds were fifty miles an hour last

night. And I'll tell you this," he leaned closer, lowering his voice, "if a fire started in the Higuera tomorrow? Pine Gap would be in big trouble. They didn't leave enough resources here. There's no reserve to tap. And it's too windy to drop retardant."

But Roxanne thought it highly unlikely Pine Gap would be destroyed. Remote fishing or hunting camps often burned up in forest fires, but only rarely towns or settlements where people lived year-round. Of course, things were different in southern California, where towns burned up every year—even long-established, well-populated, wealthy towns. She still remembered TV footage of the Bel Air fire in 1961, flames racing along the ridgetop, consuming mansions one after the other.

"Well, your brother would be proud of you," she said. He gave her a quizzical look and she added, "You work in public service."

Clay chortled. "My public service is mostly marking trees to sell to lumber companies, and keeping up the roads for their trucks. And you know what's the first thing the For'Service does after a fire? Takes bids for salvage logging. Lumber companies end up getting all the trees they couldn't have logged."

"Makes you wonder," Loretta said.

"Yeah, don't it?" Clay reached for the pitcher and refilled his glass. "But I'll be getting training this winter on how to investigate wildland arson."

"Bobby would definitely be proud of that," Roxanne said. She raised her nearly-empty stein. "To Bobby."

They all clinked glasses.

Chapter Five

Arla rose early and took her coffee onto the deck. Already the air felt warm and the sun's rays, pushing through the flowering oleander behind the pool, glinted on the water invitingly.

She was coming to love this house, as well as the things New Yorkers denigrated about California. Instead of trudging to five shops every day, she found everything in one supermarket, including not only wine and beer but hard liquor, even on Sundays. Succulent fruits and crisp vegetables were plentiful all year. She enjoyed driving, which she'd intensely disliked doing in New York. And here, she didn't have to make an appointment twenty-four hours in advance to get her car out of the garage or pay $300 a month for the privilege.

She had paid cash for the house and still had plenty of money left, thanks to the settlement. There had been no arguments about that, much to the dismay of their lawyers.

Steve had been a homesick Californian when they'd met at NYU. She'd been to Europe four times and to the Caribbean twice, but had never been west of the Rockies, and they'd gone to Yosemite on spring break. She'd fallen in love with the vast spaces, impossibly tall trees, endless mountains, vivid blue sky.

The next year they'd taken a pack trip over Cougar Pass, with Joe Pardini as the guide. After they married, their visits to Steve's family in San Mateo often included a trip to the Sierras to either waterski or snow ski, or in late spring to do both on the same day.

Arla had worked for the two years Steve was going to grad school, and for three more years while he was putting the business together. She'd actually liked the second job, as a fundraiser for the cancer hospital. But that didn't diminish the fact that she had worked and Steve hadn't. And that it was her working that had made it possible for him to start the business. And that, when the business was a year old, still not really established, she'd quit her high-salaried job and gone to work with Steve. Not *for* Steve; *with* him. It was *their* company, not his. *He* hadn't struck it rich; *they* had.

The mid-70s had been exactly the right time to open a clothing store catering to the sort of people who subscribed to *National Geographic* and *Alaska Magazine*; people who hiked the Appalachian Trail, followed the whale migration, rafted the Colorado River, climbed glaciers in Tierra del Fuego, went on photo safaris in Kenya.

One store grew to four; then Steve tired of what had become more work than passion. So they sold the company to a sports apparel conglomerate. Even after the investors were compensated, accounts settled, lawyers satisfied, and IRS paid, a considerable amount of money was left. Arla and Steve tried to rekindle their affection by moving to California. They took an extended vacation in Europe. They bought cars, artwork, and a condo in Maui. Nothing worked.

Nor did they deplete the fortune. The divorce settlement granted Arla $3 million and a lot more in stocks. Steve got the same, along with the custom-built house in Marin. They maintained joint ownership of the Hawaiian condo. And Arla got the dog. They'd had more acrimony over that than over the money.

What would her friends in New York think, Arla wondered, if they knew she had come to recognize the sound of a rattlesnake? That she could, at a glance, distinguish the web of a black widow spider from an ordinary spiderweb?

But she was on her own, and entirely free. She didn't have to work, but could if she chose. She could swim nude at midday in her own swimming pool. She could jog ten miles without worrying about being late for something. And oh, the space! In New York, land was measured by the square foot, except for Central Park, that vast expanse of 843 acres—100 acres smaller than Joe and Stella's ranch. The Higuera National Forest had almost a million acres. It was larger than Rhode Island.

And she had options. If she got tired of living here, she could sell the house and move back to San Francisco or New York. Or to Paris or London, for that matter.

The sun was creeping ever higher. Arla finished her coffee and whistled for Morgan, who as usual was sleeping in. He came out to the deck, yawned, stretched, and leaned against her, his long heavy tail thumping against the back of her knees. His lineage was uncertain; he had the running ability of a Lab, the sweet temperament of a golden retriever, and an alert intelligence that hinted at terrier.

They left the house and took the infrequently traveled Blackberry Springs Drive toward Camargo. Arla's first few weeks here, she'd jogged on the highway, thinking that since it was less isolated it would be safer. But she'd had to step off the road whenever a car went by. Men had whooped and honked at her. She'd worried that Morgan might get hit, even though she always kept him on a leash. So she'd switched to running on Blackberry Springs Drive. Some days she ran six miles without seeing a single vehicle on that road.

After the first mile came a long steep downhill stretch and, ever mindful of her knees, she walked, letting Morgan off the leash. He kept darting into the trees then back out to check on her. The sun had already burned off the morning coolness and she was sweating.

Maybe she'd go to the diner for breakfast. She'd been surprised at how good the food was at Elsie's—strong coffee, real butter on the toast, pies made from scratch. Another plus was that locals went there. Since Arla had no job and no children, how else would she ever meet anyone? So far, though, people hadn't been very friendly. Or rather, they were only superficially friendly. They chatted, but didn't ask her over to dinner or to come watch their kid's baseball game. Maybe that was because her car sported a KQED decal, while the cars and pickups in Elsie's parking lot had bumper stickers endorsing the National Rifle Association, the Teamsters, and Reagan-Bush in '84. She'd been happily surprised one morning to pull into Elsie's and see an old clunker with a bumper sticker reading 'Earth First!' until she saw the smaller print: 'We'll log the other planets later.'

Her only friends in Piñon County were Joe and Stella Pardini. Once she'd had dinner at their house; once she'd taken them out. But their busy season was not yet over, and Arla understood that they couldn't afford time off during the only time of year the ranch brought in money.

But for the most part, she didn't consider her lack of a wide social circle here to be a problem. Marin County had been too small and insular for both members of a divorced couple – almost as small and insular as Manhattan. She'd had to move to a county with only 15,000 people, its largest town holding about 4,000, to find anonymity.

When the slope lessened and the road began winding among big, gnarly oak trees, she reattached Morgan's leash. They jogged along at a steady 7:45-per-mile pace, fast enough so she never forgot she was running, slow enough to keep it up. She was still amazed that Joan Benoit had kept a 5:30 pace for twenty-six miles and had looked barely tired taking that last lap in the stadium.

At the point where the branches of two giant old oaks met over the road, Arla turned around. Now it was four miles back, mostly uphill. She intended to run the entire four miles, since running uphill was not hard on the joints and did wonders for the rear end. Mainly, though, she considered it training for the Dipsea. She intended to win the race in 1988, when she would turn forty and get a handicap of at least ten minutes.

Jogging up the long hill, concentrating on her breathing and the length of her stride and the surface of the road—anything except the ache in her quadriceps and the laboring of her lungs—she heard the whining of a car engine. She looked back and saw two large pickup trucks driving slowly up the hill. She moved to the edge of the road to let them pass.

Both trucks were purple and gray with 'Eagle Development & Construction' painted on their side panels. Arla's heart would have beat faster if it weren't already racing at 130 beats per minute, because the pickups were just like the one the beautiful man had been driving Friday morning. Adonis. That day she'd been too busy staring at him to see more than the color of his pickup; now she realized he must work for Eagle, the company that had built her house and all the houses in Blackberry Springs.

The second truck passed and a handsome young Native American sitting in the back grinned encouragement, gave her a thumbs-up. Her legs felt like rubber. The two trucks rounded a turn and were gone. She released Morgan and forced herself to continue running.

Not much further, she came upon the two pickups parked beside a dirt road. Arla used that dirt road as a landmark when she was running: from here it was two and a half miles to home. There was a cattle guard about thirty feet in, and a bullet-riddled sign that prohibited hunting.

Eight men stood in a meadow, driving stakes with orange flags into the ground. The Indian was the closest to the road, his back to Arla.

Morgan made a beeline for the men. When she called him, the men turned to look at her. She felt suddenly exposed, in her tiny nylon shorts and the crop top that bared part of her abdomen. Morgan came prancing back and she leashed him.

Then she saw him. Adonis. He knocked the breath out of her more surely than that hill.

The faded blue jeans didn't hide the muscular shape of his thighs. When he turned sideways, a jolt shot from her brain straight down between her legs.

But while men felt perfectly free to gape at women, the reverse was not customary and could even be dangerous. Unless you were at a baseball game and could freely gaze at all the athletic young men in tight pants. But she wasn't at Yankee Stadium, so she forced her eyes away from Adonis.

Ridiculous woman, she chided herself. He probably knows he's beautiful and never lets a woman forget it. Never lets his *wife* forget it.

I wonder if he sleeps with other women besides his wife?

Well, if he does, he's probably a lousy lover, like the handsome ones so often are. It's probably so easy for him to get a woman to bed he doesn't care whether he pleases her or not; if she doesn't come back, there's always some other woman waiting for his invitation.

Yes, yes, yes, but for pure beauty alone, my God, he was truly a work of art.

It took all her willpower not to glance back for one more look.

Chapter Six

The fire road started just outside town and ran alongside the North Fork Higuera River for twenty-some miles, climbing over 2,000 feet in elevation before turning sharply to the south, where it dead-ended at the east end of Blackberry Springs Drive. The Forest Service kept it up only enough for their service vehicles. Logging trucks hadn't used this road for at least twenty years.

No way could construction vehicles use it. Ray had told his boss that much already, but Mr. Cushing wanted to make certain and had told him to drive the road in order to ascertain the condition of the first fifteen miles, up to Gennessee Mine Road.

Mr. Cushing had plans for both ends of the road. Here at the northern end, on the border of the national forest and less than a half-mile from the steep canyon down to the North Fork, he had bought fifty-eight acres for a housing development.

Ray stopped his truck, looked around and shook his head. People never used to build this close to the forest, or so near a river gorge. Certainly not as close to the gorge and the forest as Mr. Cushing now intended on doing.

The development would be larger than Blackberry Springs, but not as upscale; each house would be on a one-third-acre plot. Perfect for city people who wanted a rural retirement home. All they had to do was sell their cramped little bungalows in San Francisco's Sunset district. A house they'd bought for $12,000 in 1946 could be sold for $250,000 in 1984. California real estate: the new and improved Gold Rush.

Still, Ray did wonder whether Mr. Cushing was overestimating the prospect that upscale developments would pay off in Piñon County. Five of the twenty houses in Blackberry Springs still hadn't sold, and they'd been on the market over six months. Even so, Blackberry Springs had opened the door for development, and the way these things went, ten years from now houses and shopping centers would probably cover every inch of land in the twenty-seven miles from Camargo to Blackberry Springs that wasn't owned by the government.

Ray put his pickup in gear and drove south on Gennessee Mine Road. It was steep but easily drivable, composed of hard-packed dirt and gravel. It wasn't in bad shape, considering. Only six miles long, it ended at Blackberry Springs Drive, the site of Mr. Cushing's other project. This parcel had been slated for a trailer park, but the owner went bankrupt. At the moment the site was nothing more than twelve sloping acres denuded of trees, stunted with boulders and stumps, and showing several deep, gaping holes where old mine shafts had been uncovered. This wasn't going to be an easy grading job.

With new housing developments being marketed to retirees, there would be a need for more doctors. So, Mr. Cushing was putting up a medical office building. Ray thought it was a strange place for a medical building, being so far from the hospital, but Mr. Cushing didn't seem concerned about that.

This would be the Eagle crew's first day working here, other than Monday when they'd staked it.

Ray had come early to look the place over again before the guys arrived. The trailer was already in place. He set the large thermos of coffee and the box of donuts on a makeshift table —a sheet of plywood across two sawhorses.

He was anxious to get this project completed because Eagle had a lot of work coming up. They were scheduled to begin grading for High Mountain Mall in March. They were also under contract to start the new telephone company office building late next summer. The housing development at the northern end of Gennessee Mine Road would not get underway until late spring at the earliest; the approval stage of a project always took a long time, and the Board of Supervisors probably wouldn't vote before winter. The crew would have to wait for good weather to start the work.

He glanced east, at the smooth paved road that led to Blackberry Springs. She was probably there right now, in that house that he'd built for a family of five, never imagining that one woman would live there by herself. Or maybe she was out jogging right now and would pass the site, like she had on Monday. And maybe, he said to himself, that's the reason you came out here so early.

Terri had been surprised when he'd left the house at quarter to five. "Ray, I haven't made your lunch yet," she'd said, starting to get out of bed. "It's okay, I'll eat at the Claim Jumper," he'd replied. "I have to check out a new job site for the old man." And that was true, but it was also true he hadn't had to leave quite so early.

Terri had given him a look, even though 4:45am wasn't much earlier than he usually left. But they'd been married ten years now, and Ray knew Terri's looks, and the look she'd given him this morning had definitely been tinged with suspicion. But in the next moment, he could almost see her shaking off the suspicion as absurd: *If he's having an affair, he'd hardly be going out to consummate it at 4:45 in the morning. And besides, he promised me.*

It pained him to admit to himself that he'd broken that promise twice. The last time had been over a year ago, yet it haunted him. Not what he'd done, which he considered unimportant in a sense, because it didn't affect how he felt about Terri or about their marriage. But he didn't like having to hide things from her.

Now he was concealing something again, even though he hadn't broken the promise. All he was doing was thinking about a woman. Thinking about a woman wasn't the same as making love to her. (Yet another thing Jimmy Carter had been wrong about.)

Was she thinking about him, too? She'd sure been looking at him the other day. Billy had commented, "That city woman's got eyes for somebody over here." Eddie had said, "Oh, yeah?" in a way like he assumed it was him. "Sorry to disappoint you for once," Billy had returned—they were all used to Eddie, a handsome MiWok kid, getting attention from women—"but this one's got her eyes on Ray."

Ray wasn't unaccustomed to such attention. He knew he was good looking; he felt women staring at him wherever he went, even women who'd known him since grade school. He rarely accepted an invitation. If all she wanted was to get laid, fine. But if she was the kind of woman who'd expect him to leave his wife or get into a complicated emotional relationship, forget it.

So, he said to himself, get your mind off this city woman. She's trouble and you know it. She's divorced. That's strike one. She doesn't know what it's like to live in a small town. Strike two. Besides, she's too boyish—thin and angular, and built like an adolescent, almost no breasts or behind. She's probably looking for a husband, or at least a boyfriend; it wouldn't be just sex with this one. You ran out of strikes already, boyo.

He heard the familiar whine of Eddie's ancient International pickup. Time to get women off the brain and start thinking about the day ahead. Ray finished his coffee in a long gulp and put on his hard hat.

By eight, work was proceeding at a good pace. But he should've knocked on wood, because five minutes later they encountered a tree stump that had more or less petrified and he had to call the office for an excavator. It came about an hour later, accompanied by the black Ford Bronco belonging to Hiram Cushing. Ray cursed.

Hiram Cushing was in his sixties, with the leathery look of a sun worshipper. He was tall and lanky, so bony that you expected him to clank when he walked. Yet he moved with the agility of a much younger man. Only his hair gave him away, for it was thin and entirely gray. To Cushing's credit, he didn't try to minimize that by dying or a comb-over.

He was one of those guys who'd been born on third base but thought he'd hit a triple, and was prone to saying, within earshot of the crew, that he'd worked hard all his life. Of course, what a guy like that considered hard work was one thing; the guys in the crew used a different dictionary. Not that any of them ever said a word to Cushing. They kept their opinions amongst themselves. If Cushing thought playing a round of golf with an investor or taking a state assemblyman to lunch was productive labor, Ray couldn't argue. But productive labor wasn't the same as hard work.

Mr. Cushing was proud that his family had been among the earliest settlers in Piñon County. Whenever Cushing alluded to that, the MiWok guys would stare impassively, except for Eddie, who'd grin. None of them ever said anything to Cushing, but later Eddie would fulminate.

"Morning, Ray." Cushing climbed out of his van. Ray bit back a warning about the dust. Cushing hated being treated like a suit.

"Hi, Hiram," said Ray, addressing him by his first name, as he preferred. "Got some coffee, if you want some."

"Thanks anyway, I'm trying to cut back. Did you see that game Sunday?"

"Yeah, the defense was amazing," Ray said. "But the offense should've scored more than fourteen points."

"You're right about that." Cushing stood rocked back on his heels, the way he always did, with his arms folded high on his chest.

Football was the only thing not related to work that he and Hiram Cushing ever talked about, and Ray tried not to reveal the extent of his passion. Partly that was just his native caution against letting someone with power over him know the depth of his feelings.

When Cushing had hired Ray back in 1975, he'd commented that he'd seen Ray play high school football for the Camargo Cougars. They'd won the local championship in 1968 and Ray had been the star of the team—a strong, fast halfback and a hard-hitting defensive end. "It's too damned bad about the war," Cushing had remarked. "You might've gone far with football."

"Naw, I wasn't that good," Ray had said, trying to fend off any notion that he was susceptible to flattery. "I was more interested in goofing around than playing football. And I never made it to Vietnam, anyway."

But in truth, he *had* wanted to play football. He'd been third-team All State, but his grades weren't good and neither were his SATs. The only full scholarships he'd been offered were from small schools outside California. He'd decided to work for a year, save some money, then go to a junior college, then transfer to a Pac Ten school and try out as a walk-on. But the Selective Service had had other plans for him.

After a few more minutes analyzing Sunday's game Mr. Cushing said, "Let's talk privately," and they stepped into the trailer.

Ray unrolled a map and said, "No way can construction vehicles use that old fire road. We'd have to grade and pave fifteen miles, and that's not feasible." He tapped the map. "But we can get to the site from this end."

Cushing glanced out the window at Gennessee Mine Road; at this end it looked more like a deer path. He frowned.

"This end's beat up because guys been coming in to cut firewood," Ray explained, "but once you get over that hill, it's in pretty good shape."

"But I assume some work will have to be done."

"Yeah, we'll have to pave it, and there's one part we'll have to grade, a section about a quarter mile long. But that's the only grading we'll have to do. It's in pretty good condition, considering. And it's a lot less steep than I remembered."

Cushing leaned against the desk and smiled. "This is good news. Almost no grading, and paving six miles instead of fifteen. Even better, I won't have to negotiate with the Forest Service over their damned fire road. That should make things easier when I go before the Planning Commission."

"When's the hearing?" Ray asked.

"Late November. After the Planning Commission approves the project, it'll be three to six weeks before it goes before the Board of Supervisors. So the earliest the project will be approved is January. We'll have to schedule the work to start in April."

"Okay," Ray said.

"That'll mean hiring a lot of men because by then we'll be working on the mall too."

"Shouldn't be a problem," Ray said. "There's a lot of guys looking for work right now. Probably be even more in April."

"It will help if we can get this job done by then." Cushing gestured toward the window. "What do you think, will it finish on schedule?"

"Hard to say for sure on the first day, but it looks good so far. There's a lot of rock, like we thought. Ran into a petrified stump, but that'll be gone this morning. The maps say there's two old mine shafts. I figure there's probably a few more than that. But I knew there'd be unforeseen problems and the schedule accounts for them."

"I hope you're right," Cushing said, somewhat distractedly. And then, with more force, "We've got to get cracking on that mall property on schedule. I'm thinking about starting earlier than we originally anticipated. Will that be a problem for you?"

"Hell, I could start over there tomorrow if you give me the go ahead. I could assemble a crew in a day."

Ray thought the conversation was over, but Cushing remained leaning against the desk with his legs stretched out in front, crossed at the ankles. "The quicker the mall goes up, the better. I don't want to give any of the investors time to have second thoughts."

Why would they? Ray thought, but what he said was a neutral, "Makes sense."

"These are big-name retailers. They want assurances of an adequate customer base. And that's a perfectly legitimate concern."

"Sure," Ray said uneasily. He didn't know why Cushing was telling him this.

"I'm going to have to give them that assurance very soon. I don't want any investors getting nervous about the development climate in Piñon County. I don't expect any problems from the Planning Commission, but until I've got those permits for the Gennessee Mine housing project in my hand, I'm concerned." He paused. "You know, Ray, sometimes a man in my situation doesn't hear about something that affects his interests until it's too late. You're in a different position than I am, not only at the job, but in town. I wanted you to know how things stand, so if you do hear something, you'll know its significance." He drew a business card from his pocket and wrote a number on the back of it. "This is my private phone number, in my home office. Never hesitate to call me if you think it necessary. Maybe an opportunity will present itself. One never knows."

INTERLUDE

March 1888
Stubbs Landing, California

The moon was so bright that despite the heavy iron bars on the window, she could see the beginnings of buds on the dogwoods. She thought the full moon a good omen. Tonight, she would slip through the doors and gates being left unlocked for her and find her way to the city—or at least to shelter, to some place where no one would think to look for her. Her husband would not come for her himself, but most assuredly would send men after her, as he had done the last time. And perhaps the sanitarium would send men, too.

She fingered the drapes. It was nearly time. She must finish the letter so she could hide it in the usual place before she left.

She returned to the desk and read over what she had so far written.

My dear friend,

The time has come. You cautioned me to do nothing drastic or irrevocable. Yet what I intend to do is both, for I have no alternative. By the time you read this it will be too late for you to stop me. I only hope that you make no hasty judgments, that you consider my action with the kindness and sympathy that are the hallmarks of your character.

The page was filled. She took another sheet, dipped her pen and wrote:

Soon, I shall call upon you one last time for assistance. When I am free, I shall send you a message. My faith in you is absolute; if you do not send help, it will be because you cannot. My heart beats wildly with fear, but with hope too. For the first time in so long, it beats with hope.

From the far end of the corridor came the doctor's voice, and that of the night watchman, then the echo of the doctor's footsteps in the marble passageway. Quickly, she signed the letter with her initials. She had decided not to let the doctor know about the letter, for his own protection, and for the protection of the person who would post it.

She pulled her bundle from under the bed and her cloak from the hook, and brought them over beside the desk. Checking that the ink had dried, she folded the letter in thirds and put it into a blank envelope, which she tucked into the pocket of her cloak. The person who had promised to post the letter would add the address in his own hand, another precaution.

The doctor tapped quietly at her door as a courtesy only; she could not open it. She waited anxiously as he fumbled with the keys before finding the right one. The door creaked slightly as he entered. He closed it gently and locked it again. They would not be disturbed.

He walked over to the window and peered out. "The night watchman is drinking the tea I brought him and will soon fall asleep. Here, I've brought something for you."

He took a dram of powder from the pocket of his long black coat, poured it into a glass of water, and held it out for her.

She hesitated, and the doctor smiled. "Don't worry. We have potions to make one lively, as well. That's what this will do."

She took the glass. "What is it?"

"Cocaine. It's made from a South American plant. The natives chew the leaves when they wish to stay awake and alert. That's what we want for you tonight."

"Yes." She brought the glass to her lips and drank quickly.

He watched her drink. She caught a glimpse of something in his eye, but it was too fleeting for her to quite name. A moment later a terrible heaviness overcame her head and limbs. Her knees briefly trembled and gave way. Try as she might, she could not make her arms or legs move. The feeling was like that of laudanum, but more so. *So this has all been a trick, and he has betrayed me. I should have known. I should have known better than to trust him.*

She was unable to struggle, or even to object, as he dragged her onto the bed. He began to go through her bundle of things, stopping at the crinkle of paper in her cloak pocket. He retrieved the envelope, took out the letter and read it. He then looked at her with what seemed a horribly inappropriate expression: amusement. "How easy you make it," he said.

But she hadn't addressed it. Thank *God*, she hadn't addressed it. The precautions she had followed for all these months now proved worth her efforts.

He tore the second page of the letter into shreds and returned the first page to the envelope. At the armoire he searched the pockets of her dresses, opened the two hatboxes and looked underneath the hats, and shook out her slippers. Then he put his hands on her shoulders. She knew he was very close, yet he seemed at a great distance. "Where is it?" he demanded. She was so sleepy that to make herself acknowledge his question would have been impossible. "Don't pretend you don't know what I mean," he hissed. "I told your husband about it. He asked me to retrieve it."

She felt her eyes fill. The doctor laughed once, abruptly. "Did you think I wouldn't tell your husband?"

'Yes,' she would have said, had speech been possible. 'That *is* what I thought.'

He slapped her face on one side, then the other. "Where is it?"

She had hidden it well; they would never find it. And it would haunt her husband for the rest of his life.

As the woman slipped into death, she actually smiled. The doctor would have slapped her again if he thought she would have felt it.

He undressed her only so far as to remove any signs indicating her intent to flee—boots, hat, travel jacket. She had not yet put on her cloak, which he returned to its peg. He untied her bundle and returned her things to their proper places. This task did not take long; she had not been taking much.

When she'd collapsed onto the floor, the glass had slipped from her hand onto the rug and rolled under her desk chair.

He retrieved it now and put it into her right hand, then allowed the hand to fall naturally onto the bedding, and the glass to roll out.

He took the bottle from the top drawer of the desk and heated it, then secured the envelope with her wax and seal. The letter was unsigned but her seal, administered behind her locked door onto a letter written in her hand, would convince anyone of her intent to end her life.

Only one task remained.

He had already gone through her articles of clothing. Now he looked through the bureau and the desk, even reached behind and underneath the drawers. He shoved them out and peered behind them. He lifted the bed covers and felt underneath the pillows and mattress. He trod slowly upon the floorboards in case she had found a loose one. He looked behind the framed pictures on the wall.

Momentarily he was panic-stricken. But quickly, he reassured himself. He had searched thoroughly and it was not here. She must have left it behind. According to the husband, she had been brought to the sanitarium rather hastily; perhaps she had not had enough time to retrieve it from some hiding place in or near her home. In either case, then, it would never be found. He could reassure the husband with absolute confidence.

The doctor relaxed. He smoothed his mustache and fingered the pocket of his vest, where he actually did keep a vial of cocaine. He carefully looked over the room again. Nothing was amiss. He opened the door, verified that the corridor was empty, left the room, locked the door and, stepping with a light tread and cautiously checking around every corner, made his way out of the building.

Part II

___

1984-1985

LATE FALL & WINTER

"Last night four men slept in the small room we occupied on bunks put on one above the other. We paid ten dollars apiece. That means the proprietor got forty dollars for the rent of that room for one night… I think we are all wrong on this gold-mining business. We ought to go into real estate. That's where the money lies."

—1849 diary of Andrew Gordon, quoted by Victoria Sherrow, Life During the Gold Rush, (San Diego: Lucent Books, 1998; p.70-71 [citing Woodward, The Way Our People Lived, p.273].)

Chapter Seven

Most applications before the Planning Commission for new developments were for ten houses or a mobile home park on former ranch- or farmland near Camargo or one of the other towns. So, Stella had been surprised to find that among the items on the Commission's November agenda was for a development of 100 houses in a remote area bordering the national forest. It was, in fact, very near where her Uncle Sal's farm had been: Gennessee Mine.

That site was home to one of the few remaining stands of the indigenous Higuera paintbrush. Once prolific in Piñon County, it had been carelessly destroyed throughout the last century until, by 1970, only three patches remained. One, on a ranch near the Oso Grande county line, had been recently bulldozed when the firefighting airport was built. Should the housing development be approved, there would be only one place where the Higuera paintbrush still existed: Pardini Ranch.

Hiram Cushing was not at the hearing. He'd sent two lawyers, who sat quietly near the front. Clearly they were city men, the only men in the room wearing suits and ties.

Not until nine-thirty was the Gennessee Mine item finally called. By then the intentional infliction of stuffiness was about to escalate into attempted asphyxiation. Stella glanced around the roomful of red, perspiring faces, fanning papers, and drooping heads. She got up, made her way to the windows, and threw one open. Thirty-nine-degree air rushed into the room. One of the commissioners frowned and seemed about to object, but when the audience began to applaud, he turned to Cushing's lawyers and asked if they had anything to add. They didn't, and the matter was opened for public comment.

The first speakers urged approval. It was about time Piñon County got a piece of the pie in the booming economy of the '80s. The lumber mill cutbacks were hurting the entire county; construction of a housing development would bring much-needed jobs. People need places to live, so let's build them.

Stella lowered the window to an inch and returned to her seat.

Joe spoke last and had twenty minutes because several other development opponents had turned their allotted minutes over to him. First, he read into the record the notice requirements: "Notice must be given sixty days prior to the hearing, and must not only be posted and published, but sent to property owners in the vicinity. Any decision made at this hearing won't be legal, because the notices weren't postmarked until September 26th—fifty-seven days before the hearing. So the Commission would be wise to cancel this hearing tonight and reschedule it with the proper and legal notice."

"Your point is duly noted, Joe," said Commissioner Giacometti. His father owned the car dealership. "The hearing will proceed."

"Now, I realize many of the people here tonight want this development to be approved because it will bring jobs to the county."

There was a smattering of applause.

"I'm not opposed to housing developments, so long as enough planning goes into how and where they're built. But this project is too near the border of the Higuera National Forest. Building so many houses in the middle of the forest doesn't seem like a good idea to me, but I guess you could look at the bright side and think of all the jobs that'll open up fighting fires.

"These mountains have always been mined for their wealth —there's not one of us here who doesn't know how devastating gold mining was to the land. The gold lust of the 1980s takes a different form, but it's just as motivated by greed and it's even more destructive. And it's irreversible." He briefly addressed the matters of infrastructure and traffic, before Commissioner Maggert banged his gavel. "Your twenty minutes are up. That's the last scheduled speaker. Commissioners, are we ready to take a vote? All in favor."

All three commissioners raised their right hands. "The item passes and will be sent to the County Supervisors for final approval. This meeting of the Piñon County Planning Commission is hereby adjourned." The gavel banged down again.

It was past eleven by the time they drove home. "So we'll have to go to court," Joe said.

"What lawyer are we going to see about this? I can't think of a single lawyer in town we can trust."

"We'll have to hire one from somewhere else. Sacramento probably."

They exchanged a wry smile. The presiding judge of the Piñon County Superior Court was Hiram Cushing's brother-in-law. The other Superior Court judge was Pete Jensen's cousin.

"We'll have to bring the lawsuit in another county, too."

"This place," she said, laughing.

Joe shrugged. "In a city, the judge sees your adversary at his racquetball club or they were frat brothers in college and you never know about it. Here, at least we know about it."

NOVEMBER PASSED WITH no rain or snow. The air was so dry it crackled, and every time Stella touched metal, she got a shock. Not until early December did rain finally fall, beginning one afternoon as she collected a basket of apples from the shed.

In the weeks since the hearing, their lives had been taken up by the lawsuit. The lawyer had filed it in Federal Court in Sacramento, including an application for an injunction stopping construction of the Gennessee Mine development. A decision was expected any day now.

Stella had assumed there could be no counter-argument to the bald fact that the Planning Commission had not provided the required sixty days' notice for the hearing. The county's defense was that the Planning Commission had met the requirement since it had *issued* the notice within sixty days, but hadn't *mailed* it for a few more days. The lawyer didn't think this would wash, but cautioned that one could never be sure how a judge would rule. "On the written law, one would hope," Joe had remarked, and the lawyer replied that laws were always open to interpretation.

As she peeled and cored the apples, she gazed out the window over the sink at the rain hammering down, sniffing deeply at the aroma of the ground moistening. Surely nothing smelled as good as the first rain of the season. The apples complemented it and reminded her of the aromas in Nonna's kitchen—apple fritters sprinkled with sugar, and the pot of strong coffee always on the stove, even in the summer.

The Cushings, the first owners of the Minelli house, had planted the apple and pear trees; Nonna had planted crabapple, olive, and cherry trees (the first week of June every year Stella used to eat herself sick on cherries), and best of all, an O'Henry peach tree. Stella still missed that orchard. She hadn't seen a Roxbury Russet apple in twenty years, and wished she'd had the foresight to save some seeds before the city had bulldozed the orchard. Her trees were Sierra Beauties, which produced a nice crisp apple, tending to tartness rather than sweetness, and they baked well. But they weren't Roxburys. And no one grew O'Henry peaches anymore.

She was just finishing the pie when she heard Joe come inside, hang up his slicker and remove his muddy boots in the foyer. He entered the kitchen and kissed her from behind, commenting on the nice latticework of the crust, and eating one of the leftover apple slices.

"Could you taste the Sunday gravy, Joe?"

"I think I could manage that." He grinned.

Of everything her grandmother cooked, Sunday gravy had always been her favorite. She'd watched Nonna make it hundreds of times—and had probably made it hundreds of times herself. She didn't need instructions, but always propped the recipe card on the window ledge where she could see Nonna's familiar spiky handwriting, some ingredients written in English, some in Italian.

Stella's gravy never came out as good and she'd given up hope that it ever would. But Joe hadn't grown up eating Nonna's Sunday gravy. He tasted a spoonful of sauce, exclaimed with pleasure, then put a big spoonful into a bowl and dunked a chunk of sourdough in it.

He left to take a shower. She glanced at the stack of mail he'd brought in, mostly consisting of brightly colored advertisements, and thought, we won't be spending anything on Christmas this year.

The lawsuit was costing them dearly.

Because of the nature of their business, their bank

accounts were deceptively large in autumn. They made their money in late spring and summer and lived on it the rest of the year, supplemented by the small dividends, between two and three hundred dollars a month, from the utility company stock Stella had inherited from her Uncle Sal.

But this year, they would have to stretch out even less money than usual to get through the winter. This year, they had a lawyer to pay. He was from Sacramento, and he'd given no break on his fee. He had required a big down payment.

Rain hammered on the roof. Perhaps the winter would be a wet one, the drought would end, and they would make everything back next summer.

Chapter Eight

The smell of coffee brewing drew Ray into consciousness the Saturday after Christmas. Beside him Terri slept, so he knew it was Trixie making the coffee. When he went into the kitchen, she stood on a chair before the coffeemaker, waiting for it to finish dripping, and she had got out his favorite mug, the one with the 49er logo.

When the coffee was ready, they pulled on their jackets and went into the backyard. He carried his coffee and her orange juice; she brought a bag of peanuts.

Their house was at the eastern end of Camargo, adjacent to a sheep ranch. Trixie was always hoping the sheep would wander into the grove of live oaks that pressed up to the yard, but they rarely did. Maybe sheep, like cattle, didn't like the taste of live oak leaves.

Dozens of blue jays lived here, though—the garrulous, bold scrub jays as well as the bashful, colorful Steller's jays, with their crested heads and bright blue above-the-eye teardrops.

By the time Trixie had lined the length of the back fence with peanuts, the oaks were filled with jays. She ran back to the patio and climbed onto Ray's lap. He sipped his coffee, watching her as she watched the jays swooping down to snatch the nuts, which they took off to bury somewhere. Perhaps one day the sheep rancher would discover that he'd become a peanut farmer.

"Look, Daddy, there's the one I told you about, with the crooked tail. Do you think it's injured?"

Ray followed her pointing finger and was surprised to see the jay's tail feathers growing at such a severe angle. "Maybe, or maybe it's a birth defect. How many times have you seen that one?"

"Mmm." Trixie leaned against him. He breathed in her hair, the smells of fresh air and citrusy shampoo. She was seven now; how many more years would she curl up on his lap, not mind his kisses, turn to him with her questions? "I think four times."

"So it'll probably be okay, then." And as he said that, the crooked-tailed scrub jay snatched a peanut from under the beak of another. "Yay!" Trixie exclaimed.

By then it was almost eight o'clock. It was almost a four-hour drive to Candlestick Park and the game started at one o'clock. Terri didn't have to leave for work until quarter past nine and normally wouldn't get up until eight-thirty, but he knew the shower would wake her, so he set a cup of coffee and the *Sacramento Bee* on the table on her side of the bed.

When he got out of the shower she was sitting up, pillows propped behind her. She smiled and opened her arms. "You're so sweet," she murmured as he embraced her. She was warm from sleep and he kissed the tender place where her cheek gracefully curved down toward her neck. "How soon are you leaving?"

"Soon as I get dressed." He went to the bureau.

"I just don't understand why he invited you to a playoff game."

"I've worked for the guy for ten years."

"So why's he taking you to a game now, after all those years? He must have some ulterior motive."

"He probably does." Ray pulled on his T-shirt. "But what the hell, it's a 49er playoff game."

"Well, be careful."

He didn't reply, irritated that she thought he'd let Cushing bamboozle him, or that he was such a sap he'd start thinking Cushing was his friend and forget he was his boss. He tucked his shirt into the jeans and slung a sweater over his shoulder. "I'll see you tonight."

"It's supposed to be cold down there today. You'd better bring a jacket, too."

"I'll be fine," he said, not telling her that he had a jacket out in the pickup. Yet even as he realized he was being perverse, he couldn't bring himself not to be.

She pulled the newspaper up almost in front of her face, her way of telling him she was ticked off.

HE TOOK THE Higuera Highway, the two-lane road that ran the width of the state, albeit with a different name every fifty miles or so.

The long drive afforded him plenty of time to think. Despite his irritation with Terri, he too wondered what had prompted the old man's sudden magnanimity. Hiram Cushing had owned 49ers tickets for four seasons, and knew Ray was a 49ers fan, but had never invited him to a game. Why should he? Ray was just an employee. So it took him by surprise the other day when Cushing came into the construction office and said with a wide grin, "How'd you like to see the playoff game from the forty yard line?"

He knew he'd grown pretty comfortable in his job, but he

sure didn't plan on working for Cushing forever. It wasn't that he disliked his job. The work itself he enjoyed; he took pride in his craftsmanship and never hesitated to have something done over if necessary. Not long after Ray's promotion to site foreman Cushing had commented how much time it had cost to redo a foundation. Ray had said bluntly, "If you want a foreman who's gonna overlook a bad foundation, you better hire someone else." And Cushing had said, "No, that's not what I want at all." So Ray figured Cushing had been testing him.

Once he'd let Cushing know he wouldn't compromise, either on union issues or on the quality of the work, Cushing had never asked him to again. Ray had plenty of authority, both at job sites and about hiring; Cushing didn't meddle in the day-to-day details. In fact, during Ray's first five or six years at Eagle he seldom saw Mr. Cushing, who used to spend a lot more time at his other places, one in the Bay Area and the other back east somewhere, and on extended vacations. Only in the past few years, starting with the construction of Blackberry Springs, had he been living pretty much full time in Camargo.

While in high school Ray'd had a part-time job in a yard, learning about the materials that went into building. In shop class he earned his only A. But getting drafted had put carpentry on hold. After basic training he was stationed in Germany. He had not been there long when he got a letter from home that his best friend, Bobby, was dead—not in Vietnam, but a casualty of the war nonetheless.

The news devastated Ray. For weeks he was gripped by an exhaustion so debilitating that the company commander sent him to the base hospital. He didn't have pneumonia, anemia, or TB. Not until many years later did it strike him what had been wrong: he'd been felled by grief.

The whole time he was stationed in Germany, Vietnam

loomed over him, over all the guys in the base. Ray knew that he himself might be killed or crippled, although he couldn't believe it in his gut.

He lived with the peculiar mix of boredom, misery, and absurdity that comprised the life of a soldier, yet army life afforded time for daydreaming and even for exploration. He saw cathedrals and castles nearly a thousand years old. Having known that such ancient structures existed had not prepared him for the staggering experience of actually seeing them. While the other GIs spent their time off the base in bars or trying to score dope, Ray often spent his looking at buildings. It got to be a joke in the company. Once, he managed to get to Aachen. Most of his leave was consumed in travel but he had four precious hours at the Cathedral. Another time he went to Paris, where he must have walked thirty miles looking at the layers of history revealed by the different architectural eras. Centuries were reflected in the solidity and intricacy of the buildings, distinguishing venerable Europe from new, raw California.

He daydreamed about life after the army, and imagined himself building. What he wanted was to use his hands and his back, to feel earth and wood and rock, to smell freshly milled lumber. He wanted to build houses.

He hadn't dreamed of building housing developments, office parks, or shopping malls—all the things he was building now. Places like Blackberry Springs weren't what he'd had in mind, either. The houses were nice enough, but they were the dreams of Mr. Cushing, not of the people who ended up buying them. The houses were more or less alike, with just enough differences to fool the average person into thinking each was unique.

Plus, he didn't like their location. It was stupid to build houses so close to the forest. They'd been doing it down in L.A. for thirty years, and for thirty years there had been devastating fires every fire season. Millions of dollars spent putting up luxury houses in Malibu Canyon and Bel Air and Laguna Beach; suppressing the inevitable fires; rebuilding the houses; then ten years later, another fire. Stupid or not, that blueprint was being followed not only in California, but all over the west.

The Gennessee Mine development would be almost in the middle of the forest, but he knew he would work on it. What good would it do to refuse? He'd get fired and they'd just hire another guy to build it. He'd worked on Blackberry Springs, and it was in just as dangerous a place.

After driving for an hour, Ray entered the San Joaquin Valley and felt the pull of nostalgia. But it was for a place that no longer existed: for small, scattered farm towns and miles of perfectly aligned rows of crops, for almond trees and grape vines speeding past a car window with dizzying symmetry, for the smells of tomatoes ripening on the vine, orchards in bloom, just-irrigated fields of alfalfa.

Now he drove past rows of tract houses, some standing on former floodplains. One of these days there would be an unusually wet winter and the inevitable floods would be catastrophic. FEMA—i.e., the taxpayers—would fork out millions, but homeowners never got paid back in full and renters usually got nothing at all. Meanwhile, the politicians who had approved building on the floodplains would get off scot-free, and the developers would have already walked away with a tidy profit.

The tule fog was dense this morning. That was one thing about the Valley he'd never missed. It seeped up from the ground and sat there, never moving, just getting thicker, colder, more penetrating. It made your whole body hurt, a deep bone-ache. When his family moved to Camargo it was the middle of winter, and Ray remembered being surprised that frozen snow and a temperature of 28 degrees didn't feel as cold as the tule fog of Lodi. And tule fog had a nauseating odor. Some people said that came from accumulation of pesticides and fertilizers in the ground. There weren't many organic farmers back in the 1950s and 60s, especially not in the Valley.

He turned onto Interstate 80 and drove through Sacramento, across the river and westward through the Yolo Causeway. He was startled to see it nearly dry; normally this time of year it looked like a big shallow lake. Both sides of Davis were still farm country and he passed winter-bare almond trees and grape vines, and fields where tomato vines and corn stalks had been plowed under in October. Huge flocks of sandhill cranes and tundra swans filled the fields and the sky was dotted with new arrivals stopping in their winter migration.

He wondered why it had never occurred to him to bring Trixie to see the sandhill cranes. She loved birds and she would love having an adventure with him. He promised himself he'd do it next year. Just him and Trixie.

Finally, he got to Candlestick and parked in one of the outlying lots. Cushing had left Ray's ticket at will-call. He owned four seasons' tickets and two guys Ray didn't know were there, friends or business associates of Mr. Cushing's from the Bay Area, the kind of guys who wore suits to work. Ray was on the other side of Cushing so he didn't have to converse with them.

Terri had been right about the weather. He turned up the collar of his fleece-lined jacket against the biting bay winds. "Baseball weather today," Mr. Cushing commented with a grin.

Ray laughed, but couldn't help thinking that the guys at work would cynically say that Cushing was trying to show he was a real fan, someone who knows it's colder at the 'Stick in summer than winter. Rich as Croesus, but just one of the guys.

The Niners got an early lead and beat New York 21–10. After the game, Cushing invrited him to dinner. He demurred at first, thinking the invitation was made for the sake of politeness, but when Cushing pressed and said there were some things he wanted to talk about, Ray said sure. He could hardly refuse to have dinner with the boss, especially not after the boss had taken him to a playoff game.

They went to a restaurant at Fisherman's Wharf and sat before windows overlooking the bay. After they ordered, Cushing said, "I want to talk to you about the situation with the Gennessee Mine development."

"Sure," Ray said, but the Candlestick Park hot dog suddenly felt heavy in his belly.

"What with this lawsuit, it looks like we won't be able to get started on the project until this summer, if then. So we're going to be working on it at the same time as the mall. We'll be starting the phone company building in late summer, so that means we'll be in the middle of three projects simultaneously. What I'm thinking, Ray, is that, given the size of the project, we'll act as a general contractor."

"So we won't do the work ourselves?"

"Some of it. We'll do the foundations and frames, then subcontract the rest." Cushing sipped his Scotch. "How would you feel about coordinating and overseeing the work of other companies, and making recommendations on which companies we should use?"

"The truth is, that's not something I'm real experienced at, Hiram. I'm more of a hands-on guy."

"You're a site foreman; you coordinate our work with other construction companies."

"Yeah, but not on the scale you're talking about. Don't get me wrong. I'm glad you want me to do it and if that's the way it goes, I'll make sure I know what I'm doing. But I don't want you thinking I'd be the best guy at this, because I'm not."

"I've always appreciated your frankness, Ray. That's exactly why I want you to do it: I know I can trust you. I don't want someone who's going to sugar-coat things for me or make side deals with the concrete contractor or hold back bad news until it's too late to do anything about it. So, can I count on you to be in charge of these projects?"

He took the plunge. "Yeah. I'll take it on. But if it's too much for me to handle, I'll come tell you."

"Of course. And by the way, this will be considered a promotion and you'll be compensated."

"I got no complaints about that. You've always been fair that way."

"That's just good business practice. I don't want a good man deciding to go elsewhere just because I tried to save a couple dollars." Cushing sipped his Scotch and Ray figured that was it for the business talk. He leaned back and took a pull from his beer. Then Cushing said, "But I'll tell you this, Ray. I've had a hell of a time just trying to improve things in Piñon County, and it's beginning to affect the situation with the mall."

"Yeah?" Ray said. Was Cushing trying to find out his opinion, or was he simply airing grievances and wanting sympathy?

"When we went to investors and retailers with the idea of putting up a world-class mall in Piñon County, it was with the expectation that there'd be customers. Which means building houses for those customers. We certainly didn't anticipate problems getting the development approved. Unfortunately, the opposition took us to court, and things have gone much further than I expected."

"You mean the restraining order?"

Cushing's brow creased slightly. "The problem is the length of time court cases take. We'll win, but simply being in court puts the development on hold for months. That makes investors nervous."

So the mall was in trouble unless this other deal went

through. Obviously, the retailers wanted to be assured of an adequate customer base, but a couple other developments were going up in the northwestern part of the county, and so far as Ray knew there'd been no trouble about them. Each contained about twenty houses.

"We're getting too damned much trouble from certain people." Cushing drained his Scotch and gestured with his empty glass to a passing waiter. Ray wouldn't have minded another beer, but he had a long drive home.

"I don't understand their motivation, Ray. I consider them not so much pro-environment as anti-people. Here we are in the middle of a recession, I'm proposing something that creates dozens of jobs providing homes for people who need them, and I get nothing but grief. And you can imagine how much money the lawyers are costing me."

Ray nodded and commented inanely that lawyers were expensive.

"Yes, and Pardini has to be paying a bundle to his lawyer, too. They don't take on cases like this without getting paid up front. I just wonder how the hell he can afford it."

Ray assumed the remark was rhetorical and didn't respond. But Cushing went on: "You think he's doing better at that outfitting business than people say?"

"No idea."

The waiter arrived with Cushing's drink, but he kept right on talking. "That's the rumor, isn't it, that he's hurting?"

"Thanks," Ray said to the waiter, and after he'd gone: "That's what I've heard, that he's hurting because of the drought, just like everyone else. I guess it's worse for him because of all the Forest Service restrictions during fire season."

"Well, I suppose he'll run out of money soon enough and that'll be the last of this ridiculous lawsuit. Either that, or something else will bring him to his senses."

Ray glanced out the window. The reflection of the lights made the water look black and solid, as if you could walk all the way to Alcatraz.

"You know what I mean, Ray?"

Ray thought Cushing must've said something that he hadn't heard. "What's that?"

"Never mind." Cushing smiled. "Enough shop talk. How do you think the Niners will do next week against Washington?"

"It might not be Washington. I wouldn't count Chicago out," Ray said.

Cushing waved his hand dismissively. "Chicago doesn't have a decent quarterback, not since McMahon went down."

Ray responded diplomatically. "Well, it should be a good game."

On the way back to Piñon County he silently cursed himself. Why hadn't he told Cushing that he had to think it over before agreeing to see all three projects through to completion? He shouldn't have agreed without consulting Terri. Agreeing to stay on at Eagle for what surely amounted to another two or three years was a major decision.

Despite his wariness, Cushing had caught him by surprise. Terri had been right to worry. Now he was committed, so forget about going out on his own anytime soon.

Not that she had been urging him to do so. If anything, she was more inclined to want him to stay with Eagle, where his income was assured. They had a way to go before they could start putting away money for their old age, that was for sure.

That thought echoed in his mind and he shook his head. What the hell had happened to him? To both of them? Before they married, they'd sworn not to be pulled into a middle-class lifestyle and values. But here they were—in debt and with kids to provide for, trapped in their jobs and worrying about old age.

And the other thing, too. He wasn't trapped with Terri; he loved her; but trapped in the *situation*. Ever since that time five years ago, there had been something between them that he knew would always be there; silent but always present, no matter how long since he'd been with another woman. That something was her lack of trust.

He felt that, in a weird way, his job was tangled up with it. He was pretty sure this was something that only he thought, not Terri; but it was as though because of what he'd done, he owed it to her to sacrifice his youthful dreams for the security of the job.

Chapter Nine

The way Cindy's friend smiled nervously every time she saw Kit was beginning to get on Kit's nerves. This time she didn't look up when Freda entered the living room, just kept her eyes on the latest *California Cattleman*.

Freda had just come from the bathroom, where Kit had heard her washing her face and brushing her teeth. Why would anyone brush their teeth *before* dinner? The face washing part she could understand, although Freda's complexion wasn't as bad as she apparently thought it was. She wore her hair so far over her face that her eyes were barely visible.

Freda wandered around the living room and stopped before the mantle, looking at the stockings. Mom had made them when Kit was five or six; each had individualized appliqués.

Kit treasured her family's Christmas decorations. A basket of sugar pinecones sat on an end table; she had helped Mom gather and glaze the foot-long cones almost ten years ago. There were many vases of toyon berries—Christmas berries, as people called them. The two-pound box of See's chocolates, an annual gift from Aunt Jinx, sat on the sideboard; already, half the box consisted of empty brown papers. Glittery cut-out snowflakes brightened the antique gun case, and the wagon wheel chandelier twinkled with a strand of blinking lights.

Freda stopped before the two Charles M. Russell prints. Kit had always liked how the ropes of tinsel draped over the frames transformed the scenes—cowboys huddled around a homely winter campfire in one, cattle in a snowy pasture in the other—into holiday settings, as though Russell had been thinking of Christmas when he'd painted them. But for the first time, she realized that another person might think it weird, putting tinsel around a picture frame.

She had to admit that Christmas didn't thrill her as much as it used to. She remembered being giddy with excitement and anticipation at seven, nine, even twelve years old. Of course, a lot of it had been the presents, but Christmas had so many special moments. Riding out with Dad to select a tree. She and Cindy carefully unwrapping the ornaments, some of them ones Mom had got from her own mother. The great smells: pine from the tree and from pinecones in the fire; cookies baking; cloves and cinnamon simmering in apple cider. On Christmas Eve they roasted chestnuts in foil in the fire, then dropped them warm into glasses of claret—a holiday tradition Mom had adopted from the Minellis.

One of Kit's favorite things was staying up late with Mom to watch all the Christmas movies: *It's a Charlie Brown Christmas* or *How the Grinch Stole Christmas* in the early evening, then *The Bishop's Wife* or *Meet Me in St. Louis* later. Mom always got teary-eyed when Judy Garland sang. Well, everything Judy Garland sang was sad, even the supposedly happy songs.

For the past few years, Cindy had decorated grudgingly, and this year Kit had ridden out alone to select and cut the tree. Maybe someday she wouldn't anticipate the holidays with joy. But that was probably inevitable, just a part of getting older.

And Freda wasn't doing anything except appreciating the decorations, Kit chided herself. There was no call to feel so snide and resentful, and make Freda even more self-conscious.

Dad and PJ were just coming in, their boots thunking on the hardwood floor, their voices loud. Kit went to the dining room and set the table while Mom brought the food in. Cindy and Freda got ice water and glasses.

Dad was telling PJ which fences should be reinforced with stays before the snow. PJ, nodding, helped himself to a thick slice of meatloaf and set the serving dish in front of his plate. Kit reached for it, couldn't quite get it, and nudged PJ instead of interrupting his and Dad's conversation. He ignored her. So she stood up and stretched her arm over his plate. PJ drew back in mock alarm. "Sure, reach right over me."

"You could pass the dish around the table," Kit retorted. "But I guess that's too much like housework."

"Knock it off," Dad commanded. "Princess, would you pass the string beans?"

Cindy complied, and Kit met her eyes. They sat directly across from each other. Kit made a gagging motion, which Cindy would know was a reference to Dad's syrupy tone. Cindy surreptitiously gave her the middle finger. Mom didn't seem to notice; as usual, her eyes were glassy and unfocused. Would Freda realize Mom was a bit tipsy and gossip about it later, or tell her parents and *they'd* gossip?

"We might get a foot," PJ said.

Dad shrugged. "Maybe."

"Snow won't do Cushing any good," PJ said.

"He'll start the mall on schedule no matter what," Dad said. "He won't give any investors an excuse to pull out."

"You think some of 'em are thinking about pulling out?"

"That's the rumor – a lot of cold feet since Pardini got that federal court order."

"But he got that court order on a technicality," PJ said.

Dad nodded. "Yeah, but look at it from their point of view. You're a major stockholder in, let's say, The Gap. The company's about to spend, what, two million building a store up in the boondocks because there's going to be a lot of residential development there in the next few years. Then, wham, turns out maybe there won't be residential development on the scale you'd been told there would be. Turns out there's just enough opposition to stall things for a couple years. So you'll spend two million to build, more on hiring and stocking the store, and for all your investment, you can expect no customers for another five years.

"Now, wouldn't you be thinking of pulling out before that two million gets spent? Wouldn't you be thinking maybe the money's better spent building in another mall, one with customers already living next door?"

"Hell yeah," PJ said emphatically. Day to day she'd gotten used to Dad and PJ doing most of the talking at dinner. Tonight, with someone here, she was embarrassed by it, and even more by her own complicity.

Cindy sighed audibly. "This is almost as interesting as football."

Dad's eyebrows raised. "Since when do the kids decide the topics of conversation?"

"Since never," Cindy replied.

"That's right. But we do have a guest tonight, and maybe you're right and it's rude to have a conversation that doesn't interest her."

"Oh, no, it's interesting," Freda said.

But Dad turned on his real estate salesman's charm, asking Freda questions about her own life, making references to her family as if he thought they were the solid, respectable people that kept Piñon County running, when Kit knew that he really thought men like Freda's dad were just drones without hopes or dreams or imagination, and would never be anything else.

But Dad also had a way of making it clear to Freda that he was praising her family pro forma only; that she should be honored that one of the richest men in the county was making the effort to show even phony interest in the daughter of an appliance repairman.

Kit listened and watched silently, eating seconds of meatloaf and potatoes, seething over Freda's simpering responses to the flattery, the sole purpose of which was to prove she was susceptible to it. Freda even began to enthusiastically describe how her father had fixed the heating system at the library, which had saved the county the thousands of dollars it would have cost for a replacement. "Is that so," intoned Dad, making his boredom obvious.

Freda was more astute than Kit had realized. She reddened and went silent, staring down at her plate.

Cindy acted like she hadn't noticed.

Then Mom said, "I think that's wonderful, Freda. Imagine how many books the library can buy instead of spending the money on a new boiler."

"Laura," said Dad sharply, "go get the dessert."

Kit looked at her mother, wishing she would defy him and stay at the table, tell him dessert could wait. But she stood up and went into the kitchen, returning a few minutes later with a bowl of butterscotch pudding.

After that Dad and PJ left together, not saying where they were going. Probably to Cougar Creek Tavern. Cindy didn't bother to excuse herself from helping with the dishes even though it was one of the few chores she was expected to do; she and Freda went upstairs and from behind the closed door came the faint sound of Brenda Lee rockin' around the Christmas tree.

So Kit cleaned the kitchen by herself, thinking what a coward Cindy was for letting Dad humiliate her friend, but reminding herself that she hadn't said anything, either.

She went to her room and flopped onto her bed. The book Carlos had recommended, *The Man of Property*, sat on the nightstand. He thought she was wasting her time on the novels she usually read. Actually, that was the only time she'd found herself a little put out at him, when they'd talked about books. Kit had had to ride the bus that day because Cindy had a dentist appointment. Feeling bold, she'd sat next to Carlos and asked about the book they'd been talking about at lunch the day before. It was *In Chancery*, the second in The Forsyte Saga, which his class was reading.

"What is it you get out of it?" she'd asked.

"First off, Galsworthy uses language in a way most other writers only wish they could. And he's not telling a story just for its own sake, he's showing us something about society, about how people hurt each other through hypocrisy and greed. The novels he wrote are worth all those," and he'd gestured at her paperback Dick Francis mystery, "ten times over."

"How do you know?"

"It's the same book over and over again. And what does it tell you about real life? How does it change the way you look at the world? How does it help you understand anything?"

"So you think I'm just a brainless idiot."

"No, I don't. That's why I care what you read." He'd taken out his copy of *The Man of Property*. "You know what this book reminds me of? Piñon County. The people are upper-class English, but people here have the same kinds of prejudices and narrow-mindedness. And the same authoritarian family values."

That had startled her. How did he know about her family? Then she'd realized he meant families in general.

"Will you read it?" He'd looked at her intently, extending the book.

She'd reached for it reluctantly. "What if it's too hard?"

"Come on, Kit, it's not as hard as those textbooks you read

about horses. Anyway, doing something hard makes you stronger. It's like running; sure it's hard, but the more you do it, the stronger your lungs and legs get. Doing something mentally hard makes your brain stronger."

So she'd promised. That had been three days ago. She hadn't got too far yet, but tonight seemed like a good night to read, because she wanted to take her mind off the way things were in this house. She picked up the book.

When she finally set it down, it was one o'clock in the morning. Were men with property so different in 1980s California than they had been in England at the turn of the century? Didn't they still think of women as property? Or was it just men like Dad who thought that way, men who owned land and cared too much about money?

At least divorce was legal and not hard to get now, but on the other hand people still stayed together when they didn't love each other. Mom was as securely bound by her own attitudes as Irene was by the law.

How could a beautiful girl ever be sure that a boy liked her for herself, not just for what was on the outside? Maybe it was impossible to tell; a pretty woman might end up married to a man who would decide he didn't love her anymore when she was no longer so young and beautiful.

That was probably what had happened to Mom. Kit had always thought Mom was really pretty. Then, when she was about ten, she saw a photograph of Mom as a young woman. To this day, she could remember staring at that picture, so stunned she couldn't speak. Mom had been movie star beautiful. If she'd grown up in Los Angeles that's probably what she would've been. Instead, she'd grown up in Camargo and married Dad. They didn't even like each other, let alone love each other, and Mom was a lush. So where had being beautiful got her?

Sometimes Kit was glad she wasn't pretty. Because if a boy

ever loved her, she knew it would be for her personality and her character.

Despite going to sleep so late, she got up very early the next day and went out on Sadie, not even thinking about where she was going. Sadie's hooves crunched on the icy snow, and Kit pulled her hat low against the sharp glint of ice in the morning sun. The leather of the saddle creaked familiarly, a comforting sound.

She rode all the way to the border to Pardini Ranch and was surprised to find that the barbed wire fence was still down.

Why hadn't PJ fixed it yet? She'd told him about it during the Thanksgiving holiday, just before they took the cattle down to winter pasture. That had been five weeks ago.

She'd been riding near the creek and thought it odd that she hadn't seen the cattle. Then she'd come upon the broken fence and knew that the cattle had wandered onto the Pardinis' land. No telling how long the fence had been down, but the cattle had made a path into Pardini Ranch, and it was well-rutted by their hooves.

Keeping the fences in good repair was her responsibility in summer when she didn't have to go to school, and she rode out every day to inspect them; there was no section that she didn't inspect at least once a week. But this time of year, it was PJ's job, and she'd been surprised that he hadn't found and fixed this already.

If the only thing wrong with the fence was that the barbed wire had come down, Kit could have fixed it herself. But the post itself had been snapped in half. She'd had to get PJ. She'd shown him the fence and they'd rounded up the cattle. "We better tell Joe and Stella about this," she'd said as they drove the cattle back to their own ranch.

"No need to. I said I'd fix it. Besides, we're moving the cattle to west county this week."

"But PJ, the cattle might've been there a while, and you

know we've still got yellow star thistle on that part of the ranch."

"Hey, if Pardini doesn't pay enough attention to his land to notice the cow pies and figure it out himself, then the dumb dago's in the wrong business."

"But he might not come down to this part of his land every single day, PJ. We should tell him so he can take care of it before the thistle seeds."

"All right, all right, I'll call him," PJ had said.

Now here it was the end of December, and the fence was still broken. Kit dismounted Sadie and looked closely. The broken post lay exactly as it had when she'd found it. PJ hadn't even dug a new post hole. So had he bothered to tell Joe and Stella that the cattle had been on their ranch?

Kit patted Sadie nervously. Cattle loved yellow star thistle and could eat it with no ill effects, then spread it wherever they defecated. Horses and livestock picked up the seeds in their hooves, trucks in their tires, and hikers in their boots, and transported seeds to other areas. A single seed was all it took; you could have no yellow star thistle, and two years later your land would be covered with it. It choked out the native grasses, with long taproots that stole water from everything else.

Mowing made it spread, unless done during a very narrow timeframe when the native grasses had begun drying up and the thistle was barely beginning to bud. That condition might exist on one acre and not the next. And if you had the mower blades set too high or too low, you'd spread the thistle. Mulching was prohibitively expensive and only possible on small areas. Thistle thrived in dry, hot conditions so it grew well during droughts. There were herbicides that would kill it, but would also kill everything else, and you couldn't keep animals from eating poisoned plants.

Worst of all, horses liked the taste of yellow star thistle. If they ate a lot of it, they got sick very quickly, within a few months. If they ate a little of it over a long time, they got sick slowly. Chewing disease, ranchers called it. It was like Parkinson's disease. The horse gradually lost control of its motor movements and developed a terrible twitch in its upper lip. The twitch was so bad the horse was unable to pick up, chew or swallow food, and eventually couldn't even drink water. The kindest thing to do was put the horse down at the first sign. Because there was no treatment and the horse would die, slowly and painfully.

Kit had never had a problem keeping Sadie from eating yellow star thistle, because she was kept in a corral where there was none. The corral was not large and Kit inspected it carefully and often for signs of thistle. A few years ago she'd found it starting. She'd gone to the Forest Service for their brochures and she'd managed to eradicate the weed from the corral by careful mowing at exactly the right time, followed by diligent mulching.

The Pardini horses were often turned onto their land, where they were allowed to wander and graze freely all day long. That was why Kit had insisted that the Pardinis be told.

Kit remounted Sadie. It's not right, he didn't tell them, she said to herself. She gently tugged Sadie's reins to the left and they headed west, toward the Pardinis' house.

Chapter Ten

SUPER BOWL SUNDAY, JANUARY 20, 1985

On the clear, cold Sunday afternoon of January 20th, almost every TV in Piñon County was on and tuned to ABC. The Niners were in the Super Bowl and Piñon County was 49er country. Wanda had been up half the night Thursday and Friday baking special order pies; half the town must've been hosting parties for the other half. Fred had doubled his order with the beer distributor, expecting Cougar Creek Tavern to do a brisk business Sunday afternoon. Shops in Camargo normally open on Sunday had posted hastily scrawled signs: *CLOSED FOR SUPER BOWL, GO NINERS!*

Stella Pardini didn't go riding that day. She sat at the kitchen table carefully reviewing the transcript of the Planning Commission's November hearing. Game sounds filtered in from the living room. All week long, Joe had been taking guff from 49er fans, on top of the guff he already took for remaining a Raiders fan even after they'd absconded to L.A. a few years ago.

He called in commentary to Stella. "Starting from their own six … For Pete's sake, they let Montana run for fifteen yards! … Marino to Johnson! Beautiful! … Ha, they finally sacked Montana … That wasn't an incomplete pass! It was a fumble, damn it!"

She smiled at the ups and downs in his voice, but soon was immersed in the transcript. She wanted to let the lawyer know by Monday morning of any substantial errors. The full hearing was set for next week in Sacramento and would address the county's failure to adequately address water supply, construction of a sewer system, the necessity for roads, future government expense likely to result from forest fires, and violation of the Piñon County General Plan. The California Native Plant Society had filed papers asking to be heard. Their concern was to prevent destruction of the rare Higuera paintbrush.

The lawsuit had brought things out in the open even more than the Planning Commission's hearing had. East county residents were now divided into two camps. But it was funny, Stella mused. You could go into Wanda's just about any morning and a man who was suing the Planning Commission would be sitting at the counter next to a man hoping to sell his land to the developers. Sometimes the tension was pretty thick, but there they all were, inches apart, eating Wanda's Hangtown Fry and drinking her San Francisco coffee, politely passing each other the catsup bottle or sugar dispenser.

During halftime Joe came into the kitchen and opened the refrigerator.

"Let me warm that up for you. What's the score now?"

"14–10 San Francisco," Joe said glumly.

Stella got out the saucepan. "I know you don't like that team, but they are special. You know that yourself, Joe, even if you won't admit it."

He leaned over and kissed her gently. "To you I will. To no one else."

Smiling to herself, Stella warmed the ravioli, filled his plate and generously topped it with freshly grated Parmesan. She brought the food into the living room and watched for a while.

"The 49er secondary looks very good."

"Yeah, yeah," Joe grumbled.

"Especially number 22."

"He's not the best of them, either."

"Mm. Well, that depends on your point of view. From this angle—"

"Stella! This is a serious football game," Joe said sternly.

"I'll get back to my work then." Stella laughed.

After finishing the corrections, she returned the transcript to the file, which she would be bringing down to the lawyer's office first thing tomorrow. The lawyer would notify the court of the errata.

Stella knew there was more to come. Its remote location had not exempted Piñon County from the blight. A development of 100 houses seemed impossibly large, but of course that wasn't so. In other places, developments often consisted of thousands of houses.

She didn't think such large-scale developments were feasible here in eastern Piñon County, much of which was preserved as part of the Higuera National Forest. Most of the privately owned parcels were small, ten or twenty acres. The only large properties were the three contiguous ones: the lumber mill, Joe and Stella's ranch, and the Jensen cattle ranch.

GUNFIRE PUNCTURED THE sky in Piñon County for hours after the 49ers' resounding victory. Not just pistol shots; people fired rifles and even double barrel shotguns. Impromptu parades clogged the main roads, and celebrants leaned on their car horns, whooped and yelled. Air horns blared and firecrackers exploded. Bars were filled with boisterous fans. Sheriff Stick Jensen had called in all ten deputies.

Pete and PJ spent the evening at Cougar Creek Tavern and didn't get home until just past two. PJ stumbled upstairs and barely managed to lurch as far as his bed, where he passed out fully clothed on top of the covers.

Pete was hungry and went into the kitchen, where he found Laura still up. She was reading, a glass of brandy beside her. He told her to make him some bacon and eggs. The deliberateness with which Laura moved infuriated him. "Get a move on, damn it!"

But he would've sworn she didn't move even one iota more quickly. He watched her with gritted teeth until his anger boiled up and out, and he backhanded her. He meant to hit her lightly across the face, just to wake her up. But his aim was off, and so was his judgment. He struck hard behind her jaw, and she went to the floor.

"Get up. You're not hurt."

Laura slowly got up. A welt glared angrily on her neck. Pete knew it was going to be a hell of a bruise in a day or two. Luckily her hair was long. He cursed himself for hitting her when he was not only drunk, but out of practice at not leaving marks in visible places.

Laura finished cooking while twin rivulets trailed silently down her face. She moved no faster than before, but Pete set his jaw and occupied himself with the Sunday paper while he waited. Finally, she put the plate before him. He concentrated on the food and the real estate section, and was relieved when she silently left the kitchen.

Chapter Eleven

Saturday was Terri Mathieson's busiest day. Saturday was *everyone's* busiest day, so on the Saturday after the Super Bowl all seven chairs and the manicure station at The Cutting Edge were occupied, despite the icy roads and bitter cold. The shop vibrated with the sound of dryers, scissors, razors, the telephone, and women's voices. Women leafed through magazines; sat under the dryers in the back room; stood outside to smoke cigarettes; had their nails painted or facial hair ripped off with wax strips. Not a man in the place. Had one ventured in, he would have been surprised at the sudden change in atmosphere; for a beauty parlor without women's voices seems eerie.

Four years ago, the House o'Beauty had changed ownership and got a makeover. Maya painted the walls robin's egg blue with a bright pink trim, hung plants from the ceiling beams, and put in a manicure station. The old sign came down and The Cutting Edge was painted on the window in art deco style. The shop would hereafter be called a salon, not a beauty parlor, and the hairdressers were now stylists.

Terri greeted her next customer. Laura Jensen was one of Terri's best customers: she had a regular monthly appointment, bought hair care products for herself and her two daughters from Terri, and tipped well.

Laura set down *Glamour* and brought her travel cup to Terri's station. Terri tied an apron around her neck. Laura had thick, heavy, dark brown hair, going a little gray but Terri took care of that. "I think we can go another month before a touch up," she said, and Laura nodded. "So, just a trim and conditioning today?"

"Yes. But don't trim it too much. I like having it over my ears and neck in the winter."

Terri took her to the shampoo bar and began to lather her hair. As she scrubbed low on the right side, Laura winced. "Sorry," Terri said, thinking she had accidentally hit a sensitive spot. A few minutes later, they returned to Terri's chair in the middle of the salon. All around them women were talking— talking the way women did in no other place.

Terri sometimes reflected on the code of the salon. Although she had been a hairdresser for nearly eight years, she was still sometimes startled by the things women told her. But, much as a psychiatrist was legally bound to silence, Terri considered herself ethically bound. Just as she would never reveal what she'd learned about another woman's physical shortcomings or the methods used to conceal them, her customers' confidences never went beyond her chair. Her sister Loretta called it 'beauty parlor *omertà*.'

Of course, if someone at the next chair overheard gossip, it was fair game. But customers knew that, and whenever a woman told Terri something confidential, she told it in a low voice, and even then only if the operators at the next chairs were too busy with their own customers to eavesdrop.

Terri combed Laura's hair, lifting it out. Suddenly she was

confronted, just under Laura's right ear, with a large, ugly bruise. She froze, her comb poised, and the two women's eyes met in the mirror. It was impossible to read anything in Laura's even, stoic expression.

At the next chair, Vickie was saying, "But if you love a man, you should trust him. You shouldn't be thinking about the property settlement before the wedding!"

Terri's heart raced. The bruise was a bad one, red-purple in some places, in others faded to yellow, but she knew Laura's neck must have been awfully sore.

"Love's one thing, honey," Vickie's customer said. "Property's something else."

Terri casually took another small white towel and wrapped it high on Laura's neck, gently covered the bruise, and clipped the towel closed in the front. Laura smiled ever so slightly.

"Well," said Vickie philosophically, "I guess you never know what can happen."

"Exactly," Vickie's customer said. "You could be married for fifteen years and then your husband gets male menopause and leaves you for some twenty-five-year-old."

"Or the love fades and he starts getting mean," said Angie's customer. "That happens a lot more than people know."

Fifteen minutes later, Vickie had taken her next customer back to the shampoo bar. Angie and the chair across from her were having a raucous discussion about a television show. Terri was touching up Laura's trim. She'd taken off less than usual from the length.

Suddenly Laura said, in a very low voice, "At least I did that much."

"Did what?"

"Kept some property in my name."

Terri nearly dropped her scissors. She had never, not once, heard Laura say anything to indicate she mistrusted Pete

Jensen, or anything that could be remotely interpreted as defiance of him.

"Well, that's good," Terri said cautiously.

"The high ranch," Laura continued. "The ranch in west county is his. It's been in the Jensen family for generations. But the Double-L was bought with the money I got from selling my mother's house. So we put it in my name."

While Laura used the ladies' room, Terri swept the floor in her station. She met Laura at the cash register. "Thank you," Laura said as she handed Terri the money. As usual, she gave a five-dollar tip, almost the price of the cut. "For everything," she added, briefly touching Terri's hand. Their eyes met. Laura was smiling. Terri smiled back, but she knew the worry probably showed in her eyes.

AS USUAL ON a Saturday night, Terri was exhausted. But she bathed Troy, tucked him in and read aloud *The Lorax* yet again, while Ray helped Trixie with her homework. Finally Terri put on her cozy flannel nightgown and got into bed, sitting against the pillows propped against the headboard, with a glass of Zin in one hand and her library book, *Summer*, in the other.

Normally, Ray was laid off for about a month in the winter. The seasonal construction lull was a mixed blessing; a few years ago, the last time there had been a wet winter, he'd been on unemployment for two months and they'd had to dip into their savings to get through. Even so, Terri always looked forward to that winter break, which apparently would not happen this year. It was almost February and Ray had worked straight through the season so far.

"Maybe we'll get some late winter storms and have snow at Tahoe into May," she said wistfully.

"Maybe, but it doesn't feel like it." Ray pulled off his sweatshirt and examined it. Terri could see mud splatters from his soccer match with Trixie and catsupy fingerprints from Troy's dinner. He tossed the sweatshirt into the hamper.

He went to take a shower. She sighed and took a big gulp of wine. They probably wouldn't get a real vacation all winter. If only he hadn't agreed to take on those big projects.

But life was full of compromises. She'd made a few herself, after all. Not in her job so much as other ways. She'd decided to accept his deceitfulness, something she'd once sworn was the one thing she would never tolerate.

No marriage was without problems, and a woman couldn't choose the way in which her husband hurt or disappointed her. But far better Ray's transgressions than what Pete did to Laura. She thought of that bruise on Laura's neck and shuddered. And suddenly she remembered an occasion years ago, when she'd overheard her parents talking about Pete and Laura.

She must have been seven or eight years old. They were at a barbecue at her parents' friends' house. Stuck in the boring afternoon with adults who got drunker as the day got longer, she began eavesdropping on the adults, while carefully keeping her eyes glued to *Photoplay*.

Someone mentioned the Jensens and someone else commented how they thought they were better than everyone else, and Terri's father added, "Even the ones like Pete that would've been in jail a few times if it weren't for being a Jensen."

"In jail?" one woman said. "For what?"

"He was pretty wild when he was a kid. One time he ran into old Klaus the barber, and just drove off."

"Just left Klaus lying there in the street," snorted one of the men. "Good thing he wasn't hurt too bad."

"And Pete didn't get arrested?"

Laughter, and someone said, "You kidding?"

Then her mother said, "What he ought to go to jail for is the way he treats his wife."

"Now, Joyce," Terri's father said, "don't go spreading stories that might not be true."

"If you'd seen her the other day, you'd know it was true," Mom returned hotly.

It had been years since Terri had heard any similar gossip about Pete and Laura. Of course, she didn't move in the same circles as the Jensens, and Laura was of a different generation. But maybe Ray had heard things. He wasn't friends with Laura's son, PJ, but he did know him. They'd gone to high school together and played on the football team.

Ray had finished his shower and returned to the bedroom. She couldn't think of how to ask him whether he'd ever heard rumors without betraying the beauty parlor *omertà*. Instead, she mentioned that she'd seen Laura Jensen that day, adding, "She doesn't look a day over thirty-five."

"She's always been beautiful." Ray sat in the dressing table chair and spread a newspaper under his feet. "My freshman year I had a huge crush on her."

"Really? Did she know?"

"I thought I was keeping it under wraps. But how discreet is a fourteen-year-old with raging hormones?"

"Not very." Terri laughed. "Did you see her often?"

"No, hardly ever." He leaned over and clipped a toenail. "PJ had a couple of parties for the guys on the team. That's the only time I saw her, up at the house. I don't remember ever seeing her in town." He looked at Terri. "I never liked Pete much. I couldn't figure out what she saw in him."

"I can't imagine." She grimaced.

"Maybe he wasn't so full of himself when he was young. Or so mean."

Her heartbeat quickened. "Mean to Laura?"

"I don't know. I remember there were rumors, but I never saw them together. I meant to PJ. If PJ made a mistake in a game, like fumbled or missed a tackle, he was afraid to go home and get hell from his old man."

"What kind of hell? Did Pete used to beat him?"

Ray shrugged. "We all got smacked around sometimes. I don't think PJ got it worse than anyone else, but we never talked about stuff like that. But Pete gave PJ hell verbally. And once he got started, he wouldn't let up."

"Like what?"

"One time we were up there at PJ's for a pool party and another guy beat PJ arm wrestling. Pete was on his case about it all day. Someone would ask if there were any more sodas, and Pete would say, 'Go ask sissy boy!' or 'Have the pansy get some.' Finally, PJ got mad, and that's what Pete was waiting for. 'Think you can handle me?' he says. 'Go ahead, make your move.' So PJ went for him and Pete put him down with one hand. He made sure everyone knew PJ was crying."

"What a bully," Terri said.

"Yeah, it seemed like the more humiliated PJ was, the more Pete liked it. He used to call PJ 'Re-Pete.' He'd say, 'The copy's never as good as the original.' But you know what's really weird? Now they're together all the time, PJ and Pete." Ray shook his head and bent over again.

She picked up her book and Ray got into bed with his.

He must've been more tired than usual, for within five minutes *Giant Steps* had fallen from his hand and he was sound asleep.

Terri was still wide awake. She felt uneasy about not having told Ray about the bruise on Laura's neck, as though she had lied to him, even though all she'd done was not betray a confidence, albeit one that hadn't been directly asked for.

She picked up *Summer* and was soon re-absorbed into

Charity Royall's life. Her sense of dread increased with each page. Charity would probably end up pregnant, a 'fallen woman' in a small town where ostracism was the weapon used to enforce conformity and punish rebellion. It gave her a nightmare that Laura Jensen was mixed up in, though when she woke up, heart pounding, she couldn't remember how.

Chapter Twelve

The first weekend in February was clear and bone-chillingly cold. Arla jogged only two miles Saturday morning before turning back. Every intake of breath felt like an icicle piercing her lungs. Twice, she almost slipped on black ice.

She should have gone to Marin last night. Now it was too late; to the west, the storm had certainly begun already. She'd experienced the terror of driving through winter storms in the San Joaquin Valley, sheets of rain cutting visibility to nil and flooding every dip of the highway while other drivers still sped along at seventy miles per hour—just as they did when the tule fog was so thick you couldn't see more than ten feet ahead.

Amazing the way a winter storm stopped everything out here. Not long after she and Steve moved to Marin, a storm swept down from Alaska; by noon, two feet of snow had fallen in the Sierras and another foot was expected. Let's go to Tahoe, she'd suggested, excited at the idea of all that fresh powder. But Steve had shaken his head and explained that the road would be closed until the snow stopped falling. 'Highway 80?' she'd exclaimed in disbelief. 'But that's an interstate!' Then she'd grumbled that this wouldn't happen in New York.

'No, it wouldn't,' Steve had retorted, 'because the so-called mountains there aren't ten thousand feet high.'

But she had to get some shopping done before the snow and before the 'chains required' signs went up. She had chains in her trunk, of course, kept them there all winter; but she couldn't put them on by herself.

Most of the stores had just opened and Camargo was bustling; probably everyone had the same idea as she had. After buying groceries, she also got a few more sacks of rock salt. She was surprised at how quickly she'd been going through it. Her driveway, though short, sloped enough to get very slippery.

As she drove along Main Street, the beautiful old Victorian house caught her eye. She knew this was the headquarters for the historical society as well as the county museum. Impulsively, she parked and walked to the house. It sat on a narrow lot with buildings of much more recent origin crowding in on both sides. She entered through an iron gate. An historical marker on the lawn read: *CUSHING HOUSE, 1887. Built entirely of locally harvested sequoias by Judge Hiram Cushing.*

Six stairs led up to a broad porch. As Arla pushed open the front door, a bell tinkled. "Hello!" called out a woman's voice, from a room off the entry hall. Arla approached. "Hi, are you open?"

"The information desk is, but the museum doesn't open until noon," replied the elderly woman at the desk. Her hair was a halo of iridescent white curls.

"I was just passing by and this house caught my eye. I can come back another time."

"You're new here in town?" the woman asked, peering over her glasses.

"New since August. My name is Arla Stinson."

"Pleased to meet you. I'm Mary O'Malley." They shook hands. "Where are you living?"

"Blackberry Springs."

"Ah! You're the woman from San Francisco." Arla must have shown her surprise; Mary smiled. "We're all curious whenever someone new moves up. Welcome to Piñon County, Arla. You're probably the newest resident, and I may be the oldest."

"You've lived here all your life?"

"All eighty-one years of it," Mary O'Malley said. "I was born right down the street, in the old county hospital. They tore it down in 1966 to make way for that lovely county administration building."

"That gray one that looks like a fortress?"

"The same." She smiled wryly. "The demolition of that beautiful old hospital was what prompted me to join the historical society."

"You must know quite a lot about the county."

"Eighty-one years of history personally, and the rest from reading up. And," Mary's eyes lit with amusement, "sometimes reading between the lines. This brochure will tell you about the house. I'm sorry I can't give you a tour." She glanced at her watch. "I'd urge you to wait for the docent, but with this storm coming, she may not make it in today."

"That's okay, I'm trying to get back home before it starts snowing." Arla took the brochure. "I'll read this and come back another day."

"Are you interested in history? Or mostly in architecture?"

"History more than architecture. I grew up in New York, and after I moved to the Bay Area I got interested in the Gold Rush."

"And now here you are in one of the places where the gold was being dug."

"And fortunes made," Arla said, glancing around the house.

"Oh, the Cushings didn't make their money mining gold.

In fact, very few men did." Mary shook her head. "I do go on and on."

"But I want to know."

"Don't say I didn't warn you."

"Scout's honor," Arla laughed.

"Well, it was late January of 1848 when gold was discovered, so the news didn't reach back east for some months. The gold seekers had to plan their journey around the winter, if they came by land, or around ship schedules. So even those who came as quickly as they could didn't get to California until 1849. By that time, people who'd been out west before the discovery had already been working in the gold fields for a year and had claimed the easiest pickings. A few '49ers struck it lucky, but most barely eked out enough to survive. By the early 1850s, many had gone home. Some who stayed ended up working in someone else's mining operation for a daily wage."

"So how did the Cushings get rich?"

"Ah, yes. Elihu Cushing was a '49er with a law degree. He found that, contrary to rumor, a man couldn't pick up chunks of gold from the ground or streambed; it took hard physical labor, which might not even pan out, if you'll forgive my pun. A miner had to live in the most deplorable conditions, and ran a high risk of dying from disease, starvation, accident, or violence.

"And furthermore, suppose a man staked out a good claim? The best ones might produce fifty dollars a day. Now, in 1849, a good wage in New York was a dollar a day. But in California, a man could scarcely be comfortable, let alone rich, on fifty dollars a day, which was considerably more than most miners took in. A miner spent almost every penny on the necessities of life. A pound of flour cost two dollars and a shovel was fifty. An egg cost a dollar and canned oysters were a dollar per oyster.

So Elihu Cushing opened a supply store. You might say he mined the miners."

"And the judge who built this house, was that his son?" Arla asked, remembering the sign in front of the building.

"Yes. Elihu Cushing was a judge, and so was his son Hiram and his grandson Marcus." Mary grinned. "Townspeople referred to the Superior Court judgeship as 'the Cushing seat.' Still do. The great-grandson broke tradition by becoming a developer. If I'm not mistaken, he built the house you live in."

"It was built by Eagle Development," Arla said.

Mary O'Malley nodded. "Hiram Cushing, owner and president. Of course, the Cushing seat still has a Cushing. Hiram Cushing's brother-in-law is the Superior Court judge."

"There's only one Superior Court judge in the whole county?"

"No, there's also a family law court judge, John Owens. He's descended from a pioneer family too, the Jensens."

"Jensen," Arla repeated. The name was familiar.

"They're in real estate too, and the sheriff is a Jensen," Mary explained. Perhaps she would have said more, but the telephone rang.

"I'll be off, then," Arla said.

Mary reached for the phone. "Please, take this membership form with you. I do hope you come back. Good morning, Piñon County Historical Society."

Arla tucked the brochure and membership form into her bag and carefully walked to Camargo Bicycle and Mountaineering, five blocks that felt longer in the icy wind. She entered the store and it took a few moments before her eyes adjusted to the rather dark interior. A man's back was to her, but she recognized him. There was a little girl with him, a pretty towhead seven or eight years old.

The man behind the counter looked up at Arla. "Hi, be right with you."

"That's okay, I know what I need," she replied. Adonis – Ray, she reminded herself – glanced over. Arla thought his eyes widened momentarily, but in the dimness of the shop she couldn't be sure. He nodded in a polite way, one customer greeting another.

"…think they could do it, even after they creamed Chicago in the playoffs," the shopkeeper was saying. "Heck, Marino threw four TDs against Pittsburgh."

"Pittsburgh ain't got Ronnie Lott," said Ray.

"Man, that secondary! Did you see…"

Arla tuned out and concentrated on the winter running gear. When she brought her items to the counter, the shopkeeper was avidly analyzing something called a dime defense. He broke off. "Oh, sorry. Will that be all?"

"That's all," she replied, smiling indulgently. Ray was wearing a fleece-lined Levi jacket over, of course, a 49er sweatshirt. She was startled by the incredibly deep blue of his eyes.

"You're the lady lives up in Blackberry Springs, aren't you?" he said.

"Yes, and you're the man who built it, aren't you?"

He grinned. "I helped build it. I work for Eagle Development. Ray Mathieson," and he extended his hand.

"Arla Stinson," she replied, and when their hands touched, the electric shock was so strong that a spark flashed.

"Whoa!" said the shopkeeper. "Must be the weather."

"Must be," Ray agreed, but as his eyes met hers, Arla thought she saw a small smile.

"Everything working out with the house? Any problems?"

"Oh, no, it's a wonderful house, and the setting is so beautiful. I'm surprised the rest of the houses haven't sold."

"Not many people want to move this far up in the mountains," Ray said. "Not without all the amenities close at hand, anyway."

The shopkeeper ran Arla's credit card through a machine. "Ray, when do you start working on the mall? This summer?"

"Probably. And once the mall's open, the rest of the houses will sell like hotcakes, Mrs. Stinson. You'll have plenty of neighbors."

"Please, call me Arla," she said, her eyes meeting his. She was well aware that he probably knew she was actually divorced. If even the ladies in the Historical Society knew such things about her, surely he did, too.

"Daddy, can we go now?" the little girl piped up.

"Yep, we're ready. Nice to meet you, Arla."

Arla, putting her card back into her wallet, glanced at him leaving. And she could have sworn that, as he held open the door for his daughter, he was glancing surreptitiously at her.

Chapter Thirteen

Stella liked winter, so long as it wasn't extreme. But the cold snap in early February was the coldest in twenty-two years. All over Piñon County people listened to weather prognostications with unusual attentiveness.

Cold seems colder without snow, and this was a cold spell without moisture. The snowpack at Cougar Pass was only thirty-two inches; the seasonal norm was eighty-eight. Since this winter had been so dry, the deep freeze would be especially injurious to trees. Many would die. That did not bode well for the next fire season. Some days, a wind bore down from the north and chilled Stella into the marrow of her bones. Good thing propane wasn't expensive, because they were using twice as much as normal.

On Monday, Joe headed into town to get supplies and she decided to take Tabasco out on a long ride, southwest toward the national forest and the river. She left a note for Joe, filled her water bag, grabbed two apples—one for herself and one for Tabasco—and the revolver, because you never know.

She rode past the stone wall built by Joe's great-grandfather almost a hundred years ago; it was one of the few rock walls in Piñon County not built by Chinese laborers.

Most locals had little interest in history, even that of their own families, but Joe knew his fairly well.

His Russian great-grandfather Mikhail Verkhovsky and Mikhail's uncle Andrei had been the first of Joe's family to come to Piñon County. Mikhail fell in love with Maria, an emigrant from Chile. They built a house close to town and started a farm. Uncle Andrei, who worked in a mine, lived next door in a one-room cabin. The area became known as Russian Camp.

By 1885, Mikhail and Maria had raised all their children. One daughter, Luisa, lived with them. When the fire started in the middle of the night, it spread through the settlement so quickly that there was no time to evacuate the animals; most were burned in their barns or suffocated by smoke in their pens. All seventeen houses in Russian Camp burned to the ground. One person did not escape: Andrei Verkhovsky.

At first it was believed that Uncle Andrei had started the fire accidentally, but later it was found to have been the work of two arsonists, who were hanged.

But in 1885 homeowners' insurance was not commonly held; all that Mikhail and Maria had left was their ten acres, now scorched, and a contaminated well. Without so much as a single tree to soak up the water and anchor the earth, the next rainy season would wash away the topsoil that Mikhail and Maria had spent so many years coaxing into existence out of the Sierra clay.

When Judge Cushing offered to buy their ten acres for a price that was generous considering the condition of the land, although much less than it had been worth several days earlier, they accepted. Other Russian Camp residents received similar offers. The judge was much praised for his generosity.

Their daughter Luisa, Joe's grandmother, had been bitter.

The judge robbed us, she'd told Joe more than once. *He bought the land where the fire had been and only a year later, sold it at a much higher price.*

Yet there was no evidence that Judge Cushing had known that the value of the land would increase three-fold within a year. It was plausible that he was merely lucky, as the rich so often were.

Mikhail and Maria bought twenty-nine acres high in the mountains. They started again.

Half a century ago Joe's parents had planted trees in the valley, and now the poplars towered behind the barn, adding graceful beauty to it, especially in autumn when the leaves turned bright yellow. Sycamores loomed over the house, a blessing in the summer when their abundant foliage assured that the house stayed relatively cool, and a bane in the autumn when the leaves fell for months. Since sycamore leaves were useless as mulch, they had to be raked into piles and burned. Raked and raked and raked, Stella thought wryly.

The one-story house had originally been a perfect square, but with additions over the years it was now irregularly shaped. The front porch faced south, so was often sun-drenched. The barn and stable were east of the house and were painted the same brick red. Directly across from the stable were the six guest cottages, far enough from the house to give the guests privacy, but not so far that they'd feel isolated.

Northwest of the house, where the land began a long slope upward, nature had carved a creek bed. Beside this small stream Joe and Stella had their garden. When Stella drove down the ranch road, she liked to pause on the rise and look down on the lush green sprinkled with the bright red of tomatoes and strawberries, the purple bunches of grapes, glistening yellow squash.

Over the years the Pardinis bought adjacent parcels, and by the time Joe inherited it in 1965 the ranch had grown to its present size, 967 acres. The ranch was shaped like a ragged rectangle leaning east. To the north the highway formed the property line. The entire western border was shared with Slide-Pac and included an eight-foot cyclone fence constructed at what must have been considerable expense. The eastern border was contiguous with the Jensen property, and to the south was the national forest.

These days Pardini Ranch was known for its horses, but when old-timers referred to Pardini Ranch they meant Pardini chicken ranch.

At twenty-six, Stella had long been considered an old maid. In Piñon County, few women still single by the ripe old age of twenty ever married. "I can't understand why a girl as pretty as you isn't married yet," one or another aunt would say. And Stella would reply, "Just lucky, I guess."

Her family would have been dismayed had they known that Stella had already turned down several proposals. She would think she loved someone, only to realize that she couldn't bear the thought of waking up next to him day after day for the rest of her life.

Of course, she'd known Joe for years. Piñon County was not large and the Italians did tend to stick together, even thoroughly Americanized and thoroughly assimilated Italians like the Pardinis. Joe was ten years older than her and a veteran, having spent World War II in the Philippines. Slivers of shrapnel still resided in his left leg. He had also been married for a few years—one of those hasty, short lived war marriages. The Minellis assumed that his being divorced took him out of the realm of Stella's prospective suitors. But Stella had renounced the Church as a teenager and considered Joe's rather virulent anti-Catholicism a strong point in his favor.

And when they did finally sleep together, Stella knew this was one man she wouldn't mind waking up next to every morning.

'How'd you get her to marry you?' Stella's brother-in-law once asked, and Joe answered, 'I'm the first man she ever met she liked as much as her horse.' They all laughed, but it was true.

Sitting high on her horse's back, both of them exhaling plumes of white in the crisp mountain air, Stella sighed happily. She was so fortunate. Fortunate to love and to be loved by Joe, to live in the mountains, to ride a horse to work.

She rode past the fence that marked the ranch boundary to the Higuera National Forest. At the river, Tabasco stopped for a drink and Stella filled her canteen. She had never seen the Middle Fork this low in winter. And with the meager snowpack, there would not be much spring runoff.

Last week the judge had ruled that the Gennessee Mine development did not violate the county's General Plan. Nor had the court ordered that the development be stopped merely to spare the Higuera paintbrush. Cushing's lawyers had cited numerous cases in which an offshoot of a plant species had not been allowed to impede a project that would greatly help a local economy. The Native Plant Society had been granted permission to retrieve samples of the Higuera paintbrush to be preserved by botanists.

As to the lack of proper notice for the Planning Commission's hearing in November, the court ruled that while this had indeed violated the city charter, in this case it was a harmless error since the notice had been only three days late and all of the interested persons had received actual notice. The Planning Commission was ordered to pay a sanction of $500 to plaintiffs. $500 barely made a dent in the lawyer's bill.

There would be no appeal, because Joe and Stella had no more money for lawyers. The battle was lost, and so was a large chunk of Joe and Stella's money. They had run out of ways to economize. And there was no way to make more money in the business. They did not even consider doing autumn or winter pack trips, because that meant guiding hunters. They used to offer hunting trips. Since local people knew where and how to hunt, their customers were city or suburban men and their sons. City men going hunting had an unfortunate propensity for asserting their masculinity with an inflated macho attitude. This made them unpleasant company and unreliable trail companions, even without the additional complicating factor of their being armed. Two seasons of that had been more than enough.

They did rent out the horses to local hunters, but that brought in very little money. They couldn't board other people's horses; the barn was already filled to capacity. (Not that many Piñon County horse owners had to board their horses, anyway.) There was no capital with which to start some other enterprise.

They had decided: one more season, and if they didn't at least break even, they would give up the outfitting business.

The idea of having no regular source of income was frightening, but on the other hand, they did not live extravagantly and if they weren't operating the outfitting business their expenses would be low.

And in another few years, when the bank loan was paid off, they would need even less money to get by. Between what they could grow and raise, and the social security checks that Joe would be able to draw in a few years, they could almost make it.

She and Tabasco meandered alongside the river almost as far as the lake, then went north to Cougar Creek and followed it back toward Pardini Ranch. The creek was nearly dry, and what water there was flowed under a sheet of ice.

Tabasco shook his head and shied, and a few seconds later she saw that some fifty feet ahead, where brush gave way to an open field, was a bobcat. She was surprised that it didn't flee, since bobcats were very shy around humans. Then she saw why.

It was caught in a trap. Even from this distance she could see that it was panting. She dismounted and approached cautiously. The bobcat's eyes were unfocused, clouded over in pain. It had been caught by the worst sort of trap. Sharp steel claws had ripped into and pinioned its rear leg. The cat had tried to gnaw its own leg off to free itself, but starvation and pain had weakened it too much.

She walked Tabasco fifty yards away and tied him to a tree, then went back to the bobcat. It was beyond caring that she was there. She took her revolver from the holster, put it to the bobcat's head, and shot.

By the time she got to the house she was no longer crying, but her anger had not dissipated. She called the Forest Service about the illegal abandoned trap and told them she'd had to put the bobcat out of its suffering. The ranger said they'd come get it and would she mind coming down to sign a statement sometime in the next few days.

Joe wasn't back from town to talk her down. She grabbed a box of reloads and walked the half-mile to their makeshift range. Tin cans stood in for the animal torturer. Stella shot the cans into bits. Humans were supposed to be guardians of the planet, not its depraved despoilers.

She set up another row of tin cans.

INTERLUDE

March 1888
Stubbs Landing, California

The superintendent was proud of his institution. A private facility, San Joaquin Sanitarium was run with the discretion and comfort required by the wealthy patients and their families, and the efficiency required by the owners. The buildings were designed in the Kirkbride style, and the grounds were immense, immaculate, and beautiful. The food was of high quality, well prepared and delicious.

The facility housed anywhere from fifty to eighty patients. Each had his or her own room. The west wing housed voluntary patients as well as those who, though not here of their own volition, had been judged only moderately ill.

The more difficult patients were kept in a separate wing on the east side of the administration building; their rantings and screams could not be heard by patients in the west wing. The vast majority of the difficult patients were women. Often, it was necessary to resort to such means as hydrotherapy (submersion in ice baths or alternating hot and cold baths for several hours) and sensory isolation (bandages over the eyes and ears), and in severe cases, restraints. Sometimes, unfortunately, none of those methods succeeded in calming a woman. One surgery coming into vogue for a certain type of nervousness was to remove the source of agitation by performing clitoridectomies.

The superintendent was dismayed to learn that the newest patient, who had seemed relatively serene and had been assigned to the west side, had apparently been storing her sedatives in order to end her life. He had written to the husband. Such letters were his duty and he was skillful at composing them. The letters could not be stern or abrupt, but neither could they descend into the maudlin. They must contain the correct balance of straightforwardness and sympathy.

When Hiram Cushing arrived to collect the body of his wife, the superintendent was duly impressed. More commonly, those who died in the institution were abandoned by their families, who were duly sent a bill for burial services. Furthermore, a man as wealthy as Judge Cushing might have sent others for this task; that he undertook it himself proved his devotion.

THE LOWEST PAID and lowest ranking of all the staff of San Joaquin Sanitarium was Jorge Salvador, a gardener, barely twenty years of age. After Catherine Cushing's death, rumors spread throughout the institution that Mrs. Cushing had apparently committed suicide but, as usual in such cases, no information was provided to non-medical employees.

As Jorge raked the sand walkway, he saw Mr. Cushing arrive at the Sanitarium. A tall, stout man with a slightly florid complexion, Mr. Cushing was snappish with his driver and brusque with the staff member who greeted his coach. Perhaps grief had caused him to forget his manners. But even so, that meant his manners only went skin-deep.

Jorge suspected that the husband was the reason for the troubles of the gentle, kind Mrs. Cushing. Her suffering had been apparent in her eyes, yet never once had she spoken to Jorge rudely or inconsiderately. Only at his request had she called him by his first name. That she pronounced his name correctly had led to his finding out that she had learned a bit of Spanish from a friend. Eventually, Jorge had offered to post her letters to that friend, because she did not wish to submit them for the doctor's approval.

Jorge had been expecting that she would leave him another letter to post. She had told him she would. She had said it would be in the usual hiding place. That was two days ago, when they had seen one another in the garden, where he pulled weeds one by one and she sat nearby on the bench. They had spoken softly and maintained their positions so that if anyone noticed them, it would seem merely that the patient was enjoying the flowers and perhaps commenting on them to one of the gardeners. But despite the outer serenity, her voice had contained tremors of excitement and she had told him that she was, for the first time since her arrival, happy. She had said that she couldn't tell him the reason for this, for his own protection.

And now she lay dead, by her own hand, they said.

She had been joyful. She had been a devout Catholic. She would not have done it. Something was being concealed, all right, but it wasn't suicide.

"YOU DIDN'T FIND it?" Judge Cushing's expression began in incredulity, ended in skepticism. "Surely you asked her, prior to–"

"Prior to, yes, but not that night." The doctor smoothed his mustache. "Not only would she not have told me, she would have become suspicious and would not have willingly accepted the drug."

The judge waved a hand dismissively, but by not disputing the doctor's comment, he conceded its truth. He wouldn't even have known about the diary had not his wife confessed its existence to her trusted doctor. However, the doctor had failed to learn the diary's location. He had obtained no information from Catherine except her assurances that it was safe.

The doctor hesitated. "A house has many nooks and crannies. There must be, for instance, closets filled with linens; a small book could easily fit in between them."

Judge Cushing waved his hand again. "Recall, sir, it was our moving into that house that precipitated her crisis and led to her being brought here. We had not lived there for long; our household staff was still arranging our effects. Furthermore, Catherine would not have entrusted its safekeeping to the house she refused to live in. No, it is not there. I am certain of that."

"There is another possibility," said the doctor. "She may have given it to a friend to hold."

Cushing shook his head. "No. She has no friends."

"A family member, then?"

"Catherine had become a pariah within the family. She would not have asked either of her daughters-in-law to conceal a diary, and certainly not either of our sons. None of them was aware of the existence of this diary. Nor was I, as you know too well."

The doctor nodded.

"It must be here," the judge said.

"I assure you, it is not at the sanitarium," said the doctor firmly. "She was under near constant surveillance. She wrote letters, which we reviewed prior to their being posted. Had she written any other documents, the staff would have seen her doing so. They would have had to supply ink, for one thing."

"Where, then? Where *is* the damned thing?" The scowl on Judge Cushing's face deepened into rage. Were Catherine still alive, he could easily have strangled her.

Part III

1985

ONE WEEK IN MID-JUNE

California lives by the Golden Rule: the one with the most gold rules.

—Gold Rush saying

Chapter Fourteen

"What we really need some help with," said Mary, "is cataloging."

Arla swallowed pride and dismay in one big gulp. "Sure."

Mary led her into a small room off to the left. Boxes were stacked on the floor. "This is the rest of the Childress family archives—what was considered unimportant back when the Society first went through it in 1965. That was when Miss Childress died and the Society received these archives."

"I don't think I've come across that name in the county history," Arla remarked.

"No, I expect not. They were just regular working people, and in 1965 the only families of interest to the Historical Society members were their own, or the rich families. The Childresses were an ordinary family, but they have been in Piñon County since 1849. Or they were, up until 1965. None of the descendants live here now.

"When old Miss Childress died … listen to me, 'old Miss Childress,'" Mary shook her head and laughed, "but anyway, she was the last Childress in Piñon County. Her family had moved away years earlier. They sold the farm and donated some of her things to the Historical Society."

Arla eyed the stack of a half dozen large wooden crates, all of which were covered in dust and cobwebs. Labels on the boxes depicted beautifully painted apples of all hues stacked in a red wagon being pulled by two rosy-cheeked children. The boxes alone must be rare and valuable now.

"Now, when the Society received the donation twenty years ago, they took everything they thought of historical interest. There was a cedar chest, which by then had become a historical artifact itself, and a half dozen boxes. The rest of the things were apparently unimportant historically and were stored in our attic. Now it's going to be like finding buried treasure." Mary looked longingly at the boxes. "No one made an inventory, but they did at least keep everything. So, dear, an inventory is what I need *you* to do."

What was left were trinkets and gewgaws that Arla doubted were of value or even interest, but she carefully removed and catalogued each item. The second box contained what must have been the 'bad' china, along with things that Arla thought might now be of some historical interest: an old shaving kit, two beautiful though slightly moth-eaten doilies, and five kitchen implements, including two whose purposes eluded Arla. At the bottom of this box was a small parcel, its contents wrapped in a piece of red damask tied by yarn. Under the yarn was a piece of paper that read, *Rosa Escovido Childress personal effects*.

Arla carefully untied the yarn and set aside the note. She unwrapped the material to find rosary beads, a beautiful mantilla, a pair of white kid gloves, and two missals. Why two? she wondered idly.

The cover of one was black leather, and embossed letters read 'Sunday Missal.' She carefully leafed through the pages, which were filled with colorful depictions of Mary and various saints. Each page was bordered by elaborately drawn ivy.

She thought the cover of the other was in Latin, then realized it was actually Spanish. Opening it, she was surprised to find on the first page, written in beautiful script, *'Catherine O'Hara Cushing. 1874.'* She turned several pages. No colorful depictions and no prayers. This volume contained nothing except handwriting. Religious notations, perhaps? But something caught her eye, or perhaps it was the whispering of her intuition. She stopped at a page in the middle and began to read.

This was a diary.

Her heart began to pound. What was Catherine Cushing's diary doing hidden in the effects of Rosa Escovido Childress?

Arla knew she ought not to do what she did. She carefully returned the diary to its cover and put it into her purse.

By the time she left, Mary was already gone; only the docent was still in the building. Arla bid her a good afternoon, walked to her car and drove directly home. She took the diary to her study and sat staring at it.

Chapter Fifteen

Roxanne watched out the kitchen window as they walked toward the lake, their shadows long in the late afternoon sun. Carlos's Hawaiian-patterned cotton shorts were long and baggy, and his legs seemed very thin in contrast. The legs of a boy, but his eyes were those of a young man when they lit upon that girl.

She sighed and took cheese and milk from the refrigerator and turned on the oven—as if the house wasn't hot enough already. Macaroni and cheese had been a favorite of Carlos's since he was six. Hopefully Kit liked it too.

Like everyone else she knew, Roxanne had sworn to never forget what it was like being a teenager, yet had forgotten. That is, she'd learned that there were different types of remembering. The day-to-day feeling of what it meant to be her, Roxanne Sjenstrom, at seven years old, and twelve, and fifteen—*that* was what she couldn't remember. All that was left were events, snippets of conversations, and certain moments of intensity.

Her eighth-grade class had been taken on a field trip to a

reconstructed gold mine. The tour guide had a long, gray, obviously false beard and wore the plaid flannel shirt and overalls of placer miners of 1849. He told them about the many nationalities of people who had come seeking gold, which was why so many places had names such as Frenchman's Flat, China Creek, Russian Camp, and Swede's Bar Road. That reminded him that the name Swede's Bar had been meant as a joke, because the Swedes had been terrible gold miners. 'They used to say a Swede couldn't find gold in Fort Knox. Swede's Bar was the only place along the entire North Fork that didn't produce more than a couple ounces of gold.'

In the coolness of the underground mine, she'd grown hot at a sudden insight: when Pete Jensen called her father 'Swede Jim,' he meant to be disparaging. It was his way of insinuating that he, like his Swedish gold mining ancestors, was a financial failure.

She added macaroni to the boiling water and reflected on how the small size of Piñon County exposed class differences. In cities, rich people socialized only with other rich people; but here, everyone pretty much ate at the same restaurants, went to the same events, and usually attended the same schools.

Her family had not been destitute. She'd never known hunger, or real deprivation. But they'd lived in Madrone, the unincorporated community just northeast of Camargo, where no one lived if they could afford to live somewhere else. Old-timers still referred to it as 'Futility Flat,' the name bestowed by some luckless gold miners.

She'd shared a room with her brother until she was ten. School clothes were purchased in Sacramento at Lerner's (or, in a good year, Montgomery Ward). Everything had to go with something else. She wore shoes that were durable, not fashionable. Her grandmother trimmed her hair.

Yet she didn't feel deprived, because her family was in the

same boat as the families of her friends. Bobby DiMauro, for one. Ray Mathieson, for another. Everyone in her elementary school lived in Madrone, so everyone was from a working-class family.

Then came Camargo High School, where students from every economic class were thrown together. Roxanne met girls who shopped in San Francisco for new school clothes at the Emporium or Joseph Magnin. They didn't have to mix and match their wardrobes, and even had shoes that matched their outfits. They lived in big houses with more than one common room, and each child had his or her own bedroom. Their parents bought a new car every year or two. Their mothers hired cleaning ladies. Their fathers belonged to the Elks Club, their applications welcomed enthusiastically, not seen as an opportunity to inflict humiliation via the black ball. They got their hair trimmed and styled at a salon. They took music lessons, ballet lessons, or both. They always had pocket money. They went to specialized camps every summer to perfect their skills in music or baton twirling.

After graduating in 1968, Roxanne left for Sacramento. Within a year she fell in love with Rafael, got pregnant, and dropped out of Sac State. By the time she returned to Piñon County in 1976, everything had changed in America, even in Piñon County. The war was finally over, and most people believed that the United States had been wrong for going into Vietnam, and that the government had lied about everything concerning the war the entire time. Several local boys had died in the war and Bobby had died for opposing it. Watergate had happened, too, and her parents' generation seemed not so much angry as embarrassed that the system they'd stoutly defended for years could be so flagrantly corrupt and profoundly wrong—but mostly because it had been so inept as to be caught red-handed.

Her generation had changed American society. Not that

Roxanne could take any credit. Bobby would have been disappointed with her, for she'd gone to only a few anti-war demonstrations, and those near the end. She'd read the women's liberation newspapers and pamphlets of the early 1970s without joining so much as a consciousness-raising group. Except for having married a Mexican-American man, she'd taken no risks.

But after all, she had a baby. Carlos was born in 1969, and she had to devote most of her time, energy, and consciousness to him.

Roxanne glanced out the window. She used to think that once Carlos reached his teens, she wouldn't worry about him so much. Instead, she worried more.

She put the macaroni and cheese in the oven and took the salad vegetables out of the refrigerator.

Surely Kit hadn't told her parents she had come to Pine Gap to see Carlos? So, what *had* she told them? Was there liable to be a call any minute from an angry Pete Jensen? Or worse, from PJ?

For years, she hadn't thought about what had happened. Lately, every time she got nervous, it popped into her mind. She reassured herself that PJ didn't place that much importance on it either, might even have forgotten the whole chain of events. Otherwise, wouldn't he occasionally mention it? But he hadn't, not once in all the years since.

It was dusk now. Where were the kids? Just as she had decided to go find them, she heard them approaching. "Hi, Mom," Carlos said. "Is dinner ready? We're starving!"

"It'll be ready in ten minutes," Roxanne said. "You can set the table. Kit, do you need to call your folks and tell them you're staying?"

Kit and Carlos exchanged a glance, and he said, "She already told them she'll be late."

Roxanne just nodded and didn't say anything.

After dinner the two kids cleaned up, then Carlos walked Kit to her friend Priscilla's house.

"Carlos," Roxanne began when he returned.

"Mom, if she says she's coming to see me they won't let her," he said at once.

"They—you mean not just Pete? Kit's mother, too?"

"I don't know about her. I don't think she'd mind, but so what? *He* runs things at their house." The bitterness in his voice surprised Roxanne. "And *he* doesn't like Mexicans."

"He's going to find out, Carlos."

"No, he won't. We're being careful. Why are you talking like this, anyway? Are you going to tell me I can't see her?"

"Of course not, but you are taking a risk."

"You're afraid of him."

Roxanne was about to deny it, but stopped herself. "Yes, I am. He's a racist and he's a powerful man. He thinks he can get away with anything … that he's above the law."

Carlos gave her a look of exasperation, a look that conveyed to her all that she remembered feeling toward her own parents at that age.

"You think he'd beat me up?" he said scornfully. "He's a racist pig, but he's not stupid. Even the great Pete Jensen would get in trouble for beating up a kid."

"I hope that's enough to restrain him, but it means relying on Pete not letting his temper get the better of him. And what about Kit's brother? He's just as much of a racist as his father, but nowhere near as smart. You can't count on PJ using good sense and self-restraint."

"I almost never see him," Carlos said.

"And how often does Kit see him?"

He stared at her, wide-eyed.

"You've got to consider that, Carlos. And that Pete could lose his temper with Kit."

"She told me he hasn't hit her since she was seven or eight."

"So that guarantees he won't hit her now?"

Carlos was silent for a few moments. When he spoke, his voice was filled with emotion. "So, what should I do? I don't want her to get hurt. But should I never see her again because her father and brother don't like it?"

"That wouldn't be right, either. And I doubt it would even protect her. But you have to be aware of what you're getting into, Carlos. Both of you have to realize what the repercussions might be." She paused and collected her thoughts. "Carlos, I agree it's unlikely he'll beat Kit. It's not the fifties anymore; men can't get away with that the way they did then. But he could do something that would hurt her in a different way—send her to live with a relative somewhere else, take away something she loves—"

"Sadie." Tears sprang to Carlos's eyes. "He knows how much she loves Sadie."

Roxanne waited, wanting to take him in her arms, but knowing he wouldn't want her to at this moment. He used some tissues and when he'd collected himself he said, "I hate this. Having to be on guard all the time, it feels like giving in to them, somehow."

"It's not. Awareness and acquiescence are not the same thing, not by a long shot." She opened the refrigerator and got a bottle of beer. "I don't want to invade your privacy, Carlos. I just don't want anything to happen to you."

"I know, Mom." He put his arms around her, and she held him tightly. He smelled of outside, and of the soap they used and very faintly of something else, a citrusy aroma that must be Kit's shampoo or body lotion.

He went to bed and she drank her beer, thinking of the look on PJ's face that night almost twenty years ago, and the arrogance with which he'd always carried himself back then, born of an awareness that because of who he was, he could get away with so many things. And she thought of the scar on his face and how getting it had wiped that arrogance away.

But Bobby was dead, and maybe PJ wanted nothing more than to get back at her. Maybe he'd been waiting for his chance all these years.

Chapter Sixteen

The Jensen Real Estate office was in downtown Camargo on Madison Avenue, which ran parallel to Main Street. Years ago, when Laura was a girl, she had preferred to walk home from school on Madison. One block had been lined by black oaks so tall and wide they touched at the top. In hot weather that block had been a tunnel of cool shade, and during the rainy season she could walk its length without getting wet.

All of the houses on Madison had been Victorians, of the elaborate style she later learned was called Queen Anne. Almost as big as castles, the houses sprawled across spacious lots, only three or four on each long block. Those houses on the hilly side of the street had seemed even more magnificent because they sat so high, their front yards behind stone retaining walls taller than she was.

Spring on Madison used to be intoxicating, with the smell of flowers, humming of bumblebees, bright flitting of butterflies, and the constant warbling of songbirds. Laura remembered how one fence seemed made of wisteria, one stone wall of honeysuckle, another of rosemary.

In the 1940s many of the houses had served dual purposes.

Lawyers, doctors and dentists, including hers, kept offices on the first floor and lived upstairs.

One Sunday morning while Stella was still at Mass, Laura had roller skated along the quiet downtown streets, shedding her sweater as the sun changed from glimmering between branches to steadily glaring from above the treetops. Then she turned onto Madison and slowed. The air was saturated with the delicious aromas of dew drying on fresh grass and the early April flowers releasing their scent as the sun touched them. She stopped in front of Dr. Thelen's house. The roses hadn't bloomed yet, but irises created a vivid rainbow around the lawn. A trellis leading to the front steps dripped with purple wisteria; on either side, hummingbirds darted from flower to flower.

The house was still and there was no car in the driveway. She sat down, removed her skates and let herself into the backyard. She'd always been curious to see what her grandmother dismissed with a scoff: 'Wildflowers—just a fancy name for weeds.'

It was like no garden she'd ever seen. Plants ran riot, some tall and feathery, others short and scrubby, in every shade of green imaginable. Poppies wove in between everything. The aroma of sage was powerful.

She was bent over a bush covered by blue-lavender flowers with gold centers and an exquisitely delicate scent when the back door banged open. She jumped up, her heart pounding, but he merely walked down the back stairs, gestured at the bush and said gruffly, 'That's blue witch. It's a member of the nightshade family. So is the potato.' She was only twelve then, but she understood he did not often find another person interested in his garden, let alone appreciative of it. 'What's that one?' she asked, pointing. They spent nearly an hour walking through the garden. He was proudest of the two sequoias he had planted that 'not me or you or your great-grandchildren' would see fully grown.

By the 1950s most of the large Victorians on Madison were torn down, replaced by office buildings or parking lots. Only a few survived the march of progress. The doctors and dentists moved into antiseptic modern medical buildings next to the hospital, all except for Dr. Thelen, who stubbornly kept his practice in his house. He retired in the 1960s. His wife had already died and he lived alone in the big house.

Laura thought that he'd probably had Alzheimer's disease, but back then people just called him senile. He'd died about a decade ago, and the house had stood empty ever since, the heirs squabbling over it. None of them wanted responsibility for the place, more a liability than an asset. Laura passed it every time she went to Pete's office, invariably saddened to see that once magnificent home so decayed. According to an article she'd read last month in the *Piñon County Register*, the city had condemned the Thelen house and ordered that it be demolished or repaired by the end of October.

Large Victorians were appreciated now, so perhaps someone would buy the Thelen place. Of course, it would have to be someone who could spend many thousands of dollars on renovations. Laura didn't think this was likely. Few people who could afford pricy real estate wanted to live in Piñon County, let alone in downtown Camargo.

Had the Thelen house been anywhere else, it would have been turned into a bed-and-breakfast inn, but they had not caught on in Camargo. The last attempt, in a lovely Tudor at the edge of town, had folded within a year. Camargo was too far from Escalada; skiers might stop in town for gas or a meal, but they lodged where they skied. And Camargo's gold rush tourists preferred modern hotels with all the amenities.

She continued to the treeless block containing the Jensen Real Estate office. Sunlight rebounded blindingly off the concrete sidewalks and stucco buildings. Air conditioners jutted out from most windows. On weekdays, when people were working, the street hummed with the droning of condensers and the air was faintly tinged with the peculiar odor of cold metal.

Pete employed a part-time secretary who answered the phones, typed up deeds and title papers, and arranged his schedule. She couldn't keep up with the filing, so Laura came in as needed, usually on a Sunday when she wouldn't be disturbed by the phone or drop-in customers. The answering service took calls on Sundays.

"You're late," he said when she walked inside. Laura glanced at the wall clock. It was 9:02. She didn't respond. He gulped down his coffee and explained what work he needed her to do. Laura nodded and seated herself behind the secretary's desk. He said that he wouldn't return to the office; she should make sure to lock up and he'd see her tonight at home.

Pete had told her it would take all day, but Laura was finished by noon. She had eaten a large breakfast and wasn't hungry.

And now she had real work to do.

FOR THE FIRST ten years of her life, Laura Fitzpatrick had been a happy, exuberant girl. She sometimes wondered how things might have turned out for her had fate not intervened.

When she was seven years old, her father set up a business painting houses and installing rain gutters. The Depression was over and his economic future looked bright, and for two years it was. Then Pearl Harbor was bombed. Two days after that, he drove to Sacramento and enlisted.

Eleven months later, a Western Union man holding a yellow envelope knocked on the door. She remembered her mother screaming and screaming, then not saying anything for the rest of that day, or for many days afterward. Granny and Grandpa Bream came to stay. After that, they were the ones who took care of Laura. They fixed her food, washed her clothes, got her ready for school, told her not to make so much noise.

The household was ruled by whispers and tiptoes and the things no one said. There was never a day when Mama felt good. Every morning, Laura woke with dread in the pit of her belly: what would it be today? A bad headache, a touch of fever, woman troubles?

Laura began to spend more and more time at the Minelli house. Although she was sometimes punished by being forbidden from doing something she liked, she was never told she couldn't go to the Minellis'. Years later, she realized that it must have been a great relief to her grandparents when she was gone; her absence freed them from the constant vigilance required to keep the natural exuberance of a child from disturbing the delicate nerves of a woman who'd never recovered from a nervous breakdown.

At the Minelli house, people talked and laughed and yelled. Opera music played on the Victrola. Or someone's voice filled the house with proclamations of love that, to Laura, always sounded more gushing in Italian.

Laura was learning to obey instantly when an adult said something, even when it wasn't framed precisely as a command. It took her a long time not to flinch in anticipation when Uncle Sal or Stella's mother or some other adult would lean out a window and holler, 'Hey! How many times I gotta tell you kids don't run through the flowerbeds? You come put these dishes away if you don't want a cuff!'

Children rarely got cuffed at the Minelli house. 'The yelling doesn't mean they're mad,' Stella assured her. 'That's just the way they talk.'

Laura never complained to the grown-up Minellis, partly because she was ashamed and partly because in those days people didn't interfere with the way others raised their children. But Octavia, Stella's nonna, seemed to know whenever Laura had been disciplined with her grandfather's belt or a willow switch. Perhaps it was the stiffness with which Laura moved, or her subdued state, her puffy eyes, or that she winced when she sat on a hard chair.

Octavia would gesture for Laura to come to her, and she'd put lavender oil on the spots where the belt buckle had landed. Or she'd open her arms and draw Laura to her ample bosom and soft shoulders. Or she would shoo the other girls out of the kitchen and give Laura some homemade *bugie* or *frutta candita*, even though dinner was only a few hours away.

By the time Stella entered Camargo High they had grown apart. The next year Laura married, quit school, and moved out of town, down to the west county ranch. Their friendship soon seemed a part of the past, a relic of Laura's childhood. She was married with the demands of a baby, a husband and a big ranch.

Octavia died in 1955. Laura's grief was compounded because she had visited Octavia so infrequently since marrying. PJ was four years old, but she had only taken him to see Octavia a few times.

She'd had three miscarriages after his birth, and the doctor told her she probably couldn't have any more children. For that reason she became lax about birth control, and in 1966, when PJ was fifteen, she found herself pregnant. She deliberately didn't use birth control after Cindy was born, hoping to have another child so Cindy wouldn't have to grow up alone. Three years later, Kit was born. After that, Laura had her tubes tied.

By then, they were living in the mountains. When Laura's

mother had died in 1957, Laura had sold the house on Main Street. With that money, she and Pete had bought the ranch in the high country. Pete had dubbed it Laura's Legacy, jokingly at first. The name stuck. They'd designed and registered a brand, the Double-L.

Most people had forgotten what it stood for. Laura never had.

SHE LOCKED THE office door, sliding on the chain. If Pete unexpectedly came back, she would tell him she got nervous being here alone on a Sunday. He would sneer at her for it, but she knew he'd believe her.

She turned on the copy machine to warm up and made sure it had plenty of paper. She went into his office, took the key from where he kept it hidden, and unlocked his desk.

The drawer where he stored the information on their personal finances was well-organized. She copied the 1984 tax returns first.

She wondered if she would have to tell the IRS about the proceeds from her mother's necklace. She had inherited it almost thirty years ago and didn't know anything about inheritance laws. She would probably have to hire a tax accountant next year because, for the first time, she would be filing her own tax return.

She felt only a twinge of regret for the necklace. Her father had given it to her mother on their tenth anniversary, their last one before he joined the army. Her mother had never worn it outside the house. She had, however, taken it out to look at almost every day.

But Laura could not afford sentimentality. She'd had it appraised in San Francisco during a weekend vacation last spring. She had been surprised at how much it was worth.

Then, last month, she drove to Sacramento—to go shopping, she told Pete. She asked him for money to replenish his and PJ's clothing. And she *did* go shopping—but not until after she sold the necklace.

She worried that Pete might ask her where it was. He never had before, but he might. Perhaps she would tell him that she'd taken it to be cleaned. But wouldn't he ask to see the receipt, so he could be sure she wasn't going to be swindled? No, that wouldn't work. She would have to tell him it was locked away in her boxes, up in the attic; that she didn't want to wear it anymore and was keeping it for the girls.

That much was true, she said to herself; this is for the girls.

By three o'clock she had copied everything. She locked Pete's desk and replaced the key. She put all the copies into a box labeled 'sweaters' and brought it to the trunk of her car. She covered the papers with the sweaters and woolens she had brought, neatly packed in clear plastic bags, and taped the box shut. Back in the office, she straightened the secretary's desk and neatened the whole office, dusting the surfaces and even cleaning the bathroom.

She purposely didn't empty the trash cans. He would come to work Monday and feel justified in his opinion that she was scatterbrained.

Chapter Seventeen

Now that the Gennessee Mine housing development was finally going up and construction of the mall had begun, Ray was putting in long hard days. He liked physical labor, but he wasn't doing much of that himself these days; instead, he was making sure everyone else did it. All day long he went back and forth between the housing development and the mall. They weren't too far apart, but he sometimes felt as though he spent half the day in his truck.

He drove up Blackberry Springs Drive toward the job site. When he saw a small, slender woman jogging in the distance, he knew at once it was her.

Her dog was far ahead of her, darting into the fields and the ditch beside the road. When the dog came even with the pickup, Ray stopped. Before he even thought about what he was doing, he got out and extended his hand. "Hey, pup."

The dog trotted over, tail wagging, touching Ray's fingers with a cold nose.

"Morgan!" she shouted from a hundred feet up the road. The dog's ears flickered, but he didn't stop sniffing Ray's hand. She drew nearer. "He's friendly."

That was pretty obvious. Ray scratched the dog's head and watched her jog toward them. Actually, run more than jog. She had the even, fast stride of a runner. And the legs of a runner, too. His blood rushed and he forced himself not to stare. Not to notice how short her shorts were. Not to imagine the smooth warm skin of her thighs against his lips.

"I'm sorry," she said, clipping the leash to the dog's collar. "Usually there aren't any cars this time of day, so I let him off leash."

"That's all right." Ray smiled. "This isn't what I'd call a ferocious beast."

As if on cue, the dog gave an excited yap. That broke the ice; they both laughed. "This is Morgan," she said.

"Hey, Morgan." Ray gave the dog another couple of pats, but without taking his eyes from her. "How you doing? I haven't seen you for a while."

"I've seen *you*," she said at once. Then blushed, and went on quickly, "When I drive past the mall. You guys seem to be doing a lot of work there."

He let it go. He addressed the remark about the work. But his pulse throbbed in response to what she'd said first, without thinking; and even more, in response to the blush that confirmed the significance of those words. 'I've seen *you*.'

She was saying something about how when the mall was finished, she wouldn't have to drive down to Sacramento or San Francisco to go shopping.

"That's one of the things I've had to adjust to." She smiled. "But this makes up for it." She made a sweeping gesture to the land around them.

"Can't beat it," Ray agreed.

"You've lived here all your life?"

"Pretty much. I was away for a couple years, and that's when I knew this was where I wanted to be. I love these mountains." He hardly knew her, and here he was telling her personal things, and wanting to tell her more. "You from Fris—San Francisco originally?"

She shook her head. "No, I lived in Marin County for a few years, but I'm from New York."

"No kidding? New York City, or some other part of New York?"

"Oh, the city." She laughed. "New Yorkers have an egocentric worldview. People from other parts of New York have to preface it with 'upstate'."

"Why'd you leave there?"

"I was married then, and my husband wanted to come back to California; he grew up in San Mateo. We used to backpack in the Sierras, and that's how I found this place." Then she smiled, a lovely smile that lit all of her face, and gestured expansively. "I was unprepared for spring. Wildflowers everywhere, and so many colors, every shade of purple imaginable. It was as stunning as autumn in Vermont and lasted longer. No one had told me how beautiful spring in California is."

"We keep it to ourselves." He grinned. "We got enough tourists already."

"Is it that? Sometimes it seems to me that native Californians don't really appreciate the beauty here."

"I got to disagree with you about that."

"I know some of you do," she said hastily. "But there's almost an air of taking things for granted. I could hardly drive down the highway last month without gaping at the poppies, but most people didn't seem to even notice them."

"I guess it's like that everywhere. I'll bet most New Yorkers don't notice the architecture."

She looked surprised. "You're right. They don't. Most people walk past an old building and if they notice anything, it's the grime, not the beauty underneath." She moved her eyes from his to the landscape, the browned hills dotted with oaks, threaded with dark green ribbons of brush. "It took me a long time to see the beauty in western summer. When I moved to California, I was shocked at how dry and brown it was."

Ray laughed. "When I was back east, all that vegetation seemed weird. Summer's supposed to be dry, isn't it?"

She laughed too. "I think so now, too. I've learned to see the beauty in what I never used to notice." She nodded at the hills then brought her eyes back to his.

He didn't know whether she was really flirting with him, or he was only hoping she was.

The dog rescued him by giving a short impatient bark. Arla laughed. "Okay, Morgan. Well, it was nice to see you again, Ray."

"You too," he managed.

She began jogging back up Blackberry Springs Drive toward her house. Ray turned the truck around, went back to Gennessee Mine Road, and turned onto it. By the time he reached the job site he had his nerves under control.

Near the end of the workday, as Ray and Billy were going over tomorrow's schedule, a cloud of dust drew his attention. It was Hiram Cushing's Bronco coming up Gennessee Mine Road. Ray groaned.

Cushing must have had to refinance the mall, because the grading, originally scheduled for March, hadn't started till this month. Now that it was underway, he was anxious, frequently dropping by to check on progress. But whatever was going on with Hiram Cushing and his investors didn't particularly interest Ray. In this industry, jobs sometimes shut down with no warning whatsoever, so you got used to the unexpected.

Cushing joined Ray at his pickup, leaning against the open truck bed, arms folded over his chest.

Ray finished putting things away and called, "I'm about to take off, Hiram."

"Can you spare ten minutes? There's something I want to talk to you about."

"Sure," Ray said. He and Terri were going out to dinner tonight, just the two of them; he resisted the impulse to glance at his watch. They sat at the picnic table Ray had brought up for the guys to use.

Cushing folded his arms on the table and leaned over, eyes intent on Ray's. "I'm going to take you into my confidence."

Ray held his hands up. "You don't have to do that."

"Don't worry. What I'm about to tell you isn't something that's liable to come up in your day-to-day conversations. And I have a reason for wanting you to know about this." Cushing paused. "You probably assumed I've been pestering you about these two projects because I'm having financial trouble. But the real reason is that I want to make sure they're finished, so we can start working on a new project."

Ray was intrigued despite himself. He waited through Cushing's long pause.

"I'm going to build a state-of-the-art retirement community."

"Where?" Ray asked.

"Right here in Piñon County. In a real country setting, but with our new world-class mall just a few miles away. Every house custom designed—we're going to sell them before we build them. In northern California alone there are at least three million potential buyers. There's going to be a waiting list to get in. A waiting list filled with people over 55, with fat bank accounts."

"How many houses you figure on putting up?" Ray asked.

"Just over 700."

Ray did a double take. There had never been a development of that size in Piñon County. That many luxury homes would require at least 300 acres, perhaps as much as 500. He wondered where Mr. Cushing was going to put the place. There wasn't a lot of privately owned land east of Camargo, and most of it consisted of small parcels scattered in between the state and federal forests. He must have bought property in west county, but west county was more than just a few miles away from the mall. "Where you plan on putting it? Do you have the parcel already?"

Cushing smiled enigmatically. "As we both know, the main impediment to a large development here has been the lack of a big tract."

Ray nodded.

"You'll be pleased to know we've solved that problem. The development is going to be spread over two large, perfectly situated parcels: Pete Jensen's ranch and the Pardini place."

"They're both willing to sell?" Ray asked, surprised.

"Pete Jensen is anxious to sell his spread. It's in his wife's name for tax purposes, but that's not a problem. We're still negotiating with Pardini, but it's just a question of how much money he'll accept."

Ray was dubious. He couldn't see Joe and Stella Pardini selling to a developer, especially not the same developer they'd sued a few months ago. Still, people did change their minds about all sorts of things when money was involved.

"It's a delicate situation. Pardini's delaying as long as possible to drive the price up, trying to wrangle every dollar out of us that he can." Cushing's mouth twisted. "I never suspected he'd be so greedy."

"Well, that land's been in his family a pretty long time."

"I suppose. Or it could be a remnant of his old-country ancestry, this clinging to a particular parcel of land against all reason. With what we're offering, he could buy a bigger spread in Oso Grande, or go to Oregon and buy three ranches. Well, that will occur to him eventually."

"What if you can't work it out with him?"

"That's a good question, Ray. In point of fact, Pardini's

property is essential. It's perfect for a golf course, and a golf course has to be part of the package of any retirement community. If we want a waiting list of buyers, we've got to have a golf course. Jensen's land is too rocky and hilly. It would cost a fortune to try and turn it into a golf course. And the Middle Fork runs right through his spread. We can hardly re-route the river.

"The Jensen place is perfect for the luxury houses." He tapped the picnic table. "Now, Pardini's land is almost a thousand acres, and I've studied the contours. The center of the property, where the buildings are, is a valley. It's perfectly graded by nature, has good underground water, and there aren't a lot of trees. From the valley, the golf course would wind south, toward the national forest. There's a big meadow near the property line and Cougar Creek runs through that portion, which will make it simple to design a course with ponds and waterways."

"How many acres does a golf course need?" Ray asked.

"A good 18-hole course, about 250 acres. This will be designed by a well-known professional golfer working with a respected course builder; we're holding preliminary discussions with them already. So it'll be a pro course, and that will attract home buyers. The reason I'm telling you all of this is because I'm counting on you being in charge."

"Okay," Ray said, but with a sinking feeling in his heart. Every time he started thinking about quitting, about pursuing his dream, some new project came along to which he felt obligated to commit himself.

"By next summer I expect to have title to the properties, the plans drawn up and OK'd."

"That soon?"

"I feel optimistic. Pardini is the only impediment, and the fact is, he wants to sell, but doesn't want to concede just yet."

"Oh," said Ray, getting it at last. "So, it's just a matter of working out the details."

"That's right. The 'details' being dollars, and reasonable people can always come to terms. So, you see why I'm not worried about the permits." Cushing grinned, and gestured to the framed buildings. "Joe Pardini spearheaded the opposition to this place. With him on board, we won't have any problems getting all the permits."

"I guess not."

"Don't underestimate his business acumen, Ray. Sometimes it's the men who seem the least interested in money who are the sharpest. You know, I tried to buy his land three years ago, intending to put Blackberry Springs there."

Ray's surprise must have shown, because Cushing nodded. "And he turned us down. He was taking a big gamble—that we'd build it somewhere in the proximity, which would increase the value of his property. We might just as easily have put it in forty miles away, or in another county. But we managed to acquire the land here and Pardini's gamble paid off. Now he's holding out for more money, figuring that the longer he holds out the more he'll get, and he's probably right."

Cushing leaned farther over the table and spoke in a confidential tone, even though there was no one within miles, let alone within earshot. "Pardini's finances are a long way from solid. By the end of the summer, he'll be knocking on my door. Until then, discretion is essential."

"I won't say anything," Ray repeated. But he wished Mr. Cushing hadn't told him all this.

Cushing untangled his long thin legs from under the picnic table. Ray stood too. They walked to their vehicles. Cushing extended his hand. "You're a good man, Ray. You don't know what a relief it is to me to have someone like you working for me."

Driving home he wondered why Cushing *wasn't* planning to

put the development forty miles away, in west county where there was plenty of open space on gently rolling hills. It was rocky in some parts, but not with the granite of the high mountains.

As a boy he'd been mystified that many places were filled with limestone boulders, and in freshman year he'd stopped at the desk of the geology teacher after class and asked her. Mrs. Mendenhall had seemed shocked, then delighted, at a student being that interested in anything, and had been only too willing to explain. "It's the legacy of gold mining. Not placer mining. When large companies began mining they used far more destructive methods. They cut trees to make flumes and routed creeks, sometimes even rivers, through flumes and pipes into big nozzles. The water shot out so powerfully that mountains of soil were washed away, but since gold is much heavier it was left behind. And so were the limestone boulders."

"I wonder what happened to all that soil?" he'd said.

"Ah! That was quite a controversy!" Mrs. Mendenhall had exclaimed, adjusting her glasses. "Debris was carried downstream and the riverbeds were filled with it, and couldn't then accommodate winter rains, which resulted in water and debris flooding the Valley." At his expression, she'd smiled briefly. "Yes, the San Joaquin Valley, where you used to live. Farmers objected year after year to no avail, until finally in the 1880s the courts prohibited hydraulic mining."

It was one of those esoteric bits of information that had made a big impression on him. Now he began calculating what it would take to build in west county, and even with the boulders, it had to be easier than in the mountains. But clearly, Cushing's mind was made up.

Chapter Eighteen

Carlos Tejada had come to work at Pardini Ranch at the suggestion of Kit Jensen. Kit herself would have made an excellent hand on the ranch and a wonderful guide on pack trips, but given the relationship of the two families, not to mention Kit's workload on the cattle ranch, that was out of the question. But she had sent this hard-working, good-natured boy to Joe and Stella, and they had put him to work mucking out stalls, cleaning tack and grooming horses.

Carlos was a fast learner. He was already good at packing manties, and he always remembered to double-check the cinches before the horses left the yard. Stella remembered a ranch hand a few years ago who hadn't checked, forgetting that one of the horses always puffed himself out when being saddled, so that a cinch that seemed tight was actually loose. Joe hadn't gone a mile before the load came off. The guests had to wait around while everything was fixed, which took longer than the original packing.

Carlos was conscientious, and once he'd been told how to do a job, he not only remembered every detail, but asked probing questions. It was possible that by the end of the season he could accompany Joe on the short pack trips. That was always the hardest time to find people to work as guides; students returned to college, so itinerate hands were in short supply. If a group was four or less, Joe could take them out by himself, but the rule of the thumb was one guide for every three clients. Some outfitters went with one guide for every two clients, not including the camp cook, but Joe and Stella's business was geared to people who wanted to rough it and didn't mind coming back into camp after a day on the trails without dinner already prepared, people who enjoyed building a campfire while Joe cooked dinner on the camp stove. Of course, Joe and Stella always prepared food ahead of time; much of the work in the outfitting business was in the preparation.

Early one afternoon Carlos came into the house to let her know he had finished his work and to report several things he'd noticed that might need her attention. She asked if he was ready for his next riding lesson, and he nodded and smiled.

"You've been practicing," she remarked after they had gone a half-mile or so.

"Well, sometimes Kit comes over on her horse and I ride her. Sadie, I mean." He turned bright red. Stella would have teased him, had he been a grown man, but she knew it would be the wrong thing to do with this boy. She pretended not to see the blush or to catch the double meaning of his words and said, "Sadie's a good horse to learn on. And Kit's about the best horsewoman in the county, so you couldn't have a better teacher."

"Kit says you're the best rider she's ever seen," Carlos said.

"She probably means rodeo rider. I used to do that. It's been a while, though."

"Did you ride a bucking bronco?"

"No, I never did." She glanced at him and decided to wait

till another time to tell him what was done to the broncos to make them buck. "You want to try a canter?"

When they slowed down again, his expression grew suddenly sober. "I almost forgot to tell you. When I went by the creek this morning, it was hardly running."

Stella stared at him. "Hardly running?" she repeated.

Carlos nodded. "But just last week it was running strong, with all the snow melt."

"Do you remember where you saw this, exactly?"

"Sure, I can show you."

They turned south and rode the two miles to Cougar Creek. The boy was right: it was barely a trickle. In silence, they rode back to the house.

"What do you think happened?" Carlos asked finally, when they took the horses into their stalls.

Stella shook her head. "I don't know. But if that creek has dried up this early in the season … I'll take Joe down later and we'll look around, see if something's wrong. Maybe there was a landslide that's blocking the water."

But later, she rode back to the creek by herself. Joe was due back this evening, but he would be dog-tired. She wanted to be able to tell him what had happened.

Thank goodness for Carlos, she thought as she rode. During the busy season neither she nor Joe had the time to ride the perimeter of the ranch more than every few weeks. Carlos had taken to doing this himself. He said the ranch was a perfect place for him to practice his cross-country running. He didn't have to tell Stella that the perimeter of the ranch was also a convenient place to meet Kit.

Normally, the water rushed over the rocks where the creek started and then, 100 feet or so later, the land flattened out and the creek widened. Since it was so near the river, this part of the creek usually had abundant water. Not today. Today, it was a trickle.

Stella tied Tabasco to a tree and walked upstream, past the rocks.

She had been expecting to find a tree fallen just-so; or a landslide; or perhaps even a beaver dam, although that would be unusual in this part of the mountains.

She had not expected to see an obstacle constructed by men. Someone had deposited a load of sand. Behind the mounds of sand, a backhoe or perhaps just a plow attached to a pickup had deepened the gully toward the river, so that instead of the water flowing into the creek bed, it swirled around the gully and rejoined the river.

Stella didn't touch a thing. Carefully stepping only where her boots would not spoil any other shoeprints, she returned to Tabasco and rode back to the ranch. She called the Forest Service and spoke with a supervisor, who said that he would radio one of the rangers to meet her there; Clay DiMauro was working in the vicinity.

Stella rode home, got her camera, returned to the blockade, and took two rolls of film. Then she sat on a boulder and waited for Clay.

"I'LL BE DAMNED if I know," Clay said. He was squatting by the pile of sand. They had found tire tracks where a vehicle had been driven down from the nearby fire road.

"So it wasn't the Forest Service re-routing the creek for some reason?"

"Nope. I'd've known if we had a project going on. Besides, the Forest Service always puts up signs and tape when they're working on something."

"Then someone stopped up the creek deliberately."

"Yeah, but they had to know it wouldn't last. Look, the water's already starting to come back over and wash that sand away. Another couple weeks and the creek'll be right back to normal." He grinned. "This isn't even half as well built as a beaver dam."

"So you think it was just a prank?"

"Most likely. But it could be something else." He pushed his hat back and squinted up at her. "Has someone got it in for you and Joe?"

"Me and Joe! But this is Forest Service land!"

"Yeah, but only for a quarter mile."

"True," Stella said, "but the larger portion of the creek is on SlidePac property. And there's no shortage of people mad at SlidePac."

"Yeah, but the mill hasn't used water power for decades. They tap the creek to water their landscaping, that's it."

"So damming the creek would be just a minor inconvenience to the mill."

Clay nodded. "Right. And I can't see a mill worker going to all this trouble and risk with so little to show for it." He paused, frowning in thought. "Maybe an environmentalist doing a little monkey wrenching."

"I doubt that a monkey-wrencher would do something that hurt the creek."

"Yeah, that's prob'ly right, too. So we're down to enemies of you and Joe."

"We made plenty of enemies last winter when we tried to stop that housing development. You know that. But if someone wanted to get back at us, I would think they'd find a more effective way."

"The creek's the only surface water on the ranch, right?" Clay said.

"Yes, but we don't use it. It keeps the meadow green much of the year, and all kinds of wildlife come here to drink, but we use well water for drinking and irrigation and the horses."

Clay pulled his hat back down and stood. For several

minutes he walked around studying the damage, stepping carefully and not touching anything. Stella waited silently. Finally, he said, "We might be able to figure out who did it. Depends how much time and effort the agency wants to put into investigating. First thing's to make casts of the tire track." He added, in a tone of thinking out loud, "Although I don't know if that'll help much. Most pickup trucks around here use the same brand of tires. The cast is going to match up to every damned four-wheel-drive in Piñon County, probably including the ones belonging to the Forest Service."

"It might help to check the access point the truck used," Stella said. "It must have come in through the fire road."

"Yeah, but so what? This track is only here because the ground's wet." He leaned over to look at the gouge in the mud. "And it's not much to go on."

"Maybe the ground is wet at the entrance to the fire road."

"Maybe," Clay said, doubtfully. "We might have better luck trying to figure out where this sand came from. Someone had to buy a couple loads of it. They probably got it from Kelley Building Supply over in Oso Grande. They're the biggest suppliers of dirt and sand."

"Or possibly some construction company keeps a large supply of sand on hand."

Clay nodded. "Most construction companies do. There's five or six in Piñon County with their own yards. Thing to do is take samples from each one. But that'll probably mean the agency will have to file a complaint in court and get search warrants. I don't know if they'll go that far."

"Why not? This wasn't a teenage prank. Someone who knows their way around the forest did this, and they either used construction equipment or a pickup with a plow attached. And someone either bought or had access to a lot of sand."

"You're right about that, but you never know how they'll react to something. I've seen them go all out over something as petty as some camper using a couple of dead branches for firewood, and go easy on someone driving an off-road vehicle past a dozen 'no entry' signs." He lifted his hat and wiped his forehead dry with a blue kerchief. "I'll take it back to my supervisor and see what he wants to do. But I don't know how aggressively he'll pursue it. Depends on whether he sees it as some kind of bureaucratic problem or a real violation of the public land."

Stella took Tabasco's reins in her hand, and hesitated before getting on his back. "Do you mean whether he sees it that way, or whether he *pretends* to see it that way?"

"That's what I'm worried about. I'll do what I can, but I'm only a GS-6, and on top of that, he doesn't like me."

"Well, if we can be any help, let me know."

"All right. I'd like to get a set of those pictures you took."

"I'll get them to you as soon as they're developed."

As she rode off, he was standing beside his jeep, talking on the radio. So now at least there would be an official report and she could follow up on it later and, if she believed the Forest Service wasn't doing enough, press for further investigation. It would help to have an ally, even one as lowly placed within the agency as Clay. But she had no idea whether he would remain an ally if the going got rough.

Maybe Clay had made his peace with the job already. Maybe he was afraid to rock the boat. Maybe he didn't have his brother Bobby's fortitude.

Joe and Stella had known Bobby when he was in high school; he'd worked part-time at the gas station the last year that Joe managed it. Bobby knew Joe and Stella were opposed to the Vietnam War, and had once remarked, only half-kidding, that the three of them constituted the entire anti-war contingent of Piñon County.

Once, after Bobby went to prison, Loretta passed on a request for money and they gave almost $300. Although that was a lot of money for them, it seemed so little, but Loretta said it was an immense help. They wrote to Bobby, an inner censor looking over their shoulders. They sent him books, and read books that he recommended. His visiting list was limited; close friends, like Loretta, were on it permanently; other people alternated. He died before they made it to the list.

All of that had happened when Clay was but a boy. He'd been only ten when his brother went to prison, not quite twelve when he died. How much influence had Bobby had on him? He didn't seem to have the same spunk and righteousness as Bobby, but then few people did. He always spoke of Bobby with pride, but she'd always sensed something else, too. Both she and Joe had noticed. It was subtle, but the pride and admiration were tempered by disinclination.

Sometimes, loving someone who had rocked the boat and suffered for it instilled determination in a person. But sometimes it had the opposite effect. Maybe what had happened to Bobby caused Clay to hesitate before taking a stand, to prefer compromise over confrontation.

But he was taking this creek incident seriously, and he'd been the one to suggest it could have been aimed specifically at Joe and Stella by someone with a grudge because of their anti-development stance.

Stella thought it unlikely, because anyone who knew them knew that Pardini Ranch didn't depend on that creek. The damming of it was an inconvenience, but no worse; and as Clay had said, nature would have repaired the relatively superficial damage before long. No real harm would come of it. Not like having noxious weeds growing on the land. She considered whether PJ Jensen had done it. After all, he had deliberately allowed his cattle to seed Pardini land with yellow star thistle.

According to Kit, the Jensen cattle had wandered through that broken fence around Thanksgiving, days after Joe spoke at the Planning Commission hearing. Generally, PJ kept the fences at the Double-L in good repair. That he hadn't noticed it was unlikely; that he hadn't repaired it after Kit brought it to his attention was malicious.

Spite or neglect, it had caused real damage, because sure enough Stella had found yellow star thistle growing last month. They'd had to fence off about three acres and had applied an herbicide—something neither of them wanted to do, but given the circumstances there was no alternative. But she couldn't see PJ damming the creek. As a prank it was too risky; as sabotage it was useless.

Stella grimaced. She was ruling PJ out of having pulled a harmless prank because she believed he wouldn't bother doing something that didn't cause real damage.

And as for Hiram Cushing, if he was inclined toward revenge, surely he had more effective ways. And besides, he had nothing to be vengeful about. He'd won the fight over the Gennessee Mine development. In fact, it was already under construction.

Stella glanced at her wristwatch. Joe would be home soon. She could almost hear him saying that this was probably nothing to do with Pardini Ranch, more likely someone angry with the Forest Service. There was a long list of candidates in that category.

Chapter Nineteen

Arla let Morgan out for a romp in the yard and got ready for a swim. At the glass patio doors, she shed her sandals and the kimono that matched her tiny electric blue bikini, and slid open the door. When she stepped onto the deck, Morgan came barreling around from the front yard to join her. But as they both turned toward the pool, Morgan suddenly stopped short and began to growl, the hackles on his neck rising. "What's the matter, boy?" Arla said, squatting beside him and looking in the direction he was staring. And that was when she saw the snake.

She froze, except for her racing heart. Starting behind its head, large, reddish-brown marks surrounded by white specks ran down the snake's body, thinning into stripes near the tail. And on the tail, rather large beads, all the same size. Pale and hard like faded porcelain, they resembled a human spinal column. There seemed to be quite a few of them.

At least it wasn't coiled. She remembered that a rattlesnake all spread out like this wasn't ready to attack. But still! Here it was sunning itself on her deck as if it owned the place. And how long would it take the snake to coil up—maybe two seconds?

She grabbed Morgan's collar and carefully backed into the house. Now what? She went to the phone in the kitchen and looked up the number of animal control. A machine answered and told her to leave a message, adding that if this was an emergency, she should call 911. Arla hung up without leaving a message.

If she called 911 it would soon be all over town. She would have established herself forever as a hapless urbanite.

Without thinking twice, she pulled on her kimono, stepped into her sandals, grabbed the car keys and ran out to her car. She drove as fast as she dared down the highway to Buckeye Flat. The men all looked over as she pulled into the lot. She felt slightly foolish at what she was about to do, but walked toward them. "Hi, I'm sorry to bother you, but I might need help, or at least advice."

All the men were staring at her. Her kimono had long sleeves and went to her knees, yet she felt almost indecently exposed.

"What's up?" Ray Mathieson asked.

"There's a rattlesnake on my deck and I don't know how to get it off."

"Sure it's not a gopher snake?" one man asked. "They look alike."

Oh God, Arla said to herself. If it should turn out to be a gopher snake, I won't be able to show my face in Wanda's. "Well, I *think* it's a rattler," she ventured.

"I'll check it out," Ray said. "Do you have a hoe?"

She looked at him blankly. "A garden hoe," he said, and she shook her head. He turned to the other men. "Eddie, could you get me a shovel?" The handsome Indian man looked through the shovels leaning against a shed and brought a square-bottomed shovel to Ray. He got into one of the big pickup trucks and followed her back to her house.

They went inside and she pointed to the deck outside the glass doors. Ray exclaimed, "Whoa! That must be the granddaddy of all rattlers!"

"So, it *is* a rattlesnake?"

"Yep, it sure is. And see the beads, how they're all the same size, and there's twelve of them? That means this snake's old. At least twelve years old, probably a lot older than that." He stared out at the snake, almost admiringly. "Gotta be six feet long."

"What should I do?" Arla asked. "Will the animal control people come take it away?"

"Most likely they'll tell you to leave it alone and it'll go away."

"Oh." Arla glanced out at the snake. "Well, how long before it goes away?"

"Maybe never. Maybe it's moved in under the deck and has a den there." Ray looked at her. "I can take care of it for you."

"I will be forever in your debt," Arla said fervently.

Ray went out the front door to his truck. He came back wearing heavy gloves and carrying the shovel. "Hold on to the dog," he said. Arla grabbed Morgan by the collar.

Ray quietly slid the glass door open and stepped out, carefully pulling the screen shut behind him. Arla thought he was going to scoop the snake with his shovel and toss it away into the brush. Instead, he raised the shovel and brought it down in a swift horizontal motion just behind the snake's head. The head shot off onto the ground and the long body squirmed and slithered madly, leaving squiggles of slime or blood all over the redwood deck.

Arla barely managed not to cry out, but Morgan began barking. "Don't let him out," Ray warned. "Their fangs can still bite for a couple hours. I'll bury the head out back."

"You killed it!" she exclaimed.

He mistook her horror for amazement. "If you know how to do it, it's not that dangerous. I've probably killed a dozen rattlers already this season. We're always finding big nests of them on job sites."

"Ohhh." Arla stepped back into the room, out of sight of that gruesome twitching.

"Are you okay?" He leaned the shovel against the wall, removed his gloves, and came inside.

Arla found herself inexplicably close to tears. She nodded mutely.

Comprehension spread over his features. "But you wanted me to get rid of it."

"I thought you were just going to take it away from the house."

"Not without the proper equipment. And besides, it might've been nesting under the house. Might've been hibernating there all winter. If I didn't take it far enough away, it'd come back. You wouldn't want that. Especially not with a dog around."

"No. No, I wouldn't," she agreed.

"In fact, you better call a pest control company and have them look under the house and make sure there's not a nest of baby rattlers there."

Arla shuddered involuntarily. She reached her hand out to Morgan, who came to her obediently, nudging her wrap, which fell open. Ray came over to pet Morgan too. His hand stroked the dog's head slowly, with an apparently intuitive sense of how Morgan liked to be touched.

For just a moment, their fingertips met. An electric charge shot through her body. Suddenly, she was conscious of the fact that she was practically naked. Her bikini was very small and had no extra material in the bra. Which meant that her nipples were visibly erect.

Hastily, she stepped back, pulled the kimono closed and retied its belt. The air felt charged and overly warm. "Thanks so much," she managed to say.

Ray gave Morgan one final pat. "You mind if I take what's left of the snake? Otherwise the guys won't believe it was really a rattler."

Arla laughed. "I was wondering how to ask you to take it!" The erotic tension was gone now. He went out again and scooped up the snake's head with his shovel, carried it to the back fence and out the gate. She watched as he dug a hole, seemingly effortlessly, put the snake's head into it and covered it back up. He returned to the deck and retrieved the rest of the body, holding it in his gloved hand.

"Do you want some iced tea, or lemonade, or…?"

He shook his head. "I've got to get back to the job. Thanks, though."

"No, thank you!" she said, and he waved goodbye and headed around to his pickup truck.

She hosed the deck clean but couldn't bring herself to sit on it. She went into the study, Morgan following. The diary sat invitingly on her desk; since she'd already taken it, she might as well read it before bringing it back. Or at least read some of it.

She leafed through the pages. The diary began in 1874 and ended in 1887. There were no blank pages at the end. Perhaps Mrs. Cushing had started another diary after this one. Mary O'Malley would know.

17 February 1874

The winter has been difficult. Day after day of gloomy skies, icy ground, air so cold that it hurts to breathe. Two days ago, a man from Sacramento rode into town and tied his horse to a post outside the Lost

Mine Saloon, whereupon an icicle broke from the eaves and impaled the poor beast.

I am now accustomed to our weather, but shall never forget my surprise in 1862 at the penetrating quality of the cold and the unceasing rains, for my uncle had written that the weather was always fine. We had not known how vast this state is, and thought that if the weather is always fine in San Francisco, it would be so elsewhere. I had supposed that only part of the Sierra Nevada mountains was treacherous in winter, the part over which the Donner party had tried to cross.

Arla skipped several pages and read:

6 September 1874

I find myself with child again. Hiram is pleased and prays for another son. I would prefer a daughter, wanting the companionship of a girl. And yet I would not wish the misery of a woman's life upon a child of mine.

She paged ahead again.

Christmas Day 1874

For days I have lain in bed after the loss of the child. I am told by Rosa that I nearly died too. None of the others—Hiram, the doctor, Mrs.

Cushing—thought fit to inform me. The child was a girl. Rosa is the only one to tell me this, also.

Then came an entry that took Arla's breath away.

10 January 1875

Rosa has told me that in the Jewish faith, their books speak of Lilith, who was truly the first woman, created from dust just as Adam was. Lilith was not obedient or submissive. She demanded to know why she should be in the inferior position during intimacies. She was discarded and God created a new woman from Adam's rib, a woman who was submissive and obedient. Rosa and I have laughed at the very idea of a woman making demands of her husband in such matters. Yet Rosa speaks as if she enjoys it. I have heard that women sometimes do. I endure it; it is an obligation.

My only desire is to be left alone. It is the fourth miscarriage. I cannot endure another, I cannot. My fervent wish is that he seek companionship elsewhere.

Arla set the book down, her heart aching with pity. What a terrible time it had been for women. And the effects had lasted into the 1950s, because Arla well remembered the tone of 'health' classes in school, in which girls of her generation had never been told about the existence of their sex organs (except for the vagina), only about the female reproductive system. 'Clitoris' was apparently a dirty word, for it was never uttered.

She returned to Catherine Cushing, skipping ahead ten years.

7 July 1885

Last night there was a terrible fire in Russian Camp. It is believed to have been started by the old prospector Verkhovsky, knocking his lamp over in his sleep. In a drunken sleep, for they say he was a man overly fond of spirits. There was almost nothing left of Verkhovsky's body. The other people in Russian Camp escaped with their lives and little else. Everything, everything burned to the ground. I shall collect clothing and food for them. Most of the families have children.

Arla set the diary aside.

Mary had told her that many gold rush towns had burned down several times, because they were often constructed hastily, of wood and canvas, the structures arranged haphazardly, with no thought given to fire protection. Someone knocked over a candle, and an entire settlement was gone in minutes. Camargo itself had burned down twice. Fire regulations were instituted in 1861; by then, the people still living in Camargo considered it their permanent home, rather than a temporary campsite to be occupied only until the gold held out.

But the fires that devastated California weren't only of ramshackle towns a hundred years ago, Arla reminded herself. The drought was making everyone conscious of the fires brought by Mother Nature.

She had taken all the recommended precautions. She kept the bushes and shrubs cut back fifty feet from the house and had a sprayer nozzle next to each hose. All her important papers were in one place. The roof was slate, not shake.

Thinking so much about fire made her restless and she

decided to go swimming after all. Morgan sniffed around the deck while Arla floated lazily in the water, getting out only to use the bathroom. Since she was in the house, she fixed a martini to bring back outside.

She had just taken a test sip when the doorbell rang. It was almost five o'clock. She realized that she'd been expecting it to ring.

They stood at the door in silence, and for a moment he seemed nervous and uncertain. She smiled and stepped back, and said, "Come in." He did.

"I know you're married," she began.

He reddened. "This is a mistake. I'm sorry." And he turned to go.

"No. I want you to stay."

He looked at her with his lips parted slightly, a questioning hesitation in his blue eyes. Arla took the plunge. She reached out and touched his arm with her fingertips. "I'm so glad you came back."

He stepped closer and she went into his arms.

Please be good, she prayed silently. Please give me pleasure. She reached up and touched his face, the golden stubble, the tender flesh. He started to pull back. "I need a shower; I've been at work all day."

"I like you just the way you are." She stroked his cheek while her other hand rested on his thick shoulder. He smelled of fresh air, dust, machinery—intoxicating, sensual odors, but she knew he would feel self-conscious if he didn't clean up. "But you can use the shower if you want, or the swimming pool."

"Do you have any men's swim trunks?"

"No, you'll have to skinny-dip." Arla smiled. "You must be even more beautiful with no clothes on."

He smiled too, and pulled off his T-shirt. He really could

have modeled for a sculpture of Adonis, she thought, and murmured his name as her hands caressed his torso.

Ray put his hand over hers, turned her arm over, and brought his lips to the tender skin on the inside of her arm. As his mouth moved slowly and softly up her arm, she grew dizzy with the intensity of her desire. She tilted her head back to receive the caresses of his lips. Oh my, she thought as his mouth touched her throat with an exquisite tenderness. His other arm encircled her, kept her up as she swayed. Oh my, I hadn't thought of this possibility, that he'll be such a good lover I won't want to let him go.

Chapter Twenty

Every year in late spring, when the calves were about a month old, roundups were held in west county at all the ranches. Even before she was old enough to work Kit had looked forward to roundups, awaited them more anxiously than Christmas, even. Until this year, she had never missed one.

She went to her first roundup at age five. As she watched, peering through the corral fence, the bawling animals were brought one by one into the chute. The dogs barked and nipped at the few calves that tried to step out of the line. The men on horses yelled and whistled commands to each other and to the dogs. Hot iron sizzled on the calves' flanks and they bellowed and struggled futilely against the wooden slats of the chute. The smell of scorched hide was pungent.

She heaved her breakfast into the brush, to the amusement of all the men. "The poor calves," she stuttered.

PJ mocked her, but Dad took pity. "Use your head, Squirt. See that? As soon as we let them go, they walk off like nothing happened." Kit watched. Dad was right.

Afterward, while the men sat in the shade drinking beer or whiskey and the women got dinner ready, the youngest children—Kit and the MacGowan grandchildren and the kids from the Giddings ranch—were sent into the corral. "Pick them up," one of the men would command, gesturing, and the kids collected the pink mounds lying in the dust, sometimes throwing them at each other, until the adults noticed their shrieks and ordered them to stop. As the men waited for the steaks and ribs, they tossed the mountain oysters onto the coals of the branding fire, plucked them out with sharpened sticks that would later be used by the kids to roast marshmallows, peeled back the skin and popped them whole into their mouths.

Every cowboy's unofficial initiation (well, after roping from a horse and learning not to pick up a hot horseshoe just because it no longer glowed red) was whether he could keep down his first bite. And many didn't—not because of the taste; they were delicate, tender but rich, like lobster, some said. It was the mental thing. Men, young ones especially, had trouble with it. Last year, Cal Giddings had chortled, 'Women eat 'em up no problem.' For older cowboys it was almost a point of pride, but Kit thought mostly they just liked to razz the young guys.

Over in Oso Grande every year they held the Mountain Oyster BBQ and Cook-off. The slogan was 'Come on over, you'll have a ball.'

By the time Kit was eight, Dad thought she might as well start learning about the work involved in operating a cattle ranch, so she rode out and helped round up the calves. Everyone had a specific job. 'Gid' Giddings drove the calves into the chute. PJ was respected for his ability at castration; he 'milked' the testicles to bring them low in their sac, then quickly sliced with a well-honed knife. Dad gave the antibiotic shot. George MacGowan stapled a tag onto each calf's ear. One of his sons handled branding, the other de-horning.

Years later Kit learned that at most ranches, cowboys roped

each calf and wrestled it to the ground, then held it down to be branded, castrated, tagged and injected. That was the old-fashioned way, and most young cowboys preferred it, because it gave them a chance to rope and wrestle. Dad and his neighboring ranchers used the chute, which made the procedure go faster and easier, with less likelihood of injury to cowboys or calves.

When she was nine, Dad told her she could help with the branding. They left the Double-L in the dark to drive to west county, and before the sun rose the neighbors arrived and everyone had a hearty breakfast and lots of coffee. As dawn broke the work began. Mom and the other women began baking pies and cakes, making potato salad and coleslaw, cooking a big pot of pinto beans, marinating steaks and ribs.

The branding took place the next morning. Kit joined the men and boys in the corral, clouds of dust rising as the cattle were brought into the pen. She pulled her kerchief up over her nose and mouth. The fire pit was already hot.

A red and white calf was brought into the chute. "You get this one, Kit," Dad said. The man working the pit handed over the branding iron. She looked at the calf. His big brown eyes stared right into hers.

"Hurry up!" Gid called, and she knew she had to do it now while the iron was hot, because if she let the iron cool that would be even worse. She brought it to his left hip and counted three seconds slowly, the same way as for lightning, and he bawled desperately, struggled uselessly, as the hot brand sank into his flesh and the flick of steel made him a steer and the numbered tag was stapled onto his tender young ear. He probably didn't even feel the hypodermic needle.

She had got used to it. She had to; branding was the only legal way to identify the cattle.

Carlos had never said he opposed branding; it was just, seeing how he felt about animals and how he treated them, she was thinking about things differently. So this spring, she'd told Dad she had to study for an important algebra test, offering to make up by restringing barbed wire on the fences at the Double-L.

She still worked the cattle, and there was a heck of a lot more to ranching than herding and branding. There was inspecting and mending fences. There was baling hay in the summer, and in the winter throwing it into the feeder or off the back of the pickup. There was inspecting the cows for signs of pinkeye, ear ticks, or foot rot. There was helping cows give birth and pulling cows out of mudholes, cleaning hooves and rubbing salve on wounds. There was riding out to see if the pasture needed a rest, and if so, moving the cattle. There was bottle feeding the occasional orphaned calf. She did all that. Just because she'd gotten squeamish about the branding, that didn't mean she wasn't working the cattle.

But it nagged at her. She didn't want to be like one of those city people, crying about animal rights while wearing leather shoes and eating chicken burritos. Since she believed there must be a more humane way to identify cattle, she had the obligation to figure it out. She went to the library. She hadn't found anything yet, but was convinced that some other way could be invented.

Dad didn't raise cattle the way the big ranches in the Midwest did—force-feeding the animals or giving them feed that contained cardboard fiber, feathers, and even chicken manure; keeping them immobile, then giving them antibiotics and other drugs to combat all the problems caused by abnormal feed and inactivity; taking them to the slaughterhouse when they were only fourteen months old. The Jensen cattle ate grass and alfalfa hay. They wandered around the ranches all their lives. The only time they got antibiotics was to prevent infections from branding and castration, or for a specific infection. They weren't slaughtered until they were three years old. Nor did the Jensens ship calves to feedlots once they were old enough to be separated from their mothers, the way some California ranchers were doing these days.

Kit considered the owners of those huge Midwestern feedlots more as factory managers than ranchers. She couldn't imagine one of them being familiar, as she and Dad and PJ were, with the personalities of the animals. 'Get that stubborn cow,' Dad would say, and Kit knew he meant that the first cow to be loaded should be the one who always balked at getting into a loaded trailer; Dad knew Kit could pick her out of a crowd of fifty others. Some cattle were curious, following Kit like puppies, watching her repair a fence or chop a fallen tree. Some were playful, with each other and even with the ranch dogs or people. Some were affectionate, licked and nuzzled each other and wanted their heads scratched before eating the hay Kit tossed down.

What she'd learned was to know them without becoming too emotionally attached. The cattle had good lives on the Jensen ranches, longer and far more pleasant lives than beef cattle in Kansas or Nebraska.

Certain times of year were busier for her. In October the cattle had to be dewormed, vaccinated, and have new ear tags put on. In November the herd was moved to west county for the winter and Kit had to round up strays. By the time a cow or steer was a year old it seemed to know the herd would soon be moved. Some liked that, but others hid. So Kit had to check all the hiding places she knew about, or else follow the manure trail.

In late spring, just before the cattle were returned to the Double-L, Kit had to put up new salt licks, always in the same places as last year. She liked to sneak a few licks herself, before the cattle or deer had got to them. If there was heavy rain, she had to ride out and make sure they hadn't melted.

Now that school was out and the cattle were back on the

Double-L, she had plenty of work. She got up early so she could do her chores before the sun reached full force. But that wasn't the only reason she wanted her afternoons free.

It had started during Easter break. She rode Sadie down to the creek, hesitated briefly, then followed the creek onto Pardini land. She knew the meadow was Stella's favorite part of the ranch, especially in spring. She dismounted and reclined on a field of tidy tips and, sure enough, Stella and Tabasco soon rode up. Stella mentioned that Mondays were usually off-days for her. The next Monday, as soon as she got home from school, Kit rode to the meadow.

Without making a formal plan, they began meeting there Monday afternoons. Stella always brought a snack of bread and cheese or homemade Italian cookies. Kit brought carrots or apples for the horses.

When Stella mentioned they needed a stable hand for the summer, Kit thought at once of Carlos. He needed a job and had told Kit he was afraid the only one he would get was pumping gas, or taking orders at the A&W. She knew he'd rather work outside and with animals. And if he worked for Joe and Stella, he'd be right there next door to her every day.

"I have a friend," Kit said. "He doesn't know much about horses, but he's really smart and he likes animals a lot. He wants to be a veterinarian."

"Do I know him?"

"I don't know. It's Carlos Tejada."

"Oh, Roxanne's boy. I do know him, Kit. Not well, but you're right, he'd be perfect. I'll call him tonight."

Carlos always told her what happened at Pardini Ranch, so Kit knew the creek had been blocked up and the Forest Service hadn't investigated very much. They had collected the evidence, in case it happened again, and they'd cleaned up the creek. Clay had come by and told Stella all that, and that he'd got into an argument about it with his supervisor and was now being assigned the worst jobs.

Kit also knew that two different times, people had made reservations for long pack trips but didn't show up. Now the Pardinis got deposits on reservations, so that problem was solved. Still, there was plenty to worry about. This was another very dry and very hot summer, worse than last year because the underbrush was thicker and the trees less healthy. The Pardinis were having a good season so far, but it wouldn't be long before the Forest Service stopped permitting campfires altogether.

Every day after Carlos finished his work, they rode out on Pardini Ranch (or he jogged while she rode), inspecting the land.

Kit had not told Stella that a few years ago Dad had forbidden her from visiting the Pardinis. She had sworn Carlos to secrecy, too. But Carlos thought it was wrong not to tell them. "If Dad finds out he won't get mad at *them*," Kit said. "I'm the one he'd get mad at." So they kept their secret.

***

ONE WARM JUNE day, they rode into the forest north of the highway. Kit didn't get over here very often, but she'd always liked it. It was a lot more mountainous than the ranch; the trails were carved into hillsides, and the ravines down to the North Fork Higuera were so steep that even she, a mountain girl, felt dizzy looking at them.

But the real danger was crossing the road. Someone might see them. Anyone would know it was Kit—that is, anyone she had to worry about. Dad, PJ and Stick all would recognize her and Sadie from a long way away.

When the road was clear both ways, she and Carlos galloped across and into the forest.

Stella had packed them a picnic, which they ate as soon as

they dismounted: ham sandwiches and Valencia oranges cut into slices, and homemade poppyseed pound cake, two slices for each of them. Kit could easily have eaten the whole loaf.

After eating they lay there lazily, gazing up at the sugar pines and the sky, so deep a blue it almost hurt her eyes. This part of the forest was too steep even for loggers, and since there'd been no fire here for decades, the trees were thick. Too thick: the forest didn't look healthy. Many of the trees had dried branches and dead tops. What with the density of the trees and the decrease of underground water from the drought, they had probably been too weak to withstand that bad cold snap last winter.

"Imagine how much drier it'll be in September," Carlos commented. "No wonder they declared fire season in May this year. That's the earliest I can remember. And it's so hot already."

"I know, and we've got at least three more months of it," Kit sighed.

"Usually I go down to my Grandma Dinah's for a month after school lets out. She lives in Oxnard."

"Isn't it hot there, too?"

"Naw, it's nice. It's right on the ocean. The weather's perfect, always about seventy-five."

"I guess you wish you were there right now," Kit said.

Carlos turned onto his side and grinned. "If I wanted to be there, I'd be there."

"You just stayed up here because you have a job."

"That's one reason."

What other reason? she wanted to ask, but dared not. Instead, she asked, "So you're going to UC Davis next year?"

He nodded. "I just figure if I go to college, even if something happens and I don't become a veterinarian, I'll have a chance of finding a job I like."

"Do you like your job now?"

"Yeah, but it's not the kind of job you can live on, like working at the lumber mill or driving a truck—the kind of work I'll end up doing if I don't go to college. Some low-wage job I'd hate but couldn't afford to quit." He leaned on his elbow and looked down at her. "It's different for you."

"I know," she said. They had never really talked about it before, about her coming from a family that had land and money, and him from people who survived by their labor.

"Roxanne told me she doesn't mind her job," Kit said.

"I know, because it's not boring and she sees different people all day long. But she doesn't pretend she'd go there if she didn't have to. She doesn't pretend she's not getting ripped off. I mean, Wanda's a nice lady and all, but Mom doesn't have any say about anything—her wages or hours, or how the place is run. And that's the best she can ever hope for: a job where the boss is nice and it's not real boring."

Kit was silent. She thought about what life was like for most people—as much of a prison as school, only worse because you never graduated and didn't get summers off.

INTERLUDE

March 1888
Camargo, California

THE DAY CATHERINE O'Malley Cushing was buried was as perfect a spring day as California can produce: an achingly vivid blue sky, bold sunshine ameliorated by a light breeze, riotously blooming wildflowers amid bright green grasses, serenading songbirds.

The Mass was well attended. Every member of the

Cushing family within 300 miles was there. None of the O'Malleys, though, since they all lived in Ohio.

The judge's face was grim, and observers took that to mean he was trying to keep grief from his countenance—although several more cynical mourners suspected that the judge, not a Catholic himself, found the funeral incense repugnant.

They were all mistaken. The judge's grimness was actually the result of annoyance.

The diary was still missing. He had searched every possible location. Perhaps he could safely conclude that if she'd hidden it, she'd hidden it so well that it would never surface. Yet its disappearance would, he knew, always eat at him.

The letter had been a bonus, something that he couldn't have hoped for. Should questions arise, he would be forced to reveal the devastating proof of Catherine's despair. He would 'have to admit' that he'd hidden the suicide note in order that she be given a Catholic funeral, presided by a priest, and be buried in the Catholic cemetery.

But since she hadn't *actually* been planning suicide, who *had* the letter been written to?

He concluded that the intended recipient was the person who was harboring the diary.

ROSA ESCOVIDO CHILDRESS did not sit with the Cushing family. Nor had she been asked to help prepare the Cushing house for proper mourning. But of all those present at the Mass, she was the person who mourned Catherine the most.

Rosa's employment at the Cushings' had ended six months earlier, when Catherine left for the sanitarium. Still, she was a worker, and immediately began baking pies that were sold at the farm store. She also took on commissions for special sewing—fancy work, such as veils and wedding gowns. So as things turned out, she did not want for income, only for more free time to spend with her grandchildren.

After the Mass, Catherine's casket was taken to the cemetery in a cart drawn by four black horses. Mourners followed on foot in a grim cortege.

Rosa had heard the whisperings in town that Catherine's death had not been an accident. Suicide, they said, but it was being concealed so that she could receive a Catholic burial. Rosa knew the Cushings to be capable of concealing the truth, but she could not accept that Catherine had killed herself. Perhaps a different truth was being concealed.

But whatever had happened, Catherine was gone. A sob caught in Rosa's throat and tears ran down her face.

When she pulled her handkerchief from her pocket she turned her head slightly, and found herself looking across the grave at Judge Cushing. He was not looking at the grave or the casket, or the priest. He was staring at her, Rosa. His eyes were cold and seemed unblinking.

Fear rushed into Rosa. She forced herself to move her eyes from the judge's, but casually and slowly, as if she hadn't noticed his hard gaze.

THE MOMENT SHE arrived home after the funeral, Rosa went into the parlor. The diary was hidden with Catherine's religious things in a small box. '*He must not find it!*' Catherine had whispered in a panic, the night she was taken to the sanitarium. '*Nor must my sons know of it.*'

Rosa had put the cover of her own missal around the diary and stored it with the other religious objects Catherine had given her: mantilla, gloves, a set of rosary beads, and her missal. At the time that had seemed a good hiding place. But now, she knew that it was not. The diary could not be kept with Catherine's things. And besides, no one kept two missals. Even though Hiram Cushing was not a Catholic, he would know that much.

She left the diary in the Spanish missal cover, took it into the kitchen and brought down the leather-bound notebook where she kept the recipes she'd used for Catherine's family, which ate so differently than her own. She tore out all the pages with notes and recipes, so that the diary fit inside nicely. On the outside she wrote *Pepinillos en vinagre al eneldo*. No one in her family ever ate dill pickles, let alone canned them, so the chances of anyone opening the small notebook were nil. She stuffed it back amid the chaos of her cookbooks and other recipe notebooks, changed into her normal daily clothes and went about her normal daily work.

And she waited for the knock at the door.

Part IV

1985

SUMMER

Going back to California is not like going back to
Vermont, or Chicago; Vermont and Chicago are
relative constants, against which one measures one's
own change. All that is constant about the California of
my childhood is the rate at which it disappears.

—Joan Didion, *"Notes from a Native Daughter"* in Slouching Toward
Bethlehem *(New York: The Noonday Press, 1990 edition, pg. 176)*

Chapter Twenty-One

Barely past noon and Ray was already exhausted. The temperature had reached 97 by late morning. He wouldn't be surprised if it got to 107 before the day was over.

At least this was Friday. Man, he could use the weekend. They were going to Tahoe. They hadn't gone last weekend, the long Fourth of July holiday, because it would have meant bumper to bumper traffic all the way up, and probably on the water too.

Ray went into the trailer, rolled up the site maps and collected the daily time and material logs and other papers, and put everything in a box to bring home so he could organize them Sunday night. Every year there was more paperwork, much of it mandated by the state. The past few years he seemed to spend at least as much time filling out forms as wielding a hammer or operating a dozer.

He heard the men's voices, the slamming of car doors and all the pickups driving away, so he was surprised when there was a knock at the trailer door. "Come on in," he called.

It was one of the laborers, Jerry Frye. He'd been laid off from SlidePac and had approached Ray one evening at

Cougar Creek Tavern to ask if Eagle was hiring. Ray'd had to think it over; the guy had a big mouth and drank too much. After a few days he'd told Jerry, "You start off doing nonunion labor, shoveling dirt or standing in the road with a flag directing traffic for eight hours. Pay's five-fifty an hour for laborers the first six months. No drinking on the job." He'd added, "And Jerry, first time you use a racist word, you're fired."

"When can I start?"

And Ray had to hand it to him; so far Jerry'd been fine.

Jerry stepped into the trailer and Ray said, "What's up?"

"I seen something I thought you'd wanna know about."

"What's that?"

"You better see it for yourself."

Half curious, half annoyed, Ray went with him to the furthest trench. Jerry gestured. "It's in the dirt that come up."

On the other side of the trench was a small pile of dirt. A shovel lay across the pile. Jerry stepped over the trench, moved the shovel and carefully swiped away some of the dirt with his hands.

It was part of a human jawbone.

"Son of a bitch!" came out of his mouth before he could contain himself. "Anyone else see this?"

"Nope." Jerry shook his head. "I came over here to take a leak, that's how I saw it."

Ray knew, from doing construction work so many years, that Piñon County was scattered with small unmarked cemeteries. Abandoned before the turn of the century, they had slipped off the maps and been forgotten, except for those in which old bones came back to curse construction sites. "A grave, maybe."

"Didn't see no headstone," Jerry said.

"Sometimes the miners buried people with only wooden

crosses for headstones. This could be part of an old mining camp cemetery."

"Or an Indian burial ground," suggested Jerry.

"There weren't any Indians right around here," he said firmly, like he knew what he was talking about. "Their burial grounds were all in the mountains, up by where the Rancheria is now."

"Yeah, sure."

How do I say this? Ray asked himself. How much can I trust this guy? "I know it's no Indian bone, but there's people who might try and stop the mall by pretending they *think* it's an Indian bone. Get the site shut down for two years while they excavate."

"Hey, man, I won't say nothing. I need this job."

"So do a lot of guys." Ray stepped back over the trench. "I didn't see this, Jerry."

"See what?" Jerry grinned.

Ray returned to the trailer and watched through the window as Jerry brought his shovel down on the bone, then heaved the fragments into the coyote brush and blackberry brambles behind the site.

He gave Jerry a ride to town. Nearly there, Ray said, "What were you making at SlidePac?"

"Good money. Eleven an hour."

Ray nodded and pulled over at a curb. "This okay?"

"Yeah, fine." Jerry grabbed his lunchpail and work gloves.

When Ray passed the old Minelli place, he almost parked and went in. Don't be an idiot, he told himself. You go into the museum asking, 'Was there ever a cemetery at Buckeye Flat?' and they're gonna say, 'You've been excavating there, haven't you? Did you find some graves?'

First things first. And first was to find out if it could possibly *be* a MiWok burying ground. If so, leaving early wasn't an option because he'd have to personally take care of things with a backhoe. As it was, he'd have to go back to the site anyway and make a cursory search.

At the cluster of fast-food joints on the outskirts of town he pulled over at a pay phone.

"Oh, hi," Arla said, sounding surprised. "I thought you were leaving for Tahoe."

"Yeah, pretty soon. I got something to ask you. It's business, kind of."

"Really? This is intriguing."

"It's got to do with that historical work you do. Over the weekend, can you try to find out what used to be at the mall site? It used to be called Buckeye Flat."

"Oh, Buckeye Flat? I already know what used to be there," Arla said. "A mining camp. A pretty lively one for a few years, apparently. Can you hold on?"

"Sure." He waited, glancing around nervously.

Arla came back on the line. "Gold was found there in 1850 and a camp of about 200 miners sprang up around the creek. People were getting gold for a couple of years. After it ran out, the camp was abandoned."

"What was there before that? A MiWok village?"

She took a few moments to answer. "I don't see anything about that. Oh, but listen to this. 'In February 1851, two men were caught taking gold from miners' tents. After a quick trial, the two thieves were taken to a large buckeye tree to be hanged. But the limb broke before the second man, who weighed nearly 300 pounds, could be executed.'"

"A buckeye tree!" Ray exclaimed. "They tried to hang a 300-pound man from a *buckeye* tree?"

"'He was revived, put on a horse and brought to an oak tree, which served the purpose.' God, how gruesome!" Arla said. "Now every time I go into the mall, I'll be thinking of this. Why did you want to know about Buckeye Flat, anyway?"

"Mostly just curiosity," Ray said.

"Did you find something there?"

He was about to deny at once, but she continued, "Some artifact or something?"

"One of the guys found an old bottle," Ray said. "I don't think it's that old though. I was thinking maybe there'd been a settlement there more recently."

"It seems not."

A truck drove by and she asked, "Where are you calling me from?"

"Main Street, Camargo."

"Oh no. Are you really? I'm tempted to start some love talk."

"That definitely isn't a good idea," he replied as sternly as he could.

Her voice dropped into a mock southern drawl. "I'm a bad girl. I deserve a severe licking."

"Monday afternoon," he promised, and hung up. Jesus!

He called Terri and told her he had a little more work to do, and drove back to the job site. It took him almost an hour to go through the piles of dirt and inspect the trenches inch by inch. He found one more bone, a couple inches long, and put it in his pocket, even though he had no idea whether it was human or animal.

It was past one-thirty by the time he got to the house. His personal pickup was parked out front, with the boat already hooked up; he'd done that yesterday evening. He opened the passenger side door and made sure his California Division of Forestry placard was still under the seat. Last time he'd worked a fire, the CDF had given him the placard and he always took it to Tahoe in the summer. If a fire started, the placard would get him past roadblocks.

He went in through the kitchen, greeted Terri quickly, and headed toward his office. En route he stopped in the living room to swoop up Trixie, who was sprawled on the sofa reading. She screeched, "Dadd–deee!" between giggles as Ray set her upside down on the other sofa.

His office was a small room in the rear of the house. He closed the door and dialed the number for Cushing's office. When he answered Ray said, "I have to talk to you, Hiram."

"Certainly, Ray. Shall I meet you at the site?"

"No!" Ray said quickly. "In fact, you better stay away from the site."

"All right then," said Cushing calmly. "I'll be at my house in fifteen minutes. Why don't you call me there?"

Terri was not happy that Ray had to speak with the boss and couldn't leave, as planned, at two o'clock. "If we wait to leave with you, we'll be stuck in traffic for hours, Ray! The whole point was to leave early so we'd beat the traffic and get there before dark!"

"I know that, but there's nothing I can do, all right? Something came up. If it wasn't important, I wouldn't do it."

"I know," she sighed.

"You guys go ahead and leave early. I'll drive up later."

Just then Roxanne called a greeting at the screen door. Terri let her in and exclaimed over the two pies she had brought, and took them to the kitchen to add to the ice chest. Roxanne greeted Ray and when their eyes met, he had a moment of panic. *She knows.*

No, she didn't know. He was careful. And it hadn't been that long, only a few weeks. He shook off the uneasiness and asked what kind of pies she'd brought. "One blackberry, one peach," she replied.

"All right! My favorites!"

Roxanne grinned. "I know."

Ray smiled, glanced at his watch and went back inside to his office.

Cushing picked up on the second ring and listened to what Ray had to say. "You did the right thing, Ray. But here's my concern. How can we be sure this fellow didn't plant those bones?"

"I guess we can't be, except what would he get out of it?"

"The same thing he'll get if he didn't plant them: better pay and a hold over us."

Ray had not even thought of that. Well, that's why Hiram Cushing's the boss, he thought, and silently cursed himself for having hired Jerry. But on the other hand, suppose Eddie or one of the other MiWok guys had been the one to find that jawbone?

"What is that fellow being paid right now?" Cushing asked.

"Five-fifty an hour. Says he used to get eleven at the mill, but he was there a long time and it's a union job."

"Perhaps he'd be happy with nine dollars an hour," Cushing said.

"Yeah, I think he'd be pretty happy with that."

"But don't tell him this on Monday. I want you to pay careful attention to what he does and says at the site on Monday. If he seems to be watching the spot where you found this other bone, or if he asks anything that indicates he might have known about it, don't mention a raise. And let me know as soon as you can."

"All right."

"On the other hand, he may say nothing, may not act suspiciously. If so, take him aside Tuesday and give him a raise. Make sure to tell him it's because he's been working so hard and productively."

"Okay."

"Can he be trusted to keep his mouth shut?"

"I don't know," Ray answered. Cushing was silent and Ray sensed tension over the phone line. "He's got a drinking problem."

"How serious?"

"He's got a DUI. And I've been around him in a bar. He

shoots his mouth off, insults women, makes racial comments, that kind of thing."

"An obnoxious drunk," Cushing said acerbically. "The worst kind."

"Right now he's got it under control, but you never know how long that'll last."

"Well, let's hope it will last a couple more months, until the buildings start going up." Ray could hear the clink of ice cubes against glass and Mr. Cushing swallowing. "Is this man a native of Piñon County?"

"No, he's been here around ten years. He moved here when the mill was going full tilt."

"What do you know about him? About his past? Anything he likes to keep to himself?"

"I don't know much about him." Ray hesitated. "I think the guy who probably knows him best is PJ Jensen."

"Ah. Well." Before Ray could ask what he meant, Cushing continued, "You went over the site thoroughly? You're sure there's nothing else there?"

"Maybe deeper in the ground, but we don't have to worry about that; nobody's gonna dig any deeper than we already dug, I found just the one other. It might not even be human."

"We'll never know," said Cushing firmly.

"Nope," Ray agreed. He would drop it in the lake this weekend.

"I know you're trying to get started on your trip. I won't keep you any longer. I appreciate your quick thinking and discretion today, Ray. Have a good time at Tahoe."

By the time he had showered, everyone had left except Carlos, who explained that Terri's car had been crowded. Carlos had already put out peanuts for the blue jays. He helped Ray load up the pickup and they were on the road by four. Carlos asked if they could listen to the Giants game and Ray agreed. During a commercial break Carlos commented on how many jays had come down for the nuts, and how quickly.

Ray grinned. "Trixie's crazy about blue jays. I have to buy a fifty-pound bag of peanuts just about every month."

"Mark Twain didn't like them. He wrote that a jay doesn't have any more principles than an ex-congressman and will steal, deceive, and betray four times out of five."

"That's harsh," Ray said. "Did you know there used to be a bounty for jays? Ten cents for every one you killed." When he saw Carlos's stricken face he was sorry he'd said that.

After a few moments Carlos said, "They're smart and they're brave. And they work together. I've seen them gang up on hawks trying to raid their nests."

"They do like to talk, though."

"Loudly," Carlos agreed with a laugh.

They lapsed back into silence as the game came back on. Ray was remembering a summer day twenty years ago, not long after he moved to Piñon County.

He and Bobby rode their bikes on Swede's Bar Road until the pavement ended, then clambered uphill, heading to the big meadow. They had brought snacks and their old rifles, planning to target shoot. They talked about baseball as they walked: Would the Giants bring up Masanori Murakami from Fresno? How bad was Marichal's back? Could Mays hit fifty home runs this year? Their socks collected burrs and foxtails; they skirted a mine shaft they'd marked with branches, and a rock pile where rattlesnakes lived. Finally reaching the big oak tree, they each climbed to a thick branch and sat leaning against the trunk.

Ray screwed the two parts of his Winchester back together and loaded four .22 longs. He looked up to see two red tail hawks gliding. The sun was directly overhead, so bright it shone right through their wings. He pumped the action, aimed at the closest hawk, and pulled the trigger.

The hawk tumbled from the sky. Bobby sat up so quickly his soda fell, hitting the ground and sending up a geyser. "What did you do that for?"

"I want to make a headdress," Ray said, running toward where it had fallen, hoping the feathers weren't too bloody.

To his surprise the hawk was still alive. He stopped abruptly. It turned its shining black eyes to him and he had the eerie feeling it had been waiting for him. He couldn't have looked away if he'd tried.

The hawk opened its beak, but no sound came out. Then the accusatory eyes glazed, and the hawk pitched forward and was still.

The other hawk was circling above Ray, screeching. Bobby ran up. His eyes were filled with tears. "The Indians climbed up to nests on cliffs to show courage and took a feather. You're no Indian!" He lunged and pushed Ray down.

Ray threw himself at Bobby's legs and they exchanged half-hearted punches, rolling around and matting themselves with stickers. Then a shadow crossed over them and they heard the beating of wings. The surviving hawk lit on the ground next to the dead one.

The two boys watched as the hawk pecked at its mate, then lifted its head to the sky and screamed.

For a few moments, Ray couldn't breathe. The hawk flew away and he leaped to his feet and ran. He ran until the stitch in his side stopped him, then bent over and was sick.

It had been twenty years, and he was still ashamed. Since then he'd occasionally killed animals for food—rainbow trout, his grandma's chickens, and once a pig. And he'd killed more rattlesnakes than he cared to count. But he never killed for the sport of it.

The other day, Arla had said how people almost never learned from history. But maybe the history a person *could* learn from was their own.

Chapter Twenty-Two

Laura looked at the calendar Friday morning and added to her mental tally. She had got through another day. 111 to go. She put away the vacuum cleaner and prepared to go into town.

Something was going on. He had been acting differently the past few weeks. Even with her, he'd been cheerful. And he'd been talking about the bright future.

Of course, Pete welcomed the new housing development; even if he wasn't directly involved in selling houses there, his own business would benefit from a real estate boom in Piñon County. But one day he'd made a comment that chilled Laura to the bone.

She was working in her vegetable garden, carefully pulling weeds from around the young tomato vines. She had asked Pete to help her put up the fencing that was necessary to keep the deer from eating everything. Pete brought out the roll of chicken wire, grumbling about how it was getting to be too damned much to keep up two ranches. Laura listened without comment. It was a familiar refrain these past few years, usually concluding that he would sell the west county ranch to the caretakers, Dick and Carla, if they could afford to buy it. But that day he didn't say that. He looked appraisingly at the house and barn, then toward the ranchland to the south, and said, "I could get a bundle for this place."

That was all. It was enough.

But how could he sell the ranch without her agreement? The ranch was in her name. Was there something she didn't know about, some technicality, or worse? He spoke as though any decision about the Double-L was his and his alone. She wondered whether he had somehow had it taken out of her name, without her knowledge. She hadn't thought to look for any property records besides the original deeds when she'd copied everything else at Pete's office. It hadn't occurred to her then to be concerned about the title to the ranch.

If anyone knew how to manipulate property titles, it was Pete; he had been in the real estate business for thirty years. Even so, Laura knew that the one thing he had to have was her signature. Could he have gone so far as to forge it? Or had she unknowingly signed something one night, too drunk to ask what it was? Or too drunk to even remember the next day that she'd signed it?

This fear had begun to haunt her. She had to find out. So she added one more errand to her list.

THE COUNTY COURTHOUSE was a substantial three-story granite structure built in imitation of the capitol. Fans hummed from every corner of every office, for the building did not have central air conditioning. Laura could almost hear the marble-lined hallways reverberating with all the furious objections when the county supervisors had voted to install air conditioning at the county jail, after having vetoed a proposal to put it in the court building. But after all, people did live in that jail, and couldn't step outside to sit under a shade tree or go across the street to get an iced tea, let alone leave at four-thirty every day. Not that the supervisors were motivated by altruism; they were under a federal court order to improve the jail.

She hesitated outside the Assessor's office, then entered cautiously. There was only one clerk, a young woman. Laura didn't recognize her. She sat at a desk behind the counter, staring at a microfiche reader. She frowned at the screen, wrote a note, glanced up at the screen again. Laura wished it was five o'clock so she could have had a sip of gin before coming into this building. She was going to have to ask for help, and she was sure that, without that sip, her voice would reveal her nervousness.

Just then, the girl saw her. "Oh, hi. I'll be right with you," she said, her voice friendly and apologetic.

"Take your time," Laura said. "I'm not in a hurry."

The girl made one more note, got up and came to the counter. "How can I help you?"

"I want to look up a property record."

"Sure, do you have the block and lot number?"

Laura shook her head. She didn't even know what that was.

"Oh, you're starting from scratch." The girl smiled. "I'll explain everything. You need the block and lot number to look up almost anything about a property. You can use that machine," she pointed. "Type in the address and you'll get the block and lot numbers. Then take the block and lot numbers to the microfiche."

Laura managed to take in most of the instructions. As she headed toward the machine, the girl called, "Oh, and if you want to look up any transactions within the past three months? You have to go through this binder. It's got print-outs for every day, listed by last name. You have to check every day, but it shouldn't take too long; there aren't that many."

"Thank you very much," Laura said. She had been afraid that the clerk would have to look things up for her, but this way was best. No one would know what she had looked up.

She checked the older records, finding nothing except that she was still listed as the owner. The binder with the past three months' records had nothing in her name. There were transactions in Pete's name, but none involving the Double-L.

She thanked the girl again and left.

Her relief only lasted until she reached the car, when it occurred to her that he could've had her sign something and hadn't filed it yet. Maybe he was holding it until the right time. She slid behind the steering wheel and tapped it nervously. Surely, she would remember having signed something, even while drunk. And surely, even drunk, she would not have signed the ranch away. It was the only thing that was hers. It was her only way out. No, the more she thought about it, the more certain she was that she hadn't signed anything. So maybe he had no plans for the ranch, and there was nothing to be nervous about.

Or maybe he assumed he could get her to sign the title over whenever he told her to.

She waited for the trembling to subside before starting the car. She drove slowly through town toward the grocery store.

She sometimes recognized the same submissiveness, resignation and fear in other women that controlled her own consciousness. And once in a while, she saw another woman moving stiffly, speaking in a subdued way. And she said to herself: So, it happens in other marriages too. No one talks about it, because it's understood that this is the way things are.

Or was it? Because he never touched her face or the parts of her body that other people could see. Only once had he gone so far that she'd had to go to the hospital; he'd been drunk and lost control and hit her in the kidneys. She withstood it for two days, blood leaking every time she went to the bathroom, waves of pain so intense she nearly blacked out. Finally, she went to the emergency room and told them she'd been thrown from a horse. She saw that the doctor (male) believed her and that the nurse and an administrator (female) did not. They prescribed fluids and bed rest and gave her a prescription for pain pills. She didn't dare tell Pete she had gone to the hospital, so she pretended to have the flu and stayed in bed for three days.

It had taken a long time for her to finally understand that what he was doing was wrong, and that it wasn't she who was to blame. For years she'd told herself that, but it was more a pep talk than anything. She was trying to make herself believe it. Then one day, a small moment occurred that changed everything.

The annual rodeo was being held at the fairgrounds. Pete was auctioning young bulls, PJ competing in stock events. Cindy and Kit, then aged eight and six respectively, were at the children's area, although pony rides and a petting zoo wouldn't be of much interest to them; they were probably spending their money on cotton candy and corn dogs.

Laura wore a long-sleeved blouse. Both arms were black and blue from elbows to biceps. He'd grabbed her two nights ago and had shaken her so hard it had given her a terrible headache that had lasted an entire day and night.

The first day of the rodeo was unusually hot for May and she felt the headache returning. She broke her own vow and drank before five. Just beer, but still. She downed one quickly and the relief washed through her; she had another. Not much later, she made her way to the women's restroom. A small entry area shielded the bathroom so no one could see inside when the outer door was open. Laura could hear two women talking in the hushed tones of a private conversation, and she paused in the entry area, not wanting to barge in.

One woman was saying, "… example does that set for

those two little girls?" The other woman replied, "A piss-poor one."

Then the first woman said, "I'm not trying to blame her. Pete's the one doing it. But a mother has an obligation to her kids to set a good example."

Laura let the door swing shut loudly. The voices stopped and she walked into the large room, a long rectangle with ten stalls and a concrete floor. The two women were standing in front of the sinks. Both were ranchers' wives; not friends, but acquaintances she'd known for years.

They both froze at the sight of her. She pretended not to notice, merely smiled and said hello, and went into a stall. The two women left wordlessly.

Her initial reaction was intense embarrassment: she didn't want them to be thinking poorly of Pete. Then, washing her hands, she looked at herself in the filmy mirror and was horrified at her own thoughts. Anger began to fill her; she could almost feel it rising from her feet upward, until she was gripping the sink and staring at her reflection. Anger at him. But anger at herself too. For letting it happen. For blaming herself for what he did. Most of all, for what it had taken two near-strangers to drive home: telling her two daughters it was acceptable.

For their sake she couldn't accept it any longer. But it took a few days of steeling herself before she got up the courage to say that to him. She entered his den and extended her bare arms, the bruises now turning green. "This must stop," she said. "We have two daughters."

Perhaps he sensed that something had changed in her, because he stopped.

Still, she'd never known whether he had really stopped, or whether, even if he meant to stop, he'd do it again anyway. For seven and a half years he had not hit her. There had been several times he'd threatened to, and two episodes that she shuddered to remember.

Without actually forming a plan, without ever coming to a point at which she told herself she had to divorce him, she had been biding her time with that in mind. She would wait until the girls left home. She could stand it that long. She had to, otherwise he would get custody. He could make a credible claim that she had a drinking problem and was therefore unfit to raise the girls on her own. She knew how convincing Pete could be; she'd seen him in action selling real estate. And on top of that, the family court judge was another of Pete's cousins.

Then in January, he did it again and she knew she could not wait for Kit to grow up and leave for college. She had to get out.

She was afraid that a lawyer, even a woman lawyer, would act too soon or speak indiscreetly to the wrong person. But finally, last month, the money from her mother's necklace tucked into her purse, she went to Sacramento and met with a lawyer.

The lawyer understood how it was with the Jensens. She'd grown up in a small town herself. She shuddered when Laura explained that her husband's cousin was the sheriff. "But he's retiring in October," Laura added.

The lawyer nodded. "We'll file on November first, then, after his cousin's out of office. And it's important that you stay on the ranch. Possession really is nine-tenths of the law. In the meantime, you keep collecting evidence. See if you can find that newspaper article you mentioned, about how the ranch was bought with your inheritance. The more evidence we have, the better. We'll take him for every penny he's worth."

"I only want what's mine," Laura said, "and what I'm entitled to."

The lawyer shook her head. "You deserve more, for what

he's done to you. Besides, it's best to demand more than your share, otherwise you get screwed. There's no such thing as scruples in a divorce case. *He* won't have any, believe me, and neither will his lawyer."

Twenty-nine days down. 111 to go. She drove down the dirt and gravel road to the house. To *her* house. No one was there.

She brought the groceries into the kitchen and began putting things away. Cindy would be leaving soon for college, so she would be safe. She and Kit just had to make it through the next 111 days.

PJ loved the Double-L, but she knew he would go with Pete. He had always regarded his father with a combination of awe and hero-worship, even when he reached adolescence and Pete became impatient, short-tempered and contemptuous, humiliating PJ before friends and family, goading him relentlessly. When Laura defended PJ, Pete accused her of babying him. Then PJ became a teenager, all nervous energy and simmering masculinity, and directed all his resentment at her. She had sloughed it off as a normal part of a boy growing up, growing away from his mother. She was still waiting for him to outgrow it.

Of the two girls, Cindy was clearly Pete's favorite. Nothing was too good for her, that beautiful princess. She was royalty among peasants, a Jensen among the lesser lights of Piñon County.

It was too late for PJ, too late for Cindy. She'd already failed them. She had loved them and taken care of them physically, but she had not taught them the things that mattered most. Perhaps she'd already failed with Kit, too. Perhaps she'd put a stop to it too late, and both girls thought that brutality was part of a normal marriage.

But it wasn't true. Her parents' marriage hadn't been like

that. She couldn't remember ever sensing the tension of cruelty or resentment or hurt feelings between them.

Stella's marriage didn't seem anything like hers, either. Laura didn't see Stella and Joe often, but when she did, she saw that Joe was respectful to Stella; that neither of them made each other the butt of cruel jokes; that they were friends; that they enjoyed one another's company.

She would have rekindled her friendship with Stella, had not Pete forbidden her from doing so. He had disputes with the Minellis, and his disputes were hers, he informed her. *A wife had the same friends and enemies as her husband.*

When Kit was twelve, Pete discovered that she'd been going over to Joe and Stella's. Laura herself was dismayed to find this out, but not surprised; after all, they were horse people too, and their ranch was right next to the Double-L.

Pete hadn't believed that Laura didn't know. Furious, he'd taken her into her room, closed the door, and unbuckled his belt. '*You promised,*' Laura had pleaded. So he hadn't used the belt. He had found another way to chastise her. Now, remembering, nausea washed over her. She opened the freezer for an ice cube and held it to her face.

Occasionally at dinner these days, Pete and PJ talked about how near the brink of ruin Joe and Stella Pardini were. They couldn't even afford to get the transmission on their pickup rebuilt, or so Pete gathered from their mechanic, the same man who worked on the Jensens' cars.

Why is the mechanic talking to you about Joe and Stella's private affairs? Laura nearly asked, indignant. But Pete had that look in his eye.

Stella had made overtures when Laura and Pete first moved up to the Double-L. And Laura had rebuffed them. It wasn't just because of Pete's prohibition. She had been ashamed to have anyone know. Perhaps more ashamed for Stella to know than some other woman. And she'd been afraid that Stella would insist on doing something about it. Or insist that Laura do something about it. If that happened, he would find out and things would get worse, a lot worse.

She folded the paper bags and stowed them under the sink. The clock showed 4:46. Close enough. She filled a glass with gin and tonic and ice cubes. Twenty-nine days down, 111 to go.

Chapter Twenty-Three

Terri worked four days a week at the salon, leaving time for shopping, errands and housework. The salon was closed Sundays and Mondays, as any woman in Piñon County could have told you, but only Terri's friends and customers knew she wasn't at the Cutting Edge on Thursdays.

Just before noon one Thursday in late July, Terri prepared to do the grocery shopping. Ray was at work, Trixie at summer day camp. Troy was outside, hauling Lincoln logs to the center of the sandbox with his toy dump truck. When the phone rang, she almost didn't answer it, but the habit of obeying its summons was too ingrained.

The caller was Laura Jensen. She sounded calm, but Terri was immediately apprehensive. Laura had never before called her at home. "Are you okay?"

"I wonder if I might stop by your house, if it's not too inconvenient." Laura paused. "I don't know who else to ask."

Terri gripped the receiver. "Oh, Laura."

"I don't want you to get involved. It's just that I need help with one thing. It should only take half an hour or so."

"Yes, come over," Terri said. She drove Troy to Aggie's, returned home, and waited anxiously.

Laura arrived wearing slacks and a long-sleeved blouse with a scarf, improbable clothes in the midday summer heat. "Is anyone else here?" she asked.

Terri shook her head no. "Did he hit you again?"

Laura didn't answer. She took off her sunglasses and followed Terri into the den, looked around it distractedly, and asked if she could use the bathroom.

When she emerged a few minutes later, she was nude. Her torso and thighs were splattered with black and blue bruises, and splotchy red abrasions. On her back were two bloody wounds that must have been made with a stick or belt. Her left breast bore an angry welt, and the nipple was purple and swollen into a distorted shape.

Terri cried out involuntarily. Laura went to her bag and took out a Polaroid camera. "I want pictures of this."

Terri took the pictures, holding back her anger and horror in the face of Laura's even manner. She took close-ups of the wounds while Laura held a ruler beside them. She took several pictures beside a newspaper showing the date and headline. Finally, there were over forty pictures and Laura nodded. "That should be enough."

Terri ran to the master bathroom at the other end of the house and splashed cold water on her face until she was sure she wouldn't be sick.

When she returned to the den, Laura, implacably calm, was dressed and sitting on the sofa with a glass in her hand. "I helped myself to the iced tea."

Terri poured herself some Jack Daniels. "Are you going to have him arrested?"

"Arrested?" Laura smiled wanly. "By his cousin, the sheriff?"

"What about the Camargo Police Department? There aren't any Jensens on the force."

"I'm not in their jurisdiction. But out of curiosity, I went to the library and looked at the annual report they file with the budget committee. In 1983, the Camargo Police Department was called to 'domestic disturbances' twenty-three times. Those twenty-three calls resulted in five arrests."

"That was before Nick Silva became the chief," Terri said. "Give him a chance, Laura. He's a MiWok; he knows what it's like to be on the wrong side of a local boy."

"Whatever he knows about the way things work, what he's figured out is how to use it, not how to fight it. Besides that, the ranch is twenty-six miles outside the Camargo city limits. He couldn't help me even if he wanted to. And whoever I called, there's no assurance that Pete would be arrested. Maybe all that would happen is he'd find out I tried to have him arrested." Laura trembled visibly.

"Then come down here and stay with us."

"Thank you for that, Terri, but I can't do it."

"But you have to leave him."

Laura nodded. "Yes, I know."

"Let's go pack your things. I'll go with you. I'll bring my gun, in case he comes back while you're packing. And what about Cindy and Kit? Where are they?"

It was as though Laura hadn't heard her. "I've never known when it was coming, or why. Sometimes, six months would go by. Sometimes, less than a week. One morning I could overcook his eggs and he'd eat them without a word of complaint. The next morning…" She shuddered. "He did it behind the bedroom door, but Cindy knew. She despises me for it." Laura's eyes filled. "Yet I'm glad for that. It means she won't emulate me; she won't end up with a man like her father.

"I don't think Kit knew. When she was six, I begged him to stop. I didn't want Kit to see it too. And he *did* stop. For years, he didn't hit me. I—" Laura's eyes met Terri's. "Do you know, I was about to say, 'I didn't give him any reason to.' Of course, what I mean was, he had no excuse.

"That's how I got through it." Laura gestured to Terri's glass of bourbon. "I kept to my rule and never had a drink before five o'clock. But I don't know if a night ever went by that I didn't have a drink. Because when I drank, the things he said and did no longer bothered me. I almost never disputed him. For years, we lived under a truce. But then, this winter, he slapped me. I told myself, 'It's just a slap, that's not the same as a beating.' He didn't use his fists, or anything else. He underestimated how hard he slapped, because he was drunk."

Terri remembered the bruises and welt on Laura's neck last winter, and grimaced.

"He didn't touch me for six months after that. Then last night—" Tears began rolling down Laura's cheeks.

"He should be in jail! And you're risking yourself, and maybe Cindy and Kit, by not leaving!"

"He has never done anything like this to the girls," Laura said firmly. "He used to spank them, but he's never beaten them, never so much as slapped them after they were eight or nine years old."

"Laura, if you could hear yourself with my ears, you'd know how pathetic that sounds." Terri couldn't control the anger in her voice. "I'm not trying to make things worse for you, but come on! You have to stop fooling yourself."

"I have stopped. And I have a plan. I know what I'm doing. I must ask you to trust me, Terri."

"Trust you to stand up to Pete?"

Laura sat silent for a few moments, then nodded almost imperceptibly. "He wants something I have. I've told him he won't get it unless he behaves himself for the next six months."

"The ranch," Terri said, remembering that Laura had kept title in her name.

"Yes."

"I don't understand. In six months, you're going to give it to him?"

"That's what he thinks, but what's *actually* going to happen is I'm going to divorce him. So I'm trusting you to keep it between the two of us, and not do anything."

Terri considered. "I will, on one condition: that we talk regularly so I know you're still okay. Okay physically, and okay emotionally."

"All right."

Terri gestured to the packet of photographs lying on the table. "What did you want those for?"

"For my lawyer."

And all at once, Terri was flooded with relief. Laura was serious about leaving Pete, after all. "You have a lawyer already?"

"Yes, a woman in Sacramento. She specializes in this— handling divorces for women."

"She told you it would take six months? Is that why you told Pete six months?"

"It won't take that long. We're actually intending to file November first."

"Why then? Why not sooner?"

"Because that's two weeks after Stick retires."

"Still, that's three months from now."

"He wants my signature on that deed," Laura said. She stood, slowly and stiffly. "Thank you for your help. I'm sorry to burden you with my troubles, but I'm very grateful to you." She wrapped her scarf around her neck and put the packet of photographs in her bag.

"When will I see you again?" Terri asked.

"Shall we have lunch together next Thursday?"

"Monday, when the salon's closed," Terri said, and impulsively she went to Laura and put her arms around her, gently. "But if anything happens, or if he threatens you, just walk out and come here. Don't take any chances, Laura."

"I won't. I promise I won't."

"Do you want my gun? Just in case?"

Laura shook her head. "I have one."

Terri watched her drive away.

Despite her anxiety Terri had to get the shopping done, so she collected her list, checkbook and car keys, and drove to the supermarket. She was so distracted that several times she found herself staring blankly at shelves of products. She found herself half-dreading that she'd run into Pete Jensen on Main Street, and half-hoping that she would.

Driving home she passed a squad car and suddenly remembered that the Camargo Police Department now had a woman officer. They'd been talking at the salon about an article in the Piñon County Register: Danny O'Grady had been named sergeant; someone else had taken a job with the CHP; the department had hired a new officer from a police department in Ventura County, and *her* name was…

The cop in the passing patrol car was a man, which was probably a good thing, because Terri would have been tempted to flag down the car if that woman had been in it. Which would have been a mistake. Laura didn't want the cops involved, and besides, who was to say whether this new woman cop was any better than the men? Maybe she was worse. Maybe she felt she had to out-macho the men on the force. Maybe she was contemptuous of abused women.

What Laura was going through made Terri feel almost grateful for Ray's shortcomings. Nothing he did could compare to what Pete Jensen did. What Ray did didn't hurt anyone, not that way. And besides, she was used to it. She'd even come to realize that the depth of their commitment and love and friendship was why his betrayal hurt so much. If her marriage were like Laura's it wouldn't matter if Ray slept with other women.

Of course, she hadn't always been so philosophical. They'd been married almost five years when she found out. Oh, that day! It had seared into her memory banks.

She'd needed his signature on some loan documents for the house (which they'd recently started building), so she dressed Trixie and drove to Ray's job site just before noon. She was heavily pregnant and had just begun her maternity leave.

She reached the job site and, about to get out of the car, instead sat watching him work. Even from this distance she could see by the glow of his skin that he was sweating hard. He wielded the hammer with rhythmic grace, his muscles moving evenly and steadily; he hit the nails so truly that he needed only two or three strikes for each. But what made love surge in her was the focus with which he worked. He ignored the heat, the sweat, the glare; not until he got home tonight would he admit to the strain in his back, the ache in his neck, the soreness of his shoulders.

Trixie began to squirm in the car seat. Terri remembered Ray had told her he had to go back to the office during lunch to sign payroll so the paychecks could be cut, so she drove back to the Eagle office to wait for him there.

The receptionist cooed over Trixie, pleading to hold her. Terri beamed as she watched the other woman adoring her daughter. "I'm going to sit down," she said, and the receptionist exclaimed, "Of course, get off your feet! Trixie and I will get you something cool to drink. Iced tea?"

And she went into the small room used by the construction company. It was more or less Ray's office, so that was where she went to wait. If she'd simply sat down in the reception area, she would have remained blissfully ignorant.

Instead, she sat at his desk and idly looked at the papers on it. She saw six messages from the same woman, a woman who would not be phoning Ray for business reasons. A woman who had been married for over twenty years. A woman Terri saw at work because she came in every month to have Vickie color her hair. A woman with grown children. My God, she was almost old enough to be Ray's mother!

And on the bottom of the most recent message, in Ray's handwriting, was written: 'Thurs noon.'

Terri's world crashed and broke.

She went into the bathroom and splashed her face with cold water, then waited for him in the reception area. Somehow, she managed to see and talk to him without letting him know. Somehow, she drove home and gave Trixie lunch and put her down for a nap. Then she collapsed.

She told herself that for the first time she understood the true, terrible meaning of the word heartbroken. She'd always thought it was only a cliché. But the real cliché was her life. She was the cliché pregnant harried wife, devoting all her time and energy to her child, letting herself go, forgetting about her husband. He was the cliché neglected husband, telling himself he was justified in seeking companionship elsewhere.

She was terrified at the thought of being deserted. Still, she confronted him. At first he denied it, but perhaps sensing that that only made her angrier, he finally said it was true.

"Are you in love with her?" Terri asked.

He was so shocked that she was pretty sure his vehement 'No!' was genuine.

"How often?" she asked, meaning how often with that woman.

"Four times," he said, then added, "but it was never serious with any of them."

Their marriage was in a crisis for months. She confided in no one, not even her sister, and felt terribly alone and lost. She ate her way through the last three months of the pregnancy (and, she reflected now, looking down at herself, I never lost that fat, either). As her belly grew and her ungainliness increased, she felt hopeless and helpless.

She came to certain conclusions. If she didn't want to divorce him, she'd have to get used to what he'd done. She'd have to accept it and move on. Men were like that. Ray just had more opportunities than most men because of his looks.

But in steeling herself, in forgiving his deceptions of the past and accepting that there would be deceptions in the future, she lost the intensity of her feelings for him. She loved him still; she liked being married to him; they were compatible in almost every way. But she wasn't head-over-heels crazy in love anymore. He was no longer her idol, her god. He was no longer the perfect husband. He was just an ordinary man.

One of the standards Terri had disavowed as a teenager in 1969 was monogamy. She wouldn't be content to sleep with only one man the rest of her life. She wouldn't equate sexual fidelity with true love. She wouldn't expect a man to give up his freedom just because they'd married; it was only a piece of paper, wasn't it?

Okay, she had not maintained those convictions, but maybe having once held them helped her to be more philosophical about her situation. And less likely to boil over and end up divorced, like other women did, over what amounted to meaningless infidelities.

She had never regretted her decision to stay with him. Look at Loretta and Roxanne. Or Aggie. That was the fate of a single mother: to live in a dump of a house, drive a broken-down old car, and have such a tight budget that brand-name cereal was a luxury. To live without companionship, without comfort, without protection, and usually without sex.

What galled her was that other women assumed she was in a unique situation. As if their own husbands never stepped out. As if Ray was the only guy in Piñon County who did.

What galled her even more was that other women assumed

she didn't know about Ray's affairs. Like she was too dumb to notice, or too downtrodden to leave him. It would never occur to any of them that she knew and didn't care. Well, cared, but didn't begrudge. Didn't try to stop him.

As if there was any way to stop a man from doing that. Better this than that he gambled, drank, snorted coke. Better this than that he beat her.

<h1 style="text-align:center">Chapter Twenty-Four</h1>

Arla sat in her study with the diary before her. She could never read it, or think of Catherine Cushing and her husband Hiram, without reminding herself that their great-grandson was Ray's boss. Which naturally made her think of Ray. Oh, how her body ached at the thought of him!

She looked at the diary on her lap. She knew she shouldn't have concealed its discovery from Mary. She would have to tell her, and soon. Each day she put off the inevitable, it became more difficult.

She opened the diary. She was reading every entry now, not skipping any.

9 July 1885

Last night I could not sleep, despite the draught of medicine. Hiram has always insisted that I take it, even though it often does no good. I came out intending to have some tea, when I heard voices in Hiram's study. As it was so late—after midnight, I believe—this surprised me. I crept to the door to find out who he was with, for

I feared that it must be bad news concerning the family. What else would Hiram be discussing at such an hour, behind a closed door, and in muted voice?

It sounded as though two men were with him. Their conversation was barely audible to me. I could make out only some words and phrases, and came to realize that Hiram was conducting a financial transaction with the visitors. Its purpose I could not determine. It seemed that work had been commissioned by Hiram. He expressed appreciation for its completion and counted out money. I listened but for several moments before continuing into the kitchen to prepare my tea, which I took back to my room, and sat drinking it in the darkness. When the men left, I looked out the window to see who they were. I recognized both.

One is the half-wit brother of Ollie Jensen. Half-wit is perhaps not accurate; I have been told that this fellow, whose name I believe is Bernie, was kicked in the head by a mule and has ever since been subject to unpredictable changes in temperament.

The other man is the one about whom our maid complained to Rosa; he had been attempting to take liberties with her. I would not have recognized either of the two men except that I was so recently at the mill for the Independence Day celebration held there. That is where I saw them. Hiram employs them both as millhands.

24 July 1885

The town was in a tizzy yesterday, as it became clear that arson is suspected as the cause of the fire at Russian Camp. One of the children saw two men come out of Verkhovsky's cabin only moments before the flames began. A husband and wife heard horses galloping away, though they saw nothing. Hiram hears all of these rumors and is kept apprised of the investigation, since he is the county magistrate.

25 July

A meeting of the town was held tonight, called by the leading men. Some of the people are angry and demand the immediate arrest of the suspects. Hiram urged caution and temperance. It would not do, he pointed out, to arrest the wrong men, or to arrest someone without being certain that the crime was actually committed.

I begin to believe that I am once again seeing his kindness, charity and tolerance—the qualities which accounted for my agreeing to be his wife so many years past.

28 July

Most of those poor unfortunates have accepted

Hiram's offer to buy their land, and the brother and sister-in-law of the unfortunate prospector—they are older, their children grown—removed to the eastern part of the county to buy a farm there and start their lives anew. When I praised Hiram's generosity, he reminded me that no one has ever lost money owning land, even land that seems worthless. 'What shall you do with this parcel?' I asked, for it is known that the land in Russian Camp has no gold or other valuable minerals, and now it will not be fit for grazing for at least several more years.

Hiram answered that he has no plans for it; he will simply assume it and perhaps in the future, someone else will want it for some purpose or another. It shall cost him nothing to merely own it.

2 August

I must record my fear and its unspeakable cause. My hand shakes as I write this, and I feel as though I have been struck by a terrible, crippling blow.

Rather late last night, two men were accused of arson and murder. The two arrested were Bernie Jensen and the millhand named Martin. I cannot rid my mind of the image of the two of them riding away from here that night after being paid by Hiram. My suspicions make me feel disloyal, but for all that, they stubbornly remain in my mind. And what is in my heart is the certainty of what he has done.

Arla closed the diary. These passages made it unnecessary to 'read between the lines' of history.

The ringing of the phone startled her, and when she answered her pulses began to throb, because it was Ray. He spoke in an undertone; he must be calling from home. The timbre of his voice triggered physical memories in her body.

"Can I see you tomorrow?"

"Yes. Yes. Oh, Ray. When?"

"In the morning, unless six is too early?"

"No time's too early. I wish you were here right now. I'm damp just from the sound of your voice."

"Don't," he said, hoarsely.

She knew he didn't want to have long conversations from his home phone. They both hung up, and she laughed softly. Tomorrow morning. He would be here in less than eight hours. She would miss her run again. She was not running as much as she used to because sometimes, he could only come over in the morning. Love was making her plump and lazy. No, not love; lust. Lust unadulterated by romance, purified by its honesty.

Chapter Twenty-Five

Kit had often yearned for change: change within the family, change in this town, where it seemed like nothing ever happened. But now that change had come, she was uneasy. Something was different between Dad and Mom. Mom was spending more time away from the house than she used to. When she was home, she wasn't drinking as much. But what was weird was that Dad seemed wary around Mom. And even weirder, sometimes Mom just ignored him, which made Kit's breath draw in. But he didn't get mad, and that was the weirdest thing of all.

Cindy would soon leave for San Diego; college started later this month. Kit ached with envy: what wouldn't she give to be that far from the family, with an apartment being paid for by Dad, and a car, and a whole new life! Instead, she was stuck in Piñon County waiting for sophomore year at Camargo High. Three years left on my sentence, she told herself gloomily. And then what? She still didn't know. PJ had gone to Cal Poly, the favorite college (along with Nevada Reno) of ranch boys. But she didn't want to go away to college just to be around ranchers.

Carlos was planning to go to UC Davis and study veterinary science. Davis was the best school in the country for that. If Kit went to Davis too, she could study agriculture and board Sadie nearby. But her grades probably wouldn't be good enough for UC. She'd have to spend a year or two at a community college first.

One afternoon, she sat in the kitchen while Mom prepared chicken for dinner. She'd already mixed the flour, cornmeal, and spices. Kit's mouth began to water, because there was nothing as good as Mom's fried chicken. But it was a long time till dinner. Mom always put the battered chicken in the fridge for a couple hours. She said it fried up better if you let it sit like that.

"Mom, were you best friends with Stella in high school?"

Kit watched carefully out of the corner of her eye. She was pretty sure her mother stiffened at the mention of Stella's name.

"No, not in high school." Mom pulled out the leg on one of the chickens and sliced through it with the precision of a butcher.

"But before that?"

"We were next-door neighbors, almost inseparable for years. But you know how it is in high school. And then I got married and moved down to the west county ranch. Stella seemed like a kid to me then, so…" Mom's voice trailed off.

"Did you go to the Minellis' a lot, then, when you lived next door?"

"Yes."

"Is that where you learned to cook so good?"

"Yes. Stella's nonna was a wonderful cook. I'd sit in the kitchen and watch her for hours. She'd show me how to roll out the dough for ravioli or pansotti, how to tell when the sourdough was finished baking, how to grind the basil and garlic for pesto. She'd gesture for me to taste something, then add a handful of sugar or oregano, a couple splashes of wine, and have me taste it again."

Mom took the egg mixture and began dipping chicken into it, then rolling the wet pieces into the flour-cornmeal batter. She set each piece on wax paper carefully, so they didn't touch. "Stella was two years younger than me. We went to elementary school together, and it was a one-room schoolhouse back then, so we were together all day long. We walked to school together, walked home together, spent every afternoon together, and most weekends too."

"At her family's boarding house?" Kit asked.

Mom coated the last piece of chicken, and sat at the table for a few minutes, her hands covered with clumps of the cornmeal batter, and gazed out as though looking past the outbuildings and the flower garden, toward the hill that sloped down to where a battery of sugar pines lined the riverbank.

"Why aren't you friends anymore, Mom?" Mom stiffened, and Kit supplied the answer. "Because *he* said so," she said bitterly.

Mom abruptly got up and went to the sink. She washed her hands with maddening deliberation, then dried them just as slowly on one of the embroidered dishtowels.

"You don't even care!" Kit exclaimed, biting back her tears.

"That's not so."

"It *is* so! He says something and you just do it."

Mom draped the dishtowel over the rack. "These things are complicated, Kit. There's no simple explanation."

"Yeah, right," Kit said. She jumped up and fled to her room. Why were grown-ups, her mother especially, so placid? If they cared about something, why didn't they defend it, protect it? Why were they always so timid, so cowardly?

She had intended on confiding in Mom that she was going to Pardini Ranch to visit, as she had promised Stella she would. She had even thought of telling Mom about

Carlos. But now she knew she couldn't. Mom would never stand up to him. She wouldn't even stand up to him about things that didn't affect them personally. Like a few months ago, they were watching the news coverage from Philadelphia, and the police dropped a bomb on the MOVE house.

"My God," Mom said, "they're trying to kill those people!"

"They brought it on themselves," Dad said.

"There are children in that house, Pete."

Dad shrugged. "A few less pickaninnies on welfare." He picked up the *Sacramento Bee* sports section.

Mom stared at him in disbelief, then sat watching as the whole neighborhood burned down, crying the whole time. But she didn't say anything else.

Kit pulled on her riding boots. On her way out, she glanced into the kitchen. Mom's back was to her. She was leaning over the sink. For just a moment, Kit yearned to go over and hug her and say she was sorry.

But I'm not sorry, she thought defiantly. She *should* feel bad about it!

That evening she found herself in Cindy's room, sprawled across her sister's bed watching her sort through clothes, and remarked how lucky she was to be getting away.

"You'll get away someday, too. You should be thinking about where you want to go to college."

"I know, but I hate school." Kit folded her hands under her head. "I still don't know if I even want to go to college."

"I don't want to all that much either, but it's the best way to get out of here." Cindy paused, then looked at Kit. "If I stay in Piñon County, I might end up marrying someone like Dad."

Kit gaped, and Cindy laughed. "Just because I know how to get my way with him, doesn't mean I don't see what kind of man he is."

"Do you think Mom will ever leave him?" Kit wouldn't

have asked it, except that Cindy was so much easier to talk to, now that she was almost free.

"I would've said never, if you asked me a year ago. But now … I don't know, she's different somehow. So maybe she *will* leave him." Cindy's eyes glittered with amusement. "Can you imagine how freaked out Dad would be?"

"Yeah, he can't even fry an egg or run a load of laundry." They both giggled and Kit continued, "He'd try to find some other woman he could boss around and treat like a doormat."

"He'd be looking a long time," Cindy said. "Women aren't like that anymore. Mom's a dinosaur. Her species is on the verge of extinction." She examined a blue sweater, put it aside in the Don't Take pile. "At least she's not *actually* extinct. I think it came close a couple times."

Kit looked at her in confusion.

"Come on, you know what I mean." Cindy made a fist and punched the air.

It was like the last piece falling into place. Kit could scarcely breathe. Her heart beat so hard, it hurt the wall of her chest. He hits her. *He hits Mom!*

"Seriously, you didn't know?"

She shook her head no, still not able to speak. Cindy came over and sat beside her. "I would've broken it to you easier, but I thought you knew."

"How often?" Kit asked.

"Not that often anymore. It was a lot when we were little, but it kind of stopped when I was eight or nine. Only a few times since then."

"How did you find out?"

"Sometimes I'd hear a noise and tiptoe over by their room. I could hear him hit her."

"Oh my God." Kit leaned her head over the edge of the bed.

"Hey, if you're gonna throw up, do it in the bathroom!"

"I won't throw up," she mumbled.

"Other times I could tell, because she'd be walking all stiff. Or in summer, every day she'd wear a sundress or halter and shorts, then all of a sudden she'd be wearing long sleeves and slacks." Cindy considered. "You know what? A couple weeks ago, I noticed her wearing winter clothes for a few days. I wonder if he's doing it again."

Kit felt something tear inside herself. Cindy brought her a towel and she sobbed into it for what felt like a long time. Finally she lay on her side, depleted, sadder than she thought she'd ever been in her life.

Cindy had finished packing and Kit watched her sitting on the suitcase so she could zip it. "Don't worry," Cindy said. "High school will go by fast and then you can leave. Or if it gets too weird, just come down and stay with me."

But it wasn't herself she was worried about. Why *hadn't* Mom left? Or better, thrown him out? Why did she tolerate it? What kind of woman put up with that?

THREE AFTERNOONS AFTER that revelation from her sister, Kit was resting in the shade of a grove of pines on the southeastern side of Pardini Ranch. Carlos, lying on his stomach, his head on his arms, was almost asleep; he'd been working since early that morning. His hair was pulled back in a ponytail. Kit, sitting beside him, sprinkled water from her canteen onto his neck and arms. It was quiet except for an occasional airplane droning overhead, the distant whine of chainsaws working in tandem, and the bawling of cattle.

"Are those your cows, Kit?" Carlos asked sleepily.

"Mm hm. They must be going down to the river."

She heard a distinctive voice leading the way. The red cow —the only one in the herd without the usual white face—was the Boss Lady. She was the one who always saw the approaching pickup first, or spotted a coyote pack on the horizon.

People always said cattle were stupid, but Kit knew they weren't. People mistook docility for stupidity. When they were rounded up for the slaughterhouse, they followed the horses—and each other—right into the corral, up the ramp and into the truck trailer. At such times they were tragically docile. But then, how were they to know they weren't being taken to the other ranch, as usual? Over the years she had sometimes found herself secretly hoping they would escape, break down the fence and flee into the mountains, never to be found.

They weren't always docile. They protected their calves with ferocity and fearlessness. Once PJ saw a cow charge a calf-stalking coyote, butting it with her horns; after PJ shot the coyote, he saw that the cow had actually gored it.

And no one who'd had to pull a stuck cow out of a mud puddle—Kit had spent an entire afternoon doing that very thing last spring—would underestimate the strength, orneriness, or monumental stubbornness of a cow.

"Where's the fire?" Carlos asked, as yet another plane took off from the firefighting airport to the north, near the county line.

"Forty miles north of Tahoe. On the radio this morning, they said 2,500 acres."

"Probably up to 4,000 by now."

The air base was three years old. Before that, firefighting planes were kept at the county airport and took off over a residential area just west of town. The planes, old and loaded with slurry, strained to get altitude. Then one of them clipped a pine tree and nearly crashed. After that, the new airport was built.

The state had bought the land from a man who had a small ranch. Kit remembered Dad commenting how pretty soon there wouldn't be another cattle rancher in the whole damned county. Secretly, she had been glad to see that particular one go. Every time she'd been to that ranch, she noticed how miserable Bradley's horses were. The corral was too small. The water trough was never more than a quarter full, green slime lined the sides and the water was speckled with hay, dead flies, and mud. He didn't use fly masks and the horses never had a moment's peace in the summer; flies swarmed on their eyes, mouths, and ears. And actually, winter wasn't any better, because the horses stood hock-deep in mud.

The cattle had it bad, too. Bradley had a new pickup every couple of years but was too cheap to buy hay, leaving the cattle to forage. They ate everything so far down that eventually not even weeds grew well. They were always thin and she wondered how he ever managed to sell them. Dad said he fattened them up right before auction, on grain and water. But no one ever bought Bradley cattle more than once. When buyers looked for brands, it wasn't only to choose the best cattle.

Bradley and the two sons had moved to Nevada. She hoped they weren't still ranching.

"Let's go down to the river," she said now.

Carlos rolled onto his side and looked up at her. She could see the pulse in his temple. His lashes were so long, they cast little shadows on his cheekbones. "Yes, let's."

They rode slowly. Kit thought about what Carlos had said a few days ago about Roxanne and PJ, the thing that happened when they were in high school.

PJ always said he got the scar on his cheek during a fight. *'It was nothing,'* he'd say—but he said it the way people do when they want to imply it *wasn't* nothing; that the only reason they *said* it was nothing was modesty. Which, come to think of it, was totally unlike PJ. If the fight had been life-and-death, if he'd had to deflect a deadly knife thrust, he might still *say* it was nothing, but he'd definitely make sure to recount it often, and in plenty of detail.

According to Roxanne, it wasn't even close to life-and-death. She and PJ had a disagreement; she wouldn't say what about. Her friend Bobby (who was Clay DiMauro's older brother) confronted PJ. They had a fistfight. Bobby won the fight, pinned PJ, and nicked him with the knife as a warning. Bobby got suspended from school for two weeks.

Bobby had died a long time ago, but a lot of people had seen the fight, which might explain why PJ didn't brag about it.

"What do you think your mom and PJ disagreed about?"

"PJ was saying things about Mom at school, things that weren't true."

"What was he saying?"

"She wouldn't tell me." Carlos paused. "I think it was something she felt embarrassed to say."

They looked at each other. Kit could only think of one sort of thing a boy could say about a girl so bad that another boy would punch him out over it and so bad that the girl would be embarrassed to talk about it twenty years later with her son.

"Mom wanted me to know about the fight so we'd know PJ might have a grudge against her. That he might have a problem with me and you being friends—not just because I'm Mexican." He was looking ahead, concentrating on where Griselda was stepping.

"Yes," Kit said, slowly. PJ did seem to dislike Roxanne so much. He always implied it was because she'd married a Mexican-American. But this must be the real reason for his antipathy.

"Turn left ahead," she said. "That way we'll be in park property."

Carlos nodded. Kit didn't have to add, by way of explanation, that they would thus avoid Jensen land. They had both become used to avoiding any possibility of contact with her father and brother. But sometimes she was aggrieved by how routine this had become. And she thought of what Cindy had told her, and burst out, "My father is such a jerk."

"Everyone thinks that about their parents."

"I'm not saying that because it's just some typical teenage thing to say. He really *is* a bad person." She didn't try to conceal her impatience. "Why do you deny it? Not everyone in the world is good, Carlos."

"I've noticed that occasionally."

"Well, my father's prejudiced. He's cruel to people who aren't as strong as he is. He says he loves the land, but he doesn't really; he only loves that it might make him rich." She hesitated. "He doesn't even love my mother."

"Why do you think that?"

She didn't answer for a second, wanting to tell him, but for some reason afraid to. "He wouldn't be so mean to her if he loved her."

"Maybe it's that he doesn't *like* her. There's a difference, you know. You can love someone but not really like them."

They had reached the banks of the river and both dismounted. Carlos smiled at her. "Let's go in."

They waded into the river fully clothed. The water wasn't deep and they ducked down, shrieking at how cold it was. When they got out it took only minutes to feel warm and almost dry.

"You know what, Kit?" he said. "Everyone's embarrassed about their parents, and ashamed about being embarrassed. But you don't have to be embarrassed about your mother. Maybe she drinks a little too much, but she raised you to be the person you are. You didn't get it from *him*, right?"

She could not speak. She shook her head vigorously.

"And besides, he's probably the reason she drinks."

Tears sprang to her eyes. "My sister told me he used to hit Mom." Now her words rushed out, tumbling over one another.

"He might've started doing it again. I'm so afraid for her. I keep thinking how careful she is not to annoy him, and how afraid of him she must be. I shouldn't call her a coward, but–"

"*He*'s the one who's a coward. Big strong man, such a weakling inside he has to hit a woman to feel strong. Shit!"

Carlos didn't cuss often. She was surprised at his vehemence, but comforted by it too.

"What kind of man does that?" he fumed. "Terrorizes a woman by reminding her he's bigger and stronger, then actually hits her. Your father really *is* a Nazi!"

To her own surprise, Kit began to laugh.

"I'm sorry, I mean he's your father, but…"

"Don't be sorry. That's what he is. Mom should have left him a long time ago."

"She should've *shot* him a long time ago," Carlos said.

Chapter Twenty-Six

"When did you fall out of love with him, Laura?" Terri asked. It was Thursday afternoon and they sat on the swing in the backyard. Troy was taking his nap and Trixie was at a friend's house.

"I don't know if I ever really loved him."

"But you married him," Terri said, the protest in her voice coming out before she could stop it.

"I was pregnant."

Ah, the good old days, she thought bitterly. The fifties, with all those wonderful family values: women knew their place and abortion was illegal.

Laura continued, her voice as serene as always. "Pete and I were out on our third date. I had sneaked out to see him; I told my grandparents I was going out with my girlfriend. He was twenty-three; I was still in high school. I was forbidden from dating him."

"Because of his age?"

"That, yes, and because they didn't like him. My grandfather thought him arrogant and irresponsible; a spoiled rich kid." Laura sighed. "What I felt for Pete was sexual attraction, but I mistook it for love because the feeling was so compelling. I knew very little about sex; it wasn't something that my mother or grandparents could discuss with me. The one time my grandmother said anything at all, it was that if I kept a nickel between my knees, there was nothing to worry about."

Terri grimaced. "So, what happened on your third date?"

"We were in the back seat of his car, kissing. I was fully dressed, wearing my beautiful western clothes—we'd been square dancing. He put his hand under my skirt. I said no, and he promised he wouldn't touch any further down. But his hands are quite large and his fingertips just barely touched my panties—by accident, I thought. I had an orgasm. I was so naïve, Terri. I didn't even know what it was, except that it was the most exquisite physical sensation I had ever had. And then he held me down. I tried to stop him. I wanted my first time to be somewhere special, not like every other hapless girl taken in the back seat of a car. But Pete wouldn't stop. It was quite painful. And that one time was enough. I missed my period. I went to a friend to find out about herbs and other methods that could cause a miscarriage. I tried everything she told me. Nothing worked."

They sat silent for a few moments. "Tell me the rest," Terri said.

"My grandparents said they'd disown me. Pete was pressured, too. I was underage and that made him vulnerable, since he was over twenty-one. Later, I found out that a little committee had visited him—my grandfather, and Lino and Sal Minelli."

"Stella's family." They'd been almost legendary in Camargo.

"The only person who thought I shouldn't marry Pete was Octavia, Stella's grandmother. She thought it would be better if I went to a home and gave the baby up for adoption."

"Why didn't you?"

"Everyone in town would have known why I'd gone away. My grandparents said that would disgrace the family, and I couldn't come back and live at home. What would I have done —seventeen with no money, no home, no family? I didn't have the courage to find out." Laura stared toward the oak trees on the other side of the fence. "I told myself it wouldn't be so bad, that I could learn to love him."

"So you got married."

"Off to Reno we went, with an escort. And for all I know, a shotgun in the car. There have been times since that I've thought that I might have been better off, after all, being an unwed mother. But I suppose I'm exaggerating my problems."

"I doubt that," Terri said. It took several attempts to light her cigarette.

"I sound philosophical about all of this now, but it's taken me years to get to this point. To look at the situation objectively."

"Objectively, the situation is that he's a pig." Terri blinked back her anger. "It frustrates me that I can't help you."

"But you *do* help me. You must realize that. I'm not drinking nearly as much as I used to. That's your doing."

"Mine? I've never talked to you about that."

"I didn't need someone telling me I drink too much." Laura reached over and touched her cheek. "I needed a friend."

THE CUTTING EDGE was hectic, its normal state on a Saturday mid-afternoon. Every chair was occupied and every stylist was working two customers at once. A dozen women waited and the phone rang constantly. There'd been no time to do more than keep the disarray at each station from becoming pure chaos. They were about to run out of towels; Maya was on her way with a clean batch, but if she didn't get here soon, someone was going to have to run over to the five-and-dime and buy some. The air conditioner repairman who'd been promised by noon still hadn't arrived at three, by which time the outside temperature was ninety-six. They'd set up fans behind tubs of ice.

But at least she wasn't on her period. Last weekend she had been, with terrible cramps and a flow so heavy that she'd had to cancel all her Saturday afternoon appointments. Ray had taken care of the kids and picked up her codeine prescription.

"Terri!" called Vickie, holding up the phone. Terri stuck it between her shoulder and ear, and continued combing out her customer.

"Hi," Ray said. "Sounds pretty crazy there."

"It is."

"Well, I won't keep you. I'm about to go grocery shopping. I've got the list; is there anything else?"

"Yes, I'm glad you called. We need orange juice."

"Okay. You think you'll be back by six?"

"I hope so. I'll call if I'm going to be later."

"We could drive down tomorrow morning if you're too tired tonight," Ray said.

"No, let's go tonight. It's only an hour drive."

After they hung up, her customer asked where she was going. "Down to my folks' place," Terri answered.

"They live down below, don't they?"

"Yes, at Mossback Lake," Terri said, carefully sectioning Nadine's hair, "from May until October or November."

"We used to call it 'Mosquito Lake,'" Nadine remarked.

"Everyone still does." Terri laughed. "Mom and Dad had to screen the porch all the way around. I always slather myself with Deet. It's been really bad this year, worse than usual."

"Everything's been worse this year. I don't know how much more we can take of this drought."

Underneath the hum of mundane conversation, she was thinking how glad she would be to see her sister tonight. She was still thinking of Loretta when the shop finally closed and she was cleaning up. Sacramento wasn't all that far, but it was far enough when you have busy lives and two kids each. Loretta had weekends off, but Terri worked Saturdays, which left them just Sunday to be together. Neither of them wanted to waste any of that precious time driving, so they'd been meeting at their parents' place at Mossback Lake, which was about halfway between Sacramento and Piñon County.

Terri remembered all the nights spent in the darkness of the bedroom she had shared with Loretta as girls—nights spent whispering and giggling, cursing and crying. Do you know what I heard *him* say yesterday? You'll never believe what *she* was doing. Two girls, blonde and slender, blithely confident that what was theirs by the grace of youth would never change. That teenage indolence would magically transform into effortless vitality. That they would never become like *her*, letting herself go. That only careless, lazy women were afflicted with jiggly thighs and tummy fat and sagging breasts. "It's because she doesn't take care of herself," Terri whispered. And Loretta said, "She's sloppy about everything. That's what being old means. I'll *never* be like that!" "Me either!" Terri swore. Oh, the scornful superiority of an adolescent girl!

And here she was now, with her skin no longer rosy and smooth and sleek, but dry and often blotchy from the chemical potions she used in her work. Rarely dressing nicely—since the kids would just spill something on her, she might as well wear already-stained clothes. Never exercising or eating right or losing the thirty-five pounds she needed to get back to her wedding weight—because there was always some reason not to start a diet, or not to go to the gym.

She looked just like her mother.

By now her station was spic and span, surfaces shining and tools organized. She stuck her head in the back room and waved goodbye to Vickie, who was still on the phone, and left.

She got home at the same time as Ray and the kids. Trixie's face was flushed from the heat; Terri gave her a Popsicle, which produced a smile, and put a cold washcloth to her forehead, which produced a protest. "Just for a few minutes, Trixie." Terri brushed back the strands of her daughter's wet hair.

Terri and Ray unpacked the groceries and exchanged news of their respective days. Ray pulled out the large chocolate bar and put it in the refrigerator. "No, that's to bring," Terri said. "It's for smores for the kids."

He smiled. "I thought it was getting to be that time of month, you craving chocolate and sex."

She stared at him. How could he have forgotten that she'd just had her period? "I just had it last week, don't you remember?"

For a moment Ray looked perplexed, then awareness spread over his features, and then something else, so fleeting so she couldn't even be sure it had been there: alarm. Then it was gone and he said, "Oh, that was just last week? It seems longer ago."

"Well, it wasn't." She felt hurt that her discomfort wasn't important enough to him to remember.

Ray slid his arm around her waist and kissed her ear. "I'm sorry. I didn't forget; it's just that when things are hectic on the job, I lose track of time."

"No, *I'm* sorry. You've been working so hard, Ray."

"Not as hard as I used to work, but I'm not used to taking care of three job sites at the same time."

"He should've hired a foreman for each one of those sites. He's just saving money having you do it all."

"I know that. But I can handle it, so far anyway," Ray said.

"I told him a long time ago, if things get to be too much, I'll come tell him and he'll have to hire another foreman."

"But when is it 'too much?' After something really bad happens?"

He faced her again. "Come on, honey. Don't worry so much."

Terri felt a rush of emotions: contrition for giving him even more to worry about, appreciation for his good nature, longing to be as good to him as he was to her. She went to him, circled her arms around him, and whispered what she wanted to do. Those six words were enough to draw his immediate physical response. She took his hand and led him into the bedroom.

BY THE TIME they left, the sun was about to set. Ray drove, Terri watched the scenery, and both kids were quiet for a change. The wooded foothills began to soften into rolling meadows, and Terri smiled because nothing had changed on this route, not even the road itself, since she was a girl. Of how many roads in the state could that be said?

Later that night after dinner and smores, the kids finally in bed, Terri and Loretta sat outside. As was so often the case these days, one of their main topics of conversation was their parents. They'd spent more time with their parents in the four weeks since Loretta moved than in the previous five years combined. Loretta had been here since Saturday morning and had just about reached her personal boiling point. She let it all out with Terri, until Terri held up her hands in a stop signal. Loretta laughed. "God, Ter, I'm sorry, but if I couldn't let it all out with you, I'd be in the nuthouse."

"Last time I was the one who vented, remember?" It was almost midnight, quiet except for the crickets and a pair of dueling bullfrogs. On the other side of the lake someone was having a party; occasional bursts of laughter drifted over the water.

She had always considered her sister to be her best friend, but it suddenly occurred to her that she felt more intimate with Laura. They hadn't been friends very long and only saw each other once or twice a week, but she found herself able to talk about things with Laura that she couldn't imagine discussing with anyone else, not even Loretta.

Idly, Terri wondered how much life insurance Pete had and whether he had high blood pressure or clogged arteries. Laura would be better off with him dead, but him dead with a big lump of money would be even better.

She remembered thinking that once about Ray, not long after she'd learned of his first betrayal. That thought, having voiced itself in her mind, haunted her to this day. Yet for just a moment she'd been so angry she could have killed him. She'd been so angry with him that she'd lost all perspective.

Could intense fear do the same thing? Did Laura lie awake plotting ways to kill Pete without getting caught?

Chapter Twenty-Seven

Roxanne took a cool shower and went into her bedroom to get dressed. I'll just rest for a few minutes, she thought, and the next thing she knew it was pitch dark and an owl was hooting. She heard voices from Carlos's room, strained her ears, and recognized Kit's laugh.

Oh, lord. Ten o'clock at night and they were in his bedroom.

She'd tried to broach the subject of birth control with him last month, but he had cut her off. "Dad already told me all that stuff." Later, she'd called Rafael.

First thing Rafael said was, "Does he have a girlfriend?"

"He won't say. There's a girl who's his friend. I don't know if it's more than that. Rafe, he knows to always use a condom? And how to use it?"

"Roxanne," Rafael said gently. "I told him everything I think he needs to know."

She lay in bed now, worrying that Carlos hadn't taken his father's words seriously enough, remembering how little she'd listened to her parents as a teenager, agonizing over whether she should try to get up quietly and find out what they were doing, or just get up normally and give them time to stop doing it. But maybe they weren't doing anything except talking or listening to music. In fact, she could hear music, the now-familiar voice of Joe Strummer.

She got up, making no attempt to be quiet, and saw from the angle of the light that his door was open. She heard Kit exclaiming, "You did too! I saw you spill the whole bucket!" and Carlos laughing, "No, I swear, I didn't." They both laughed, then hushed each other between giggles.

She smiled in relief and continued on to the kitchen. She had her dinner, cereal with banana, half-eaten before they came out.

"Did we wake you up, Mom?"

"No, but I wish you had," Roxanne said. "I slept the whole evening away. How are you, Kit? All ready for school?"

Kit grimaced. "Yeah, I guess. Mom and me went shopping last week and I got some new jeans and shoes and stuff."

"New jeans." Roxanne smiled. "My freshman year, boys weren't allowed to wear blue jeans to school. Girls couldn't even wear pants."

Kit and Carlos both stared in disbelief. "You had to wear *skirts*?" Kit asked, aghast. "I don't think I wore a skirt or dress all last year!"

"I don't blame you," Roxanne said, then wondered, "Is there even a dress code anymore?"

Kit and Carlos exchanged another look, this one conveying uncertainty. "I don't know!" Kit laughed. "People wear pretty much whatever they want."

A few minutes later, Kit phoned her house. Pete and PJ were both out, so Carlos drove her home.

Watching them leave, Roxanne sighed and lit a cigarette. She knew she should tell Carlos what had happened with PJ all those years ago. It hadn't been enough to simply say there'd been a disagreement.

PJ's attack had been so quick and so unexpected that he'd taken her totally by surprise. He'd very nearly had his way, but another boy walked by and she'd escaped.

Sadly enough, it hadn't been a big deal to her at the time. If everything had stopped there, she might not even remember it. The reason she hadn't forgotten it was because of what had happened afterward, even before PJ got that scar: the other boy seeing her come out of the bathroom, PJ talking about it as if she had been in there voluntarily, the word spreading around school that she and PJ had been 'doing something' at the party, and the sickening realization that to protest that he'd tried to force himself on her would be no different, so far as her reputation was concerned, as the lie he was telling, or allowing to be told. Because in those days, if a boy you knew forced sex on you, it was your own fault.

But Carlos, who had the sensibilities of his time, would look at it very differently.

Now he was friends with PJ's sister. And Roxanne knew that every morning when PJ shaved, he saw that scar.

Soon. She'd tell him soon.

She walked over to the tavern and was momentarily taken aback to see both Jensen men there. They glanced at her but said nothing. She went to the far end of the bar and ordered a draft. The TV was tuned to a variety show. The jukebox no longer played strictly country; heavy metal was preferred by many of the young, still-employed mill workers. Roxanne's temples began to pound and she wondered why she'd even come here. Loretta was gone. The people still living in the Gap were on edge most of the time, testy and short-fused. Fewer people came to the bar, but there were more fights.

Then Clay DiMauro come in. She patted the stool beside her. Fred had a beer in front of Clay by the time he sat down. Clay held the cold bottle against his face. "Every summer about this time, I tell myself I'm gonna move somewhere on the coast where it's temperate. Santa Cruz, maybe."

"What, leave this wonderful place?"

"It's been known to happen."

"What about your mother?" she asked, keeping her tone casual.

"Yeah, that's the thing," Clay sighed. "She needs me. I take care of things for her."

Roxanne nodded.

"She's still bitter about Dad, not getting a full pension after getting hurt at the mill. Then Dad became a drunk." Clay took a swig of beer and gestured to Fred for another. "And everything with Bobby. She's had a hard life."

They both sat silent, remembering. It hadn't been a secret that Bobby had strong opinions about the war, but what he did had taken everyone in Piñon County by surprise. He joined a protest in front of the Oakland draft board, and burned his card.

Not every man who burned his draft card was prosecuted. But the UPI photograph had appeared in newspapers all across America and even made the cover of a national magazine: Bobby holding aloft his flaming card. So, he was prosecuted, and they sent him to federal prison.

When he got sick it was early in the week. The guards later claimed they thought he was just shamming. They didn't take him to the infirmary for three days. By then it was too late.

These days Mrs. DiMauro had turned Bobby into a martyr, but in 1969 she'd been ashamed of him. Roxanne had heard that she hadn't even visited him in prison. It was doubly infuriating that she was now using his death to guilt-trip Clay.

Out of the corner of her eye, she saw Pete and PJ Jensen standing up to leave. "Guess who was the only guy in Piñon County to qualify for a deferment?" she said.

Clay glanced at PJ. "On what grounds?"

"He was appointed to the sheriff's reserve."

"Christ," Clay said angrily.

PJ was not walking very steadily. He shouldn't be driving, Roxanne thought. She wouldn't shed any tears if he ran his truck into a tree, but he might run into another car instead.

Then Fred called out, "Pete, you leaving PJ's truck here?"

"Yeah, one of us'll come by for it in the morning."

"In the morning," PJ repeated, slurring the words.

"At least he's got enough sense not to drive," Roxanne said.

But that interrupted the conversation, and it was one of those conversations you couldn't go back to after an interruption. Clay glanced at the clock and drained his beer. "Better get going. I gotta go to work tomorrow."

"Me too."

"I'll drop you off at your place."

"It's just up the street, Clay. I can walk."

"Come on, I wouldn't feel right."

They walked through the parking lot toward his car. Suddenly he stopped. "Wait a minute. That's PJ's truck we just went past, right?"

"The blue one, yeah."

Clay retraced his steps and peered into the truck bed. "I don't believe this. I do not believe it."

"What's wrong?"

"Roxanne, hang on just a minute. I have to do something." He went to his Forest Service jeep and got out a gallon-size ziplock plastic bag. He came back, leaned into the bed of PJ's pickup, and put something into the bag.

Roxanne glanced at the bag. "Is that sand? Why'd you take it?"

"To satisfy my curiosity." He glanced at her. "But you didn't see me do that, all right?"

He dropped her off at her house. Before going to bed, she went through the stack of mail. There was an envelope from

Slidell-Pacific, but not one of the usual ones with computer-generated labels; her name was typed, and the envelope was thin. She opened it.

It was a letter from the company headquarters in Coos Bay, offering $30,000 for her house. The offer was good through October 31. She was confused. *Why are they offering to buy* my *house? And why $30,000? The house is only assessed at $22,000.* She set the letter aside, too hot and too tired to try and figure out what was going on.

<hr>

AT WORK THE next morning, she was boxing up three pies that Stella had ordered, when Arla Stinson pulled into the parking lot. Stella was just getting out of her pickup and they talked animatedly for a few minutes before coming in. Roxanne brought the pies to the counter. "You staying for breakfast or coffee, Stella?"

"Yes, do," Arla exclaimed. "It's so rare I get to see you this time of year!"

Stella smiled. "All right, but I already ate, so I'll just have coffee."

They took a table on the far side of the restaurant from Pete, and Roxanne couldn't be sure that Stella had even seen him. But he had seen Stella. Pete Jensen kept stealing glances at Stella, and finally, as she turned to leave, he called, "So you're still in business, hey, Stella?"

Stella looked at him. Her eyes briefly widened in disbelief. She paused on her way to the door. "Do you know any reason why I wouldn't be?"

"Heck no," Pete said, in a parody of cheerfulness. "Can't think of a single one."

Stella left.

"What was that all about?" Arla said, when Roxanne brought her food.

"What it's about is Pete's a jerk. He knows everyone's hurting with the drought. He'd probably say he was just kidding, but I think he enjoys rubbing salt in people's wounds."

Arla looked over at Pete. "I've heard other people say similar things about him, so I stay away."

"Smart decision."

Chapter Twenty-Eight

He used the phone in the trailer. From outside came the rumble of concrete rolling down the chute and the shouting of men's voices; from Arla's line came a pointed silence.

"What's the matter, Arla?"

"Will you come over this afternoon? Just for a while?"

"I can't, Arla. I've got–"

"Oh, please, Ray. Please. When you get off, can't you just stop by? I won't keep you long."

"But Trixie's got a volleyball game and I'm going straight there after work."

"Oh. All right then." Arla sounded resigned. She prided herself on not coming between Ray and his kids.

"I'll try to get over Friday. We might be going out of town, but I'm not sure about that yet. If not Friday, then I'll come Monday during my lunch break."

"But Ray, my God, Friday's four days away, and it's already been almost a week!"

"I know, Arla, but–"

"And don't even say Monday; that's a week from now. Please don't make me wait that long!"

"By then you'll *really* want me."

"Damn it, Ray!"

"Come on, baby. I'm just teasing."

"It's not funny! I'm so … oh, Ray, don't you know how I feel just thinking about you?"

His penis was reacting in predictable fashion, and he instinctively covered himself even though no one else was in the trailer.

"—and you know what it does to me to see you in your work clothes."

"Arla—"

"Please come over and make love to me."

"But I'm at work," he said feebly.

"You're the foreman; can't you leave early?"

"Maybe," he said, thinking about it. "I'll try to arrange it. But if I can't, don't be upset."

"I will be upset!" she said, but laughed. "I can't believe you're making me beg you."

"Believe me, I want to be with you just as much. But once in a while, there's an emergency here at work. So don't worry if I don't show up, okay?"

"I won't worry. I'll suffer."

Ray hung up and sat there allowing his racing blood to slow, his passion to subside. He had to see her. He could leave Eddie in charge. And then he'd call in at quarter to five to make sure they'd got everything done. Mr. Cushing never questioned Ray's schedule, and no one else had the right to.

He waited until one-thirty, then said casually, "Eddie, I'm going to check on a couple things this afternoon. I'll be taking off pretty soon."

"Sure," Eddie said, looking at him briefly, but not asking any questions. That worried Ray, that he didn't ask any questions. Would Eddie, or some of the others, speculate about where he was going? Was there already speculation about Ray's occasional early afternoons and two-hour lunches?

He gave Eddie instructions for the rest of the day, thanked him in advance, and said, "I have to get to my kid's volleyball game at four-thirty," and glanced at his watch.

"Trixie?" asked Eddie.

"Yeah. You should see her spike," Ray said proudly.

"Got the killer instinct, huh?"

Ray climbed into the company pickup. "Why don't you come down for a while if you get the chance? They're playing at the rec center."

"Maybe," said Eddie. And Ray could tell he was trying to come up with a gracious explanation of why he wasn't interested in going to an eight-year-old girls' volleyball game. "Thing is, there's a pow-wow at the Rancheria this weekend and everyone's helping get ready for it. I'm supposed to clean up the sacred burial ground."

About to start the truck, Ray froze with his hand on the key and stared at Eddie. For just that second, he thought Eddie was hinting that he knew about the bones Ray had destroyed.

"You can come to it," Eddie added. "There's always white people at the pow-wows."

Not a bad idea, Ray thought. The kids would like it. He got more information from Eddie before leaving.

As soon as he hit the road, he called the office and said he'd be offsite the rest of the day. He drove up the highway and turned onto Blackberry Springs Drive. The three-quarter-ton GMC painted in Eagle Development's trademark purple and gray couldn't be left somewhere obvious, like in front of Arla's house. He drove a short distance up the fire road and pulled the pickup into the tunnel he'd made in the brush. It was barely big enough for the truck to fit into and not be visible, either from the road or from above. He walked the short distance to her house, going to the back door as usual. He tapped on the door.

Arla opened it without even asking who it was. She wore nothing except a black satin slip. He remembered that the very first time he'd seen her, he had thought her boyish. Now he could not understand how he had ever thought that, even for a second.

He went to his knees and began to kiss her through the black satin.

THE AIR CONDITIONER was turned to a low temperature and the heavy drapes were drawn. Neither light nor heat from the strong afternoon sun penetrated the house. In the king-sized bed, Ray was cool, comfortable, sated.

He watched her walking toward the bathroom. Her body, toned by regular weight training in her home gym, swimming, and of course jogging, didn't jiggle the slightest bit when she walked. Her hair, glossy and healthy, was perfectly cut. No matter what she was doing, or had just done, she still looked neat. Ray knew a haircut like that cost a lot, and had to be kept up. She didn't get it done at the salon where Terri had a chair; she went out of town. She probably thought as little of driving to the Bay Area once a month to go to the hairdresser as other women did of driving to Camargo to go to the grocery store.

Sometimes, he couldn't believe how pretty she was. She was in her late thirties but had never had a baby, so she still had a body like a teenage girl—beautifully shaped and perfectly proportioned. He especially loved her thighs—slim, strong, and evenly browned, the skin as smooth as silk. Truly, one glimpse of them was enough to arouse him, even now when he had just spent an hour and a half making love with her.

Arla often told him, and showed him, that she liked his body, too: the thick wrists he'd developed over years of construction work, his sinewy arms and muscular thighs. Their first time together she'd told him he had the most perfect torso she had ever seen. He was glad she felt that way, because he had expected her to be one of those women who preferred the airbrushed torsos of men in advertisements. "Kind of hairy," he'd said, and she had smiled, "Oh, yes," and lowered herself to him.

Each time they were together, she came more easily and more often; she was more relaxed, trusting his desire to give her pleasure and accepting that he would not try to rush her.

He felt almost dizzy from the thrill of being so intensely desired, from the taste of her, from the vibrations of her pleasure.

Now, he glanced at her clock. He had forty minutes before Trixie's game. He opened his arm and Arla got back into bed, lying against him. She stroked his shoulder, her fingers straying down to his bicep. "Remember I was telling you about the county history I've been reading?" she said, when they had settled back down into each other's arms.

"Uh huh."

"Have you ever read it?"

"Nope."

"You aren't interested in Piñon County history?"

Ray didn't want to disillusion her, but he'd skimmed that book and had found a sanitized version of the past, primarily praising wealthy settlers for being self-sacrificing, fair minded, and pure of motive.

He answered, "Sure, but I already know where the biggest gold deposits were dug up and how many saloons Camargo had during the gold rush. The juicy stuff." He grinned.

"So how many saloons were there in Camargo?"

"Twenty-seven," he answered promptly.

"Amazing." Arla laughed.

"Yeah, that's a lot of saloons."

"No, *you*'re amazing." She gently tugged at his chest hair.

She wasn't interested in sports, so he didn't explain the reason that the fact had stuck in his mind. 27 had been the uniform number of one of Ray's childhood heroes, R. C. Owens of the 49ers, another underappreciated genius athlete. He'd invented the alley-oop pass, his blocked field goals at the goal line had caused a rule change, and his low salary prompted him to sign with another team, leading to *another* rule change. Ray had been ten when that happened, and still remembered his father complaining about 'that nigger' R.C. Owens's 'ingratitude' to the 49ers. Those episodes of gross injustice had opened Ray's eyes to oppression. And his disrespect for his father, now well entrenched, had been born with that remark.

Arla was saying, "… a lot of Jensens in the history. I would imagine your old teammate PJ, or his father, are interested in it."

"Maybe they are, I don't know. I never talked about that stuff with PJ when we were kids, and we don't hang out anymore."

She rested her chin on his chest. "Ray, is there some history there, between Pete Jensen and the Pardinis?"

"I always heard they don't get along, but I don't think I ever heard why."

"He made a sarcastic remark to Stella today in Elsie's. There seemed to be a lot of tension between them."

No wonder, Ray thought. Pete Jensen stood to make a lot of money if the deal with Cushing went through, but the deal wouldn't go through if Cushing didn't get Pardini Ranch too. "She's your friend," he answered Arla, "why don't you ask her?"

"Mm, maybe I will. You know, that's why I moved up here,

of all the beautiful places in California I could have moved to —because Joe and Stella taught me to love it here. We used to take pack trips with them."

"Who's 'we'?" Ray asked. "Your ex-husband?" Against all reason, he felt a pang of jealousy.

"Yes, and sometimes one of his brothers or his father, too. Steve loved the mountains, and I came to love them too, although at first they almost scared me. They're so much bigger and wilder than the mountains back east."

"There's mountains back east?" Ray asked with mock innocence.

"Yes, there's mountains back east," Arla replied with mock indignation. "But they aren't nearly as high as the Sierra Nevada.

"And Joe and Stella taught me how to respect the land," she went on. "Joe's very particular about certain things when he takes you into the mountains. He knows how to leave the land as if no one had been there. He won't even let people smoke on the trail, just in camp."

"You can't be too careful of fire," Ray said.

"That's what Joe taught me on my first visit here. Wildfires aren't such a danger back east. And I think because it's so dry here, it's easier to damage the land in other ways too. Joe said he has to be careful about choosing horses. High-strung horses cause more damage to the trails and campsites because they're always pawing and trampling."

"You like riding horses?"

"Oh, yes," she said, passionately. "Stella invited me to come up and ride to the pass after they close for the season. She's got a nice mare, Griselda. I just love that old girl. Joe and Stella are very good to their horses."

"Horses are their business."

"Yes, but even so, they both have such rapport with them. When we used to come up early in the season, before the horses were in prime condition, Joe always brought two extra horses for packing. And he was always careful about what order the horses were ridden on the trail; they have a kind of pecking order." Her hand was warm on his chest.

"I'd love to be on a horse with you riding it too, sitting right behind me." Her index finger delicately traced around his nipple. An electric charge of desire ran up and down his body. He slid his hands down her back and pulled her all the way onto him. "How soon do you have to leave?"

Ray glanced at the clock. It was 4:05pm. He groaned, cursed, told himself to stop, but gave in.

Afterwards, disoriented, drained, wanting nothing so much as to lie with her in his arms while his heartbeat slowed back down, wanting to stay, wanting to make her come again and again, he allowed her to pull him out of bed. He dressed quickly. She came to kiss him goodbye at the back door. She was naked. He glanced nervously out the open door, but of course no one was there except blue jays and squirrels, and they didn't seem to be watching.

"Will you be back Friday afternoon, then?" she asked.

"If I'm in town."

"And Monday too?"

Ray laughed. "If I can."

"I know I'm greedy. I can't get enough of you. It's your fault, you know." She kissed him tenderly.

He drove toward town in a daze. We should stop seeing each other, he said to himself as he got to town; and the moment he thought it, he thought of the texture of her skin, the feel of her smooth flat belly against his, the sound of her ecstasy, the taste of her hunger. And he knew he could not stop. No, he told himself, you know you *will not* stop.

And suddenly he remembered that he hadn't washed up. *Jesus*, that was close! He pulled over at the Texaco station and rushed into the bathroom, soaping and rinsing his hands three times, until all of her scent was gone. He scrubbed his face until the skin was red and raw. He even put a drop of soap on his tongue and swished soapy water in his mouth. He could only hope that his clothes wouldn't give him away; fortunately, the odors of construction work were powerful, and he was reassured by the concrete dust, red clay, and oil on his Levi's.

This was the second close call. The first was a few days ago. Terri asked him to bring the chocolate and was anxious to make love, and he remarked about what time of month it must almost be. She gave him a look of surprise and said she'd just had her period last week, didn't he remember? He realized he was getting their menstrual cycles mixed up; it was *Arla* whose period was due.

You're getting careless, he told himself now. You can't afford it. You've got to tighten up.

He arrived at the rec center at 4:25 and hurried to the clay courts behind the building just in time to see Trixie's team taking their positions. His heart softened at the sight of his daughter, all legs and arms in her green and white uniform, her hair pulled back in a ponytail, her exuberance apparent even from this distance.

As Ray approached Terri, who stood on the sideline, she threw him an angry look. He pretended not to notice. "Hey, Terri."

"Why are you so late?" she demanded, her mouth set.

"I'm not late," he said, and he wasn't; the game hadn't started yet. Usually, he got to the games early enough to talk to Trixie, but just because he hadn't done so today didn't mean he was late, technically.

"Where the hell were you today?"

"Huh?"

"I called at two and they said you already left for the day."

"No I didn't," he said, looking puzzled, he hoped. "I left

the job site and went around the other sites to check up on things. They didn't even offer to get me on the CB?"

"Damn it, Ray, I told you what they said."

"Who'd you talk to?"

"It wasn't Alice or Ellen, that's all I know."

"They've been hiring temps to help Alice with the phones," he said, and allowed irritation to creep into his voice. "How many calls did I miss today because someone at the office is too lazy to call me on the CB? What time was it?"

"Two o'clock, Ray." Terri drew it out, but he could sense that he was beginning to convince her. Meanwhile, Trixie's team had won the coin toss and would serve. He knew she'd make that first serve, because she was the best server on the team.

"You should've asked to talk to Cushing," he said, knowing that Cushing would never allow himself to be cross-examined by a workman's wife. "Look, Terri, I don't want to get anyone in trouble, but you've got to try to remember who you talked to. I can't afford to miss my calls. I mean, what if something happened to one of the kids?" Now he allowed himself a slight impatience. "Didn't you even ask her name?"

"No, because I didn't know you were going to make a federal case out of it."

"Next time, find out, okay? I won't tell the boss and get her in trouble, but I'll have to talk to her about it. And Terri, the office can almost always get me on the radio. Don't let them tell you different." He made a mental note: *Bring your walkie-talkie into Arla's house!*

Terri stood there stubbornly, but mollified, he could tell. She simply didn't want to admit defeat. He granted her that privilege.

Her pale skin was blotchy in the heat. Her pants were too tight, causing the fat in her stomach to bulge, and he was irrationally annoyed. Then he was ashamed of himself. She had borne children, she worked; she couldn't spend two hours a day exercising.

Trixie stood poised behind the end line, the volleyball balanced lightly on her left palm, her right arm behind her, her eyes focused on nothing but net and lines. Ray resisted the urge to wave at her; he simply watched her, with a lump in his throat.

Chapter Twenty-Nine

There were no guests at Pardini Ranch that night, but a small group would arrive the next morning for a day trip, a twenty-mile loop along the old emigrant trail. Joe and Stella worked late preparing the food.

She brought the bowl of sourdough to the big wooden table, and dipped her hand in the flour bin, sprinkling a handful of flour onto the table and powdering her hands with another handful. "Joe, I just thought of something."

Joe was at the cupboard putting away the pots and pans he had dried. "Uh oh. Let me sit down before you tell me, Stellaskaya."

"Giuseppe, I do not want to hear you say it sets off alarm bells when I have an idea." She turned the dough onto the table.

"I try always to please you, dearest. You will not hear me say it."

Stella punched the lively dough. "My mother warned me not to marry an Italian. My own grandmother, born on Italian soil, warned me not to marry an Italian. And did I listen?"

"No, because no one could tell you anything when you

were a girl," Joe replied. "You've become reasonable only in middle age."

"Far too late to do any good," Stella said tartly. She put the dough back into the bowl to let it rise again, and spread a towel over the top.

"But then, for me it's worked out very well." They both laughed and Joe dried the last frying pan. "All right, *cara*. Tell me what you've been thinking."

She went to the sink to wash her hands. "There will be vacancies on the Board of Supervisors in the next election."

"Yes, two seats of the five. You think we should try to organize an anti-development ticket?"

"Yes." Stella paused. "With one of us on it."

"Ah, Stella. Where would we get the money? And how could we run our business if one of us was running for office, let alone serving in office?"

"I know, I know, but if we agreed that it was important to do, we could try and figure out how to do it without going bankrupt." She dried her hands and continued. "Joe, something has to be done before it's too late. If we don't do something, this place will go the way of Contra Costa and Yuba Counties—nothing but mini-malls and business parks and housing developments from the county line all the way to our ranch. It's already started, with Blackberry Springs and Gennessee Mine Road and that mall. We've got to stop it!"

"We tried to, and we lost."

"So that's it, then?"

"We didn't lose only in court, Stella. We lost with the people. We didn't get enough support to get those commissioners thrown off the Planning Commission and we wouldn't raise enough support to win a seat on the Board of Supervisors."

"No, but we'd raise the public consciousness. Development would become part of the debate. Maybe we'd make it possible for someone else to win on an anti-development platform in the next election. If we don't do it this election, Joe, the Board will be pro-development for four more years."

"Let's go outside." Joe took down two of the heavy glasses they used for wine. She waited for him on the porch, staring out into a night so dark the silhouettes of the trees were almost invisible. A few moments later, Joe came out and handed her a glass of Sangiovese. In the distance coyotes yipped, and in the stable the horses spoke to one another in gentle whinnies. Overhead the stars glittered fiercely, a reflection of her mood.

Stella leaned back and sighed. "I've been thinking a lot about Kit. So many people her age don't really care about nature. We weren't concerned about it when we were fifteen, either; we took it for granted. And we grew up and it was still here. Battered and bruised and poisoned, but here. But when Kit's generation grows up, it won't be here anymore. Remember when we were talking with Arla a few weeks ago, she was describing the way people think back East?"

"It's hard to fathom that people can be so out of touch with nature."

"But it can happen here, too. Most of the people who move to California come from places that have already lost touch with the natural world. They don't even understand what it is! And most of Kit's generation is growing up out of touch with nature, too, especially young people growing up in places like Los Angeles or San Jose. And when there aren't enough people who treasure nature, then it won't be protected. All the wild places will be gone, because no one will understand how important they are. It's already happening."

"Yes, because when all that counts is money, why consider the effect of what is being done? Our ancestors didn't consider it when they trapped otters and dug mines and cut down thousand-year-old redwoods." Joe paused, and when he continued, his voice held bitterness. "Were the people who came here in 1849 any better than the people we're complaining about now? They were willing to destroy the land getting gold out of it, and weren't especially concerned with their fellow humans either."

"That's probably true." She took a long drink of the dark wine. "Sometimes I understand what motivates those people who put sugar in the gas tanks of bulldozers and chain themselves to trees. It's pure desperation, because there just seems no other way to stop this … this juggernaut of development. California really was a paradise on earth, once."

"Damn that James Marshall!"

Stella laughed. "Of course, if not for him and the gold, we wouldn't be here."

Joe stood up and stretched. "Speaking of gold. How do our accounts seem, so far?"

"No better than last year," she said.

They were both silent for a few moments. A barn owl hooted and in the next moment she saw the gleam of white as it glided over the valley. "Maybe we shouldn't have taken out that loan."

"We had to replace the septic tank," Joe pointed out. "We had to re-roof the house. And we had to pay our taxes and the veterinarian."

"And now we've got a thousand-dollar bank payment every month."

"We'll get through it, Stella. We might have to make further economies, sell one of the pickups or some of the horses, but we'll get through it."

"And what about making monumental changes?"

Joe took her hand. "That's our obligation and our opportunity. We just have to figure out what is to be done."

"CARLOS DOESN'T FEEL that way about me," Kit said, looking straight ahead at the trail.

Stella watched the girl's expression and body language. At first, she had assumed Kit was saying this the way another teenage girl might say it, merely to be assured of what she had already concluded—that the boy was mad about her. But Kit's denials were heartfelt. Her eyes glistened with tears and, even more tellingly, she gripped the reins tightly.

"Come on, let's go over to the rocks and let the horses rest."

They were very near the border to Slidell-Pacific property. Sadie and Tabasco were happy to stop and drink from Cougar Creek while Kit and Stella clambered onto the boulders beside the creek. The large, lumpy, red rocks had been formed by lava a millennium ago. This cluster was all that remained of what had been, before the lumber mill was built, a mile-long line.

Stella sat on the flattest of the boulders, leaning back against the tree trunk. "I want to talk to you, Kit."

"You don't have to tell me about sex. Mom already did that. I mean, she didn't talk to me, but she gave me a book last year." She joined Stella on the boulder. "I think Mom's worried I'm gay."

"Oh? Why?"

"Just things she says sometimes. About how sometimes people are more attracted to their own sex." Kit sifted dried oak leaves through her fingers. "People always think just because you like horses and being outside, and you don't wear dresses, you must be gay."

A sign of the times, Stella mused. In her day, such girls were called tomboys, and their parents assumed they wanted a husband but wouldn't be able to attract one. "Laura just wanted you to know that she'd love you no matter what."

"I don't think there's anything wrong with being gay. If I was, I'd just tell Mom. Well, I *think* I'd tell her, except I wouldn't want her to tell my father … Stella, you and Mom were pretty close, right? So, I want to ask you something. Why'd she marry him?"

"Well," Stella said cautiously, "Laura didn't confide in me her feelings about Pete."

"I know she was pregnant," Kit interrupted impatiently. "I figured that out a long time ago. But what I meant was, why'd she date him in the first place? She's so pretty; there must've been other boys she could've dated besides him!"

The passion of Kit's disdain surprised Stella. "Laura was more than pretty. She was the town beauty. I think boys her own age were almost intimidated by how beautiful she was. Pete was older, and he did have a certain charm; people said he was outgoing, fun to be with."

Kit looked at her quickly. "'People'? What about you?"

Stella hesitated only briefly. "I never liked him."

"But Mom did," Kit said bitterly.

"It was so different for girls back then, especially for girls who weren't told very much about the facts of life, like Laura. She wasn't allowed to date until she turned sixteen, and even then she could only go on double-dates, and only if one of the parents did the driving. Certainly, she wasn't allowed to date someone she didn't go to school with. Pete was twenty-three when they began seeing each other. Laura was barely seventeen. She sneaked out to see him." Stella sighed. "I helped her. Much to my subsequent regret."

"And then she got pregnant."

"Yes. And off to Reno they went, escorted by my father and uncle."

"So that's how it was for Mom." Kit picked up an acorn and threw it hard at a tree trunk.

"You would have to ask *her* that." Stella resisted the urge to reach over and put her arm around the girl. "She wanted you to have that book so the same thing wouldn't happen to you; so that you'd have enough knowledge to make good decisions."

"There's nothing for me to make any decisions about," Kit said bitterly.

"Oh, Kit, you're wrong about Carlos. I know he feels strongly about you."

"Did he tell you that?"

"He didn't have to." She could see that Kit still didn't believe her. Well, it was probably best that she find out for herself.

But Stella had suggested taking this ride in order to tell Kit what she'd done; there was no point in delaying it any longer. "Kit, I want you to know that I spoke to Laura last week."

"What?" Kit started and sat up straight. "About what?"

"I told her that you visit Joe and me, that we've become friends."

"Stella! I *told* you I'd talk to her!"

"Yes, honey, but you never did." Stella paused. "I can't deceive someone who's been a friend. And you being a teenager complicates things. That's not your fault, but it's something you have to realize."

"What'd she say?"

"She thanked me for telling her. And she said she already knew."

"She knew! But how?"

"She said you've been talking about me and Joe often, and wanting to know about when she was young. That all summer you've been spending long hours away from home and she didn't think you were riding; she said you would never ride Sadie so long in the midday heat." Stella paused again. "I believe she knows about Carlos, too. And I think it would be best if you talked about him with her."

"Did you tell her that, too?"

"No, but your mother's more insightful than you give her credit for."

"Whatever. But she's not–" Kit broke off and looked down.

"Not what?"

She shrugged and dug at the surface of the boulder with a twig. Stella waited. Finally, Kit burst out, "She doesn't have guts."

It was not what Stella had expected, but hers was not the point of view of a girl who saw in her mother a woman who did not even stand up for herself, so couldn't be expected to stand up for her daughter. Perhaps Kit had seen and heard things in that house that increased both her pity and her contempt for Laura. But she hadn't known Laura as a girl. She hadn't lived next door and heard Laura's grandfather yelling for his belt.

"You know," Stella said, "in many ways Laura's had a difficult life."

For a few moments, Kit concentrated on the twig. When she finally spoke, she still did not look at Stella. "What were they like, Mom's parents?"

"Laura's father was kind and calm, and he just adored Laura. And her mother was so beautiful and tragic, like someone in a novel. Everyone always said they'd been very much in love, those two. After he died, she had a nervous breakdown. So her parents came to take care of her. They had to take care of Laura too, and weren't happy about that." A lump filled her throat and she could not say more.

They rode back in silence, broken only to say goodbyes when Stella turned off onto the Pardini Ranch trail.

LATER, WHILE PREPARING breading for the catfish she'd be frying up for dinner, Stella thought about Laura and Pete and their marriage. Back then everyone had spoken of the situation as though Laura had trapped a member of the wealthy Jensen family into marriage.

But that wasn't true. After her third date with Pete, Laura refused to see him and wouldn't tell anyone why, not even Stella. Pete, on the other hand, was anxious to see Laura—so anxious that one night he even came over to the Minellis' looking for her. He'd had too much to drink and Stella's father and uncle escorted him out of the boarding house.

Then came that terrible night. Panic-stricken and weeping, Laura pleaded with Nonna to help her. Nonna was a devout Catholic, but she brewed the herbs that women sometimes used to 'bring their monthly.' She got down the castor oil and began running a hot bath. But nothing worked.

A few days later, there was a conference: Laura's mother and grandfather, Nonna, Stella's father and uncle. A delegation was sent to the Jensens, and soon thereafter Pete and Laura were driven to Reno, following the path of so many young Californians who went to Nevada to obtain not a quickie divorce, but a quickie marriage.

Stella had her own theory about the whole situation. She believed that Pete, despite his proclaimed reluctance to marry, got exactly what he'd intended all along. Pete wouldn't have stood a chance of marrying Laura once she grew a little older and wiser. She believed Pete knew that. But Pete got Laura pregnant, and he got Laura—the most beautiful girl in Piñon County.

Pete used to go around town denouncing the Minellis for having interfered in his private affairs. 'Of course,' he would add grandly, 'I would have married her anyway; I just don't see what business they got sticking their (big dago) noses where they don't belong.'

He was prone to put forth that complaint when he'd had a few too many, an occurrence not so rare that the Minellis didn't hear about it. Eventually, he said it under circumstances in which the only honorable thing to do was for Stella's Uncle Sal to confront him. That had happened when Stella was living at Uncle Sal's place. He came home that night with a bloody mouth and a black eye, grinning happily because he'd broken Pete Jensen's nose good.

When Stella married Joe and moved onto Pardini Ranch, Pete and Laura had already been living on the Double-L for four years. Stella thought that she and Laura might become friends again, although they had hardly spoken in the twelve years since Laura's marriage. But not only was Pete still carrying a grudge, but Laura had changed.

Stella used to hear gossip now and then, and paid little attention. But the third time someone made an allusion to Pete Jensen keeping his wife in line, she bucked up her courage and went to visit Laura. She kept giving Laura openings, but Laura never took them. Finally, she got up to leave and said awkwardly, "If you ever want to get away, you can come to me. I promise I'll help."

Stella never forgot Laura's response. Laura was still young then—just thirty, in the prime of her beauty—and as she looked at Stella, first hope, then terror, and finally despair moved across her features. "I don't know what you mean," she whispered.

Chapter Thirty

Arla knew the time was long past when she should have told Mary about the journal. She knew too that the journal should be at the museum, not in the desk drawer in her study.

She sighed. She would soon be leaving to visit New York. After she got back, she would tell Mary what she'd done and turn the diary over to her. No matter what. In the meantime, Catherine Cushing was waiting. Arla cranked up the air conditioning and read.

10 August

I took confession this morning, even though I have not yet been confirmed, for the need to confess is strong, and Father Farley is wise and kind. I asked him, 'What should a person do when he is sure that an injustice is being done? When someone is charged with a crime for which he was commissioned by another?'

Father Farley told me that unless one is truly

certain of the facts, it would not be right to bring difficulties upon another's head.

'But if one knows in one's heart? Suppose what one knows is not enough to denounce the person to the authorities, perhaps, but is enough to cause certainty in one's heart? Should one say nothing to that person? Should one remain friends with that person?'

'Follow your heart, my dear,' said the priest. 'But remember that the heart can be mistaken.'

24 August

I was not there, but Rosa told me later what transpired.

When the men were brought up to the structure with their hands tied behind their backs, Jensen began to shout. 'It was Hiram Cushing! He paid us to do it! We didn't rob the old Russian! The money you found on me was from Cushing!'

Then the hood was placed on his head and he screamed.

It is said that Martin comported himself with dignity to the end.

Of course, no one believes the hysterical accusations of a condemned killer trying to save his own neck, a half-witted condemned killer.

I must speak with Hiram. I must put my suspicions to rest.

1 September

Eight days have passed since the hangings. There has been no talk in town of investigating the matter. Not even the displaced families have made such a suggestion, or if any of them has, it has not reached my ears.

What is it that I fear? Not that Hiram will strike me, for that is not his way. Not that he will no longer speak with me as the mother of his children, as companion, as friend; for I have over the years suffered his silences far more than I have enjoyed his companionship. Not that he will abandon me, for he values the respect of his fellows and they would surely disapprove of a man deserting his loyal wife of twenty-five years.

What I fear is that he will tell me that he did indeed commission the crime, that he is therefore responsible for the death of the old man and the displacement of all those people, and for the hanging of the two criminals.

Suppose he tells me that—what shall I do then?

Arla was so absorbed in the journal that when the tap came on the back door, she was disoriented for a few moments. Then Morgan went prancing to the kitchen, for he had grown fond of Ray and was always excited to see him.

She quickly put the journal in the desk drawer and went to greet him. As usual, they went straight to her bedroom. Sitting on the side of the bed, leaning over to unbuckle her sandals, she told him she'd just bought her airline ticket for New York.

"Do you have to stay that long?" He turned on his side and she felt his breath on the small of her back.

"Two weeks isn't very long, angel. Especially in New York, two weeks goes by awfully fast."

"It's a long time here," Ray murmured, as his lips touched her spine and moved up. "It'll be a long time for me without you."

Arla closed her eyes as his mouth reached the nape of her neck.

"Won't you miss me, baby? Won't you miss me kissing you?" He nibbled along the slope of her shoulder. "Or maybe you won't even think about me." He delicately lifted her arm and kissed forward. She gasped and turned toward him slightly, but he moved just before his lips would have touched what she was presenting. "Maybe I should just spend the next ten days getting you excited without making you come." He slowly blazed a trail of kisses down her side. Arla's thighs opened without conscious effort. "Maybe that would guarantee you wouldn't stay more than two weeks." His hands held her hips in place. "I know your body so well, Arla. I could do that; stop just before you come."

When he did, she assumed he was just teasing, and she laughed and moaned at the same time. "Don't you dare stop, Ray!"

"Or what? What will you do? You're already leaving me for two weeks."

"My God, Ray, it's only two weeks, you go away every other weekend! Don't stop, it's not funny, damn it!"

He laughed. "You have a sense of humor about everything except sex, you know that?"

Later, much later, she lay almost entirely on top of him and had fallen half-asleep. She thought that he was nearly asleep, too. But suddenly he hugged her tightly, enveloping her to his broad chest with those thick muscled arms.

"You won't stay longer, will you? Or maybe not come back?"

"Not come back!" Arla raised her head and stared at him. "But I live here!"

He started to pull her back down onto his chest, but she stopped him. "Why did you say that? Do you really think I wouldn't come back?"

Ray hesitated, his eyes cast down; she touched the lids gently, to urge him to look at her. "Sometimes you act like you don't really live here. It's like Piñon County's not real to you, like what happens here doesn't really matter."

She was silent for a few moments, because she knew what he was saying was true. She had not made an emotional commitment; it would not be wrenching for her to simply pack up and leave. Well, she amended silently, it wouldn't have been wrenching before June. Before Ray.

"Maybe all of this is just a vacation to you—Piñon County, the history work, everything here."

He didn't say 'me.' He didn't have to.

"That's why I'm worried about you going to New York. You'll remember all the things you liked about living there, and all the things you don't like about living here."

"I left New York five years ago. I don't want to live there, Ray." She saw that he wasn't convinced and continued, "New York has about one tree for every thousand people. Maybe one tree for every *ten* thousand people. There aren't any animals except at the zoo. Well," she amended, "not counting the rats."

"Rats! Christ!"

Arla laughed. "You kill rattlesnakes, but you're scared of rats."

"I'm scared of rattlesnakes, too."

"You did kill that rattlesnake without batting an eye."

"You think I enjoyed it?" He put his hands on her shoulders, gently moved from under her and sat up. "I don't like killing, Arla, not even rattlers. I don't hunt."

"I'm sorry, angel. I thought everyone here hunts. And you mentioned having guns–"

"Not for hunting. For protection. You ought to have one, too. I can't believe you lived in New York and didn't have a gun."

"New York has strict gun control laws," Arla said.

"Yeah, and there's eight million people and probably fifty thousand of 'em are violent criminals."

"I hope it's only fifty thousand."

He shook his head. "Pretty risky to live there and not have a gun. You need a gun there more than here."

"Listen to you. You tell me you don't hunt, but you'd shoot a human being?"

"That's right, for the same reason I killed that rattlesnake: to protect people I care about."

"Well, if you lived in New York you could kill some of the rats," she said. "The four-legged ones, I mean. Sometimes you see five or six of them just scurrying along the street or sitting on a subway platform, bold as can be."

"Because they know the people aren't armed," Ray said.

Arla began to laugh. "Don't worry. I just walk or take cabs. Even if the subways *were* safe, they're so uncomfortable this time of year. New York can be pretty hot in September, too."

Ray settled back down and opened his arms. "C'mere, tell me what else you like about California, so I know you're really coming back."

"You're all the reason I need." She rested her head on his chest. "But I'll tell you the things I *don't* like about New York. It's awfully muggy in the summer. The air, well, it doesn't smell like the air here. On trash day the sidewalks are stacked with bags of garbage, mountains of green plastic. And every day is trash day somewhere in the city."

"Don't they have dumpsters?"

"There's no room for dumpsters. Restaurants store trash in their basements, and on the night before trash day they bring the bags up and stack them on the sidewalks. The rats know the schedule, so…"

Ray's nose wrinkled in distaste. "Seems unsanitary."

"It is. That's why New Yorkers have tough immune systems."

"Must smell pretty bad in the summer."

"Oh, God, the whole city reeks! That's bad enough in the normal summer, but about five years ago there was a garbage strike. It lasted three months. That was the last straw for my ex, actually. He refused to live in New York any longer."

"I don't blame him," Ray said, shaking his head. He glanced at the clock. He had told her he was taking his wife and his mother to dinner, so he had to get home by six to shower and dress. Their reservation was for seven o'clock at MacGowan's.

Arla glanced at the clock, too. It was 5:20. "You've got a little time," she said. "Believe me, angel, Piñon County's a Garden of Eden compared to New York. It's just, sometimes a girl wants to spend a little time in Sodom and Gomorrah."

"I wouldn't care if I never saw New York. I've seen better cities."

She instinctively bristled, and he nudged her. "You can take the girl out of New York…"

"Well, one thing you'd find to your taste in New York," she said. "There's always so much construction going on. They say it's the city that's always being built."

"Would you take me with you?"

Arla was taken aback. She had never expected him to say something like that.

"Don't worry," he said gruffly. "I didn't mean it."

"Ray, of course I'd take you there. I'd love to show you the city. Just not this time. This time I've already made plans with my old homegirls. But I am taking you with me."

"Huh?"

"I'm going to bring some pictures of you." She caressed his face with her lips.

"We probably got some I could give you."

"I want to take them myself." Arla pulled the sheet up so that it barely covered his genitals.

She had him adopt all the poses she could dream of, stopping just short of the sort of photos that might cause consternation in the darkroom.

"Where are you going to develop these?" he said suddenly.

Arla laughed. "Don't worry, angel. I'll bring it to a one-hour place in Marin when I take Morgan down there. I'm going to leave him with my ex and his girlfriend," she added. "Now, put your work clothes on. I want pictures of you in them, too."

He buttoned the blue jeans. She clicked the shutter. "Now from behind." She remembered when she first moved up to Piñon County and jogged past him working at the job site, how she'd wished she could pose him any way she wanted, walk around just admiring his perfect physique. Her dream had come true.

She ran her hands all over him, his T-shirt, his biceps, his concrete-flecked Levi's.

"I have to leave in a few minutes," he reminded her, but his body was already responding to her touch.

Later, she re-buttoned his jeans as he tried to orient himself. He rested his hand on her head. "And you wonder why I don't want you to go?"

Arla laughed. "I don't wonder at all."

INTERLUDE

March 1888
Camargo, California

When Rosa's husband came home the evening after the funeral, she saw at once that he was worried. But not until they prepared to turn in for the night did he tell her what was troubling him. "Rosa, the judge came to me after the funeral," he began.

She stopped buttoning her night dress and looked at him.

"He thinks Mrs. Cushing gave you something to keep for her. A book she was writing."

Rosa didn't reply at once. She was filled with sorrow, for she had not thought Albert would do this. Of all her family and friends, she had not thought it would be Albert.

"And he wants you to get it and bring it to him?" Rosa said.

"He wants to read it, to make sure she didn't say anything about taking her life," Albert said.

"So *that's* what he says he's worried about," Rosa murmured. She met Albert's gaze. "And what did you tell him?"

"That I didn't know if you had this book, but that you'd never mentioned it to me. Do you have it, Rosa?"

She went to the dressing table and began to brush out her long thick hair—once as black and shiny as a wall of coal, now streaked with white but still lustrous and plentiful.

"Rosa," he pleaded. "The judge is powerful. He could cause us harm."

"Yet you wish to help him. This man you believe to be vengeful and cruel when he doesn't get his way." She began to braid her hair.

Albert sat on their bed and rested his hands on his thighs. "If Mrs. Cushing was still alive, it would be different. But what harm can it do now, to let the judge read the book?"

"Perhaps none," she said. And did something she had never before done with Albert: she lied. "But I don't have it. Caterina didn't give me such a book."

Albert's expression didn't change.

"He won't believe you if you tell him so?" Rosa asked. "All right then, Alberto. Invite him here to find out for himself."

THE NEXT DAY, Judge Cushing appeared at their farm, hardly concealing his distaste. He took no apparent notice of the scent of lavender as the sun touched it, the buzzing of all the worker bees flitting from blossom to blossom, the nearby hillside alive with poppies, the hens chattering and pecking at pebbles, the eight-week-old kittens wrapped around each other as they slept in a box on the porch.

Rosa offered coffee; the judge declined. "Your husband explained why I asked to meet with you?"

"Yes, Judge," Rosa said. "You wondered if Mrs. Cushing gave me a book of hers to keep safe."

"That's right."

"She gave me the things she uses ... *used* for Mass: her mantilla and gloves, her missal and a set of rosary beads."

The judge sat silent for a moment. So did Rosa. Then he said, "May I see them?"

Rosa hesitated, so as not to seem too willing to comply, then nodded. "They are in that basket." She stood and retrieved the basket, and handed it to him. He looked through it, even going so far as to riffle the pages of the missal.

Thank God I moved the diary, Rosa said to herself. She

asked him, "Is that the book you seek? You may take it back, Judge. It's written in English, so I cannot read it."

He looked up quickly. "But Catherine taught you to read."

"She taught me the alphabet," Rosa said, "which is mostly the same in Spanish, and provided me with basic Spanish books." That was true. And if he took it to mean that Catherine had not also taught her to read English...

Judge Cushing nodded. He stood to go.

"So, I may keep these things?" Rosa didn't have to pretend that tears filled her eyes. "They remind me of her every time I go to Mass."

"Yes, yes," he said impatiently.

When he had gone, she glanced at the recipe shelf in her kitchen. She dared not return the diary to the box of Catherine's religious artifacts. Best to leave it where it was, safely disguised as a collection of dill pickle recipes.

Part V

SEPTEMBER 1985

FIRE SEASON

Whenever we see a new subdivision go up and the developer is boasting it abuts national forest land, we figure our firefighters are going to be getting to know those new homeowners up close and personal in a few years.

—Matt Mathes, U.S. Forest Service, California Region spokesperson, quoted in *San Francisco Chronicle*, October 28, 2003

Chapter Thirty-One

Kit set the table while Joe and Stella cooked. There were no guests at the ranch today. In fact, no parties were booked for the week; overnight camping was still prohibited. If it rained, the Forest Service would probably lift the ban. Not that anyone expected rain. None was in the forecast, and the air just didn't feel like rain. But Kit hadn't given up hope that this would be one of those Septembers when the weather changed quickly, the way it used to in Septembers before the drought.

The big kitchen was filled with good smells: spaghetti and meatballs, percolating coffee, and yeasty sourdough bread, baked by Stella using the starter her grandmother had used. Mom used the same starter when she made bread and had told her Stella's grandmother brought it from Italy.

She set the bread on the big trestle table, along with the cutting board and a serrated knife, and glanced out the window at Carlos. He had just finished cleaning the stalls; he'd taken off the long rubber boots and was hosing himself off. It was so hot outside that steam rose from his back when the water hit it. Then he soaped up and rubbed the lather all over his bare torso, arms and neck. Her heartbeat quickened.

Soon, they sat down to eat and Joe asked Carlos about college. Carlos talked enthusiastically about UC Davis. Kit wasn't looking forward to next year. They'd made plans to see each other on weekends, but she knew that once he started college and had new friends and interests, he wouldn't want to drive back to Piñon County every week.

Then he smiled at her, as if he knew exactly what she was thinking. She smiled back, a brief flicker of a smile, just for him.

She finished her stuffed zucchini and nodded yes when Stella offered the plate for more. The conversation had shifted; Joe was now talking about the Livermore Valley. "… three small towns between all that ranch land, but now it's twenty miles of malls and housing developments."

"But why did the ranchers sell?" Carlos asked, reaching for the jar of Vallecitos wax peppers.

"Their land was rezoned," Joe explained. "It was changed from agricultural to commercial-residential. Their property taxes went from a couple thousand dollars a year to over fifty thousand, or more."

"So they used taxes to force farmers to sell?" Carlos exclaimed.

"Yes, and it's been happening in California for decades," Joe said. "But it's particularly sad when it happens to fertile land. Like in Santa Clara. All the fruit orchards got turned into Silicon Valley."

That wouldn't happen here, Kit thought gratefully. Livermore Valley was on the outskirts of the Bay Area and Stanford was in the Santa Clara Valley. But Piñon County was far from any city, too far to commute from, and unlikely to become a technology hub.

AT THREE O'CLOCK that afternoon, Carlos's room was almost dark because the heavy drapes were drawn. They had just been swimming at Cougar Lake. Carlos wore his Hawaiian shorts, Kit a swimsuit with a T-shirt over it. Sandalwood incense was burning and music filled the room as they lay side by side—apart, not touching—on his bed. Baba Looey had stretched out between them.

She liked that he had no 'sexy girl' posters. Instead, he'd put up posters of Bob Marley smoking a cigar-sized joint; Dwight Clark making The Catch; Willie Mays making the other great catch; *Free Nelson Mandela* and *Viva La Huelga;* and a poster announcing the movie *Chan Is Missing.* It was his favorite movie ever and yet Kit hadn't seen it. Actually, she'd never even heard of it until he told her about it. He'd seen it in Sacramento, where there was a theater that showed unusual movies.

Carlos put on a tape. She hadn't really paid much attention to these groups until she found out he liked them. Romeo Void, The Clash, the Eurythmics, Joe Jackson. Right now, The Pretenders tape was on. A woman was singing. Kit felt both excited and embarrassed by the words in the song, by the frank eroticism of the woman's voice, and how sure of herself she sounded. She didn't beg quietly, she demanded.

"Have you ever seen Chrissie Hynde?" Carlos asked as the tape ended.

Kit shook her head.

"She kind of reminds me of you."

"Me!" Kit was flattered, and mystified. "Why?"

"She's not like most rock and roll singers, trying to look like movie stars or something." He put on *Rastaman Vibration* and lay back down. Baba Looey climbed onto his stomach. "You're not phony. You don't try to act like everyone else just so you can fit in."

"So, you wouldn't rather I was more feminine?"

He turned onto his side, dislodging Baba, who stretched luxuriously and leapt from the bed to the chair. "Kit, you're totally feminine. To me, that doesn't mean a girl who wears ruffles and makeup; it means a girl who's happy being the way she is."

She was lying on her back, so she couldn't see his expression as well as she wished, especially not with the lamp light behind him. She swallowed, trying to get up her courage. And then she felt his hand on her cheek, his longish fingers reaching back into her curly hair, the palm of his hand warm, almost hot. Kit looked into his eyes and, at last, she knew. Stella was right.

She leaned over and tentatively brought her lips to his. She felt funny about not really knowing how to kiss. Maybe she would be so awkward that he wouldn't want to kiss her. But oh, his mouth felt good. His lips were so soft and warm. And when she stopped, when she pulled back a little to make sure he didn't mind her kissing him, Carlos murmured her name and brought his mouth to hers again.

Their bodies pressed together. She felt the runner's muscles in his thighs and hips, his chest that seemed to have grown broader in just a year, his flat abdomen, and the maleness that surged against her. His arms were around her, and when the tips of his fingers gently touched her lower back where it curved in just above her hips, a jolt of electricity rushed through her.

They kissed all the way through Side B and when the tape flipped itself over, Carlos pulled away from her slightly. "We'd better stop."

She pressed herself against him again. "I don't want to."

"You're only fifteen."

"So I'm a year older than Juliet Capulet."

"Besides, my mom might come home any minute."

"You said she won't be back till five. It's not even four yet." Her eyelids dropped down. "I guess I'm being too forward."

"No, Kit. I think you're so great. Don't you know how it makes me feel, that you want to be with me?"

She shook her head.

"It makes me feel so lucky," he whispered.

Happiness filled her to bursting. Oh, she knew who the lucky one was.

"I just want you to be sure."

"I've been thinking about it for a long time, Carlos."

"So have I." His thigh slipped in between hers and Kit's breath drew in sharply. "I don't have any protection," he said. "I mean, I do, but they're old and I don't think you're supposed to use them if they're old."

She couldn't have explained why, but she was touched that he hadn't expected this, or planned for it. "There's other things we can do."

Carlos smiled. "Yes, lots of things."

She brought her body to his, nothing else between his thigh and her flesh except the thin material of her swimsuit.

JUST BEFORE FIVE o'clock, Carlos murmured, "My mom's probably on her way home."

"Mm."

"We should get dressed."

"Mm." But she didn't move, and neither did he. Their arms and legs were entwined and she snuggled her head even closer to him, against his skin where his shoulder sloped up to his neck, breathing the scent of him and the warmth of him and the essence of him that she, only she, could taste and touch. She was so filled with happiness that she felt it physically; she felt like crying, like laughing, like dancing.

At first, she'd been embarrassed by her hands. The palms were callused and tough, scarred from rope burns, barbed wire, a flying ember from the burning leaf pile. She kept her nails short and squared so they wouldn't break below the quick when she worked. She had stopped touching him, removed her hands from his tender skin, and when he'd said, "What's wrong?" she began, "My hands are rough," but he brought them to his mouth. Both of her hands, he brought them up and kissed them—right on the palms with all that alligator skin, on the blunt fingertips, and on the backs where the skin was sun-darkened and weather-dried. "You have good, strong, hard-working hands. Hands like the ranch girl I love."

Love, she had said to herself. *Love!*

And then he'd smiled and put her hands back where they had been, on him. After that she wasn't embarrassed or self-conscious about anything. There was no right or wrong way to do things, no rules to break or guidelines to follow. They were making their own world.

She wished they could just stay here all night and all day tomorrow and the night after that, too. She wished it didn't matter that his mother would be here soon. She wanted to stay forever in this world that she and Carlos had created, a world of exhilarating intensity. She didn't want to go back into a world where adults didn't think teenagers should love each other, even when they were careful not to make a baby. Into a world where her father would not be happy for her, and would not care that Carlos was good and kind and smart and sensitive, only that he was Mexican-American.

He nuzzled her cheek and said, "Do you want me to do it again?"

And that was when they heard Roxanne's pickup. They scrambled for their clothes, pulling them on frantically. Carlos put his shirt on backwards, but it was too late to fix. When Roxanne came into the house, they were sitting up on the bed, side by side, not touching. The bedroom door was open and a Romeo Void tape was playing.

"Hi, kids, have a nice swim?" Roxanne said cheerfully.

"Hi, Mom."

"It was great," Kit said fervently. Out of the corner of her eye she caught Carlos's smile.

"Are you two hungry?"

Kit realized that she was ravenous. "Kind of."

"We're starving," Carlos said.

"Good, because I brought macaroni and cheese from Wanda's, and a fresh lemon meringue pie."

"Lemon meringue!" Kit exclaimed.

Roxanne laughed. "Come out to the kitchen."

They started to leave the room, but Kit gestured to him to fix his shirt. He did, then grasped her hand to detain her. He quietly closed the door and put his arms around her. His kiss was tender and she could taste a little of herself on his lips, and she could feel desire starting up in her all over again, could feel it beginning again in him, too. "Carlos, can we do it again tomorrow, after school?"

"I have cross-country practice," he reminded her. "You don't want me to skip it, do you?"

"Well ... um..."

He laughed, and she did too. "Okay, then. After school we'll drive somewhere." He opened the door, but before they left the room, he gently tugged her hand again. He put his mouth to her ear and murmured, "I love you, Kit."

"I love you, Carlos. I love you. I love you."

Chapter Thirty-Two

When they'd received a letter from the lawyer last week, Stella had seen no reason to meet with him. She'd assumed Joe would feel the same. But he'd surprised her. "Let's hear what he has to say."

She'd looked at him with curiosity. "We're not going to sell, so why bother talking to him?"

"For one reason: to get a better idea of just what's going on around here."

Not until fifty minutes after the meeting time did they hear tires on the gravel and went onto the porch to greet their guest. Joe winked at her, stepped off the porch, and walked to the Lincoln. The lawyer wore a suit and tie and brought a slim briefcase from the car. He extended his hand. "Bob Sutcliffe. You're Joe Pardini? Mrs. Pardini?"

"Stella," she said. They all shook hands and exchanged pleasantries. On Sutcliffe's part the greetings didn't seem strained; perhaps he thought he was coming here to tell them something they had been eagerly awaiting.

"Sorry I'm late," he said, and explained about a problem at the airport.

"Can we offer you lunch?" Stella asked.

"No, thanks very much. I'm afraid I'm in a bit of a time-bind here. I've a meeting in Reno at four," he glanced at his watch, "and the pilot tells me we'll have to leave by three."

Joe showed Sutcliffe to the best chair, then joined Stella on the sofa. She was aware, which she ordinarily was not, of how shabby the room must seem. None of the furniture matched and most of it was old. A few pieces might even be described as threadbare.

"Well, we may as well get started," Sutcliffe said, opening his briefcase. He pulled out some papers, set them on the coffee table, and gave them a business card. The card was on heavy cream-colored stock embossed with black lettering.

"On behalf of our client, we have an offer to extend to you for the purchase of this property. This agreement explains the offer in detail; I'll leave it with you so you can consult with your own attorney. But to summarize the offer: our client proposes to purchase Pardini Ranch in toto for a price of just over $500 per acre."

The offer three years ago had been for $700 an acre. Stella dared not look at Joe. She knew that he was thinking the same as she, that whoever was behind the offer knew how close to bankruptcy they were now.

"That is, for all 967 acres, a total of $500,000."

Lower price or not, hearing that amount spoken aloud, *five hundred thousand dollars*, was staggering.

The lawyer continued. "The offer is for the entire property only, and is valid until October fifteenth. If you do not accept the offer by October fifteenth, it will be deemed withdrawn. Any counteroffer will, of course, be construed as a rejection of the original offer."

"Did you say this offer is for the entire property only?" said Joe.

"Yes, that's right. Our client is not interested in purchasing only a portion of the property, due to the nature of the intended purpose of the purchase."

"What is the intended purpose?" Stella asked.

"To build luxury homes."

"On all 967 acres?"

"They will be on large lots, one to two acres each. Our client intends to build along the natural contours of the land and to maintain as many of the natural features as possible. It will be a gated community but, as in any development, a fair amount of land will go to public works—parks and recreational facilities."

"I have a question, Mr. Sutcliffe," Stella said.

"Bob."

"Yes, Bob, who is your client?"

The lawyer hesitated. He looked from Stella to Joe. "I can't see how that matters."

"Oh really?" Stella said, but Joe pressed his foot against hers.

He smiled at the lawyer. "I'll try to explain our perspective. If you don't mind my asking, where are you from originally?"

"Like everyone in San Francisco, from somewhere else," Sutcliffe grinned. "In my case, Illinois."

"San Francisco's a beautiful city and people move there from all over the United States."

"From all over the world," Sutcliffe said.

"Sure. But it's different in Piñon County. People have deep roots here. Stella's family and mine have both been here since the gold rush. I've lived on this ranch all my life."

"In the same place, all your life?" Sutcliffe's eyebrows shot up. "That's unusual in California."

"In San Francisco and Los Angeles it is, but it's not so rare here in the Mother Lode," Joe said. "What *is* rare, even for here, is that I live in the house I was born in. My great-grandparents bought this land and my grandparents built this house; it's ninety years old. I was born in a room right down the hallway. Stella grew up in a house that's now the county museum. I tell you this so you'll understand how Stella and I feel about the land—not just our own land—all of the mountains. It's important to us to know whether the person or people wanting to buy our ranch are local people, or at least northern Californians, or whether we're talking about a horse of a different color."

The lawyer watched Joe intently. "I think I understand," Sutcliffe said. Stella thought he looked relieved.

"Here, let me give you a refill," and Joe poured more iced tea into the lawyer's glass. "I know that probably seems old-fashioned to you. But Stella and I take a lot of pride in being Californians—northern Californians. And we don't much like the way so much property is being bought by foreign investors. There's a lot of money from Canada and the Far East coming into our state."

"Well, I think I can give you some relief on that score," Sutcliffe said. He looked from Joe to Stella and smiled reassuringly. "This offer is from local investors. The bank is in Los Angeles, and the package was put together by a northern California investor."

"Who is that northern California investor?"

"Joe, I'm sure you can appreciate the need for discretion during the early stages of organizing a package like this."

"Sure," Joe said, in a bitter tone that no one but Stella would ever suspect to be exaggerated. "Wouldn't be the first time some city people came up here with their plans. They don't know anything about this place, but they've got the money to do what they like."

"That's not the situation," the lawyer said hastily. "I can assure you of that. The main investor is not a city person. It's someone who … Let me just say that the project could not be in the hands of anyone more conversant with the local situation, or more sympathetic to it."

"I'll take your word for that," Joe said. "I guess that's about all the questions I have. You've given us a pretty clear idea of things. But it's mostly for my own peace of mind I wanted to know. I don't want to mislead you; we aren't–"

"Excuse me, one other thing," Sutcliffe said. "We didn't discuss the method of payment, but you'll be paid in full within three months, with one-third immediately, if you accept the offer."

"We don't need until October to give you our answer."

Sutcliffe held up his hands, like a cop stopping traffic. "Please, consider this at your leisure. Talk it over with each other, your families, your lawyer. Even if you're inclined not to accept, there's no need for haste." Sutcliffe smiled. "Give yourselves a few weeks, at least, to decide."

He stood, and so did Joe. Everyone shook hands. Stella went into the kitchen as Joe escorted the lawyer out to his car. She sat down at the heavy wooden table, her knuckles drumming a fast staccato. She heard the lawyer saying again what a lovely property this was. She heard Tabasco nickering at Joe.

He came back in and sat across from her. "Cushing," she said.

Joe shook his head. "That's what the lawyer wants us to think. But the mall is sitting there with almost no work being done. Same with the other places Cushing was building. He's in trouble."

"You think so?" she said skeptically.

"To us, in Piñon County, Cushing seems very rich. But in the overall scheme of these things, he's small potatoes. That offer, half a million, I doubt Cushing has that kind of money anymore. He's fronting for other people. To them, Cushing's nothing, and if he fails they won't care. They'll simply come in and seize the remains."

"But Joe, whoever they are, they know we're about to go bankrupt. They probably figure they can wait us out and get our place for nothing." She felt fear rising in her throat. "If we can't pay off the loan, the bank will take the land. They'll foreclose. We're running out of options."

"So, you want to accept that offer?" he asked quietly.

"I don't *want* to accept it. I just don't know what we're going to do. We're no different than those ranchers being zoned out of existence. If we sell, we could buy land somewhere else, up north or even in Oregon."

Joe's eyes were steady on her. But in them she saw the beginnings of something she had never seen there before: disappointment. "Here's what I think," he said. "We'll try to get through one more season. If we can't, then we'll close the business. We'll sell all the horses, except Tabasco and Tippy. We can even sell the new pickup."

Stella smiled, despite herself. He'd been looking for an excuse to sell that car. She said, "But the most we can get for everything is maybe $15,000. The bank payments are $1,000 a month, Joe. We still owe thirty-four thousand on that loan."

"Selling the stock and some of the equipment will give us time. We can wait them out."

"But selling everything won't get us more than six months."

He nodded. "That's just what we need. In six months we'll be digging our way back out."

Stella hesitated. "Isn't it possible that you're thinking with your heart instead of your brain? The land is in your blood. It's in mine, too. But we're beaten and it's my fault. If we hadn't started the packhorse business, if we'd stuck to chickens—"

"Stella, dear, it's you who are thinking with your heart. If we do sell the stock and gear and the new pickup, we can use that $15,000 for the bank payments while we figure out what to do. We could make a year's worth of loan payments and have $3,000 dollars left over."

"That would give us time to establish a horse boarding and training service." She was thinking out loud. "I could give riding lessons, Joe."

"We'll have plenty of time to figure something out. We're actually very fortunate. Some people have to figure out things like this with only a month before they're evicted from their apartment and sleeping on a subway grate. We've got the ranch and the house. And each other." He brought her hands up to his lips and kissed her fingers. "Now, let's have some dinner."

"We should have eaten it two hours ago." Stella went over to the stove and turned the pasta water back on. "That damned lawyer."

"I must admit, it's hard to think kindly of a man who keeps me from my fettucini."

Chapter Thirty-Three

Ray was in the construction trailer at the site of the new phone company headquarters, when Hiram Cushing's secretary called and asked him to come by the office at 5:30 for a meeting. "Sure," Ray said. "Do you know what it's about?" But Ellen didn't know. Or said she didn't.

Ray figured it must be bad news. A few weeks ago, Cushing had told him to hold off before starting the next phase of High Mountain Mall, the electrical work. At first, Ray assumed there was some problem with the electrical subcontractor. Then, a few days after that, another order came down: Ray was to shift some of the crew from the Gennessee Mine housing development to the phone company building. So, although the framing work was still going on at the housing development, with fewer men it was proceeding at a slow pace. Ray warned Cushing that they were liable to start running behind schedule. Cushing said he realized that, but they had to risk it.

That was the kind of bad news that could turn good. For years, fear of losing a regular paycheck had kept him at Eagle. But if things started looking bad for the company, or even if he was going to be temporarily laid off, it would be a good time for him to go it alone, to finally do what he'd always wanted to do.

Sometimes it was hard to remember that before marrying, he and Terri had vowed not to get trapped by all the things that now had them firmly entrenched: house payments, car payments, boat payments, credit card payments. Trapped by the luxuries they'd bought to help them get through the daily routine of work.

You had to work, unless you hit the jackpot. Arla had hit it, but she'd come from upper-middle-class people to begin with. It was people from that class who had spare money to risk on, say, IBM stock in 1975. But how often did someone from his class hit the jackpot? People like him or Billy, like Loretta or Roxanne, never hit the jackpot, because they never had extra money to gamble with.

Who the hell could say that it wouldn't be worse if he owned his own business? Maybe he'd have even less of a say over his own time. Business owners often made that complaint.

He looked longingly toward the mountains. He hadn't been able to get to Tahoe much this summer, not with all the work. And he had to admit, he hadn't wanted to be away from Arla, even though he rarely saw her on weekends. But it was not getting there last winter that he'd really missed. In a normal winter, construction was often idled for weeks at a time because so many construction jobs couldn't be done in heavy rain or during a freeze, but the drought meant that work didn't have to be postponed until spring.

He loved snow and the High Sierra was beautiful after a snowstorm. He loved waking up to a glittering white world, knowing he was 7,000 feet above the floor of the San Joaquin Valley, with even taller peaks towering above. He liked the sound of wind through pines and the tinkle of icicles melting, and even the booming of dynamite as ski patrols set off avalanches. Like control burns set to preempt forest fires, avalanches were started purposely so skiers wouldn't start them accidentally.

Ray sighed and returned to work: to dust in his nose, sweat stinging his eyes, a sharp ache threatening to seize up his lower back, a pounding headache from the remorseless sun, and the constant pressure to make decisions and give directives and respond to sudden changes.

After work he had a while before the meeting with Cushing, so he drove out to Arla's, parked in the brush and let himself in through the back door. Hopefully, none of the neighbors would see him and call the cops. It might be hard to explain to a sheriff's deputy why he happened to have a key to Arla's house, and why he was letting himself in when she was away on vacation.

He walked through the house to the front door, cautiously opened it, peered outside, saw no one, and retrieved the mail. Along with several bills, credit card statements and some junk mail was a letter addressed to herself, but the return address was 'Cleo,' so he knew it was for him. It was short and newsy, only one page, telling him about an off-Broadway play she'd seen and explaining that the enclosed photograph had been taken in Central Park before the play. The photograph made his heart beat harder and faster: Arla in a slinky black dress with spaghetti straps.

He left the letter on the table in the breakfast nook, with the small stack of others that she'd sent. He found a blank envelope in her study and put the photograph in it, and stuck it in his pocket. He knew he'd probably be taking it out ten times a day.

It was now quarter past five. Ray jogged back to his truck in its hiding place on the fire road, and drove quickly to the Eagle office. The office staff had already gone; Hiram Cushing was the only person there. "Ray, thanks for coming by." He steered Ray to the conference table in his large office.

Bookshelves lined two walls; one actually contained books—treatises on water rights and building codes. The rest displayed trophies and memorabilia: first place in a marlin fishing tournament, a football encased in glass with signatures of Joe Montana and Dwight Clark.

There were also photographs. In one, Cushing wore a suit and a hardhat as he cut a ribbon with ceremonial scissors. The caption read: 'The opening of Sea Breeze Estates at South Lake Tahoe, 1963.' In another, he stood beside Governor Reagan, both grinning as if one of them had just made a joke about having seen that one redwood tree.

Cushing sat across the table from Ray. He untied a roll of paper and spread the plans for the mall on the table. "It's time I had a talk with you—a frank talk about the state of the projects."

"Okay," Ray said, and his heart felt as though it was literally sinking in his chest, because he was sure he knew what was coming. He might be able to turn it into a good thing, but still that didn't mean he looked forward to hearing it. And he didn't like laying guys off, which he'd certainly have to do if the mall project was shelved.

"Some of the investors in High Mountain Mall are nervous; they were counting on the new development being built to give the retailers a strong customer base."

"With a full crew we could be done by the end of the year," Ray said.

Cushing shook his head impatiently. "I'm not talking about Gennessee Mine; I mean the retirement community and golf course. The investors expected it to be at least in the planning stages by now."

Ray was shocked to find out that Cushing had promised that the project would be built before he even had title to the land. He looked down so Cushing wouldn't see the surprise in his eyes.

"Pardini's holding out for a lot longer than I expected, but that's not something you have to be concerned about. I wanted to tell you what the situation is, not how it got that way. To get right to the point, two tenants have pulled out of the mall: The Gap and Tower Records. And now our anchor tenant, Lucky Stores, is getting cold feet."

"They're threatening to pull out too?" Ray asked.

"They're hinting at it, but I consider it a negotiating tactic to gain concessions from us. Rather expensive concessions."

Ray knew full well that if Lucky pulled out, that was the end of the mall. So whatever concessions they were demanding, Cushing would probably have to make. They had him over a barrel.

"The uncertainty is the reason I've held up your end, Ray. I didn't want to incur high labor costs that may ultimately prove unnecessary. And on the other hand, if the labor will be needed after all, I'd like to figure out a better plan for utilizing it."

Ray's stomach tensed. The word 'labor' out of the mouth of management was always alarming.

Cushing continued, "We've all taken shortcuts; as experts in our field, we know where a shortcut will cause no harm, no degradation of the product." He paused. "It's really a matter of not alarming people with petty details about which they have no expertise. Or as they say in the military, information is provided on a need-to-know basis. Do you see what I'm getting at?"

Ray replied carefully. "I'll build the place however the plans say to build it."

"Certainly, that's what I expect you to do," Cushing said smoothly. "Of course, sometimes a contractor can make an honest mistake. Perhaps a plan calls for basement walls thirteen inches wide, the plans are misread, and the walls end up eleven inches." Cushing gestured to the architectural plans, pointing at one of the mall buildings. "Here, for instance, the plans call for steel beams one inch thicker than the Building Code requires. It could hardly be questioned if the crew used the standard size steel beams."

He felt Cushing's eyes studying him and suspected that Cushing could see his anger. A guy didn't get as far as Cushing without reading people.

"Well, Ray, we'll talk over the details at some later date. I mostly wanted you to understand why we've had to lay off some of the crew and why there's so much uncertainty. But I expect to have things worked out, one way or the other, by the end of this month. As to Pardini, I expect to make some progress there very shortly. I won't go into details, but things look promising. All of this is strictly confidential, Ray. I don't want you discussing this with anyone. Not even your wife."

"I won't, Hiram."

"That's good." Cushing looked at Ray gravely. "And be careful about speaking indiscreetly with any other intimate friend."

A bolt of white heat shot into Ray's head. For a few moments, he couldn't breathe.

Cushing got up and went to the birdcage. The cockatiel scampered back and forth on its swing and squawked excitedly. Cushing fed it pieces of fruit.

Ray stood up and left.

He drove home with his heart pounding and his blood rushing. How did Cushing know? Was someone at the office or on the construction crew reporting things to him? Was he having Ray watched? Was he intending to use it as leverage? He must be, because why else would he have mentioned it? Was that the way Cushing figured he could get Ray to build differently than the plans called for?

How could he keep working for Cushing?

Chapter Thirty-Four

On Monday morning, after Ray left for work and Trixie for school, Terri dashed to the store for fresh fruit for her brunch with Laura. They were having an English-style tea today; Laura would make scones, Terri would provide a pot of Earl Grey tea and fruit.

She washed the berries, then changed out of her shorts and T-shirt. She always wanted to look good for these brunches with Laura. Laura dressed with a simple elegance. Terri wasn't emulating her; she couldn't do that even if she wanted to, for she and Laura were very different physically. But there was something in Laura's demeanor—her way of carrying herself and, despite everything that had happened to her, her dignity —that made Terri always want to make an effort for her, to treat their Mondays as special.

She fixed her hair, then walked quickly through the house, straightening up. There wasn't much of a mess, just some of the kids' toys and a few dishes here and there. She collected up the clothes and towels to run a load in the washer.

Ray's shirt and Levi's were still on the floor in his study. Terri added his clothes to the washing machine, and only thought to check his pockets a scant second before the jeans were inundated by warm soapy water. Normally, Ray cleaned out his pockets himself, but he had probably forgotten that he'd left his jeans in the office.

Terri pulled out a package of gum, pizza and ice cream receipts, and a folded envelope. She turned the envelope over. Nothing was written on it. There was something inside that felt like a snapshot. She opened the envelope.

She stood there hardly breathing, staring down at a Polaroid of that woman from Blackberry Springs, the snotty one who'd moved up from the Bay Area. The one who jogged all the time and had a stomach as flat as a teenager's and drove around in a red Mercedes and never got her hair done in Piñon County. Ray was carrying a photograph of her in his pocket! She was in a park, standing on a lawn with a city skyline behind her, skyscrapers towering over the distant trees. She wore a little black dress: spaghetti straps, a hemline above her knees, her figure lithe and slender. She looked very pretty.

Terri cried out and stumbled backward.

She must not have heard the doorbell. The next thing she knew Laura was there, in the laundry room, on the floor with her, holding her.

"It may not be what you think," Laura said.

"No, no, that's what it is; why else would he have her picture in his pocket? Oh my God." She moaned into Laura's shoulder.

Laura's eyes filled, too. "I'm so sorry, darling. I'm so sorry."

She helped Terri get up and they went into the kitchen, where Laura steered her to the tea kettle. And oddly enough, it did help, to go through the ritual of filling the pot with the fragrant leaves, to put cream in the good creamer and sugar in the matching bowl, to slice cantaloupe, watermelon and strawberries and arrange them on one of the good china serving plates. And all the while Laura, who had tied an apron around her silk blouse and slacks, hummed softly. Soon, the smell of baking scones filled the kitchen.

"He must be in love with her," Terri said as they sat in the nook with their food.

"I was wondering if you … if this is the first time Ray has ever done this."

"No, *that's* not what I'm upset about!" Terri burst out. And then, as the implication of Laura's hesitation struck her, "Does everyone in town know Ray sleeps around?"

"There's been gossip," Laura said.

Terri felt herself redden. Laura spread lemon curd on a scone and handed it to her. "Why do you think he's in love with her?"

"Because he isn't making love to me," Terri said miserably. "Last night he did, but I'm the one who asked, and before that it was almost three weeks. Usually when he's got someone, he makes love to me a lot. That's how I know when he's—but this!" She didn't think she could eat the scone without choking, and set it down. "There have been things that seemed insignificant until now. He's been coming home late two or three nights a week. I thought he was working so hard. Oh, I'm such a fool!" Anger rose in her throat. "Sometimes he leaves for work way before five. He's been going to her house at five o'clock in the morning!"

She looked at Laura through a film of tears. "There's never been another woman he made love to that often. The other times, it's been once a week or less. But he's going to her house every chance he gets. Don't you see, Laura? He *must* be in love with her." Her stomach churned with the fear of being abandoned. Would he leave her? Could he possibly do that if it meant leaving the children too? The children! They loved him so much! He couldn't hurt them so badly, could he?

Laura's gentle hand stroked her hair and Terri sobbed against her, clinging to her as a drowning person to driftwood.

Finally she stopped, wiping her eyes and nose with tissues from the box Laura handed to her. "I'm sorry to dump this on you."

"After what I've burdened you with, you say that? I only wish I could help."

"You *are* helping. There's no one else I could talk to, and I don't think I could deal with it all by myself." She gulped some tea. "Now that I think about it, he's been acting kind of funny this week; he seems distracted. And he's been coming home on time, except one night he said he went to the tavern. He did, because Troy got sick and I called him there." Her hopes soared and she looked at Laura. "I wonder if she broke up with him? Or if something's wrong between them?"

Laura frowned slightly. "I thought I heard…" Then, to Terri's shock, Laura went to the telephone.

"What are you doing?"

Laura held her finger to her lips. "Hi, Stella, this is Laura."

Terri was surprised. She thought that the Jensens and Pardinis were feuding. But here was Laura, speaking to Stella as though they were used to speaking with each other.

Then the rest of the conversation drove those thoughts right out of her mind.

"No, fine, but I'm wondering if you happen to have Arla Stinson's telephone number? I understand she drives down to Sacramento fairly regularly, and I thought I could get a ride with her … Oh, she's in New York right now?" Laura looked at Terri. "Do you know when she's coming back? … Tomorrow, I see … Two weeks, that's probably longer than I'd want to vacation in New York!" Laura laughed. "Yes, thank you. I'll call her a few days after she's back, give her time to settle in." After pleasantries, Laura hung up.

"That explains it, I guess," Terri said bitterly. "She's been out of town, so he's distracted and unhappy, and coming home on time."

She had always heard that love and hate were so close that

they were almost the same thing; she'd considered it a platitude. But now she got it. She was close to hating him. She hated what he'd done so much that she could feel hatred for him threatening to engulf her. Anger gripped every inch of her body. Her stomach clenched, blood pounded painfully in her head, even her skin felt tight and stretched. She went to the sink and retched.

Laura waited until she stopped. "What are you going to do?"

"I don't know. I don't want to talk to him when I'm this upset."

"No, you shouldn't."

"What I really want to do—" Terri broke off. She wanted to hit something—no, to hit *him*. To really hurt him. To make him suffer as she was suffering. To show him what betrayal and duplicity felt like, physically.

She sat down again and her head dropped into her hands.

Laura sat beside her. "For the time being, act as if nothing has happened."

"I don't know if I can. I don't know if I want to."

"You can, and you have to." Laura's voice was firm. She took Terri's hands. "Put that picture back in his pocket and don't mention it to him." When Terri nodded, she went on, "I want to see you again this week. And I want to talk to you every day. We can talk as long as you want. You can get it all out with me, if that will help. But don't say anything to Ray. Not yet. You've got to get hold of yourself first."

Chapter Thirty-Five

San Francisco was cool and foggy, but as soon as Arla got over the Bay Bridge the sun glared down. By the time she got to Camargo, the time and temperature sign showed '1:12 PM 101 degrees.' Ah, she smiled, clicking the AC up a notch, home sweet home.

She drove past the mall site, slowing slightly. Oddly, it was deserted.

She had been back less than two hours when Ray called. "Can I come over?" he asked at once.

"Yes!" Arla said, surprised and thrilled that he would come over at three o'clock on a workday. She'd been expecting to have to wait to see him. "But if you want to wait until after work—"

"I want to come now. I missed you, Arla."

He was there within twenty minutes. She couldn't believe he was so apparently unconcerned about giving any of his coworkers reason to gossip or speculate.

"What did you tell them at work?" she asked as he carried her into the bedroom.

"I shut down early today. We can't work in this heat." He was nuzzling her neck. "And I laid off half the crew last week."

"Is something wrong? I thought this was going to be the busiest part of the job."

He brought her to the bed. "Let's talk about that later."

They made love with an uncommon urgency. Two weeks' worth of unfulfilled desire became something like desperation; she came, he came, and he laughed and said, "Let's rest for a minute. Then we'll get to the real lovemaking."

He enclosed her in his big arms, and held her as her heartbeat returned to normal.

Finally, he sighed and said, "I don't know what to do."

"What do you mean, angel?"

"Things can't stay like this forever."

"Why not? Aren't things fine as they are?"

"I guess so." He turned onto his back and pulled her onto him. "I was going half crazy, I missed you so much."

"You just missed the sex."

"I know how I feel," he said, and she could tell she had hurt his feelings.

"Oh Ray. I missed you, too." She sat up a bit, leaning her chin on his chest to look at him. "I kept one of the pictures of you in my purse and I was always taking it out to look at it."

"Which one?"

"Do you want to see it? You're like a work of art." She went and got the picture, handed it to him, and settled back down.

He seemed taken aback. "I never saw a picture of myself like this."

"You're wonderfully photogenic. Not every beautiful person is, you know."

"It looks like something out of *Playgirl*." He set the photograph on the bedside table.

Arla laughed. "That's what my friend Jen said, too."

Ray's face suddenly reddened. "You showed this to someone else?"

"Don't be mad because I bragged about you."

"Bragged about what about me?"

But some things, Arla cautioned herself, are better left unmentioned. She doubted that Ray, being male, could handle knowing the extent to which women sometimes shared their intimate lives with one another. So she answered, "Nothing all that personal."

"Nothing personal?" he repeated, and to her surprise he got out of bed. She had never seen him this agitated.

"Ray, please don't leave. Please. Can't we talk about this?"

"What's to talk about? Call up your girlfriends in New York, tell them the piece of ass got mad."

Without even realizing she was on the verge of tears, Arla began to cry. He stepped into his jeans. "That's not gonna keep me here."

"I didn't mean to cry—I'm not doing it for that—if you walk out we won't be able to talk about it. I can't call you. I can't come see you. This is our only chance."

He had been looking for his T-shirt, but he straightened up and looked at her. "All right. Let's talk in the kitchen."

Arla quickly pulled on a shirt and shorts. When she got to the kitchen he stood leaning against the counter, arms folded across his bare chest. She sat at the table in the bay windows. For several minutes, neither of them spoke.

"What if I did that to you?" he said. "Had a picture of you naked, showed it to a bunch of guys and bragged about how hot you were?"

"Men do things like that all the time."

"I don't. I don't talk to other people about private things."

She folded her hands on the table and focused on them. "Ray, I'm sorry I did that. It didn't even occur to me how wrong it was, and I'm sorry for that, too."

"I know women talk to each other about private stuff. I had an older sister I was pretty close to, and I've had close female friends all my life. But what you did shows I don't mean anything to you, except for sex."

"That's all we've ever agreed to be to each other."

"That's all it was at first." Finally, he came over and sat across from her. His blue eyes were bright and clear. "You're a beautiful woman and you were hot for me. And then we got together and the sex was hot, too." He rubbed his face. "This is hard for me to tell you, but I didn't think you'd be very deep, you know? I figured you were just a city woman having a good time with the kind of guy you'd never look at twice in New York or 'Frisco.

"But this isn't only about sex for me, not anymore." He looked right into her eyes. "So when you talk about me that way to your friends, I see it *is* only about sex for you."

"No, that's not true, but—" She hesitated.

"Go on. Like you said, it's our only chance to talk."

"That's it, Ray. That's it right there." The truth, which she had not dared acknowledge even to herself, began to spill out. "I haven't wanted to even consider you being more to me than a lover, because what if I did? I can't call you to try to get together; I have to wait for you to make the arrangements. I can't call you in the middle of the night if I'm feeling blue. We can't even go out to dinner and a movie like normal people." Annoyed with her tears, she hastily swiped at them. "I don't want you to leave your wife and you don't want to leave her. So, we have only one option: to never see each other outside the bedroom."

"You're right. That's the way it is and I don't know how it can be anything else." He sighed deeply. "Maybe we should just call the whole thing off."

Arla couldn't answer him right away. Now, at the thought of really losing him forever, she realized how very badly she wanted to keep him. But perhaps he was looking for an out, she thought, and said, "Is that what you want to do?"

"No!" He looked startled. "It's definitely not what I want to do, but if it would make things easier for you, I will."

"What do you want, though?"

"Me, you know what I want. But you got a point. So if it's too hard for you to deal with, things being the way they are, the world we live in being the way it is, then I'd understand. I admit I wouldn't like it, but I'd understand." He paused, looked at her searchingly. "So, what do you want to do?"

Arla's voice was low with emotion. "To spend every moment with you that I can. However few moments there are."

Later, as they lay in each other's arms, he murmured her name and pulled her even closer. "I love you."

"No, no—"

"Yes. I love you. I was afraid to tell you before, but when you were gone, I realized it. The sex wouldn't be this good if I didn't love you, don't you know that?"

"But Ray," she began, but he said "Shhh," and with his cheek he stroked her hair back from her face. His breath was warm on the back of her neck. "It's okay that you don't love me. It's better if you don't. Just love this. Love this."

For a few moments Arla hardly breathed. She dared not raise her eyes to his, dared not let him see what she knew was in them. He was married. He had children. Naturally, she felt momentary surges of love for him. Momentary surges, that was all they were.

"Are you cold?" he asked.

"A little," she whispered. Yes, that's why I'm trembling.

She fell asleep in his arms. When she woke at midnight, he was gone.

She got up and unpacked her suitcases, as well as the boxes of clothes that had arrived ahead of her. Morgan of course had got up with her, and he followed her through the house as though afraid to let her out of his sight.

When she brought the receipts into the den she saw the diary, just where she'd left it on her desk. She picked it up. There were only a few more entries and they were widely separated in time, at least compared to the earlier entries.

December 1886

Hiram told us that just today, he completed an agreement to sell a parcel to the county, upon which shall be constructed the new high school and the town library. It is the land where Russian Camp once stood.

For that land, ninety-three acres in all, for which Hiram paid $1,000, the county has paid $3,000. Hiram also stands to gain from the contract to build the high school and library, for his company shall do the construction and his mill shall supply the wood. The county has approved the cost of $50,000 for both buildings. Bonds have been issued for that purpose.

But the news of which Hiram informed us was that this windfall means that he shall build a new house, the grandest in Piñon County.

10 August 1887

Rosa and I worked in the garden today, tending the roses. We then walked through town and saw the lot upon which the new house is being built. I laid a red rose upon the soil.

That house is being built with blood money. I cannot live there.

When I told Hiram that I shall not live there, he said that I am suffering from nervous disorders and that unless I cease troubling him with vague accusations, he shall send me to a sanitarium for a rest cure.

He has poisoned the minds of our sons against me, for they too all treat me as gingerly as they would treat an ill person. I am not hysterical; I have no nervous disorder. I suffer from conscience. But that is a fatal affliction when one is married to a man such as Hiram.

November? 1887

It has been many months since I have written in this journal. I do not even know today's date, although it must be late in the month, as Thanksgiving has passed.

I cannot live in this house. I tried to leave in September and he sent men after me. They brought me back. But I cannot live on the fruits of his deeds. Why not name those deeds here, in the privacy of this book, which shall be given to my dear Rosa later tonight, for safekeeping? I shall name them. Arson. Fraud. Murder.

He burned those families out of their homes. He commissioned arson, which caused the death of one man. Two other men hanged for that crime. He then bought their land, pretending to do so at great financial sacrifice, yet he knew all the while the land would be purchased subsequently, at three times the price he paid for it.

I had thought that when Hiram sold the land at Russian Camp on such favorable terms, people would recall the accusation made by Bernie Jensen before he was executed. But if anyone recalls, they have remained silent. Instead, people chortle that Judge Cushing has the Midas touch; as an act of kindness, he purchased that worthless land, and it has turned to gold.

At Thanksgiving dinner, I listened as Hiram and our sons and the other men discussed the Haymarket case. Three of the convicted men had just been executed, and another committed suicide in prison. Hiram was well satisfied with the events. 'The Supreme Court was right to turn down the appeal,' he said. 'I don't know, Father,' Frederick replied. 'They are anarchists, true, but none was accused of participating in the bombing. Does the law truly provide for execution of a man merely for spreading ideas, however abhorrent those ideas may be?'

Hiram replied, in his most magisterial voice, that of course it did, and that he had faith in the judge who had heard the case, and all the judges thereafter who had ruled on the appeals.

And I said, 'So a man may be judged guilty when he has merely inspired a crime. What, then, if he actively plans one?'

They all stopped speaking and stared at me, for I so rarely voice an opinion on legal or political matters.

'Now, Catherine,' he said, a tone in his voice that

probably no one present but me understood to be a warning.

And I told them. I told them what he had done—their father, their uncle, their brother, the patriarch of their clan.

Not a single one of them believed me. They believed Hiram. He did not show his anger with me, not then. He shook his head and said that, 'Sadly, Catherine has been suffering delusions of late; she has a nervous disorder, so please be kind and understanding to her. Do not hold this against her, for she cannot help what she says.'

The women—my son's wife, the wives of Hiram's brothers, even Hiram's sister—lowered their eyes and said nothing. For they know what happens to a woman who displeases men.

And I do not think the men truly believe Hiram; I think they merely pretend to believe him. For he is powerful and wealthy and they, like he, crave power and wealth.

He is sending me away, in a way that disgraces me.

I feel grateful that my daughter died at birth, for had she lived, I could not bear what is to be done to me. So, I see now that God was right to take the child, though at the time I did not understand.

There is only one person who believes me: Rosa. But she is a woman, too. And she is married to a man with no power in this town.

This morning, when Rosa and I walked together after Mass, I said to her that I have just come to understand that mankind has suffered from the original sin in a way that is not commonly understood. When God expelled the first man and woman from the Garden of Eden, part of the punishment was that thereafter, the man would rule, and the woman would have no power. Humanity has since been ruled by men. And our world is dominated by war and greed and cruelty, for that is the nature of men.

And because men rule, they have lied about woman, put the blame on her for our fall from grace and used this accusation to bolster their contention that women are unfit to rule.

Rosa looked at me with fear in her eyes and whispered, 'That is heresy.'

Tomorrow I shall be taken away. He is sending me to a sanitarium. Rosa will come tonight to help me pack. I will ask her to secrete this book where no one shall find it, where it may be kept safely until it can perhaps serve to do good.

That was the last entry in the journal. Arla set it down.

Mary was still at her grandson's in Eugene. She would be back in Piñon County late next week and Arla knew that she would finally have to tell Mary about this journal. She knew that she ought to have done so long before now. She would have to tell Mary about it and accept the consequences of not having told her, of having taken it from the offices of the society without permission, and from then having concealed it.

Chapter Thirty-Six

Kit lolled her head against the car seat and closed her eyes as the cool night wind rushed over her face. With each passing moment, the barely lingering light of the day faded and a dozen more stars began to glitter. Thanks to the football game there were no other cars on the road, and Carlos's Volkswagen's headlights scarcely penetrated the darkness.

Tonight, she would call Priscilla, so that if Dad said anything Kit could pretend she'd been at the football game. She didn't have to know every single play, just how the game had gone in general. More important was to know what the other kids had been doing and whether anything memorable had happened, like a fight behind the stands or vandalism of the visiting team's bus.

She stole a glance at Carlos just as he was glancing at her. He smiled and a full feeling warmed her. His hand was on the gearshift and she almost felt jealous of it. Jealous of anything else lucky enough to feel his touch.

Too soon, they reached the turnoff to the Double-L. Carlos pulled in only far enough to turn his car around. Kit leaned over to kiss him goodnight. "Have fun," she said. "But be careful, too."

"I'll do both," he said, his lips caressing her cheek. "Call me Sunday afternoon. I should be home by five, after I get all the horses combed down and everything cleaned up and put away."

"I hope you won't be too tired."

"You're kidding, right?" He laughed. Oh, to move from his embrace felt like torture, but they both knew better than to linger here. He drove away.

Kit stepped over the cattle guard and jogged down the driveway. Sadie recognized her steps and whinnied, and Kit went over to say hello. "Oh Sade," she whispered, as the mare's rubbery lips nibbled at the sugar cubes in her hand. "I love him so much."

Mom was in the kitchen, just finishing cleaning up the dinner dishes. "Hi, Mom."

"Hello, darling." Mom hung the dishtowel on the rack. "Are you hungry?"

"Starving. What did you make?"

"Pot roast." Mom took a foil-covered plate from the refrigerator.

"Yum, let me have a bite." She peeled back the foil and took a chunk, then Mom put the plate in the oven.

"Sit down. I'll get you some salad." Mom set the food before Kit and sat across from her. Kit wondered why she didn't have a glass of booze.

"I'm so hungry." Kit added dressing to her bowl of salad.

"Didn't you get something to eat at the football game?"

She paused with her fork halfway up. It was one thing to have told Mom that she was friends with Carlos; she wasn't about to tell her that she and Carlos had just spent three hours together in a meadow west of town, and that they hadn't watched the sunset and hadn't had dinner and definitely hadn't gone to the football game. "Um, well, it was a while ago, and the food's so bad there."

She glanced up and found her mother looking at her intently.

"What?"

Mom shook her head and smiled.

WHEN SHE CAME down for breakfast Saturday morning, Dad was there already, irritable as always in the morning. Following his rule, there was no conversation. On weekdays he usually had breakfast at Elsie's, but Saturday was his busiest day at the real estate office and he liked to get an early start, so he ate breakfast at home.

Kit sat down and picked up the section of the paper with the comics. She noticed out of the corner of her eye the way Dad just held out his cup without saying anything. Didn't even look at Mom; just held out his cup without taking his eyes off the sports section. Kit gritted her teeth and busied herself with putting sugar and cream in her own coffee.

After a few minutes Dad gulped his coffee, set aside the paper and said, "Sometime this morning, Kit, go check on the paddock fence by the east ridge. PJ said the old bull's been over there a lot lately. Make sure the fence is holding up."

"Okay. I'll go right after breakfast."

"Laura, either you or PJ are gonna have to run down to the west county ranch today. Dick's got that guy coming out to fix the baler and he needs a check."

"What time will he be there?" Mom asked.

"Eleven. Get me some more orange juice."

"I'll have to squeeze some more, Pete." Mom went to the refrigerator. "It'll just take a few minutes."

A look of annoyance came onto Dad's face. "Here, Dad," Kit said quickly. "You can have mine. I feel like having milk."

"Thanks, Squirt." Dad drank the orange juice and left.

As his pickup tires crunched on the gravel, Mom said, "I'll get you some juice, Kit."

"It's okay," Kit replied, but Mom made the juice anyway.

By seven-thirty Kit was on Sadie, riding out. She'd loaded her saddlebags with tools and a small bag of concrete powder, a gallon of water, and a bucket. The turkey vultures were already gliding overhead, the sun was already relentless. She let Sadie set her own pace.

She wondered how far up the trail Carlos, Joe and the customers had got. The men they were guiding had come for golden trout, plentiful in Surprise Lake, which was about twenty miles this side of the pass. Perpendicular granite cliffs surrounded the lake on three sides, cutting it off from the forest enough so that overnight camping was allowed. But not campfires. Joe and Carlos had brought two portable cookstoves, and plenty of warm clothes for after the sun went down.

The grasses, leached almost white, crackled under Sadie's hooves. With each step, a cloud of frantic grasshoppers materialized, leapt to the right or left. Some didn't leap far enough, and the whole way across the field, Kit was picking them off herself, the saddle, and Sadie's mane.

They reached a grove of sugar pines and rode in the shade all the way to the fence, following it north until it took them back into the merciless sun. A hot breeze ruffled the air with an almost electric quality. Coming up over a hill, she spotted the old bull in the distance, rubbing his head against the double prong wire. She rode down the hill and sure enough, the fence posts leaned in like they were whispering to each other and the wire was all over the ground between them. "Oscar, why can't you just be nice and mellow and not cause any trouble?"

The bull stared at her, but his tail wasn't up so she dismounted, brushing off a couple of persistent grasshoppers. "I'm not gonna rope you, you old grouch." Oscar chewed his cud serenely, but kept an eye on her. At least now he was merely grouchy; he'd been awfully mean when young. He wasn't all that old, really—about ten—but past the age of being good for breeding. They had to keep him away from the cows to let the younger bulls take on that duty. If they didn't keep Oscar in his own pasture, the young bulls might not have a chance. He was bigger and more belligerent than any of them. Handsomer, too, she thought, glancing over.

Last year he'd broken a fence and got in with the herd. When PJ rode up, Oscar was mounting a cow. No telling how many others he'd mounted but three of last year's autumn calves bore his distinctive markings. The problem was, his calves weren't as sound as the calves of the younger bulls. But Oscar wasn't ready to retire yet.

She mixed up a batch of cement and poured it around three of the fence posts. But that was only a stopgap. She'd have to come back with PJ and put in new posts. She tightened up the barbed wire, for all the good that would do; Oscar would have it messed up again in no time.

If only there was something else for Oscar to scratch himself on, maybe he wouldn't keep ruining fences. And then, struck by inspiration, she stared at the two oak trees thirty yards apart. Well, why not? she asked herself, and set to work. She strung two strands from one oak tree to the other, pulling the barbed wire so tightly that it sang. She secured the wire with double-headed nails. The bark seemed thick enough that the short prongs and the quarter-inch nails wouldn't hurt the trees. She tore her kerchief into long strips and tied them to the barbed wire, so no animal would accidentally run into it.

Oscar watched her all the while. "You smart enough to

figure this out, old boy?" she said. "See, it's nice and tight and even you won't be able to bend these trees."

She rode away and, on the way up the ridge, glanced back. Oscar was standing in front of the wire. He seemed to be considering.

On the ridgetop she turned Sadie loose to munch whatever grass she could find and sat down to eat her lunch, looking down at the highway threading west and smoke rising from the mill. Cougar Lake twinkled in the bright sun.

When they got home, Mom's car was in the carport and PJ's pickup was gone. She was relieved that PJ instead of Mom had gone to west county.

She rubbed Sadie down, cleaned the tack and went into the house, leaving her dirty boots on the porch. Mom was making chili and the whole house smelled of it. Kit lifted the lid and took a couple spoonfuls to taste. Mom wasn't in the house and Kit went out back to look for her. She was in the garden, stooping over the tomatoes wearing her big straw hat, pulling weeds.

"Mom, it's too hot to be doing that."

"I've let it go too far already."

"Come get something cold to drink and let's go for a swim. I'll help you later on, after it cools down."

Mom smiled. "Those offers are too tempting to refuse."

A little later, they were on the patio sitting side by side on lounge chairs, both of them dripping wet, glasses of iced tea next to the chairs. Mom said, "Kit, could we talk for a few minutes?"

"What about?" Kit asked warily.

"About Carlos."

"There's nothing to worry about," she said firmly.

"I wish that were so, but we both know better."

Kit tried to figure out how to tell her that she and Carlos only made love in ways that didn't risk pregnancy. She couldn't figure out how to say it in a roundabout way. Then Mom said, "I'm not worried about what you do, Kit. I'm worried about what *other* people might do."

Dad, Kit said to herself. She was stunned that Mom was talking to her so openly. Mom must be scared of what he'd do to *her* if he found out, because he'd blame Mom, that was for sure.

Mom hesitated. "Kit, if you could just…"

"Just what?" she prompted, when Mom's voice trailed off.

Mom looked at her with a troubled expression. "Just be discreet, darling. And be very careful."

Chapter Thirty-Seven

For the sixth consecutive year they had lost money. They had already cut expenses to the bare bones. They had economized in every way possible. There was no way to get another loan even had they wanted one.

And now the letter. The final blow.

They had received a similar letter over a year ago. Then, the premium had been raised. Now, it was being doubled.

They would not be able to pay it. But they could not operate the business without liability insurance; that was the law. And there was nowhere to buy insurance other than through Patrick. They'd tried that already.

That first increase had been steep. This new one was simply impossible. They would have to close their business.

That was bad enough. But the situation was even worse: they owed money to suppliers, to the bank, and to the government. Without substantial income, there was no hope of paying those debts. They wouldn't likely find jobs, not at their ages and not in this economy.

So, what were their options? Earlier, they had speculated that they could sell the new pickup and all the horses except

Tabasco and Joe's horse, plus the saddles and gear. That would stave off the inevitable for a few months.

But only for a few months.

Stella closed her eyes. It had been her idea to start the outfitting business. Joe had been enthusiastic too, but she knew he never would have done it without her urging. They'd never regretted it, although they had struggled economically for years. And then, when they finally seemed to be over the hump, the drought struck. They had gotten themselves too far in to pull out, and the drought had gone on longer than anyone had imagined it would. Had they still been raising chickens they would've been fine.

She rose heavily to her feet to go and tell Joe they had lost. To tell him that this land he loved—even the original twenty-nine acres that had been his family's for a hundred years—must be sold, or else it would simply be taken.

"SO THAT'S WHY Cushing's lawyer wanted us to wait two weeks." Joe carefully fitted the board into the slot on the cabin stairs. "He knew our insurance was about to be doubled."

"But how could he know that?"

"Someone told him."

The import of Joe's words sank in, and Stella was incredulous. "You think *Patrick* told him?"

"It's a hell of a coincidence." He gently pushed the new board in as far as it would go.

Stella handed him nails, not speaking as he pounded in six of them. "That's good for now." He rested his gloved hand briefly on her forearm. "Let's go up to the porch and talk."

She took the old rotted board to the burn pile, then went to the porch and sat in the swing. Joe came out of the house with a pitcher of ice water and two glasses, and sat beside her. Then he said abruptly, "I want to ask Arla for a loan."

"Oh, Joe. We can't do that."

"We're out of options."

"But not that. No. We don't ask friends for money. We'll get jobs."

"You yourself told me we wouldn't be able to make the loan payments and feed ourselves and even just two horses on the sort of jobs we're liable to get. We'd each have to get a job with a paycheck after taxes of $300 a week. Do you know what that means?" He looked at her. "It means both of us have to find jobs that pay ten dollars an hour."

"I know." Stella sighed. Few businesses in Piñon County were hiring. And none were offering that much. "But Joe, you know all the reasons why it's a bad idea to borrow money from friends. And besides, we really have no idea how much money she has. For all we know, she spent everything she has to buy that house."

"For all we know, she has considerably more. It might mean nothing to her to loan us what we need."

"Money never means nothing, not even to rich people. *Especially* not to rich people. Good lord!" Stella groaned. "She'll be appalled that we asked her. It will end the friendship. And it's not as if we're close friends! We don't know her that well, not well enough to ask her for that kind of money!"

"Stella, don't forget," Joe said gently, "Arla moved to Piñon County after we helped her learn to love it. She might be more appalled if we lost the ranch to developers without offering her the chance to save it."

"But how would we ever repay her? We can't keep afloat on the business anymore. No matter what happens, I think we've got to face that."

"I know. We can go back to raising chickens. There's a growing market for good chicken, raised the way we always did

—chickens that roam around the yard and eat good grain and insects, not spending their lives in cages and getting antibiotics and having their beaks clipped. We both know the business; we could do well."

"Yes, I think we could."

"If she can loan us $34,000 we'll pay off the bank. Then we'll sell the stock like we planned and use that money to set ourselves up."

Stella thought regretfully of how cheaply they'd sold the egg washer and chicken coops, and how much it would now cost to replace them.

"But to repay her might take years. And maybe we wouldn't be able to."

"Then she would have the land as collateral. I would rather *she* repossess it than the bank."

"Maybe she'd just turn around and sell it to developers."

"No, she wouldn't. She doesn't want Piñon County to look like Contra Costa."

"Things will be different around here in ten years," Stella said. "There might be three more malls besides this one they're building, and twenty more developments like Blackberry Springs. And she might think that's fine, that it's better than the alternative of houses all squeezed together the way they are in the Bay Area. After all, she *lives* in Blackberry Springs; to her that's a country home."

"Arla knows what it would mean to have ten or twenty more developments like that in Piñon County."

"But maybe in ten years, if the county's built up even more than it is now, she'll think it's useless to try to preserve this land."

"On the contrary. In that circumstance, wouldn't she be even more inclined to preserve the land?"

"But in ten or twenty years, she might need money."

"She might," Joe agreed.

They sat in silence for a while. Finally Stella said, "Let's draw up a proposal, Joe, something in writing. Explaining our current situation and what we need to get us through. I'll start putting it together today."

Joe nodded. "I'll call and ask if we can talk to her next week sometime."

Chapter Thirty-Eight

Ray stared at the foundation wall. A month ago, he would've insisted on tearing the whole thing out and starting over. But he thought of Cushing's oily voice saying "…with any other intimate friend" and thought, the hell with it! "Let's try and fix it," he said.

Billy and Eddie exchanged a brief glance. "I don't know," Billy said dubiously.

"If we put in another brace right here, and pour in some more concrete, that might work."

"Might not," Eddie commented.

"Yeah, I know, so if it don't, we'll tear it out and start over. But let's try."

Perspiration poured from Ray as he pushed the wood hard while the concrete came down the chute. The men were yelling instructions and warnings to each other. He just pushed, pushed until his muscles trembled from the strain. Finally, it was done and they inspected it. "Looks all right," Billy said.

"We'll let it sit overnight and look it over in the morning," Ray said. "If it still looks good then we'll leave it."

They knocked off twenty minutes later. Ray thought

yearningly of Arla, but he knew he wouldn't be able to see her today. She'd been back a week now. They'd been together three times since, and it wasn't enough for him. You're in trouble, boyo, he told himself.

A few days after that conversation, he'd decided to just ask Cushing, man to man, what he meant; whether Cushing was referring to Arla, or just to Ray's reputation for having lady friends. So he'd driven up to Cushing's house after work one night, intending to have it out.

When he got there he'd been surprised to see PJ Jensen's pickup truck parked out front. Well, no way was he going to talk to Cushing with PJ there. He had turned around and left.

That was the only time he'd even considered confronting Cushing. Every day since then, he just went straight home after work, like today.

He pulled up in front of the house and went inside. Terri was sitting at the breakfast nook with a glass of iced tea. Her eyes were red and swollen. His heart began to pound with fear. "Terri, what's wrong?" he said. "Are the kids…?"

"The kids are at your mom's. They're fine. You and I have to talk, Ray."

And his heart lurched because he knew what was coming.

* * *

IT WAS ALMOST dark by the time Ray staggered out of the house, got into the Eagle pickup and drove away. The truck bounced over ruts and skidded on rocks as the argument replayed in his mind.

First, he'd started the Dumb Male act, but Terri had held up her hand. "Stop, Ray. You'll just piss me off even more. I know. Okay? I know. I'm not going to tell you how I found out, but I did and it's indisputable. So let's go from that point."

He'd been too stunned to respond to what she said and

resorted to a different form of denial. "So, you just assume your source is telling the truth and I'm lying?"

"Damn you, I told you not to do this!" she'd retorted, and it all went downhill after that. "…You humiliate me in front of everyone in town and you betray your family—not just me—the kids too. Trixie has to go to school with the teachers and half the kids knowing she has a father who sleeps around. Doesn't that bother you at all?"

And then she began to cry. "I didn't mean to yell and scream. I wanted to talk calmly. I just want to know why, Ray."

But of course, nothing he said made a difference, except to make her even angrier. "Oh, for God's sake, spare me that! 'I love you, Terri.' Yeah, sure! That's why you can't keep your pants zipped … I know, I know, you can't explain it, it just happened. I've heard it before, Ray. All that means is you don't think with your brain; you think with your dick."

"This is different!"

"What's different is she probably has a nice tight–"

"Terri, don't say that."

"Oh, so sorry, mustn't use an indelicate word when I'm talking about your piece of ass."

He flushed at that, that she'd used the exact phrase to describe Arla that he'd accused Arla of using about him. "That's not what she is!"

"It's *exactly* what she is!"

"No, it's not, goddamn it! I love her!"

She jumped back. Her hands came up to her face as if to ward off a shockwave. Then she turned and made her way unsteadily toward their bedroom. After a few moments, he went in after her. She was lying face-down on the bed.

"Terri," he began, but she lifted her arm to silence him.

"No more."

The pickup suddenly whomped against a big hole in the

road. He saw the windshield coming toward him and then didn't see anything.

He came to crammed against the door. His scalp was speckled with tiny pieces of glass and blood. The windshield was cracked. Gingerly, he stretched his limbs and finally got out of the truck. Except for a couple cuts and a bump on his head, he felt fine. But the pickup had gone off the road into a dry ditch. He got back in and tried to drive forward, but the wheels spun. He put it in reverse, but that didn't work either. The damned gully was so deep and sandy that even with four-wheel drive, he was stuck fast. Or maybe he'd broken an axle. That would really top the day off, if he'd broken the axle in a company truck.

Get a hold of yourself, he chided. He walked around for a few minutes until his anger and irritation subsided. Then he got on the CB and called for a tow truck.

"What the hell you doing out there, Ray?" the guy at the local Triple A said.

"Can you get a tow truck here or not?"

"Sure, I'll send Mickey. He oughta be there in about twenty minutes."

It was just as well. Twenty minutes gave him time to calm down even more. He picked bits of glass out of his hair and wiped the blood from his face, checking his reflection in the side mirror, which also showed an angry lump on his forehead.

"You wanna go to the hospital, Ray?" asked Mickey as they hooked up the tow truck.

"No, just get me on the road, I'm fine."

"You been drinking?"

"Not yet," Ray said grimly.

Mickey towed him out to the paved road and waited while he crawled underneath the pickup to inspect it, and while he test drove it. The truck seemed fine mechanically and Ray could still see through the windshield enough to drive.

Tomorrow, he'd bring it into the shop to make sure, and to get the spidered windshield replaced. He waved Mickey off and headed toward the highway.

And all at once his anger and confusion dissolved, because he realized that since everything was out in the open now, he could be with her. He wouldn't have to live this double life anymore. No matter what calamities awaited him, he had that.

He wondered how she'd feel about living with the kids. Because he wasn't going to just give up custody; they would have to share it fifty-fifty. Terri would have to agree that was best for the kids. If she got spiteful … well, no point in trying to figure things out that far in the future.

"Hey, Raymundo," called PJ when Ray walked into the Tavern. PJ was at a table with Jerry Frye. Jerry had been one of the casualties two weeks ago, but he hadn't seemed all that concerned about it, telling Ray that he would just live on unemployment until Eagle began hiring again.

Ray stopped at the bar to order Jack with a beer back. Seeing PJ reminded him of having seen PJ's truck the other day up at the old man's house. Come to think of it, why had PJ been up there? PJ didn't own any of the Jensen property, and he wasn't exactly the brains of the family either.

He got his drinks, paid Fred and joined PJ and Jerry. "What the hell happened to you?" Jerry said.

"Ran off the road and bumped the windshield."

"Better get that looked at, man."

"It's fine." He drank the shot in one long gulp and his eyes watered.

PJ started in immediately. "You gonna chug whiskey, why the hell don't you drink rotgut?"

"I like Jack Daniel's," Ray said.

"He used to do that when we were in high school," PJ told Jerry. "Didn't matter what we were drinking, he'd chug it down." PJ proceeded to tell Jerry a couple of stories about

Ray's escapades. Ray remembered them differently, but why bother to correct him? PJ remembered things the way he wanted to.

Ray went to the bar with his empty shot glass and Fred filled it. He returned to the table.

"That was when Ray was always pissed off at his old man," PJ was saying. "So, who're you pissed off at tonight, Raymundo?"

Ray didn't respond, not even to look up and glower at PJ. He drank half the whiskey in one gulp.

"You get into a fight with the old lady? Huh? She read you the riot act?"

PJ and Jerry both chortled.

"Yeah, that must be it. The old lady laid down the law. Now, some women won't do that; they know better than to try that. But Raymundo's always been too easy with women."

"Women can smell that in a man," Jerry said.

"That's right, and when they do, they go for the soft spots."

Ray finished the Jack and started on the beer.

"My old lady used to try that shit with me," Jerry said. "She found out right quick she better not."

"Yeah," Ray said, "I'm talking to two experts on women here."

"I don't claim to be an expert on women, but I damn sure know you have to let a woman know who's boss," PJ said. "That's your problem, Ray; you don't do that."

"You think I need you telling me what my problems are?"

PJ held up his hands in a stop gesture. "Hey, take it easy."

"Relax, man," Jerry chimed in.

"I'm relaxing just fine. Got a ways to go to catch up to you two." Ray drained the rest of his beer, caught Fred's eye and held up the empty mug.

"Don't worry about this," Jerry said, gesturing to the bottle.

"I ain't drinking again, not like before. This is all I'm drinking —beer, and just this brand."

"What the hell is it?" Ray asked, not recognizing the bottle.

"Bear piss." PJ chortled.

"*Watered down* bear piss," Jerry corrected.

Ray looked at the label. "Oso Grande Pale Amber Ale. There's a brewery over there?"

"Yeah, it started up a year ago. Fred's been carrying it a couple months. This here's three-two, that's why I'm drinking it."

"You could have Bud Light," Ray said. "Probably cost you half as much."

"Yeah, but this stuff tastes ten times better'n Bud Light. It ain't bad. Wanna try some?"

Ray shook his head and retrieved his drinks from the end of the bar. He half-listened as PJ talked about the guy who was replacing Stick as sheriff. Ayres wasn't a Piñon County native; he'd grown up down below. (Sixty miles from Piñon County, Ray noted, but that made him an outsider.) He was a college-educated, by-the-book guy.

Finally, Ray said, "Didn't Stick pick him as his replacement?"

"Yeah, yeah." PJ waved dismissingly. "But he had to. The supervisors wanted Ayres, and they're the ones got the final say-so. They figure if Ayres is acting sheriff for a couple years, he's a shoo-in next election because he's the incumbent."

"Same way Stick got the job," Ray observed.

Jerry told a story about a sheriff in Mendocino that concluded with a rant about the tree huggers ruining his life.

"Ain't that simple, Jerry."

"The hell it ain't," Jerry returned. "The mill's down to one shift. And now the mall's on hold."

"How can you blame that on the tree huggers?" Ray said, watching PJ out of the corner of his eye. He didn't want to hear Jerry's rants, but he did want to hear what Jerry knew about the situation, or thought he knew. Because whatever that was, it had to be coming from PJ.

"Look, Ray. I know I'm not the smartest guy around, but even I'm smart enough to figure out what's up. Cushing sold that mall with the idea there'd be more people living here. That means building houses."

"Like the places we're building up off Gennessee Mine Road."

Jerry snorted. "I ain't talking about pissant developments with a hundred houses."

"Then what the hell *are* you talking about?"

Jerry looked around to make sure no one else was listening. "Something big. Something real big, right here in east county, close to the mall."

Ray glanced at PJ. He was looking off toward the pool table, as though the conversation was of no concern or interest to him. Then Jerry said, "Somewhere like the Double-L, for instance."

PJ's gaze returned to the table and collided with Ray's. He patted the pockets of his shirt. "Jerry, can you go out to the truck and get my tobacco?"

"Yeah, sure. Is it locked?"

PJ tossed him the keys. When the door swung shut behind Jerry, PJ said in a low voice, "I know you know about this already."

"About what?"

"The development."

"I heard a rumor," Ray said. "I didn't know it had anything to do with you, except you might be selling him your ranch."

"Yeah, we're selling him the spread, and Dad's gonna handle the real estate after the lots are cleared." Annoyance crossed PJ's face. "Why the hell am I telling you this? You already know."

"Why do you think I already know?" Ray returned.

"Cushing told you all about it."

"So you been talking to Cushing about me."

PJ's scar gleamed in the dim bar light. "No, I never talk to Cushing. I hear things from other people that talk to him."

Drunk as he was, Ray's antenna for danger still worked. He forced himself to look away from PJ. *Someone's been talking to the old man about my private life, but it wasn't you. You don't talk to him; you just park your pickup in front of his house.* "You're selling him your ranch," he said carefully. "You doing that without talking to him?"

Jerry arrived back at the table, handed PJ the can of Skoal and his truck keys, and sat back down. PJ pushed a wad of tobacco into his cheek. "Go ahead, Jer, tell him the rest. You figured most of it out yourself."

Jerry grinned. "PJ's place is a good size, but the acreage by the river's too rocky to build on. So I figure the old man wants Pardini's land, too. Some of it, anyway. If he gets the northern half of Pardini's place and the northern half of the Jensen spread, then he's got all that nice flat land right next to the highway to put houses on."

"Sounds good," Ray said, "but it'd all depend on Cushing being able to get both those parcels."

Jerry took a long swig of his Oso Grande Pale Amber. "PJ's old man promised to sell his land, so that leaves the Pardinis."

Ray paused with the shot glass almost to his lips. "Maybe they don't want to sell."

"For the time being," Jerry said. His eyes narrowed slyly and he cast a sideways grin at PJ. "But hey, don't worry. Everything's gonna work out just fine."

"That's right," PJ agreed. "It won't be long. By this time next week, I wouldn't be surprised if Pardini signs the whole place over."

Ray drained his beer and stood up. "I gotta go."

"You think you oughta drive?" Jerry said. "Liable to end up with a DUI in your condition."

"Yeah, and with that bump on your head, the booze'll be hitting you harder than usual," PJ added.

Ray started to object that he was fine, but when dizziness suddenly swept over him, he realized they were right. There were only three cabs in the whole county, but Roxanne lived just up the street. She could give him a ride. He stepped into the hot heavy night and headed up the hill toward her place.

Chapter Thirty-Nine

Roxanne knew she wouldn't be able to get to sleep that night without cooling off. She took a quick shower and got into the long T-shirt that doubled as a nightgown. God, she hated this time of year! Like a guest whose charm had worn off hours earlier, impervious to everyone else's yawns, summer lingered—and not unobtrusively, but hogging center stage—until autumn got impatient and realized that polite hints were not enough and finally, with claps of thunder and torrential rains, hustled summer out the door.

But that was probably weeks away. Until then, everyone suffered and worried. So far, there had been only a few grass fires, quickly extinguished. But forest fires were burning all over the west; fire season was in its peak.

Today, Clay had come into Wanda's shortly after the lunch rush. He'd told her that a Red Flag Warning had been issued that morning, but some local crews had already been sent to fires in other places.

"Oh no. So we're short-handed here?"

"Yeah." Clay nodded. "If we get a fire they might have to

draft local men to fight it, like they did back when we were kids."

"That was still happening when you were a kid?"

"Hey, I ain't *that* young!"

"That's a matter of opinion." She'd grinned, and refilled his coffee. "I remember my dad was once gone for a week on a fire. It's strange to think how back then, they used mostly working men and prisoners to fight fires, but the fires did get put out."

"Wildfires were different then," Clay had said. "Not so close to civilization. But we got a lot more civilization now. The population's almost double what it was in 1960."

"It used to rain a couple times every summer back then, too. That probably kept the fire danger down."

"I can't remember the last time we had rain in the summer," Clay had said morosely. They'd both looked out the window at dirt and trash swirling around in the parking lot, and had exchanged a worried look: wind without rain.

Now, sitting in her living room, remembering that conversation, she shuddered. A big fire probably wouldn't endanger the towns, but houses and ranches in the outlying areas could be lost and the forest itself would be devastated. That could put a big dent in tourism for years to come; people didn't want to hike or ride into wilderness areas devastated by fire. They wanted tall pine trees and grassy meadows.

If the Higuera caught fire, Wanda might get a contract to supply meals. She'd close the café to the public and call in all the staff to work overtime serving hot meals to any firefighting personnel that came in, usually the supervisors and coordinators. They would also prepare sack lunches for firefighters on the lines.

The last such contract, Wanda had been paid well, which was fair because it was her only business for as long as the fire lasted.

There would be plenty of overtime for the employees. And even though the people who came in to Elsie's for a hot meal didn't have to pay, just sign for it, they did leave tips. Good tips, since they weren't paying for the food out of their own pockets.

Suddenly, footsteps sounded outside. Baba Looey leaped off her lap and ran down the hall to hide. For a few moments Roxanne froze in fear: her first thought was that Pete Jensen had found out about Carlos and Kit and had come here drunk, with mayhem on his mind. She thought of her revolver in the drawer next to her bed.

But it was Ray's voice saying, "Roxanne, it's me."

She opened the door and as he stepped inside, she saw a nasty swelling on his forehead and spots of blood in his hair. "What's wrong?"

"Nothing, I'm fine." He gestured dismissingly. "Ran off the road and cracked the windshield with my head."

Roxanne winced. "You must've hit it hard."

"Naw, I hit it just right." He touched the bump gently. "I was hoping you could give me a ride. But I see you're about to go to bed; maybe I could just use your phone?"

He was pretty drunk, slurring his words a little and not too steady on his feet. "I'll give you a ride home, Ray, but maybe you ought to go to the emergency room and make sure that's not serious."

"This happened hours ago. Seven-thirty, eight, around there. If it was serious I'd be passed out by now."

"Well, it's your call. I'll get dressed." She went to her room and hastily pulled on clothes and shoes. When she returned to the kitchen, Ray was still standing exactly where he had been a few minutes ago.

"You ready?"

"I don't wanna go home."

"Oh Ray. No, no, no, don't say anything you'll regret telling me."

"I wanna go to Arla's. She's out, but I'll wait for her there."

"Damn it," Roxanne groaned. "Why do you have to get me in the middle of this? No, I'm not driving you to her house! Terri's my friend, Ray!"

"Terri knows about it." He sank heavily into one of the kitchen chairs.

"You had an argument?" Roxanne sat across from him. "That's why you went out and got drunk and had a wreck?"

"Nope. Had the wreck first, then got drunk." He laughed harshly. "Figures I'd do it ass-backwards."

"Did Terri kick you out?"

He shook his head.

"Go back home, then. Don't make a rash decision tonight, not in your condition and not after an argument."

"It's not rash. I love Arla."

Anger began to simmer in Roxanne. You're all alike, she wanted to say. All of you! Marry a woman when she's young and pretty. Make the usual promises. Start a family, knowing it means she'll become a different person and your marriage will change and give you your excuse. Knowing that because of motherhood, she won't any longer devote her every breathing moment to you, the great manchild. But she'll trust in your love and devotion as husband and father, thinking that it won't matter that she has to think of the kids' needs more than yours, won't matter that she doesn't have the time to spend on a stationary bike getting rid of the extra weight she put on to bear the children (*your* children), won't matter that your interests aren't running on the same tracks anymore.

Instead, the next thing she knows, he finds himself a woman who thinks of no needs but his, a woman who devotes her time to making herself beautiful for him, a woman who makes his passions and interests her own.

It was tempting to let him go to Arla Stinson's and find out that she didn't want to live with him. And that wasn't inconceivable; after all, Arla didn't depend on any man … not economically, anyway. But it wasn't only Ray's life that would be ruined.

Roxanne sighed. "Maybe she'll think you just turning up is an invasion of her privacy."

After a few moments of silence, Ray began to talk, more to himself than to Roxanne. "Yeah, I gotta ask her first. Can't just assume. She's not the kinda woman who appreciates assumptions." He pushed back from the table. "You can drive me home?"

Roxanne nodded yes. Carlos's light was out now, but she left a note. As they got into her pickup, she chided herself for playing the usual thankless eternal feminine role: supporting a man and keeping him from getting into even worse trouble.

But maybe it was simply that she was being a good person, she thought, starting the engine as Ray slumped against the door on the passenger side. Maybe it was just one more instance of doing the right thing without expecting thanks or appreciation, in the hopes that her karma would one day even out the scales of her life. Besides, she was doing this more for Terri and the kids than for Ray.

She glanced over at him. She hadn't seen him this drunk since high school. It wasn't until after his father left Piñon County that he stopped treating it as though it were his job to get drunk—something grim and necessary.

"What?" he muttered, apparently feeling her eyes on him.

"I was remembering when we were kids and used to get drunk."

"I'm probably gonna feel just as sick tomorrow morning as I used to feel then, trying to get up and go to school."

"Well, it probably won't be that bad. Unless you had a jug of Red Mountain, a half-pint of sloe gin and a six pack of Hamm's."

"Oh Christ," Ray groaned. He leaned out the window and

Roxanne rolled to a stop as he heaved out whatever it was he had actually drank at the Tavern. Finally, he was finished. "Could you stop at the gas station?"

She pulled into the closed Chevron station. Ray turned the hose on himself, rinsed his hair and face and hands, then washed off the side of her pickup while she smoked a cigarette. "You all right?" she asked, getting more worried about that head injury.

Ray nodded. "Roxanne, I know you go to work early in the morning, but do you feel like just riding around for a little while?"

"I don't mind. It's too hot to sleep, anyway."

They drove at random on the old roads that wound around in the hills that encircled Camargo. Roxanne realized she was on Yosemite Road, which dead-ended behind the cemetery. She drove all the way up and pulled into the dirt.

"The old hangout," Ray commented.

"I come up now and then." She turned off the engine and it ticked in the night air. "Want to get out, or sit in the truck?"

"Let's get out. Maybe the fresh air'll clear my head."

They walked down onto the paths between the graves. When a barn owl suddenly lit out in front of them with a flash of bright white, they both jumped, then looked at each other and grinned.

They sat down on the grass. Roxanne leaned back and stared up at the stars. "What are you gonna do, Ray?"

"I don't know." His sigh was more like a groan. "Christ, I don't know."

"Well…"

"I know, got no one but myself to blame."

"Obviously," Roxanne said, and he gave her a wry smile.

"Hey, don't hold back, Rox. Tell me what you think." He paused. "But you know, I been remembering how it was when we were young. We didn't have these attitudes. We didn't want to be thirty years old with the same old values our parents had."

"But Ray, we were kids. Things were different."

"That's what I'm getting at: why? Why were they different? What happened to all of us? Is it just getting married that makes people change their ideas? Or is it getting old?"

"I don't know, but I'm getting mad!" Roxanne exclaimed. "You're trying to justify something after the fact. If you wanted an open marriage, why didn't you talk about it with Terri *before* you slept with another woman? Afterward is too late, Ray." She looked at him and shook her head. "Sometimes I think you've got empathy with women. Then you go and act like every other man."

"What do you mean by that?"

Roxanne hesitated, then said bluntly, "*She* doesn't sleep with other people, and you do."

Before he could answer, she waved her hand. "Come on; I'll drive you home now."

Chapter Forty

Walking toward Roxanne's pickup, Ray felt a lot more clear-headed than he had when he left the bar. Although he was sure, what with all the alcohol and kissing the windshield, that he was going to wake up tomorrow with a vicious headache.

"Ray, will you tell me something?"

"I dunno. Ask me."

"Do you still love Terri?"

"Yes, I do. And I like her. She's my best friend."

They reached her pickup and got in. He slumped against the door and stared out the open side window. His clothes were still damp from when he'd washed off at the gas station and, reaching up to scratch his head, he felt little bits of glass all over his scalp.

For a while he'd started feeling better, but Roxanne had brought him back to reality with a thud. He'd lied to Terri and then he'd hurled the truth at her like a knife. Even if he was free to love Arla openly, assuming she wanted it too, he had hurt Terri and had changed everything between them irrevocably and forever.

"I got another question," Roxanne said as she turned the ignition. Her pickup whined before the engine finally caught.

"What?" he asked, warily.

She cast him a sidelong look. "Relax, Ray. It's nothing to do with what we were just talking about."

He picked another chip of glass from his hair. "What, then?"

"Have you heard any rumors about SlidePac?"

"You mean besides the one that they're gonna close the mill for good?"

"Right, besides that." Roxanne turned her eyes from his face to the rear window and backed the pickup out.

"No, but what else is there to hear?"

"Something about Pine Gap. Something like they're buying out everyone in town, or trying to. They made me an offer for thirty thousand. I couldn't figure out why they'd want to buy my place; I'm not a laid-off mill worker."

He made an I-don't-know shrug.

"I talked to a couple other people who own houses in the Gap and don't work at the mill. They got offers, too." She shifted into low for the steep hill into town. "All we can figure is they want the town empty as some kind of tax write-off."

"Yeah, maybe."

"But then I started wondering if there's something else going on. You work construction. If SlidePac was going to sell Pine Gap, you'd have heard a rumor, wouldn't you?"

"Yeah, probably, but I haven't heard anything like that."

"Would you tell me if you had?"

Ray looked at her quickly. He couldn't quite see her expression in the dark, but he heard the bitterness in her voice. He felt wounded that she'd think he would withhold something like that from her. She was one of his oldest friends, almost like a sister.

"Don't take it wrong. You work for Hiram Cushing, so–"

"He doesn't own me. Christ, I'm getting sick of people talking like I'm his goddamned bootlicker." Ray stared out the side window for a moment. "I'm gonna quit Eagle."

The pickup slowed to a stop in the middle of the deserted side street. He glanced over; she was looking at him, wide-eyed.

"When did you decide that?"

"I've been thinking about it for quite a while. I don't want the kind of pressure he's putting on me. I'm not keeping anything from you, but that's the kind of guy he *wants* me to be. The kind who'd keep something like that from his oldest friend."

Roxanne leaned over and hugged him. Surprised, Ray hugged her back.

"I thought you'd forgotten who your oldest friend is," she said.

"Same here."

"You thought I'd forgotten?"

"Yeah, except only an old friend would talk to me the way you do."

They both laughed. Roxanne put the pickup in gear again. Almost to Main Street, she said, "You think there's any place open? I really have to pee."

"The Argonaut." He gave her a sidelong grin.

"Not without my wading boots."

"Pull in to the Eagle office. I've got a key."

Ray unlocked the door, deactivated the burglar alarm, and directed Roxanne to the bathroom. He was surprised to see Cushing's office door ajar. Normally the office was kept locked when Cushing wasn't in it. "Hiram?" he said, then told himself of course Cushing wouldn't be here; the burglar alarm had been on. Someone—Cushing or his secretary or the receptionist—had forgotten to lock the door.

He peered inside the office. The cockatiel's cage was covered and no lights were on. He reached around the door to push the lock. But something caught his eye. Straight ahead, on the big conference table, sat a large architectural model. He walked over to it and turned on the lamp above the table.

At the bottom of the model was a brass label: 'Gold Slope, Piñon County, 1990.' He stared down and oriented himself, compared what the model showed to what existed in the real world right now, and as he realized what he was seeing, he drew back in shock. Because what he saw was a development that spread across not only the Pardini and Jensen ranches, but over what was now the lumber mill, and over Pine Gap, too.

Pine Gap was covered with luxury houses. The lumber mill was gone, replaced by what looked like condominiums on the western half. On the eastern side were two tall buildings surrounded by parking lots, a pool and a park. This was labeled 'Assisted Living Facilities.'

On the section of Cougar Lake owned by SlidePac, the small pier had been replaced by a sprawling resort building and several wharves, replete with lifelike details like docked houseboats and a walkway lined by date palms.

To the east, on what was now Pardini Ranch, was a large golf course. Not an 18-hole course, Ray realized, but 36 holes. Cushing had said an 18-hole course used about 250 acres, so this one must use at least 500. In the valley, where the Pardinis' house and outbuildings currently stood, were a clubhouse and restaurant.

East of the golf course, over the rest of the Pardini Ranch and covering most of the Double-L, hundreds of houses dotted the terrain. This section was labeled 'Gated Community.'

And below, coming from the west, was a freeway. Two lanes in each direction, it ran through Piñon County like an arrow, bypassing downtown Camargo and ending at High Mountain Mall, where it rejoined the Higuera Highway.

"Ray?"

"In here. You better come see this."

"What is it? A miniature train set?" And then, as she looked more closely, "Oh Ray."

"Guess you should wait for SlidePac to raise their offer," he said grimly. He felt stone cold sober.

"So this is why they're trying to buy out everyone in Pine Gap." Then she exclaimed, "But you told me you didn't know!"

"I didn't. I knew he had something in mind, but not this." Ray looked around the office and went to the large filing cabinet. It wasn't locked. He opened the first drawer. "You go ahead and take off, Rox. I can walk home from here."

"What, and leave my oldest friend to get busted all by himself?"

"Okay then. You know how to run a copy machine?"

"If it's not too fancy."

"It's out past the reception desk in the next office. It has to be warmed up."

He looked through all four drawers and found nothing. He went to Cushing's desk. It wasn't locked and in one drawer he found a folder identified as 'Gold Slope.' Inside was the contract between Slidell-Pacific and Eagle.

There was also a correspondence folder; letters were filed chronologically, with the latest on top. One letter caught his eye, because just beneath the address was 're: PARDINI.'

```
Bob,


People familiar with Pardini's financial
situation tell me he's in debt up to his
neck, with nothing coming in. He won't
be able to refuse to sell any longer,
not even if we offer him less than we
```

<pre>
did the last time. Call me next week and
let's talk about how much less …
</pre>

So Cushing had lied to him. Pardini did not want to sell his land.

The letter was to a lawyer in San Francisco. At least he thought it was a lawyer; the company was only a bunch of last names not separated by commas, and the address was Four Embarcadero Center.

There wasn't time to read through everything. He brought the two folders to the copy machine. Roxanne made the copies and Ray returned the originals to the files. It took half an hour.

He put the files back in Cushing's desk drawer and turned off the lamp while Roxanne shut down the copy machine. Leaving, he hesitated outside the door to Cushing's private office.

"What?" Roxanne said.

"It's usually kept locked, but it was open when we got here. Cushing or his secretary must've forgotten to lock it tonight."

"Then leave it the way you found it."

"I don't know if I should. He'll be able to tell from the alarm company records that I was here—and for how long. I don't want him guessing I went into his office."

"Won't he come in tomorrow and remember he forgot to lock it, then wonder why it's locked now?"

"I don't think so. You know how it is; you're always thinking you forgot to do something like that and it usually turns out you didn't forget." He pushed the lock and pulled the door closed, then tested to make sure it was locked. As they left the building, he reactivated the alarm.

"What are you going to do with that stuff?" Roxanne asked as they drove through Camargo toward his house.

"Probably better if you don't know." Not that he knew

himself what to do with it, except for one thing. He had to let Joe and Stella Pardini know what was going on.

At home, he let himself in as quietly as possible and went into the spare room. It was well after one o'clock before he finally fell asleep.

Chapter Forty-One

It was after midnight when Arla got home from the Historical Society dinner. She let Morgan out and went into the kitchen for a glass of ice water. The diary was on the counter. She'd intended on bringing it tonight before she'd found out that Mary wouldn't be there; she had the flu.

Tipsy enough to worry about spilling water on the diary, Arla put it into the gadget drawer. Then she saw her answering machine blinking. Ray had left a message that he would come by around lunch time.

She went for a run early, before the sun was up. The winds were hot and dry and the air felt full of electricity. Unsettled, she cut her run short.

Just before noon she heard Ray's truck. To her surprise, he pulled right into her driveway.

"You're hurt!" she exclaimed at the big purple bump on his forehead.

He didn't answer. He swept her into his arms and held her tightly.

"Just hold me," he said. She led him into the living room. They sat on the sofa and she did hold him, and he held her too: held her close, buried his head against her neck. She brushed his hair back and rested her hand on his cheek. Tiny shards of glass glinted in his hair. They sat there a long time like that.

Finally, Ray sighed and began to talk. "I don't know what to do. Everything's falling apart. Cushing called me in when you were in New York. He knows about us."

"He knows about us!"

"Yeah. He never said your name, just hinted he knew, like he could blackmail me into doing what he wanted."

"What did he want you to do?"

"Cut corners on the job." His face reddened. "Yesterday, I told the guys not to redo a bad foundation wall, just try to patch it up. I'm doing the old man's dirty work." He groaned, his head falling back onto the sofa. "And I found out he's even dirtier than I thought, and he's been playing me like the gullible fool I am."

"What do you mean?"

But Ray didn't answer that. He shook his head and said, "And things aren't going too good at home, either."

"Did she find out?"

"Yes, she found out."

"Oh Ray. I'm so sorry."

"So I went out and messed up the truck and got drunk."

"Is that how this happened?"

He touched the swollen black and blue lump on his forehead. "Yeah. Felt like hell this morning."

"Your head must hurt something awful."

"Not as much as my ego." He laughed abruptly. "Christ, am I a jiveass. All full of pride how I'm not like other guys, when I'm not a damned bit different."

"Yes, you are."

"No, I'm not. And full of pride about my high standards on the job, but letting that son of a bitch flatter me and pull the

wool over my eyes. At least *that* one I can do something about."
He looked at her. "When I got to work today, you know what I
did?"

She shook her head.

"Told the guys to take out the bad wall and start over.
Ordered another load of concrete. And you know what I'm
gonna do tonight? I'm going over to Cushing's to tell him I
quit."

Arla softly stroked his cheek. He had not shaved today and
his beard was bristly. He looked so very tired. "Don't do
anything rash, Ray. Think things over first."

"Too late for that. I was rash last night."

"With Terri?"

"Yeah. I told her."

"That's how she found out you're sleeping with me—you
told her?" Arla tried to keep her voice calm.

He shook his head. "She already knew that much."

Arla sat beside him, not moving, scarcely breathing.

"And then I told her–" He groaned again. "I shouldn't
have. It was cruel."

"What did you tell her?" Arla whispered.

"That I love you." His voice cracked. He brought his hands
up to his face and began to cry, in that terrible choking way of
a man, as if the tears had to break him to get out.

He tried to get up, but she held him against her and stroked
his head, his golden hair with its familiar scents. She held him
tightly even when he tried to stop crying, tried to pull away as
if ashamed … not for crying, but because he was in her arms
crying for his wife, for his broken marriage.

"Do you want to rest a while?" she said, and he shook his
head and rubbed his face. "I can't. I gotta go back to work, get
that wall put in right and tell the boss I won't be back. And I
have to go see Joe and Stella Pardini."

Arla looked at him curiously. "What about?"

"Business. I'll tell you about it later. Do you think I could have some coffee?"

"Of course." She gently disentangled herself. When she had taken but one step toward the kitchen, he reached out and grasped her hand. "Why does everyone say it's impossible to love two people at the same time?"

"Because they're afraid," Arla said.

"*You* know it's possible, don't you?"

Arla went back to him. She leaned over and kissed him on the cheek. "Yes, Ray. I do. And I don't think it's wrong."

"Can I stay here?"

"Yes," she said, after only a slight hesitation.

It wasn't so slight that he didn't notice. "What?"

"It's just that I want you to be sure."

He didn't answer.

"Let's talk tonight," Arla said. "We'll have dinner together and talk about it."

"Are *you* sure? Is that what this is about?"

"No, Ray. It's about you."

"Is it? But what if I decide I want to leave my wife for you and then you say that's not what you want?"

"I don't think you should leave her for me. If you leave her, it should be about you and her."

He stared at her with surprise, and then he smiled and traced a finger tenderly down her cheek to her lips. "That's one of the reasons I love you. You aren't afraid to tell me what you think."

Unexpectedly, Arla's eyes filled.

He gently lifted her chin. "I want you to say it."

"I love you," she said.

Chapter Forty-Two

The heat kept Stella awake until nearly midnight and she woke abruptly an hour later when Puddles, on the floor on Joe's side of the bed, lifted his head with a soft clinking of his collar, and growled. Then he trotted toward the living room. Stella sat up. Probably it was just a deer, but it might be coyotes, or even a mountain lion or a bear.

Puddles began to bark. Stella shook Joe, gently. "Something's outside," she said. "I'll go look."

He sat up, looking dazed with sleep. Stella went to the front door. She could hear the horses moving about in their stalls and Tabasco whinnying. They wouldn't be nervous about deer. She took one of the rifles from the rack, turned on the floodlights, and stepped outside.

The lights had spooked whatever it was; there was movement to the side of the stables. Behind her, Puddles' barking increased in volume and intensity. Stella racked a round into the chamber and fired into the sky over the meadow. Coyotes knew that sound meant trouble. She wasn't so sure whether a mountain lion or a bear would know, but it was loud.

The animal crashed away in the brush as Joe came out. "What was it?"

"I don't know. Something that made the horses nervous. I'll go calm them."

"I'll come with you," he said.

Ten minutes later, as they left the stables and walked back to the house, a car engine started in the direction of the highway. She and Joe exchanged a look. The intruder had been human.

Stella was glad she'd fired that round. A gunshot was an effective way to prevent return visits from *human* trespassers, too.

For the next quarter hour, she and Joe inspected the property. Nothing seemed amiss. The cabins had not been broken into and nothing had been taken from the stable or barn. They went back to bed, but not before Stella praised Puddles for his alertness.

***

STELLA WAS INTRIGUED when Ray Mathieson called Friday afternoon and asked if he could come see her and Joe. She knew Ray only the way you knew everyone in a town the size of Camargo. The Mathiesons were friendly acquaintances, no more than that.

"Joe won't be back until about four," she said. "Do you want to come then?"

"Maybe I could come now, if you'll be there?"

"Yes, of course."

Stella fixed herself a cup of coffee. After going back to bed last night her sleep had been restless. The single-digit humidity made her skin and eyes itchy, her throat almost raw. And she'd been groggy all day, a condition aggravated by the heat. Groggy, but unsettled too; she didn't like this hot wind. She turned the radio to KMTN, Piñon County's station. The Red Flag Warning issued Thursday by the National Weather Service was still in effect, and the Forest Service had closed all campsites and trails in the Higuera National Forest.

She had just finished her coffee when Ray arrived. He looked terribly tired himself, and had a black and blue lump on his forehead. She gave him some iced tea, and they sat at the big kitchen table. He carried a manila envelope.

"Stella, I've done you and Joe a disservice. Hiram Cushing told me something about you. I should've known better, but I just swallowed it, hook line and sinker." Ray shook his head. "He told me Joe wanted to sell him the ranch, but was holding out for more money. He said it had to be on the QT because Joe's always spoken publicly against development and didn't want word leaking out that he was selling the place to a developer."

"That dirty liar!" Stella exclaimed.

"I know."

"We aren't selling the ranch. We've turned down several offers."

"Yeah. Now, I know that."

"And the offers are getting smaller, not larger."

"That's because he knows you're having economic problems."

She looked at him levelly. "Ray, what's going on?"

"I saw something in his office. I don't think he wanted me to see it. It's an architectural model of what he envisions for Piñon County—for the lumber mill and your place, and the Jensen ranch. Pine Gap, too. He wants to put up housing developments, condominiums, and a big resort at Cougar Lake. And on your place? Luxury houses and a golf course."

"A golf course!" Stella was aghast. The lawyer hadn't even mentioned that.

"Yeah, a 36-hole golf course over about 500 acres."

"That's more than half the ranch."

Ray nodded. "On the model, it goes from this part of your spread, all the way to Cougar Creek."

On the meadow, she said to herself. Here, where the house is, and on the wildflower meadow.

Ray slid the manila envelope toward her. "These are the only copies."

Stella didn't touch the envelope, although she was burning to see what it contained. "Are you sure you want to do this?"

He nodded. "I'd already decided to quit, even before this."

"Will anyone know this was taken?"

"I don't think so. It's all copies. The originals are all back where they were in the first place."

Stella hesitated over the envelope. "If I were to take action based on whatever facts are in here, would that reveal you're the person who told me?"

"No. Not just knowing this stuff. But if it was known you had these documents…"

"No one will know that except Joe and myself," Stella said.

"You don't know what's in there, yet. You might want to use them."

"We won't, not if it would cause trouble for you."

"It might." He shrugged. "But I'd rather have him think it was me who gave them to you than the secretary. She's probably the first one he'd suspect." Ray stood. "I have to get back to town."

Stella walked him to the door. "There's no way for me to thank you, Ray."

"I just hope it does some good."

Ray drove off. She went back inside and waited for Joe. He got home shortly and she explained Ray's errand. "Should we open it?" she asked. "Could he be setting us up in some way?"

"I don't know. It's hard to imagine how."

"We don't really know him, Joe, and he does work for Cushing."

"You talked to him. What's your gut reaction, *cara?*"

"That he's not double-crossing us."

"That's good enough for me," Joe said, and shrugged. "But even if we're being set up, let's at least find out how."

They opened the envelope and emptied the papers onto the table.

One document was a contract between Eagle Development and the lumber company. It was long and filled with much legal language, but Stella gathered that it basically called for Slidell-Pacific to sell Eagle the mill property and Pine Gap, and for both town and mill to be vacated by the end of 1986.

In another document Eagle agreed to sell the property to an outfit called Gold Slope Enterprises.

A letter from Hiram Cushing to someone at Slidell-Pacific Lumber & Paper Company headquarters in Coos Bay, Oregon stated:

...that your company is close to securing the agreement of eighty percent of the occupants of Pine Gap, after which any remaining homeowners can be compelled to sell their houses to the company at the assessed values. During our discussion yesterday, you told me that the eighty percent figure will be met if just five more homeowners agree to sell.

Reluctance on the part of any homeowner to sell might well be overcome by higher offers for their houses. Therefore, you are authorized to offer amounts up to one-fourth higher than assessed values until five homeowners

```
agree  to  sell.  Gold  Slope  Enterprises
will,  of  course,  pay  those  additional
percentages.
     This  should  serve  to  hasten  the
process of vacating Pine Gap…
```

A letter to the lawyer, Sutcliffe, was dated two weeks ago—just before Sutcliffe had called Joe and Stella to arrange his visit. The letter was stamped, in large letters, 'CONFIDENTIAL.'

```
Bob,


I'm  pretty  sure  Pardini  is  on  the  verge
of  bankruptcy.  Now  is  the  time  to  extend
another offer for his property.
     You  said  you  think  Pardini  will  be
reluctant  to  sell  if  he  has  to  leave  his
house,  since  it's  been  in  his  family  for
so    many    years.    The    house    and
outbuildings  are  in  the  center  of  the
future    golf    course.    Under    no
circumstances  will  Pardini  be  able  to
keep  that  portion  of  the  land.  However,
the  house  could  be  moved,  and  we'd  be
willing  to  allow  reasonable  time  for
that,  and  even  to  allow  him  to  remain  on
some   small   portion   of   the   property,
perhaps  on  the  northeastern  border.  But
this  should  be  offered  only  as  a  last
resort.
     As  a  matter  of  historical  interest,
Pardini's  great-grandparents  were  only
able  to  purchase  that  property  due  to  a
```

generous buyout of their farm by my own
great-grandfather, after whom I am
named.

 It may help us down the road in these
negotiations if we promise to honor the
original settlers by naming the golf
course 'Pardini Greens.' Sometimes, what
seems trivial can make the difference in
a deal being made, or not. But let's
hold that in reserve for now.

Stella set the letter aside, walked to the window and stared out at the land.

Joe took her hand in his. They stood there together as the winds howled outside.

Stella gripped Joe's hand. "Never. No matter what, Joe."

"You're sure, Stella dear?" Joe smiled. "We may never get another chance to have a golf course named after us."

Chapter Forty-Three

By the time school got out Friday, the winds continued to gust and wail. Puffy clouds swarmed over the mountains to the north and east, but the air didn't feel like rain. The clouds were towering and white—the sort of clouds that brought dry lightning.

Carlos had cross-country practice; rather than wait for him, Kit took the bus home. She wanted to get back to the ranch and, if Dad or PJ hadn't already done so, bring the horses into the stables.

Usually, the bus driver took these familiar roads at a brisk clip; today he drove with a slow caution so uncharacteristic that it frightened Kit as much as the wind itself did.

She got off at the end of the ranch road and was immediately besieged by fine dust that pricked her eyes, hair, and skin. She pulled her T-shirt up over her mouth and nose, ducked her head down, and jogged most of the way to the house.

Mom's car was gone, which was odd; usually she was getting dinner ready by now.

The horses were already in their stalls, stamping and

snorting. Kit stopped to visit them, saving Sadie for last. "Maybe we can go out tomorrow morning, Sadie. But you have to stay inside now, in case there's a lightning storm." Sadie pushed her nose into Kit's hand and whinnied softly. Despite her nervousness, she looked at Kit with trust in her eyes.

Kit entered through the kitchen door. A note was on the refrigerator: 'I have a doctor's appointment and won't be home until six. I'll pick up Chinese food for dinner. Mom.'

She drank a large glass of milk and ate a thick slice of carrot cake. Her hair and skin were speckled with grit; she craved a shower. She took the stairs two at a time, but before she got to her room, Dad's voice called from the study. "Kit, get your ass in here."

"I was just gonna take a shower, Dad."

"Get. In. Here. NOW!"

Kit's legs obeyed stiffly. Her heart pounded so hard it hurt the wall of her chest.

He was sitting at his desk with his booted feet on top of it, crossed at the ankles. A bottle of Jim Beam and a shot glass were on the desk, too. Kit stood there and looked at him impassively, hiding her disgust and hatred behind as bland an expression as she could muster.

"You know who Fred Arledge is?" He spoke in a conversational tone, around a toothpick that moved when he talked.

"Yeah, he owns the Tavern."

Dad took the toothpick from his mouth and studied it. "I saw him today. He told me something he thought I'd want to know."

He knows, she thought, fighting panic.

"So. I've got just two rules, but even that's too many for you." He tossed the toothpick onto the floor. "What's the problem, you got a bad memory?"

"No."

He sat upright, bringing his boots down with two loud thunks as the heels struck the wood floor. "Rule Number One. Stay away from Pardini Ranch. Rule Number Two. No race mixing. Easy rules. Not so complicated. But you break them both. You've been going over to the Pardinis behind my back, while I'm in the middle of a dispute with them. You've been meeting the half-breed wetback there. And you've been going to his house in Pine Gap." Dad poured his shot glass full. "I always said the one thing a man can't have in his own house is back talk from his own wife and kids. And that's all I get anymore from you and your mother."

Kit's mouth felt like a desert. She swallowed, trying to activate her saliva. She would not have been this scared if he was yelling, if he was visibly angry. But he was sitting there saying these things in an even tone of voice.

"I'll tell you how it is." Dad drank the contents of the shot glass in one gulp. "When I'm not paying for the food you eat or the clothes you wear or the roof over your head, or for the upkeep of your goddamned horse, you can do whatever the hell you want. The day you turn eighteen, you can walk out of here. But as long as you're in *my* house, you'll follow *my* rules. You got that?"

"I got it, all right," she said, unable to keep the loathing from her voice.

In an instant he was on his feet and in front of her. His right hand slapped her hard across the face, then backhanded on the other side. Kit's eyes teared up involuntarily. She brought her hands to her cheeks. They felt red and hot. She tasted blood in her mouth.

"There's gonna be some new rules around here. Listen up." He poured another shot. "One. Stay away from Pardini Ranch. Yep, same old rule number one. Two. No race mixing. Same old number two. And half-breed Mexicans aren't white."

He drank the whiskey and set the glass down hard. "Three. No riding that horse of yours unless you're with me or your brother. Four. No after-school events. You wanna go to a football game, you go with me. You wanna join the Latin Club, that's out. Five. You want to make a telephone call, you ask me. I'm putting locks on the dials, and you aren't getting a key.

"You want to break the rules again, go right ahead. First transgression, the horse gets sold."

Kit's resolve broke. A sob tore from her throat.

"And hell, she's too old to get anything for. I guess I could sell her to the rendering plant."

Her legs gave out and she sank onto the floor, weeping. "Not Sadie!"

He shrugged. "Up to you. You follow the rules, she stays right here in my stable." He snapped his fingers. "I almost forgot. One more thing. You listening? Look at me when I'm talking to you!"

She looked up through her tears.

"The greaser get his dick in you yet?"

Kit covered her face with her hands. Dad was in front of her in two strides and he yanked her up by the arm. "Answer me!"

"No! He's not like that!" she exclaimed. She wasn't lying. They had not done what Dad so crudely charged. She was still technically a virgin, by Dad's definition.

Dad snorted. "Can you really be that goddamned dumb?" He left the room, clumping noisily down the stairs.

She stumbled into her room and collapsed on her bed.

He came in not much later. Outside, thunder rumbled and rolled and the sky had darkened. "I took out all the phones except the one in the kitchen. It's locked. You want to make a call, you ask me or your brother. Got that?"

She nodded.

"I said, got that?"

"Yes," Kit said, dully.

"I don't know yet about your mother—if I can trust that bitch with a key to the phone." He stomped downstairs, got into his pickup and drove off.

She waited until she was sure he wasn't coming back, then went down to the kitchen. He'd hooked up an old-fashioned phone, the one from the stable which had always had a lock on the round dial so hired hands couldn't make long distance calls. Kit went around the house and found the other phones were all gone. But the jacks would still be live; she could just plug in a phone to one of them. She had to call Carlos and warn him, too.

But after a cursory search she couldn't find any of the telephones Dad had unplugged.

She had to get out of the house. It felt like a prison.

She found herself grabbing one of the revolvers from the gun case and sticking it into the waistband of her jeans. She went outside. To the south it was bright and sunny, but clouds darkened the northern sky and lightning danced on the horizon. The horses whinnied and stamped in their stalls. There was no smell of rain. Kit walked away from the house, toward the hills. She began to weep again, the sobs sticking in her throat along with the dust, her face stinging from his slaps and from the blowing dirt.

Maybe she'd get struck by lightning. That would be better than having to live here for three more years. She climbed the rocky projection and stood atop a boulder. She prayed for the lightning, but it was too far away, off to the north still. Maybe she could stay here until it came, stand up and raise her arms to it.

She pulled the revolver from her waist, cocked the hammer and took aim at a rock some hundred feet distant. Whang! The rock shattered. Next, a pinecone even farther away. It took three shots before she hit it.

Her rage spilled out and she screamed with the wind. And it wasn't just to her that he was cruel. He was a horrible person! He was mean to people who weren't powerful, he cheated any customer too naïve to know they were being cheated, and he'd always been mean to Mom.

She turned to the north again, to plead with the storm to hurry. And saw a column of smoke. It was in the part of the forest north of the highway.

She studied the smoke. She couldn't tell how far away the fire was, but the wind was blowing south. It would propel the fire toward Blackberry Springs and then Sequoia State Park, perhaps even across the highway into Pardini Ranch and the Double-L. And since the lookout was no longer manned, there was a good chance no one else had seen the smoke yet.

She scrambled off the rock and began to run home. She wished she knew how to run without getting a stitch in her side. Carlos had told her it was all in the breathing. She tried to breathe more slowly, more rhythmically, but fear made controlling her breathing impossible. She clutched at her side and ran.

About to return the revolver to the gun case, she hesitated, then stuck it into her knapsack, shouldered the bag, and went to the phone. For a moment she stared in shock at the lock. Then she wasted five minutes trying to get it off with needle-nosed pliers. Finally, she ran out to the stable, led Sadie from her stall and climbed onto her bareback. "Come on, girl," she cooed. "I know it's bad outside. We'll run, as fast as you can, Sadie, over to the closest telephone. It's at Stella's. So we're breaking two rules, girl."

They ran madly over the hills, Kit with her arms wrapped around Sadie's neck and her head against Sadie's hide to shield her eyes from the blowing dirt. The clouds swarmed closer and she urged Sadie on. Then a thick bolt of lightning shot across the sky with the sharp crack of a rifle's report. A second later, a clap of thunder boomed, so loud and close the ground reverberated. Sadie squealed and reared up. Kit clung to her mane, barely managing not to be thrown. Sadie's eyes rolled wildly with fear and her nostrils flared in and out. Kit spoke soothingly to her and decided it might be better to go more slowly.

They cantered into the compound minutes later. Stella must have heard them; she ran out of the house. "Kit, is something wrong?"

"Fire," Kit panted. "North of Blackberry Springs, in the forest. By Jackrabbit Gulch, I think."

"Did you call it in?"

"No, I came here to call."

Stella nodded and hurried back inside. Kit led Sadie to the barn and quickly rubbed her down, gave her water and hay, then ran to the house. "I've notified them about the fire," Stella said. "Is anyone over at your place to take care of the horses and cattle?"

Kit shook her head no. "Mom has a doctor's appointment in Oso Grande. Dad left. I don't know where he went, maybe the Tavern."

Stella dialed the phone. "Fred, hello, this is Stella Pardini. Is Pete or PJ Jensen there now? … Oh, good, both of them … No, but could you let them know there's a fire up north of Blackberry Springs? … And tell Pete Kit's with us; we'll bring her down into Camargo."

She hung up. "They're both there, your father and brother. They'll get the stock."

Kit went to the phone and called Carlos's house; cross-country practice should be over by now. But there was no answer until the mechanical clicking of the machine. "Carlos," she said into it, "he found out and he's really mad. He hit me. You have to tell your mom."

Stella's eyes grew black with anger. When Kit hung up,

Stella opened her arms and Kit went into them. She wanted to tell Stella what had happened, but when she opened her mouth the only thing that came out was a sob. She gasped for breath and couldn't talk. Stella just held her tightly, and Kit cried against her shoulders. Outside, the wind roared. A branch hit the roof with a loud crack. Finally, she managed to say, "Please keep Sadie for me. Whatever else happens, please don't let anyone take Sadie! Especially my dad or my brother. Please promise me, Stella."

"I promise. Now come on, honey. Let's get Joe and load the horses in the trailer. We'll take them down to Camargo, to the fairgrounds. Just a precaution in case the fire comes this way."

INTERLUDE

1888 – 1966
Camargo, California

Although the Gold Rush was now safely in the past and its history had become a matter of pride, the seedier aspects were still concealed. The town's 'leading men' were never portrayed as having had less than sterling character, and poorer families were excluded from history entirely. Rosa suspected that if she brought the diary to the Historical Society, it would be destroyed to protect Hiram Cushing's reputation.

For she knew its contents.

Shortly after Catherine's funeral and Hiram Cushing's visit, Rosa had wondered why he so badly wanted to find the diary. So she read it. She was shocked by what she learned and knew that to ever reveal the diary's contents would bring horrors upon herself or, worse, upon her family.

She bore the knowledge of Hiram Cushing's crimes with silence and stoicism—and at times, a great sadness.

After Albert died in 1904, Rosa's son and daughter ran Childress Apple Farm, with help from their children.

Perhaps it was the great success of the apple farm that prompted a neighboring landowner to file a lawsuit alleging encroachment. The lawsuit was heard in June 1912 by Judge Marcus Cushing. He was Catherine's son.

While court was in session, Rosa scrutinized Marcus Cushing. She had known him when he was a young boy prone to climbing too far up trees and having to be rescued like a cat; then as an almost-man with an appetite so voracious that Rosa had had to hide pies or cakes she'd baked for the family's dessert; and as a young man, a newlywed and new property owner, whose lack of grief over his mother's death had shocked and sickened Rosa.

Now he was fifty years old and it was clear to her that he hadn't outgrown his youthful tendencies; rather, they had ripened into character traits. When he turned his cold gaze upon her, Rosa shuddered. She thought of how well Catherine had known her sons—and had known that neither of them would ever allow the diary to see the light of day.

That very night, after she returned home from court, Rosa went into the kitchen and took down the book labeled, '*Pepinillos en vinagre al eneldo.*' She removed the diary, which was still inside the Spanish missal cover, and tucked it into her sewing basket. She added the small box of Catherine Cushing's religious artifacts and walked across the orchard to her granddaughter's little cabin.

Helen was unmarried, twenty-seven years old, and the most level-headed person Rosa had ever known. Helen understood her grandmother's concerns perfectly. She took the diary, along with Catherine Cushing's religious artifacts, and put them in her cedar chest.

Rosa did not live to see her son convert the apple barn into a store. One winter night in 1922, her heart gave out as she slept.

Helen died in 1965, the last Childress in Piñon County. Distant heirs retrieved her personal possessions and all the family heirlooms, and sold the farm.

At about that time, the Piñon County Historical Society acquired title to the house that Judge Cushing had built in 1887, known since 1911 as The Minelli House. For the first time, the society had plentiful space: rooms for displays, a library, offices, and abundant storage space.

Catherine Cushing's religious artifacts were included in the batch of things that Helen Childress had left, with strict written instructions—both in her will and in a note attached to the cedar chest—that they go to the Piñon County Historical Society. The society was thrilled to receive the Childresses' lovely china, the cattle brands made by the blacksmith who'd come looking for gold, a near century's worth of school records, account books that solved several mysteries concerning other families and individuals, and photographs of the Childresses that, when enlarged, provided an historical record of Main Street in Camargo.

Other items in the bequest were not as valuable or interesting, since they were no more than personal memorabilia of a not-prominent family. Two society members sorted through them and wondered whether these things were even worth saving. But in the end, it was simpler to keep the items, and less expensive than hauling them to the dump. And so they were tossed into two wooden apple boxes and placed in the attic storage area, forgotten for another twenty years.

Part VI

THE FIRE

A Red Flag Event occurs when critical weather conditions develop … strong, gusty wind; very low relative humidity; highly unstable atmosphere; significant wind shifts; lightning … Red Flag Events represent a threat to life and property.

–National Weather Service

DAY ONE

SEPTEMBER 27

Arla, 4:30–5:30 pm

Driving past the museum, Arla was surprised to see Mary's car parked out front. She went in and sure enough, Mary was there. "Mary! I was going to call you when I got home. Can we get a cup of coffee or tea somewhere?"

They went a few blocks down Main Street to the Claim Jumper and ordered tea. And there, finally, Arla told her about the diary.

Mary sat back, stunned. Her blue eyes were wide with astonishment. "This is a tremendous find! And to think that all this time, it was right under my nose."

"I know I should have told you before now," Arla said.

"Yes, and you certainly should not have taken it."

Neither of them spoke for several minutes. Their tea sat untouched before them.

"Well, dear, you must bring the journal to the society first thing tomorrow. We'll want to make a copy of it at once. It's priceless and irreplaceable. Should anything happen to it…"

"I'll make a copy of it, Mary. *Two* copies, if you want. I'll stop at the Copy Shoppe."

"Copying old documents can be tricky. It would probably be best if you brought the diary to the museum. We'll have one of the people trained in archival preservation reproduce it."

Arla nodded.

"Tell me what it says." Mary leaned on her elbows.

"It's fascinating and very tragic. She tells a story about her husband and a horrible crime he was accused of by a man about to be hung."

Mary began to tremble. "Arson?"

"Yes." Arla stared at her. "How did you know? I didn't see any reference to it in the county history."

"Several years ago, I came across an account of the hanging written twenty years afterward. The article said that one of the men accused Cushing from the scaffold. But there was no evidence against Cushing and the rumors were far too tenuous to be mentioned in the county history."

Arla remembered Catherine Cushing's comments in her journal. "Did anyone ever look into the land records? Catherine said he made a lot of money on that land."

"The property records do show he made a tidy profit. But I couldn't find any evidence that Cushing was actually behind the arson. Not that I expected to." She paused, shook her head. "And if he was responsible for the fire, then he was also guilty of manslaughter, perhaps even murder."

"Because of the man who died in the fire," Arla said.

Mary nodded affirmatively. "By the way, that man was an ancestor of Joe Pardini."

Arla was confused. "But I thought the person who died was the Russian prospector."

"Yes, he was the great-uncle of Luisa Pardini, Joe's grandmother."

"I had no idea Joe … I just assumed he was Italian on both sides."

Mary smiled. "Luisa's parents were Russian and Chilean, and she married an Italian. Which makes Joe a rather typical Californian."

"I think it *was* murder." Arla lowered her voice. "She recorded what she'd seen in her diary. When she tried to tell her family, her husband sent her to a sanitarium so no one would believe her; they'd think it was all a crazy woman's fantasy. That was when the diary ended, the night before she was sent away."

"Sanitarium," Mary said scornfully. "That's what they called it, but it was really an insane asylum. She wasn't there six months before she died."

"Oh my God."

"I have a copy of the death certificate. *'Death attributed to accidental overdose of laudanum.'*"

Arla put a five-dollar bill on the table. "I'll get the diary now and bring it straight down to your house. There's no reason to wait until tomorrow."

When they stepped outside people were hurrying in an odd way, as though every person they saw was dealing with an emergency. Somewhere in the distance, sirens shrieked.

"There's a fire," Mary said.

Arla fought the feeling of dread as they began walking back to Mary's car.

Mary scanned the cars heading east. "There's a young man who might know—Brian!" she called to the man in the Forest Service pickup.

He looked their way and Mary said, "Where's the fire?"

"Up behind Blackberry Springs," he said. "Looks like a bad one."

Ray, 5:00–5:30pm

It was just past five when Ray pulled into the parking lot at the Eagle office. He wanted to quit in person—and to tell Cushing why.

But Cushing's Bronco wasn't in the parking lot. Ray cursed under his breath, but went inside anyway, in case Cushing was here without his car for some reason. But the only person still in the office was the receptionist, who was getting ready to leave.

"Hi, Ray," she said, slipping a cover over her typewriter.

"Hey, Alice. You know where the boss is?"

Alice shook her head. "He left a little while ago." She added wryly, "Too much trouble to tell the receptionist where he's going."

"Yeah, tell me about it," Ray said sympathetically, but his mind was only half-focused on what she was saying. Maybe he should call Cushing's house? He was determined to have this over and done with. He went into the small construction office just as the phone rang. Alice called out that she was sending him a call from Eddie, then leaving.

"Okay, have a good weekend," Ray said. He picked up the phone. "Eddie, what's up?"

"I just left to go home," Eddie said, "and before I got three miles up highway, I seen the smoke at Jackrabbit Gulch."

Jackrabbit Gulch was a couple of miles north of Blackberry Springs, as the crow flies. Ray's heart began beating faster.

"The wind's whipping up here, Ray. That fire's gonna move." Eddie must've been calling from a payphone; Ray could hear truck engines and sirens. "This is the big one, man, and it's burning south, toward Blackberry Springs." Eddie hesitated. "Just thought you'd want to know."

It was the first time he had ever alluded to Ray's friendship with Arla. How long had he known about it? Oh, well. It was all out in the open now, anyway.

Ray asked, "How close?"

"Close. Just over the ridge."

Less than two miles. If the fire moved fast, it could be at Blackberry Springs in an hour or two. He glanced out the window, to the north. The thunderheads were moving so quickly they didn't hold a shape for more than fifteen seconds, if that.

"Is the For'Service evacuating people there?"

"I haven't heard, but I guess they must be. They're evacuating higher up, I know that."

"You can't get to the Rancheria?" Ray asked.

"No, they're not letting no one through. Mandatory evacuations."

More than anything else Eddie had said, this convinced Ray of the imminence of danger.

They hung up and Ray wasted several precious seconds dialing before he had a clear dial tone. Finally, he stopped himself, waited for the tone, and punched in her number. The answering machine picked it up on the fourth ring. "Arla, if you're there, please pick up the phone. There's a forest fire and you've got to get out of there."

She didn't pick it up. He hung up.

Because he was a volunteer firefighter with the CDF, had fought on many fires, and especially because he could operate a bulldozer, he knew he'd be called soon and asked to report to wherever they were setting up a command center. So how much time did he have? He wanted to make sure Arla was okay before he subjected his time and whereabouts to the CDF.

"Ray?" a woman's voice called from the reception area.

"I'm in here."

"I saw your pickup and was hoping you'd be here." Roxanne came into the office. "There's a fire in the Higuera. I have to get into Pine Gap."

"Is Carlos there?"

"No, he's over at your house, actually. We were on our way home and they wouldn't let us past the roadblock, so I came back to Camargo and went looking for you. It's our cat I'm worried about."

Ray frowned. "They won't let people into Pine Gap? The fire's at Jackrabbit Gulch."

"Yes, but they want to keep the roads open for firefighting vehicles and people being evacuated from up highway," Roxanne explained. "They told us to wait at the high school and later on they'll let us go home. If the fire comes our way, they'll escort people into the Gap, give us ten minutes to get our things."

"Maybe you better get over to the high school, then," Ray said.

"Ray, I have to get to my house and get Baba Looey. If they don't let us in till later tonight, he might take off before then. You know cats; there's no way to find a cat in ten minutes if he's scared and hiding."

"I can probably get you into Pine Gap. I don't know if I can wait there, though."

"Just get me in. I'll figure out a way to get back out with Baba."

Perhaps it was fortuitous that he'd banged up the company truck. He was driving his own pickup today, and that was where he kept the CDF placard. He'd be able to go through roadblocks, so he could drop Roxanne in Pine Gap on his way to Arla's.

"Okay. Let's go."

They stepped outside and looked to the east. Smoke obscured the mountains.

Laura, 5:30pm–6:30pm

Laura had gone to the doctor in Oso Grande. It wasn't her regular doctor, and she had not gone for a routine visit. This was the doctor she'd gone to for treatment in July, after Pete beat her. Today, she met her lawyer there and they got copies of Laura's medical records.

The road back into Piñon County wound through a towering tunnel of sugar pines that uncharacteristically swayed in the strong winds. She held the steering wheel with both hands.

If only she could get through the next few weeks without Pete finding out about what she was doing, and what Kit was doing. She'd nearly asked Kit, 'Can you not see him for a few weeks?' But the words had stuck in her throat as she understood that things had gone too far for that. So all she had said was, 'Be very careful.' She would say more soon, before the lawyer filed the papers. It was only seventeen more days.

She turned west and soon the forest gave way to rolling golden hills. She drove to The Great Wall. Laura and Pete had been coming to The Great Wall for the entire fifteen or so years of its existence. It wasn't far from the west county ranch, so was a convenient place to stop for lunch or dinner.

Mrs. Choi took Laura's order then joined her at the counter and they chatted. Half the tables were occupied and the waiters hurried between the kitchen and the dining floor. Mrs. Choi kept an eye on everything and occasionally spoke in Mandarin to one of the waiters.

"They let you go back to your house?" Mrs. Choi asked. Laura looked at her in confusion and Mrs. Choi added, "The firemen."

"There's a fire? But where is it?"

Mrs. Choi looked stricken. "I thought you knew already."

She gestured to one table of customers. "They tell us they see smoke, and we go outside and see it too."

Laura went to the front door. Sure enough, smoke was boiling up in the sky to the east. And by the looks of it, she guessed it was awfully close to the ranch. "Oh, more smoke now!" Mrs. Choi exclaimed.

Laura ran back inside the restaurant and used The Great Wall's telephone to call the house. But there was no answer. Nor did anyone answer at Joe and Stella's. Could everyone be evacuating that quickly? She called the west county ranch. Carla, the ranch manager's wife, told her Pete and PJ were on the way down from the Double-L with the horses and both trailers.

"You take the food with you," Mrs. Choi insisted. "He's putting it in boxes now. People still have to eat."

"Thank you," Laura said, pressing Mrs. Choi's hand as she handed her a plastic bag full of food containers.

"You pay later. Go now."

Arla, 6:00–6:30pm

The highway east was already clogged with official vehicles and the cars of residents frantically trying to get home. Sirens shrieked and horns blared. When Arla finally reached the Blackberry Springs turnoff, it was cordoned off. She would have driven around the roadblock, but two highway patrolmen were there, and their patrol cars blocked the road. "I live in Blackberry Springs and I've got to get to my house," she told one of the men. "My dog's there!"

"I'm sorry, ma'am," he said. "No one is being allowed in. It's too dangerous."

"But officer, my dog!"

"We'll be sending in people to help with the evacuation and we'll be getting the animals, too. What's your address?"

Arla recited it and he wrote it down. "But he's inside, and the doors are locked."

"That development has Knox Boxes," he said, and at her apparently uncomprehending look. "The fire department has access to emergency keys. And if they have to, they can break in. I'll make sure they know about your dog."

The mall site appeared to be a staging area; it was filled with California Division of Forestry and Forest Service vehicles, and several people were putting up a very large tent. Arla pulled in and parked at the farthest spot from all the activity so she wouldn't be in the way. On the highway, people were driving down from Blackberry Springs; she recognized some of her neighbors' cars going toward Camargo. She saw Joe driving his pickup, hauling the big horse trailer.

And then Ray's pickup turned into the site. Someone was in the front with him and Arla's temples pounded. She didn't want to have to ask him for help with Terri right there. But oh God, she didn't know who else to ask.

He must have seen her, for he drove right up to her. To her relief, the passenger was Roxanne. As he caught sight of her, his face lit up. "Arla!" he exclaimed as she ran to his window. "I was just coming up to make sure you evacuated."

She was surprised to find herself suddenly sobbing. "Ray, Morgan's at the house. They won't let me go get him."

"Don't worry, baby. I'll go up and get him."

She glanced nervously at Roxanne, who was getting out of the pickup and either hadn't heard, or wasn't surprised by, that 'baby.'

"But they said they won't let anyone up the road," she said.

"I can get up." He gestured to the windshield of his pickup, where a placard read, 'CDF OFFICIAL FIRE VEHICLE.'

"You wait here. If they kick you out, wait at Wanda's."

"Oh! And the diary!" She couldn't believe that she'd almost forgotten it.

"Diary?" Ray's eyes widened.

"It's not mine," she said hastily. "It was written in the 1880s and belongs to the Historical Society. It's an irreplaceable document and the only copy is at my house."

"Don't worry, I'll get it. What's it look like?"

"It has a black cover. It's inside a Catholic prayer book. I keep it in the study, on my desk."

"Okay." He put his truck into drive and Arla reached in through the window and rested her hand on his arm. "Don't do anything dangerous."

"I won't."

"Ray, I mean it. If it's risky, don't do it. Promise me!"

Later, Arla remembered how the next half hour seemed the longest of her life. But that was early in that long, long night.

Ray, 6:30–7:00pm

Behind Arla's house the smoke billowed up, obliterating everything. Dust and ashes churned in the winds. The fire was burning closer and moving faster than Ray had realized. But it hadn't jumped the river yet, and the winds felt like they were blowing mostly easterly. So maybe Blackberry Springs would be spared.

When he opened the door Morgan came rushing over, barking agitatedly and insistently. Ray leashed him and took him out to the pickup, locking him in the cab. He grabbed a box from the bed of his truck and went back inside. Arla hadn't asked him to get anything but the dog and the diary, but she'd need her irreplaceable documents and pictures. She could probably use some clothes, too. He went into the bedroom and got a few sets of clothes, and a pair of running shoes. The box of her photographs and other memorabilia was in the closet, and he took that too.

He went into the study and quickly found all the house papers she kept neatly labeled in manila folders in her two-drawer filing cabinet. He grabbed some other folders after looking at their labels: birth certificate, passport, dissolution, and even Morgan's license. Her checkbooks and savings passbooks were in another drawer; he put them in the box, too.

But there was no diary, no Catholic missal on the desk. He opened all the drawers of her desk, looked underneath all the furniture in the room. He went back into her bedroom, but it wasn't on her bed or the bedside tables. He walked through the house quickly, scanning the surfaces. Nothing.

Well, it sure wasn't here. And he'd already been here too long. He had to get the hell out. But he didn't think he'd get another chance to make a call, so he phoned Terri to let her know he'd be going out on the bulldozer soon.

In the pickup, he patted the frenetic Morgan and told him to sit. He put on his flashers and drove on the shoulder of the highway, past the line of vehicles inching toward town, and reached the mall site in ten minutes. Arla was still there, parked at the far end of the lot, probably trying to be unobtrusive enough not to be ejected. Hard to be unobtrusive in a red Mercedes, he thought, grinning. Relief washed over him; she was safe and so was the dog she loved so much.

Before he even stopped, she was out of her car and running toward his truck. He watched her and Morgan greet each other, Arla kneeling and the dog jumping all over her.

A man's voice called loudly, "Ray! Been looking all over for you! We gotta get going!"

It was the fire boss, leaning out the window of a truck. Ray waved. "I'll be right there." Arla stood up and he took her in his arms.

"But someone will—"

"It doesn't matter anymore."

She told him she'd be at Mary O'Malley's and he promised to call her there in the morning.

Laura, 6:00–7:00pm

Laura arrived at the west county ranch just as Pete turned onto the road in his pickup, towing the long trailer. PJ was right behind in his truck, hauling the second trailer. She got out of her car and Pete pulled up alongside her.

"It looks like a bad one," he said. "They're evacuating everyone from Pine Gap east. Lucky we weren't too far away when it started."

She glanced at the trailer and saw the horses inside. "What about the cattle?"

"We couldn't get any of 'em and they won't let us back up the road."

At the thought of what might happen to them, tears sprang to Laura's eyes.

"Well, they're insured," he said. "We left the gates open. They'll probably go down to the river and wait it out."

There was not much that could be done; Laura knew that. "Did you get anything else?" she asked.

"No time," Pete said tersely. "The important stuff's all downtown in my office, anyway."

He meant property and livestock records, banking documents, stocks and bonds—things that could be replaced, albeit with some difficulty. But what about the kids' baby pictures, the drawings they'd made in kindergarten? What about her father's Purple Heart, her mother's quilt? Heirloom Christmas ornaments? The sourdough starter Stella's nonna had given her thirty years ago?

"You bring dinner?" he asked.

She nodded. "Where's Kit?"

Pete's face darkened. "She went to Pardini's to call in the fire. I guess they're at the fairgrounds now."

Laura frowned. "Why was she out riding in that weather?"

Pete didn't answer. He steered his pickup toward the pasture gate and began to back the trailer in. Laura waited until he got out of his pickup and asked, "Do you want to offload the horses before you eat?"

"Yeah, just have it ready. This should take about half an hour."

She took the Chinese food over to the picnic table. She got camping dishes from their storage shed, set the table, and thought about what he'd told her. Kit wouldn't have been out riding in that weather. Something was wrong. Her heart raced and she went inside for a glass of water, drinking it slowly to calm herself.

Kit would tell her. If it was bad, they wouldn't come back down here.

Actually, she'd have a reasonable excuse not to return: there wasn't room to stay here. Pete wouldn't expect her and Kit to bunk in the barn, although he and PJ might do so.

She went back outside and walked toward the car, just as Pete began coming toward the house. "Where you going?" he asked gruffly.

"I'll go into town and get Kit."

"Listen, Laura. I had to lay down the law with her."

"What do you mean?"

"I was talking to Fred today and he told me she's been hanging around with the Tejada kid over in Pine Gap."

Laura's heart pounded and she could feel weakness in her

legs. But she'd had years of practice at seeming calm when gripped by terror. "She's friends with him, but I don't think it's more than that."

He stepped closer to her. His body radiated anger. "That's what I figured: you knew she's been seeing that kid and you didn't tell me."

"Pete, I don't think she's dating him, if that's what you mean by seeing him. They go to school together."

"God damn you." His hands balled into fists. Instinctively, she jumped back and flung her arms protectively over her breasts and abdomen. "That's not all." He held his clenched fists tensely at his sides, as though only great self-control was keeping him from using them. "She's been spending time at Pardini's."

"Are you sure?" Laura asked, before he could accuse her of having known that, too. "How do you know that?"

"PJ followed her the other day. That kid works for Pardini. Don't give me any crap, Laura. I know you knew about that, too." He glanced around, perhaps to see if anyone was within earshot; the others were paying them no attention. He stepped closer and jabbed his finger at her. "After the fire's over and we get back home, you're gonna explain yourself. And it better be good."

Every nerve in her body screamed at the memory of pain. Every fiber of her being screamed in rage and hatred. But the part of her that was planning escape cautioned: *Don't let him see you're angry. Don't let him guess what you might be planning. Make him think you're scared of him, the way you always were before. Make him think you're worried about what he'll do to you later. Make him think you're cowed.* "Don't be angry with me," she whispered, cringing. "Pete, please don't be angry."

"Get up to town and get a hotel room until the fire's over."

"But it could be days, Pete. The fire might–"

"Shut up. I got work to do, and I don't want to see your

face while I'm trying to do it. Hers either. The two of you make me sick."

Laura got into her car and drove away. It took her fifteen minutes to get to the fairgrounds, where livestock was brought in emergencies. She saw Joe's trailer, then Joe backing a horse down the ramp. And as she got closer, she saw Kit. Trembling, Laura parked and hurried over to her.

"Mom," Kit exclaimed. And when they were closer to one another Laura saw that Kit had been crying.

"What's wrong, darling? Is Sadie here?"

Kit nodded. "She's here. But Mom—" and she began to cry again. Laura led her into an adjacent empty barn.

After hearing what Kit had to say, Laura slid down onto the hay-covered barn floor.

"Mom?" Kit leaned over her. "I'm okay. He didn't hurt me that bad."

Laura pulled her daughter into her arms and wept. It was her fault that things had come to this. She'd gambled that he wouldn't hurt the girls, but she'd been gambling with their health and their safety, and she didn't have the right to do that. Her *own* health and safety, yes, but not theirs. Not Kit's.

"Let me see what he did to you." She looked carefully at Kit's face; the skin was red, but not broken. But on the inside of both her cheeks, the skin was torn. "I'm going to take you to the hospital."

"I'm okay. It doesn't hurt now, just when he did it."

"I know, darling. But we need to make a record of it. I want you to tell the doctor how it happened. Then your father won't ever be able to get custody of you."

"Custody?" Kit repeated. "You're gonna divorce him?"

Laura nodded yes. She had been worried about telling her, but a wide smile spread over Kit's face. "It's about time! I only wish you'd done it a long time ago." Then the smile vanished. "But what if he—what if he gets so mad, he..."

Kit's eyes filled again. "Cindy told me, Mom. What he does to you."

Her heart fluttered and she rested her hand on Kit's head. "Oh, baby. I'm sorry."

"Why are *you* sorry? *He*'s the one who should be sorry!"

"I just wish you didn't have that to worry about on top of everything else. What I've always been afraid of is you and Cindy might think it's acceptable. That it's a normal part of marriage."

Kit shook her head hard. "We don't think that. Guaranteed. We don't."

Laura swallowed the lump in her throat. "I'm glad. Because I'd rather you despised me than end up with a man who hits you."

Kit's eyes filled. "Oh, Mom. I've been praying for you to divorce him and take me with you for *years*! Way before today, and way before I found out he hits you."

"I promise you, darling. You'll never have to live with your father again."

"What if the judge says I have to? Dad knows all the judges."

"Only the judges in Piñon County. But if he does get custody, you and I will run away together."

"Yeah. Me and my mom on the lam." Kit settled back into Laura's arms, smiling. "I told Stella and Joe what happened."

"Good. And what about Carlos?"

"He knows. He was in town and heard about the fire, and called Stella's. She told him about Dad. Where is Dad, anyway?"

"He and PJ are at the west county ranch. They brought the other horses down." Laura stroked Kit's soft curly hair. "He told me he doesn't want us to come down there. He wants us to stay at a hotel in town until the fire's over."

Kit grinned. "Oh, what a bummer."

"I think we can stay at Terri and Ray Mathieson's. What about Joe and Stella, where are they staying?"

"I don't know. I don't think *they* know. I guess there's gonna be an evacuation center over at the high school gym."

"That won't be very comfortable," Laura said, thinking aloud. "Maybe Joe and Stella can stay at Terri's, too. The house is pretty big. I'll call Terri. But first, let's see if Joe and Stella want to have dinner. I left all that good Chinese food down at the ranch."

"Oh! I almost forgot!" Kit said, and reached into her knapsack and produced a revolver. "It's still got bullets, three, probably." Then she seemed to read Laura's expression. "It's okay, Mom. I went target shooting to let off steam. That's when I saw the fire. And then I thought I might as well bring it in case we need it. You never know."

"No, you never do." Laura put the handgun in her purse.

They went back into the stables. Stella asked Kit to water the horses, and when she had gone, she turned to Laura. Her eyes were steely and no-nonsense. "All right, Laura," she said. "What are you going to do about Pete?"

"He'll never get near Kit again," Laura said. Stella must have seen the resolve in her eyes; she stepped forward and embraced her.

She knew what she was going to do. She had been thinking and planning for a long time. She would have to modify the plan and put it into action now, not wait until November.

Terri, 5:30–8:00pm

Terri put on the radio and began peeling potatoes. KMTN was broadcasting nothing except news of the fire. So far there were no human casualties; nor had any houses burned, not yet. But the fire was bearing down on Blackberry Springs and Sequoia State Park. The newscaster said that all of the houses in Blackberry Springs had been evacuated, and so had the Rancheria.

The firefighters always tried to save first, people; second, structures. But if this fire burned hot and fast enough it would destroy Blackberry Springs, and everyone who'd warned against building houses there would be shaking their heads in sad I-told-you-so's.

Her parents called and they spoke briefly, then she phoned Loretta, but kept that call short too, explaining that she wanted to keep the phone line clear. Which was true, but she also wasn't ready yet to tell Loretta about Ray, and knew that if she talked to Loretta for very long, Loretta would discern that something was going on.

Just before seven, right after she put the meatloaves in the oven, Ray called. It was the first time they had spoken since last night. They were both polite. Civil. This was not the time to go back to their conversation of last night. Get through the crisis first.

She couldn't help but worry. Usually he didn't work close to the fire; the CDF's own dozer operators did that. But there were plenty of dangers. He'd told her the one he most feared was a rollover. Cliffs weren't easy to see in smoke, nor were abandoned mine shafts. Sometimes a firefighter would walk ahead of the dozer watching for hazards, but there wasn't always someone available to do that.

And he would be breathing smoke all night long. The inside of the cab could get incredibly hot. Plus, he would be exhausted; he hadn't slept much last night and wouldn't sleep at all tonight, and running a bulldozer was not easy even in normal work situations, let alone in a fire. Any time he wanted to change the direction of the blade, he'd have to get off the dozer, change the pins and push the blade.

"Do you know what time you'll get off?" she asked.

"No, but probably before noon. I'll call you when I can."

"It looks like we're going to have a lot of people staying here," Terri said. "So if you end up coming back to the house tonight, don't be surprised."

"Who'll be there?"

"Joe and Stella are on the way. They can use the spare room. I'll put Roxanne in the den. Carlos can share Troy's room and Kit can share Trixie's. And if you really won't be back tonight, I guess Laura can stay with me."

"All right. If I do get back tonight, I'll just sack out on the couch."

While the potatoes simmered, she chopped celery and pickles. Carlos was in the den with Trixie and Troy. They both adored him; when he was around, Terri never had to worry about them.

She heard Stella and Joe driving up, and greeted them at the front door. A shaggy, old-looking dog was with them. "Terri, I hope this isn't too much of an imposition," Stella began.

"Of course not. Come in, dinner's almost ready." Terri leaned over and petted the dog, whose tail wagged with an energy at odds with the rest of his demeanor.

While Joe and Stella washed up, Terri set the table. She thought of all the animals and sighed. Roxanne and Carlos' cat. The Jensen cattle. Who knew how many other pets and livestock, let alone wild animals, would die in this fire. It might destroy Laura's house, and Joe and Stella's house.

It might destroy *her* house, too.

Good! Terri thought, savagely.

But that wouldn't change things. He'd still love *her*.

She quickly grabbed an onion and began to dice it. Her eyes stung and began flowing with tears that would nicely conceal those that had come first.

Arla, 7:00–8:00pm

Mary not only assured Arla that she and Morgan could stay with her, but insisted. She suggested that Arla stop in town and get something they could make for dinner later. Maybe a can of coffee, too, since it looked to be a long night.

After buying the groceries, Arla put them in the trunk of her car. The two boxes were there, so she decided to get the diary. But when she rifled through the box with the papers, it wasn't there. Alarmed, she went through the box of clothes. It wasn't there, either. Her heart fluttered and she gripped the fender of her car. She took a deep breath, turned over the box of papers and went through everything more carefully, then did the same for the box of clothing.

Why hadn't he got it? She'd stressed how important it was! She'd told him what it looked like and where it was … Oh God. She'd told him it was in the study, where it always was. Except she'd forgotten to return it to the study last night. She'd put it in a kitchen drawer for safekeeping.

If her house burned down, the diary would burn with it. She *had* to get back to the house herself. She couldn't get through on Blackberry Springs Drive or the highway. But what about the dirt logging road? She doubted they had bothered setting up a roadblock, at least not a manned one. She even knew exactly where it started: from a dead-end street called Blue Hills Road, just north of downtown Camargo.

With all the potholes Ray had told her about, she didn't think her car could make it. But Mary had a pickup truck.

Arla arrived at Mary's at seven-fifteen. Mary was listening to KMTN with its continuous fire coverage. The fire had been given a name: the Jackrabbit Fire, because it had started at a place known as Jackrabbit Gulch. It had already burned over

2,500 acres, and had now changed direction and was moving east-southeast.

They had a light dinner, with ice cold beers. Morgan sprawled out between them, immediately at home in the way only dogs can be.

"Arla," Mary said. "Did he get the diary?"

She mustered a smile and a lie. "Yes, but the box of papers is in his pickup. Which is parked at the base camp that's been set up at the mall site. He's out on the firelines operating a bulldozer."

"Oh, I was hoping to read it tonight," Mary said.

"Well, I was just thinking. Suppose I leave Morgan here and go up to the fire camp to help however I can? And I'll get the diary from Ray's pickup."

"Good idea. And you'd better take my pickup. They'll probably put you to work hauling things. The keys are hanging next to the back door. It's a stick shift," Mary added.

"I'm old enough to have learned to drive on a stick shift." Arla smiled. She left five minutes later.

Roxanne, 7:00pm–8:30pm

Roxanne had parked her pickup at Wanda's, then she and Ray headed toward Pine Gap in his truck when he saw Arla's car pull into the mall site. Once Roxanne heard about Arla's dog, she knew Ray had to go there right away. Blackberry Springs was right in the path of the fire. So she'd said, "You go ahead, Ray. I'll get someone here to take me to my place."

But half an hour later, she still hadn't got to Pine Gap.

She went to Wanda's to call Carlos and let him know she might be here for a while. Because she wasn't going to leave until she got Baba Looey.

"Be careful, Mom. Don't go in if the fire's headed that way."

"I won't. But it's not close; don't worry. Are you okay staying at Terri's for a couple hours?"

"Yeah, Stella and Joe just got here, and Kit and her mom are coming later."

She was relieved. He wouldn't want to go anywhere, not if Kit was going to be there.

"Mom, Stella told me Pete found out."

Her heart lurched. "About you and Kit?"

"Yes, and he slapped Kit and threatened to sell her horse."

"Can I talk to Stella?"

She hung up a few minutes later, reassured that everyone knew to be on the lookout for Pete and PJ. Stella didn't think they would come looking for trouble, but if they did, Joe had his revolver and Laura had one too. But Roxanne's stomach was in knots and she was more determined than ever to get up to her house right away.

She left her pickup at Wanda's and walked the short distance to the fire camp. The mall site was no longer recognizable as such. A large tent was in the process of being erected; smaller ones were already up. Portable outhouses were being unloaded at the far side of the lot. Dozens of Pulaskis were piled up, ready for the additional teams of firefighters that, hopefully, would soon arrive.

Frustrated, Roxanne looked toward the highway. Clay DiMauro was just driving into the camp in his jeep. She rushed toward him. "Clay, I need your help."

Quickly, she explained the situation. He frowned. "I shouldn't do this. But you're in luck Roxanne, 'cause I gotta go into Pine Gap anyway. I'll take you. But hang on, first I have to find someone who can…" He looked around distractedly. His eyes lit on someone and when she followed his gaze, she saw PJ Jensen, who was just getting out of his pickup. Jerry Frye was in the passenger seat. PJ saw her too, and for a long moment their eyes locked.

Clay went over and talked to them. PJ nodded and got back into his pickup. When Clay drove out of the parking lot, PJ was right behind.

"What's going on?" she asked.

"PJ's gonna go empty out the LNG tank at the store."

The general store in Pine Gap sold propane and natural gas, stored in big tanks adjacent to the building. If the fire did come into town, fire crews had a better chance at containing it if the natural gas tank was empty. As far as the propane tanks, there was nothing to do except spray them with fire retardant foam and hope for the best.

PJ pulled off at the general store. Clay continued driving.

"Are they dropping retardant?" Roxanne asked.

"Yeah, but I don't know why they're bothering; the wind's blowing it all over the place. They're gonna have to rely on ground crews, and it wouldn't surprise me if none of the crews have even got to the fire yet. You ever been to Jackrabbit Gulch?"

Roxanne shook her head.

"There's no fire road in there. After you get off the closest road, you have to hike up and down three steep hills for almost two miles before you get to Jackrabbit Gulch. The hills are so steep you can't even get there in an all-terrain vehicle. Some spots are so steep, you can only get up on all fours. Those firefighters are on foot, carrying sixty-pound packs and equipment. It'll take 'em a couple hours to hike in and I doubt they even tried, this close to nightfall. Besides, you can't have firefighters in there at night with the winds like this."

"So what about the smokejumpers?"

"It's too windy. They might be able to get them in there in choppers, but not at night." He stopped in front of her house.

"I have to unlock the gates to all the fire roads. I'll be back in about twenty minutes."

Of course Baba Looey wasn't in the house. That would be too easy, she grumbled to herself. She called him and left the door open, then went into her bedroom. She got her .38 from the bedside table, opened the cylinder to make sure it was loaded, then stuck the revolver in the waistband of her jeans. She turned over a box of books and began filling it. She tossed in the papers for the house, including the offer letter from SlidePac, insurance and title documents; banking stuff; and Carlos's baby pictures. And a box of extra cartridges.

She approached Carlos's room. She rarely went into his room and even in this crisis it seemed an invasion of his privacy to just start rooting around. So she phoned him at Terri's. He told her what things to get, and suggested she bring each of them at least one change of clothes. Roxanne laughed. "Good thing I called you. I didn't even think of that!"

She finished gathering everything, but still no Baba Looey. Time for the ultimate weapon: the can opener. That did the trick. Once he was inside, she closed the door and while he slurped down kitty stew, she brought his carrier into the kitchen. Baba mewed in protest as she shoved him inside.

Clay returned and parked out front, motor running. They loaded her two boxes and the cat carrier into his jeep and headed back out of town.

PJ's truck was still at the store, parked near the gas pumps. Both PJ and Jerry were squatting, their backs to the road. When Clay's jeep turned in, both men jumped up. PJ walked quickly toward the jeep. Jerry surreptitiously shoved what looked like a gas can behind the pickup. "Just about done here, Clay," PJ called.

"All right, hurry up. See you at base camp."

"Be there in five minutes," PJ replied.

Clay drove back toward the highway. "God *damn* them two. I send them in to help out and they steal gasoline."

"Maybe the firefighters need it for a control burn."

"Then why didn't PJ tell me that? Why'd they try to hide the can when I drove up? And I saw four more cans in the back of PJ's truck." Clay cursed again.

As they drove over the little rise and entered the long downhill slope toward the highway, the northern horizon appeared before them. They both gasped. Not even trees were visible; all they could see was smoke boiling in, turning over itself in great waves—and above that, a huge white puffball so tall it seemed to fill half the sky.

"That's one damned hot fire. Know what that is, Roxanne?"

"It looks like a mushroom cloud."

"Meteorologically speaking, that's pretty much what it is. Nuclear bombs, volcanoes, and massive wildfires—they're the only things powerful enough to make one of those."

"Does it have a name?"

"Pyrocumulus." Clay sounded almost reverent. "When the heat from a fire is super intense, it forces the air upward, all the way to the jet stream. Then vapor forms and merges with the smoke and you got a pyrocumulus."

Roxanne looked at the massive white cloud, which absurdly resembled a giant cauliflower, or a whole bin full of them, suspended in mid-air. "It's part of the weather system a fire creates," Clay added. "But to see a pyrocumulus this soon after a fire starts, well, that's unusual."

"So can it produce rain?"

"They can, but usually don't. Usually, they produce dry lightning."

Ray, 8:00–9:00pm

Ray was relieved when night approached. Fires were most explosive in mid-afternoon; at night they tend to 'lie down.' Winds usually subside. The air cools, maybe only ten degrees, but every degree helps. Firefighters stay on the job, taking advantage of the improved conditions.

But the weather that night behaved differently. And so did the Jackrabbit Fire.

Ray was sent to Blackberry Springs, where the hotshots had already started a fire line using Pulaskis and chainsaws to clear the brush and small trees. Ray and others—some of them CDF or Forest Service employees, some of them guys who worked for PG&E or the phone company or, like Ray, construction—would take bulldozers over those rudimentary fire lines and widen them. It was an attempt to create a break too wide for a fire to jump. Sometimes that worked. Sometimes it just slowed down a fire enough so it could be attacked with water and retardant. Sometimes the fire jumped the fire line and kept right on going.

To his surprise, the fire bosses weren't using the old logging road to bring in equipment and firefighters and to work from behind Blackberry Springs. They must be worried about people getting trapped. Which meant the fire was fast, ferocious, and unpredictable.

They'd barely turned onto the eastern end of Blackberry Springs Drive when the supervisor changed the orders. Everyone was to get the hell out of the area. The winds were shifting; the fire was heading south and west now. It was spotting, too, starting fires a quarter mile ahead of the firefront.

"Those houses," one of the CDF men said. The state guys were, Ray knew, all thinking the same thing: When expensive houses go up in flames, heads go on the line.

"It's too risky," the supervisor said. "The only thing that can save those houses now is if the fire shifts direction."

So they all stayed on the bus and it headed east, passed the 4,000 foot elevation marker, and turned in to the MiWok Rancheria. One of the firefighters pointed out the window to the north, where the fire was running along a ridgetop. Everyone watched in awe as trees burst into flames before the fire even touched them.

Arla, 8:00–9:30pm

The radio had said the fire was burning east. So it was burning in the opposite direction, away from her house. Arla would be following behind it, not meeting it head-on. Plus, for the fire to reach Blackberry Springs it would have to travel down the long canyon, jump the river, and come back up the other side. So, she reasoned, she should be able to get into her house and back to Mary's within an hour with no one the wiser.

As she'd expected, there were no roadblocks. There were no other vehicles, either. That was reassuring; the fire must be a long way off, otherwise there would be firefighting vehicles on what was, after all, a fire road. Still, she wished she had one of those placards in the windshield.

The road was unpaved, in some places covered with gravel, but mostly just soft dust that billowed up thickly from the tires. There were large ruts every few feet. It was impossible to drive fast; she dared not go over fifteen miles per hour. She wasn't used to the clutch and stalled out several times.

Finally, she was behind Blackberry Springs. She was surprised to see no firefighting vehicles here, either. The orange smoke was thick and opaque, impenetrable to the eye. She turned from the dirt road onto Blackberry Springs Drive. A reddish glow reflected off the viscous sky, painting houses and yards and cars a vivid orange-pink. She heard sirens not far away. She heard airplanes overhead. She heard smoke alarms shrieking in all the houses. But what she heard most was the roar of the fire. She had never suspected a fire would be so loud.

She ran into the house. Her smoke alarms were going off too, and the whole house rang with warning screams. The diary was right where she'd left it, in the gadget drawer in the kitchen. Turning to leave, she noticed her camera bag on the table, the simple zippered one made for an Instamatic. She removed the camera and replaced it with the diary. At least that would give the diary some protection.

Going back toward Camargo was even worse than it had been coming up. She was hardly a mile down the road when it occurred to her that she should have simply taken the highway. They were evacuating people; they wouldn't keep her from going back *down* the highway. In fact, they'd probably help her.

She turned the pickup around and headed back toward Blackberry Springs.

But something had happened with the fire. It was heading west now—toward her. And it was closer than it had been even ten minutes ago. Don't panic, she told herself. Just turn back around and go. Go as fast as you can, but drive carefully. This is no time to stall out or get stuck in a rut.

She turned west again and drove as fast as she dared. It seemed far too slow. Behind her, the red flames seemed to be chasing her and all she could hear was that awful roar. Her eyes watered so badly she could hardly see. How could she possibly drive the entire distance back to town in this smoke?

Suddenly, she remembered something Ray had told her. His job site was on Gennessee Mine Road, which ended at this road, and that intersection was the halfway point between Blackberry Springs and town. If she could make it there, she'd be safe. He'd told her that the trees had all been cut down, so that land would be entirely cleared with nothing to burn. She could stop there and wait until the smoke cleared. And maybe there was water at the job site; she could wash her eyes, turn onto Blackberry Springs Drive and be at Mary's within a half hour.

Time was all out of whack; she had lost any sense of it. She didn't know whether she might have passed the Gennessee Road cutoff, or whether she was still miles shy of it.

Then, going around another bend, she confronted a red wall of flame. The lightning she'd been seeing all the way up must have started another fire. She was in between two fires that seemed to be racing toward each other. Winds whipped in every direction. Flames danced at the top of the ravine, crowding up against it and pausing at the edge, as if deciding whether to try and jump. She was shocked at how tall they were.

Her heart hammered, fast and frenzied, against her chest. She forced herself to breathe slowly. I've got to get to the river. It's my only chance.

She pointed the truck, aiming the headlights in the direction she intended to run. She took the camera bag with the diary inside it and left everything else: her purse, the keys in the ignition, whatever Mary had in the glovebox. She turned toward what she thought must be north, toward the river, hoping it was the right direction. She was no longer able to tell where the fire was coming from, or which way it was moving, or how far away it was. The roaring seemed to come from all around and the smoke was thick and swirling. But she had no choice; she had to trust her first instinct. You can run, she told herself. That's what you do best. Pace yourself. Your daily pace is seven minutes a mile. You ran a 10K at 6:17 a mile. That's very fast. You can outrun the fire. You've got a head start on it. You're wearing sneakers and shorts. It's just another run.

But she hadn't taken the smoke into account. Almost immediately, her nostrils burned and pain seared her lungs. Gasping and coughing, she stopped and took off her shirt, and tied it around her nose and mouth. It wasn't much, but it would have to do. She set off running again. Within seconds, she had gone past the range of the headlights and was running in the darkness. Forget the six-minute pace; not with her lungs burning, not in the dark, not with her eyes streaming so hard she could barely see, not in a forest with no trail. She held her hands stretched out ahead of her to avoid running into a tree. Once she tripped on a root and went down, dropping the camera bag and having to grope around to recover it. She barely noticed the bruises and scratches and cuts that, during a normal run, would have made her stop and go home.

The fire sucked heat and oxygen from the air, consuming anything and everything, all of life around it, turning every molecule into fuel. Yet the air was cold, incredibly, bone-chillingly cold in this vortex from which all oxygen had been sucked. Her lungs found nothing to breathe except that little pocket of air under her makeshift kerchief.

The roar of the fire grew louder. To both her left and right the world was brilliant orange. But finally she saw a clearing, and hoped it meant the river. She ran faster, and reached the edge.

How far down? She remembered it was at the bottom of a deep canyon. Here at the top, the canyon wall lacked trees or bushes, but at least it was composed of dirt, not granite. She began stepping down sideways, to keep from falling. But it was too steep. She gave up, sat down, and let gravity take her. The wall was not as smooth as it had appeared; she kept striking rocks. A small landslide of dirt and rocks followed her down the slope. The cyclonic wind roared overhead, taking some of the debris along with it to the east as it raced toward the other fire.

But suddenly she heard the water, and then she could smell it. Almost sobbing with relief, she willed herself to go faster. Then something struck her head.

Ray, 9:30–11:00pm

Ray and another bulldozer operator were told to make a twelve-foot-wide fire line around the Rancheria, a desperate effort to save the fifty or so MiWok homes and a general store. They wouldn't even try to save any outbuildings.

Hotshots forged ahead, their chainsaws whining in tandem. This crew was doing a good job, leaving only small stobs, and they were working fast, creating a fire line three feet wide that Ray would widen.

Despite goggles and a mask, his throat was raw and painful and his eyes stung. This fire was so hot, and the forest so dry, that entire trees were gone in ten to fifteen seconds. More like exploding than burning. Ray had seen plenty of forest fires and he'd never seen pine trees go that quickly.

Somewhere not too far away, a propane tank caught fire. Heated gas rose through the emergency release valve, shooting a long plume of fire upward. Moments later the tank blew up with a thunderous boom, then settled into a steady roar like a jet engine revving, until finally the propane burned out.

All night he'd heard grumbling that if they'd had a bigger crew in Piñon County, the fire might not have got out of control so quickly; they'd've had a better shot at containing it. But he wasn't so sure. When Mother Nature was ready to burn a forest, it burned. The conditions had been perfect for a fire and sometimes all the men and machines in the world couldn't stop one. The Higuera National Forest was almost a million acres. The way things looked so far, he wouldn't be surprised if the whole million went up in flames.

Southeast of the Jensen ranch, one of the spot fires had grown to a couple hundred acres, big enough to get a name—the Bobcat Ridge Fire. The risk was that the Bobcat Ridge and Jackrabbit would unite. Fires were drawn to each other. They created their own weather system and wind patterns, and for all Ray knew there was a more mystical explanation, too. If the Jackrabbit jumped the highway and burned south, and if the Bobcat Ridge jumped the Middle Fork and burned north, both entirely feasible, well, then Eddie was right and this really was the Big One.

It was bad enough already. Ray knew that the supervisor's decision to give up Blackberry Springs meant that this fire was even worse than people realized.

"All right," the crew chief called now. "Let's move 'em across the road and do the south side. Ray, I want you to do this area," and he gestured to the relatively treeless stretch. "This is habitat for the Western Burrowing Owl. We just last year found them nesting here and it's the only colony in Piñon County. I want you to make a high pass."

Warring against the fatigue threatening to overwhelm him, he took a pull from his water bottle and nodded. He doubted that a high pass would spare the owls' burrows, but it was worth a try. All night long they'd been seeing animals fleeing, their fear of the fire overwhelming their fear of men and machinery. Deer, foxes and coyotes went right through lines of firefighters. One guy had almost run over a family of quail that darted in front of the dozer. On the east side of the Rancheria, a couple hotshots had seen a bear and two cubs running southward, which meant they'd be heading for the Bobcat Ridge fire, but there was no way to redirect them.

Suddenly the smoke darkened, no longer the white that their lights reflected off, but almost black. This wasn't just trees and brush burning. Somewhere nearby, buildings and probably cars were burning, too.

"There goes Blackberry Springs," one of the firefighters commented.

At some point—Ray didn't know what time, because he couldn't see the hands on his watch—they took a short break. Everyone soaked their kerchiefs in water and tried to wash the grit from their eyes; somehow, it crept in behind the goggles. Suddenly, one of the guys stared open-mouthed to the southeast and exclaimed, "Holy Christ!"

Everyone turned to look that way. It was downhill from their position, so they had a good vantage point. Strange translucent balls were rolling up the columns of smoke and when they reached the top of the smoke, probably a couple thousand feet up, the balls exploded into flames.

The crew chief, who'd been fighting fires for twenty-some years, said in awe, "I've heard about this, but it's the first time I've ever seen it."

"What the hell is it?" someone asked.

"Balls of gas. They form down in the heart of the fire, but there's no oxygen there. So they rise up looking for it." They watched another ball explode. "It means this is the hottest damned fire I've ever seen."

Arla, 10:00pm to Midnight

Arla came back to consciousness when she landed in the water. Not only water: the river, like all western rivers, was filled with boulders. One sharp edge struck the shin of her left leg. Pain shot through her and she screamed then lay panting, her head on the riverbank, the rest of her in the water. It was icy cold. Perhaps it would both wash the wound and numb the pain.

The camera bag was no longer in her hand. She must have dropped it when the rock hit her head. She sat up and looked around, but didn't see it. She could only hope it had lodged on the slope, that it had not fallen into the river and been carried away. Oh God, she moaned to herself. You really screwed everything up.

Her leg hurt terribly. She reached down tentatively. It seemed to be more bruised than cut. Perhaps, she thought, I should try to stand on it. Just to see if I can.

She scooted back from the water onto the rocky riverbank. She could see the red on her shin and was afraid that it was worse than she'd thought, that it was bleeding badly. But then she realized the red glow wasn't just on her shin. It was everywhere—in the water, on the cliff walls opposite her, on her body. It was the fire. The fire had come right up to the edge of the ravine. The roaring had intensified, too, and within moments, it was deafening, as if a jet were taking off a few feet over her head.

She looked up to a ceiling of flame. Red and orange and yellow, alive and moving, the fire leapt across the ravine. The awesome power of it, the exquisite beauty, brought tears to her eyes.

I must be losing my mind. This fire nearly killed me, and has probably destroyed my house by now, and I'm in the same emotional state as when I stand before Monet's waterlilies.

And then it was gone. The glow, the roar, the wind. The night was quiet. Only after her ears adjusted, did she realize that it was not quiet at all. From above came cracks as tree limbs snapped, thuds when they hit the ground. Occasionally a popping explosion, as though the trees were bursting from the inside out. An owl hooting. The sound of the river. The blessed river.

She tried to stand up, and nearly passed out. The bone must be bruised, or even broken. Rather than trying to stand again, she slid back to the water and drank her fill. And then she lay in it, happily shivering from the cold. She would need strength to get back up that steep, slippery hillside.

Remembering how she'd slid down out of control, she thought that it made more sense to find another place to go up. Downriver, upriver, somewhere not as steep, and where there was enough vegetation to keep her from sliding two feet back for every one foot forward.

That would mean waiting until dawn. But why not? she asked herself. I have water. I'm safe. It makes more sense to stay here until it's light out. And besides, if I were to climb to the top now, what would I find? The pickup burned to a crisp, and a walk of miles. No, not on this leg. I'll have a better chance in daylight. If nothing else, a plane might see me. Or someone will come looking. She crawled out of the river, lay on the bank and relented to exhaustion.

She was sleeping deeply when a crashing boom woke her. She barely had time to wonder what it was before she realized that something was tumbling down the hillside above her, something huge and hard that shook the ground each time it struck. A boulder? A shower of dirt and rocks cascaded down and she knew then that she was directly in the boulder's path.

Terri, 11:00pm–1:00am

Just after eleven, when Terri was in the kitchen loading the dishwasher, the KMTN announcer said, "Jackrabbit Fire has jumped the Higuera Highway and is now burning in a southeasterly direction. It remains out of control and in the last hour, has grown from 4,000 to 7,000 acres…"

Laura finally came back into the kitchen, having helped set

up all the beds and sleeping places. "You have a very full house tonight."

Terri didn't mind that. In fact, she preferred it. Anything to keep from fretting over Ray. They took glasses of wine and went onto the back patio, sitting together on the swing, arms and legs touching.

"So," Terri said. "Tell me what happened."

She listened in horror as Laura related the events and concluded, "That's why we were late getting here; I took her to the hospital."

"How badly is she hurt?"

"She's okay. The doctor did put a few stitches on one of her cheeks, on the inside." Laura paused, looked directly into Terri's eyes. "I'm so ashamed of myself."

"What are you going to do now?" Terri asked.

"When we were at the hospital, I called my lawyer and told her to be ready to go into court Monday to request a temporary restraining order against Pete and PJ, ordering them to stay away from me and Kit, and to stay off the ranch. We're going to file another document to the effect that Pete's cousin is the family law judge in Piñon County, and another cousin is the sheriff, making it necessary to file the papers out of the county. We're filing in Sacramento."

"The lawyer thinks you'll get the restraining order?"

"Yes. I'll have to go down and be in court, too. First thing Monday morning. After the restraining order is issued, the Sacramento sheriff's department will serve it on Pete and PJ. We're filing the divorce petition, too. He'll get that at the same time."

"So you've got this all worked out already."

"Yes." Laura sipped her wine. "After he's been served, I'm going to make him a settlement offer. I'll offer to settle for the Double-L and $100,000 cash. Also, he has to pay my lawyer."

"He has that much?"

"If he sells our stocks and bonds, yes. Actually, they're worth considerably more."

"Then you should ask for more. You're entitled."

"I know. But I don't need more. If he accepts, he'll still have the west county ranch and the cattle, or the insurance for them." She grimaced. "He'll have the ranch equipment, and his real estate business, and whatever money is left. So he has no reason to refuse the settlement."

"What if the house—"

"If it burns down, I still want the ranch itself, and whatever money the house was insured for."

"And what about Kit?"

"I get sole custody. That's not negotiable." Laura's voice was firm.

"What if he doesn't accept the settlement offer?"

"Then I'll file for dissolution. I'd rather have it settled now, quickly, but I'm prepared to fight it out in court. But I think once he's thought it over, he'll settle."

"You could probably get more. He's getting off easy."

"Perhaps he is. But I want it over, and I want it over quickly."

Not until midnight was everyone in bed. The house was quiet except for the soft humming of the air conditioner, which Terri had kept on for a change.

She fell asleep and dreamed that the fire was bearing down on this house; she woke with her heart racing. What a relief that it was only a dream. Laura was on her side, facing Terri's direction. Terri reached over and carefully brushed the tendrils of Laura's hair back from her face. But Laura must have felt it; she frowned and then actually flinched. Then her eyes flew open. As they lit on Terri, she smiled. "For a moment I forgot I was here. I thought it was him." She put her hand over Terri's and held it against her cheek. "I'm so glad it's you."

Arla

She came awake screaming. The thing pinning her down, covering her right leg completely, was dark but glowed from within. She tried to pull free, but couldn't move. She knew she was wasting energy by screaming, but she couldn't stop herself, and when she finally did it was because she was sobbing.

She fell back, stuffing her shirt in her mouth to keep from biting off her tongue. She couldn't even shift her position; she was on her side with rocks pressing into her. In any other circumstance it would have been unendurable. She tried to push the thing. It was too heavy. And she could get no leverage. She smelled the burning of her own flesh as the smoldering thing sank down onto it, deeper and deeper.

She forced herself into calmness and drew a deep breath. It was a tree trunk, or maybe a treetop. No limbs protruded. She gathered herself and pushed with all her strength. It did not budge.

She didn't know how long she lay there before she realized that the pain was decreasing. It kept decreasing until she felt nothing at all; her right leg had gone numb. She knew that probably wasn't good, but didn't care. The pain had stopped and she sobbed with relief.

She looked at her watch and thought the hands showed 2:10. Another four or so hours until daylight. She could only hope that they would start searching for her then. At some point, Ray would call or come by Mary O'Malley's, find her not there, and come looking for her. Or would he? Hadn't he told her that sometimes firefighters were kept on duty twenty-four hours straight?

But he'd said he'd call her at Mary's in the morning. Oh Ray, please call. Please be near a phone.

Her right leg was numb, but her left leg began to throb.

She couldn't move it; it was twisted unnaturally and pressed against rocks. And she was thirsty again, but the river was out of her reach. She stretched down, turning her body as far that way as she could, but the water flowed two tantalizing feet out of reach.

She untied her shirt from around her neck, held on to one end, and flung the other toward the river. It touched just enough. She pulled it back and greedily sucked the water. Did it again and again.

She kept falling asleep, or falling unconscious. And whenever she woke, she was groggy in a strange way—not sleepy, but something else. *Am I delirious?* she wondered. *Is this what it feels like?*

Suddenly a loud, eerie cry echoed off the canyon walls. It sounded like the cry of a woman, and she wondered if she'd made it herself. Then came an oddly amplified meow.

Oh dear God. A frightened, hungry predator coming her way, and there was nothing she could do. Another cry echoed off the canyon walls. It sounded closer. The mountain lion must be making its way down to the river. To her.

She passed out again, and woke to an odor. A powerful, gamy odor, but not like a skunk; something different, and right beside her. *It's come,* she thought; *the mountain lion has come.* She was afraid to breathe. She was afraid it could hear the pounding of her heart. She was afraid if she turned her head to look at it, it might be startled into leaping. She wanted a few moments to prepare herself—a few moments more, before those knife-like teeth sank into her throat. *Be quick about it, lion. At least be quick.*

Something cold and wet touched her left arm. Slowly, slowly she turned her head toward it. At least these last precious seconds would be a gift. She would see something that almost no one ever did: a mountain lion in a natural setting.

But what she saw was big, bulky and furry with a longish

nose. A bear! It backed away and sat down not more than three feet from her. It was moaning, and began rocking back and forth. The smell was partly his bear smell, partly a burning smell.

Eventually, he ambled to the river and stuck his feet in the water. He snuffled loudly.

She drifted into unconsciousness again. When she woke, not knowing whether it was five minutes or two hours later, he was still there. He sat on the slope about fifteen feet from her. She felt a kinship with him; they'd both been injured fleeing the forest fire. Far from being afraid, she was grateful for his presence. No further harm would come to her with him there. The mountain lion wouldn't come with him there.

She was unable to shift the position of her body; the discomfort had become pain. She groaned and the bear looked at her, his black eyes gleaming. "Push it off me," she moaned. "Please, bear."

He made a noise like a short bark, then slowly got up and began walking downriver on all fours.

"Oh, bear. Don't leave. I'll stop talking," Arla wept.

Perhaps it hurt his feet to walk. He sat down again after going only fifty feet or so. Poor bear. The poor suffering bear.

She knew now that she was going to die. Perhaps it would be better after all if he would leave and the lion would come. That would be faster than the way it was happening now, life draining from her breath by breath.

DAY TWO: SATURDAY

SEPTEMBER 28

Stella, 6:00–8:30am

Joe was already awake when Stella opened her eyes just before dawn on Saturday. "Did you get any sleep?" she asked.

"Not very much," he said. "How about you, *bella?*"

"I slept like a log," Stella admitted.

Joe laughed softly and kissed her. "All that anxiety made you tired. But don't worry. Even if the fire went through the ranch, the house should be all right. It's in a hollow and we keep the grounds clear. The roofs aren't flammable."

She couldn't bear to think of the alternative. She lay in Joe's embrace for a few minutes while the sky began to lighten. But that was as far as it got; the light stayed dim, as though the sun had got stuck just below the horizon.

They washed up as quietly as possible. When they went out, Puddles padded along behind them and Stella gave him a boost into the pickup. They stopped in town to pick up coffee and donuts. The sun was a red blur. Ashes floated down like snowflakes, leaving thick gray blankets on parked cars.

The town was unusually active for this early on a Saturday. Pickups and caravans of firefighting trucks headed up highway, their headlights on. The Elks Hall parking lot was filled with cars and a few large tents; it had been turned into the fire command center. From somewhere to the east came the whop-whop of helicopters and the droning engines of the old planes straining with heavy loads of fire retardant as they headed out to bomb the fire. Yes, Piñon County was under siege.

They tended to their animals at the fairgrounds, then took a walk through town. "If the house is gone but the cabins are okay, we could live in one of them," Stella said. "We'd have to cook outside on the barbecue. But what if *everything* burned down?"

"We can't ask Arla for a loan now. Not when she's lost her own house."

"No," Stella agreed. Even though Arla probably had plenty of insurance, losing one's home was difficult. Arla would have to start over and perhaps, Stella reflected, she might not even want to stay in Piñon County.

"Suppose," Joe said, "the worst has happened, and everything's burned down—all the outbuildings, too. We'll have the land itself, and the insurance payout of $30,000."

"If we sold all the stock except Tippy and Tabasco, and the new pickup and the big horse trailer, we might get $20,000 for everything."

They looked at each other. They'd have no home, no business and no source of income. Not immediately, anyway. But they would have the land, the ranch pickup, and about $50,000, of which $34,000 was owed to the bank.

"Heck, that'd leave us with $16,000. That's plenty," Joe said. "We could get a trailer and put in a vegetable garden and raise livestock, enough to feed ourselves." He grinned. "Be just like when I got back from the war, living in a trailer on the ranch. Only this time, I'm about ready to collect social security."

"Good God! Are we really that old?" Stella burst out.

He laughed. "Not you, just this old man you're married to."

They went back to Terri's house, where people were starting to get up, and joined Laura in the kitchen.

"I'm going to go to the fire camp, Joe, see if I can find something out there." Stella put her hand on his arm. "You stay here and try to rest. Or if you can't rest, maybe you can put up a Sunday gravy for dinner tonight."

Ray, 8:00 - 9:00am

Ray had gone beyond exhaustion and back again several times, and when dawn finally came on Saturday, his third or fourth wind gave out. He almost fell asleep at the wheel while making a catline, so the supervisor pulled him off the dozer and sent him back to fire camp. He tried to remember how much sleep he'd had the past few days. None since that troubled four hours Thursday night, and since then he'd been up more than twenty-four straight hours, most of it working, much of it breathing smoke.

The Bobcat Fire had joined up with the Jackrabbit, and together they'd burned almost 15,000 acres. The lightning strikes had stopped, but the winds had actually increased. The fire boss grumbled that every time the officials analyzed the fire and put together a tactical plan, the fire was already doing something different. Not because the supervisors were too slow, but because the fire was too damned fast. Last night one CDF guy had remarked, "This one's not playing by the rules."

Ray got into his pickup, but when he nearly fell asleep

before turning the key in the ignition, he realized he couldn't drive. He hailed Mark Willits. Mark had been working all night too, but he wasn't in as bad a condition as Ray, and gave him a ride home.

Kit and Carlos were outside and when Ray stumbled getting out of Mark's pickup, they rushed over.

"Oh Ray," Terri exclaimed in dismay as the kids led him inside, one on each arm. "You're dead on your feet. Let's take him into the bedroom."

"I'm dirty," he began, but Terri waved off his objection. Ray collapsed on the bed and Terri pulled off his boots. When she peeled down his socks, she gasped and he knew it was because his feet were covered with blisters. He had forgotten to douse them with foot powder before going out on the lines.

Sleep began to wash over him, an inch at a time. But he had to call Arla before he passed out. After Terri left the bedroom, he called Information and got Mary O'Malley's phone number. Mary answered and he identified himself, and asked if he could speak with Arla.

"She's been at the fire camp since last night," Mary said.

Ray tried to clear the confusion from his brain. "I was just there. She's not there."

"Well, she borrowed my pickup and left her dog here with me. She hasn't come back yet, so I—"

"Mary, excuse me for interrupting, but what time was that?"

"Around 7:30 last night. She said she wanted to help out, and to get the box of her things from your truck."

Ray sat on the edge of the bed. "Wait, what box? There were two boxes and she put them both in the trunk of her car. One was clothes, the other had all her papers and pictures."

"You're sure she put them in her trunk?"

"Well, I left before she did it, but they weren't in my pickup when I got back from the fire." He concentrated. "I didn't look for them, but I'm pretty sure I would've noticed if they were still there."

"And did you also get the diary?" Mary asked. "She had a diary from the 1800s that belongs to the Historical Society."

"Right. She told me about it, but I didn't find it; it wasn't where she said it was. I figured she must've left it in her car."

Mary's voice trembled. "You know, Ray, we had just been talking about that diary, Arla and I, when we found out about the fire. It's a rather long story, but the gist of it is that she had discovered this diary, which is a very crucial historical document, but hadn't told me about it. The first I even knew of its existence was yesterday. I'm afraid I was upset with her. Perhaps you see what I'm thinking?"

Ray did. Arla had told him where the diary was, had forgotten that it was somewhere else, had remembered too late, and had decided to retrieve it herself. "Don't worry. She couldn't have gone to her house last night. Somebody might've taken her in this morning. I'll go back to the fire camp. Someone there will know where she is."

"Her house…" Mary began.

"It's gone. All the houses there are gone."

They were both silent for a few moments. "Please keep in touch with me," Mary said.

He hung up and almost gave in to panic. He had to keep his head, because he was going to have to look for her. He went into the kitchen, where Terri and Roxanne were stacking dishes, and Carlos and Kit were eating scrambled eggs and fried potatoes. Everyone stared at him. "I have to go back out."

"That's ridiculous!" Roxanne said. "There's enough guys who can run a bulldozer! You need rest!"

"No. Not that. It's…" There was, he realized, no easy way to say it. So, just say it. "Arla's missing. She took Mary O'Malley's pickup last night at 7:30 and hasn't got back yet.

She told Mary she'd be at the fire camp, but she's not there. I think she might've tried to get back to her house."

Terri was silent and grim, but made him a cup of coffee loaded with sugar. Roxanne called the hospital, the police, and the two hotels in Camargo. Arla wasn't at any of those places. Roxanne said that must mean she was at the fire camp after all.

"No!" Ray said. "I was just there!"

"She's got a pickup you wouldn't have recognized," Roxanne pointed out. "She could've been in a tent, or the Forest Service sent her into town on some errand. She couldn't have got past the roadblocks into Blackberry Springs, right?"

"Then where the hell is she?" He gulped down the coffee.

"Ray," Terri said, "you're exhausted. Maybe–"

He tried not to let his anger come out in his voice. "I am, and maybe I'm not thinking straight, but I'm telling you, something's wrong. And I won't be able to sleep until I know she's safe."

He thought he saw Terri and Roxanne exchange a glance. Carlos spoke up. "Why don't we drive up to the fire camp and look around?"

They began to make a hasty plan, and then Terri looked at him and said levelly, "It might help if you have a picture."

He reddened, but he said nothing more, and neither did Terri. He retrieved his wallet and made sure the envelope with Arla's photo was there.

Minutes later, he was in Roxanne's pickup. Carlos and Kit sat in the back. He still hadn't washed the soot and dirt from his face. His feet were so swollen that he hadn't been able to get on the boots he'd worn last night; Terri had found an older, more stretched out pair in the garage and he'd managed to pull them on, gritting his teeth as the leather scraped his blisters even through socks and bandages. They took the usual precautions when driving somewhere during a fire: they brought a few jugs of drinking water, candy bars, and two flashlights.

No one at fire camp had seen Arla or knew where she was. Had she somehow persuaded a firefighter to take her up to her house, 'off the books?' And even if she had, where was she now? But one of the firefighters Ray knew disabused them of the possibility that a firefighter had taken her into the evacuated zone. "No way," said Brian, firmly. Like Ray, his face was blackened from smoke and soot and dirt, only his eyes showing, raccoon-like. "It was too dangerous. We had a blowup at Blackberry Springs; you know that. We couldn't get in. Nobody would have taken her in there, no way."

All at once, Ray knew. "Oh no. Oh, god*damn* it."

Roxanne grabbed his arm. "What?"

"The logging road." At her lack of comprehension, he added, "Parallel to the North Fork."

"Oh, that old dirt road, with the long drops down to the river?"

"She knows about that road. She jogged on it when she first moved here." His jaw clenched. "She must've known there wouldn't be any roadblocks there. And she knew she couldn't drive that road in her car, so she borrowed Mary's pickup."

"Let's go look," Roxanne said simply.

They put all the equipment they'd brought into Ray's truck. He sent Kit to grab a couple Pulaskis, hardhats and fireshirts. Carlos ran down to Elsie's to tell Wanda that Roxanne would be late for work. Kit returned with four hardhats but had only been able to get two fireshirts. Ray gave one to Kit, and one to Carlos. "Put these on. The hardhats, too. They'll make your head hot, but don't take them off, okay?"

They all got into Ray's truck. Roxanne drove. Ray gestured east. "Let's go in from the Blackberry Springs side."

They drove up the highway, Ray's CDF placard getting

them waved through the roadblocks. The fire had moved eastward too, and the higher they got, the more devastation they saw. The Higuera had become a forest of snags. In the back seat of the pickup, Kit and Carlos were completely silent.

He turned around to look at them. They held hands and stared out the windows, eyes wide, expressions grim.

Smoke was thicker the higher they got. Roxanne had to slow to a crawl because the visibility was so poor, and even with the windows up she began to cough. "Ray, maybe we should call someone."

"Yeah, but I don't know where she is, or if she's even up here. Let's take a look first, ourselves. If we don't find her, we'll get help."

Neither of them mentioned the other possibility; that they would find her not alive. They drove on in silence.

Stella, 8:00–9:30am

"I'm off duty, so I can take you," Clay said. He had a cast on his right arm and explained he'd sprained it. "But you'll have to drive. And we'll have to take my jeep so we can get through."

As they drove up the highway he must have noticed Stella gaping at the smoldering totems that had once been trees, and said, "In this area it was a crown fire. It was moving fast as hell. But that's good for you, Stella, because it probably just went across the treetops all the way to the forest."

She turned onto the ranch road, her heart pounding so hard she could feel it in her throat. She had driven down this road thousands of times in the past twenty-three years. This was the first time she had approached the rise not with anticipation, but with dread.

She stopped the jeep, and stared down at the valley.

The house, barn and stables were gone.

Across the pond, the trees still stood, but only half as tall as before. The fire had decapitated them. The cabins had disappeared. Not even ruins remained—nothing except small piles of smoldering charcoal.

She had thought she was mentally prepared for this. Now, she knew she wasn't. She opened her mouth to speak, but only a strangled cry came from her throat.

Clay reached over and briefly rested his hand over hers. "Stay here, Stella. I'll go down and look around."

When they'd left yesterday, they'd brought a change of clothes each, various business documents, and the title papers for the property and the cars. They'd brought the veterinarian file, although probably they could have got duplicates from the vet, and receipts for the purchases of the horses. They'd brought their heirloom family photo albums and the framed photographs from the walls. Joe had brought his handgun, the saddles and some of the tack. That was it. She had left behind her favorite cooking pots. The dress she'd been married in. Joe's jazz and blues albums, a lifetime collection. The recipe cards, many in her mother's or Nonna's handwriting. Nonna's sourdough bread starter that Stella had kept alive for thirty years.

She got out of the jeep and walked about the edges of the still-smoldering rubble, poking it with the toe of her boot, looking for anything that might have been spared. The only thing she found was the cast iron Dutch oven, warped into an oblong. It seemed so horribly alone there amid the ashes that she picked it up and brought it with her.

Clay had gone over to the guest cabins, or to where they used to be. He was squatting and looking at the ruins. He stood up and walked back from the foundations, watching the ground as if following a trail. When he was about fifty feet behind them, he squatted again, looking at the dirt.

She wandered to the pond. Ashes and debris floated on the water. Behind, where the cabins had been, smoke drifted up from the charred ruins. All that remained were silver trails in the ground. She realized it was melted aluminum from the window frames.

She returned to the jeep. When Clay finally joined her, he was distracted and frowning.

"What were you looking at?" she asked.

"Just trying to figure out how it happened."

She nodded. She felt a strange veil of numbness descending, felt it physically, and welcomed it.

"Awfully hot fire it must've been," Clay remarked. "Even all the porcelain melted." He paused. "If it's all right with you and Joe, I might bring an inspector up to the ranch later."

"Okay," Stella said. "Why?"

"Just to get a better understanding of what happened. You know, we dug a line right next to the highway, figured it wouldn't jump the highway and the line. But crown fires can jump pretty far."

Stella started the jeep. "If it was a crown fire, why did the buildings burn?"

"That's what I want to try and figure out. My guess would be flying embers, and that's how the propane tanks blew up."

"They're so far from any trees," Stella said. "We always made sure there was no brush or fuel around them."

"Yeah, I guess the winds were pretty strong."

"Just an ember to do all this?" Her voice was hoarse and she swallowed hard.

Clay was silent for several moments. "Had to be more than one ember. Well, that's even more reason to get someone who knows this stuff better than I do to come up, look at the trees and at the direction the fire was going, and how it could've caught the propane tanks."

Stella turned the jeep around and they drove in silence to the Double-L. The southwestern sky was a psychedelic patchwork of orange, purple and dark gray. The fire had burned through the trees on the western portion of the Double-L, but all the buildings stood unscathed. Stella sighed in relief. She stayed in the jeep while Clay checked for any sign of the cattle. He came back shortly to report that he'd heard them, way down by the river, it sounded like.

Neither of them spoke the whole way back to the fire camp. Stella parked the jeep and Clay hesitated before getting out. "I'm sorrier than I can ever tell you, Stella."

She just nodded, not wanting to cry.

"You better get hold of your insurance agent and let him know."

Stella swallowed the lump in her throat. "The house wasn't insured."

Clay stared at her, speechless.

"We couldn't afford to keep it up."

Stella took the warped Dutch oven and walked to her pickup. She sat with her head resting on the steering wheel. Now she had to go and tell Joe that the house his grandparents had built, the house in which he'd been born and where he had lived all his life, had been destroyed.

Roxanne, 9:30am–10:30am

Blackberry Springs was a shambles. Not a single house stood. Broken chimneys rose eerily from the piles of smoldering rubble. The Blackberry Springs Estates sign was gone and the two-ton boulders had split from the heat. No trees remained, except for sugar pine corpses.

The power lines were down and might be live, rendering the road impassable. But it wasn't necessary to drive any farther; they could see from here where Arla's house had been. There was no pickup, nor the remains of one.

Ray gestured, and Roxanne turned onto the dirt road. As they headed west, every turn increased her dread. Not to say Ray's; he was scarcely breathing.

Not a single tree was unscathed. Majestic centuries-old Douglas firs had been reduced to stumps. There were no singing birds, no chittering of squirrels or rustling of voles; the only sounds were the irregular pops of tree trunks exploding and the cracks of branches breaking.

They came around a bend, and there sat a shell of a pickup. Both front and back windshields had shattered. The tires had melted right off the rims. The paint had been scorched off, leaving the entire pickup a strange reddish color. Roxanne's heart pounded hard against her chest. Ray groaned and buried his face in his hands. "I can't look. I can't look in there." He shook so hard his teeth chattered.

"I will. Stay here." Roxanne got out of the truck and trotted toward the pickup. Carlos was right behind her, and she gestured for him to stay back.

Steeling herself, she looked into the cab.

"She's not in here," she called back.

"She must have gone down to the river," Carlos said.

"Why didn't she come back up?" Ray said. "It's daylight; she should've come back up to the road."

"Maybe she did; maybe she's walking to town," Carlos said, pointing to the west.

"She would've been there already. She runs fast." Ray's voice was breaking.

Roxanne rested her hand on his arm. "Stay here while we look, Ray."

"No. No, I'll come. I've got to find out."

"Are you sure?"

"Yeah. Let's hurry."

Kit knew how to operate the CB. Roxanne said, "Call for help now, Kit. Explain the situation. If we find her, we'll yell up to you."

They started down the hill. Ray went first and quickly lost control. He descended in a half-tumble, half-slide. "Carlos," Roxanne said, "use the Pulaski. But if you have to, just sit and go down on your butt."

"I see her!" Ray screamed. "Arla! Arla!"

Roxanne saw her, too. She was lying near the river with a long, thick blackened treetop across her body. She wasn't moving.

Ray, 10:30–11:30am

Please, he prayed—to no god, but to the earth, to the forest, to the fire. Did she move? Wasn't that movement? Oh, sweet Jesus. Let her be alive. Arla, please be alive. Arla!

Her eyes opened. Her mouth formed his name. "Water!" he called to whoever was behind him. Carlos held the bottle to Arla's lips. "Slow," Ray said. "Be careful."

Her skin burned with fever. She drank the water that Carlos carefully dribbled into her mouth. Ray took her pulse. It was weak, but steady. Roxanne arrived in a scattering of pebbles. Ray gestured. "Let's see if we can move this."

On the count of three, they lifted. The tree didn't so much as budge.

"What about if we try to roll it off?" Roxanne said.

"It'd roll over her foot," Carlos said.

"I don't think that's going to matter."

Ray looked at Arla's foot. Only the toes were visible. They were blue-black.

So they tried to roll it. But the limb, or treetop more likely, had to be thirty feet long with a good two-foot diameter.

Ray turned to the boy. "Carlos, they'll have to bring a chainsaw, a tarp and a stretcher. Make sure they know it's a life-and-death emergency. After you call them, bring down my jacket; it's on the back seat."

Carlos nodded. The slope they'd slid down was too steep to go up, so he jogged downstream. Ray suppressed the urge to scream, *'Go faster!'* Then he turned up the hill and vanished from Ray's sight.

He stayed right beside her, giving her water, talking softly. She slipped in and out of consciousness. At one point he asked her about the pain and she murmured, "Don't hurt." That worried him, because it ought to hurt. It ought to hurt like hell. She had, he saw, used her blouse to get water, but at some point she must have become too delirious to do so anymore. She was shivering with fever, and wore only her bra and cotton shorts. He began to take off his shirt, but Roxanne said, "I'll give her mine." His shirt, he realized, was filthy with dirt and smoke and soot, soaking wet with his sweat. Roxanne pulled off her T-shirt and covered Arla's torso.

Suddenly, Arla's eyes flew open and she sobbed out, "Ray, I'm sorry."

"Oh, baby." He put his arms around her, not all the way, for he was afraid to lift her or move her. "Help's on the way," he said. "We'll get you out of here and fix you up. Just hang on, Arla. Please don't let go."

Carlos came back down. It hadn't even quite registered with Ray that Roxanne was there in just her bra, until Carlos gave her his fireshirt.

Ray managed to get Arla to take a few more drops of water. Suddenly, she said in a clear voice, "Is it here?"

"We're here." He stroked her forehead. "Me, Carlos, Roxanne."

Roxanne and Ray exchanged a glance.

"The bear. His feet." Now her voice was slurry and low. Her eyes closed again.

Ray shook his head. She was delirious and hallucinating. Why was the ambulance taking so long?

Carlos went back up to the road, to show the rescuers where to climb down, but it was fifteen more minutes before the ambulance arrived, accompanied by a Forest Service jeep. The rangers, three of them, had brought tarps and a chainsaw. He was relieved to see that one of the rangers was Brian. The two EMTs came down with a collapsible stretcher.

"We'll cut it here and here." Brian gestured to the tree.

"We have to cover her," Ray said, "in case this thing has live embers inside."

"Better let me do the cutting, Ray," said Brian.

Ray nodded. "Arla," he said, kneeling beside her, "we're gonna use a chainsaw and cut this tree off. So I have to cover you up for protection. It won't take long."

He and Roxanne held the tarp over her, and Brian started the chainsaw. It took only a few minutes for him to slice through the tree limb, which was indeed still hot inside. After that, it was easy for four of the men to lift the rest of the treetop.

There was an audible collective gasp as they saw her leg. It was completely crushed, a horrible pulp of flesh and blood. Roxanne emitted a strangled cry, stepped back and nearly fell, but one of the EMTs grabbed her.

Ray knelt beside Arla. How could this not hurt? The EMTs opened their stretcher, talking to each other about how they would lift her onto it. Suddenly, it occurred to Ray that the reason she had not been feeling pain was because the log had been crushing all her nerves. In the next instant, the blood began flowing into her leg, and so did sensation.

Her screams echoed off the walls of the canyon. "Give her something!" Ray yelled. "Hurry, give her something!"

One of the EMTs was already pulling out a syringe and small vial. The other one held her, but with the concentrated strength of pain and desperation, she flung him aside and grabbed her leg. "Help me hold her down," the EMT said.

They injected her and she passed out, but even then, she moaned the whole time they were carrying her.

One of the ambulance guys nearly slipped as he started up the slope. "Stepped in something slippery," he said.

Brian, the Forest Service firefighter, was right behind them. "Looks like fresh bear scat."

It seemed to take so long to get up the hill, but finally they were there. "All right," one of the EMTs said, as they slid the stretcher into their ambulance. "Let's kick ass outa here."

"Follow us," Brian said. "We'll go back the way we came in. Go slow until we get to the pavement."

Ray heard this as if at a great distance. He was standing beside the ambulance, then he was on the ground with several faces looking down at him. "Better load him too," one of them said. "He's had it."

People were holding his arms, helping him to his feet, then helping him into the ambulance where he lay on a cot right next to Arla's. They were doing things to her—an oxygen mask and he couldn't tell what else.

"Is she going to make it?"

"She's not in too good a shape right now," one of them said. The other one interrupted. "We'll do our best."

They put something over *his* face, too, and a black curtain descended.

Roxanne, 6:00–7:30pm

"Only thing makes me feel not so damned tired," Wanda commented, "is to look at these firefighters. Now *that*'s tired."

They were making sandwiches in an assembly line. Wanda halved the Hoagie rolls and spread them with mustard; Roxanne stacked on meat, cheese, and lettuce; and Jill wrapped the sandwiches in plastic. These sack lunches would be the only food some firefighters would have for twelve, eighteen, or even twenty-four hours.

Roxanne was tired, too, even though she'd only been working since about noon—not even a full shift on a normal workday. But she hadn't slept well last night. Comfortable as Ray and Terri's house was, it wasn't her own house, her own bed, and then there'd been the anxiety over the fire and about Pete—despite everyone's assurances and the S&W .38 special under her mattress. But mostly, she was tired from what had happened this morning, and from waiting to hear about Arla.

She had the weird sense that this fire was what she'd been expecting all her life.

Every summer there'd been fires—some small and quickly extinguished, others consuming huge swaths of land and burning for weeks. Every year, a Forest Service ranger would come to her elementary school and show movies about the devastation caused by forest fires. Back then, she had thought of the Forest Service as the rescuer of Smokey the Bear, not associating it with the logging trucks constantly rumbling down the highway. She'd never questioned the perceived wisdom that fires must always be put out. She hadn't doubted their slogan that, 'Only YOU can prevent forest fires!' but now knew that most fires were actually started by lightning strikes. She now knew that when overgrown forests hadn't been allowed to burn for decades, hotter, deadlier fires were the result.

She worked by rote: *turkey, cheese, lettuce. Turkey, cheese, lettuce.*

This morning, she'd been thinking only about Arla's leg and that it would have to be amputated. It hadn't occurred to her that infection had already developed, and that she might not survive. "They're giving her fluids and antibiotics," Terri had told Roxanne about an hour ago. "It's still touch and go."

Half an hour and two hundred sandwiches later, Roxanne and Jill began assembling the lunches into bags, adding two pieces of fruit, potato chips, and slices of pound cake. Finally, that was done and so was she. She paused outside to have a cigarette before driving back to Camargo.

Wanda came outside for a smoke too. "You going back to Ray and Terri's?"

"Yeah, but I think I'll go see if Clay's around first. He said he'd be getting off about now."

She walked to the fire camp and found Clay at the main supply tent, about to go off duty. He greeted her and she said, "Feel like having a beer?"

"Oh yeah!"

"I've got a six pack on ice in my truck."

"Where's your truck?"

"At Wanda's."

They walked the short distance in the new gloomy world. Gray and black ash had settled over every surface and continued to fall, so thick that car headlights were barely visible. The air had the eerie half-light of a solar eclipse.

People were hanging out at the parking lot. There were a few firefighters or staff who'd come to pick up food, but most were local people. A group of men, current or former mill workers, had gathered around their pickups and were drinking beer. One was Jerry Frye.

"Roxanne, look over there, and tell me what kind of beer Jerry Frye's drinking."

She glanced over. "Looks like what he drinks at the Tavern.

It's from that new brewery over in Oso Grande. I forget the name, but it's got a bear on the label."

"A bear like the one on the state flag."

"Yeah, come to think of it. Why?"

Clay shook his head and cursed under his breath. "You think we could go back to the fire camp?"

"Sure, but you mind telling me what's going on?"

"I want to go to Pardini Ranch. But I have to get a few things to take with me."

At the fire camp, he gathered some equipment into a satchel, then they drove in silence to Joe and Stella's ranch. "Park over here," Clay said, tersely. "And don't walk around; if you get out of the truck, stay right around here, okay?"

He opened his carryall and took out a pair of booties, asking for her help getting them over his boots. For a good ten minutes he took pictures, then returned to the pickup. "I think I know where it started," he said, almost as if talking to himself. "You can see where the weeds aren't incinerated—they're only partly burned and they fell over." He faced her. "Roxanne, I want you to do something."

"What?" she said, cautiously.

"I want you to drive down to command post. It's at the Elk's Lodge. Ask for the arson investigator, and bring him back up here. Have him follow you in his car."

She hesitated. Her heart pounded. She knew that arson was a crime most often committed by the property owner himself. And she knew that there was no way Joe or Stella had done this. But she also knew that innocence was no guarantee against prosecution. "Clay—"

"I know Joe and Stella didn't do it. They don't even have insurance, for Christ's sake." He gestured impatiently. "Put on that other pair of booties and come with me."

They walked over to a row of foundations that must have been the guest cabins. Twenty or thirty feet behind what had once been a propane tank, in an area bypassed by the fire, Clay squatted and pointed to something on the ground. It was an empty, ash-covered beer bottle. The label on the bottle was Oso Grande Pale Amber Ale. Roxanne gasped. "Oh, Clay. Oh, no."

"Like I said, I'm making a wild guess. So don't say anything just yet. Not even to Joe or Stella."

"It's not all that wild a guess."

"Might be another explanation," Clay said. "Maybe Joe and Stella stock this brand for their guests."

"Joe and Stella don't stock alcohol for their guests," Roxanne said. "And they don't drink beer themselves. They drink wine. And besides, no guests have stayed in the cabins for at least two weeks. I know, because Carlos works here."

Clay, grim faced, didn't answer. He frowned and bent over, examined the scorched grasses. Eventually he said, "So, you going to get the arson investigator?"

"Yes, I'll go back and get him."

"Tell him to bring a magnifying glass, too."

"You aren't going to come?"

He shook his head. "I'm staying here in case whoever did this gets worried and comes back to destroy evidence." He paused, and his eyes met hers. "Hurry, Roxanne. But be discreet."

Terri, 7:30–8:00pm

Ray was awake by the time Terri got to the hospital, despite having only had six hours of sleep in the last sixty.

Most of the day, he'd paced between the waiting room and the doorway outside the ICU. Now it was evening, and he still didn't know whether she'd live or die. Terri had tried to get him to eat a few times, but he couldn't. She had insisted that he drink water. Meanwhile, she'd fumed: Why weren't the doctors worried about Ray being dehydrated? Or about infections? Shouldn't they have hooked him up to an IV of fluid right away? Okay, so all day the hospital staff had been coping with emergencies, both those related to the fire and the usual kind that happened every day. But still.

Eventually, they brought Ray into an examination room and Lydia picked out the bits of windshield glass which, Ray told them, had been in his scalp since Thursday night. And finally Dr. Pretzinger, who'd come on duty at four, bustled in.

The doctor found several small burns scattered over Ray's arms, as well as a cut on his leg, which he hadn't even noticed. Terri sat in a chair across from the examination table.

Dr. Pretzinger made notes and finally said, "So, Ray, you've got a mild concussion that we'll be keeping an eye on. These burns we'll treat topically, and I'm going to stitch up that cut on your leg. We're giving you some antibiotics for all these abrasions and burns and the blisters on your feet. We don't want to take a chance on a major infection developing. We'll put you on an IV for a couple hours and get you hydrated. That'll bring your energy level back up. But what you need most is sleep."

"I can't sleep," Ray said.

"That's common in situations like this. We'll give you something through the IV that'll help you get some rest. It'll put you out and you'll sleep like a baby."

"No."

"You need sleep," the doctor said. "You're fatigued, and that puts you in more danger of infection."

Ray shook his head. The doctor pursed his lips, and Terri steeled herself and said, "Doctor, the reason he can't sleep is because he's worried about his–" She'd been about to say 'friend,' but caught herself and finished, "–his cousin, Arla Stinson."

Ray's glance at her was quizzical for a moment. Then he nodded almost imperceptibly.

"We'll have a better idea of the prognosis tomorrow," Dr. Pretzinger said. "We're keeping her as comfortable as possible."

"You won't know until tomorrow?" Ray said. "That's not what the other doctor said."

"No? Well, I'm afraid he was mistaken. But I'll check on that." He walked out of the room.

When five minutes passed without the doctor returning, Terri stepped into the corridor to see what she could find out. Dr. Pretzinger was approaching with another doctor, nodding as the other doctor spoke.

They entered the room and Terri hesitated, wondering whether she would be intruding. But Ray would need her, if the news was bad. She went in.

The surgeon was already speaking. "…understand you're a relative and that you're the one who found her?"

"Yes," Ray said.

"Just this past hour, she took a turn for the better. She's out of the woods; she's going to make it. We've finally got control of the infection. She's no longer in shock, but now that she's conscious she's in a great deal of pain."

Ray swallowed hard several times.

"We've given her as heavy a dose of painkillers as we can, given the circumstances. We'll have to amputate her leg, but there's still a question as to how much of it has to be removed. A colleague is on his way from Modesto, in fact he should be here any minute. I expect the operation to be sometime tomorrow."

"Is it dangerous?" Ray asked.

"The operation, no … Certainly, it's far less dangerous

than not operating. That is to say, the longer we wait, the more dangerous her situation is and the more delicate the operation becomes." He glanced at his watch. "Now if you'll excuse me."

Terri realized that Ray couldn't speak. "Thank you," she said, and the surgeon left.

"Now," Dr. Pretzinger said, "I really believe we're going to have to give you something to help you sleep."

"I'll be okay now that—" Ray's voice cracked.

Terri moved to his side and put her arms around him. He clung to her, shuddering. She knew by the wetness on her shoulder that he was crying.

"We'll be back in five minutes," Dr. Pretzinger murmured.

"I'm sorry, Terri. I'm sorry."

"Shh. It's all right. Don't worry, honey; it's all right."

She realized she was truly glad Arla wasn't going to die. It would be nice to think this was because her love for Ray was generous, but she knew it was actually a form of selfishness. Because what she was most afraid of was that, should Arla die tragically, he would be more likely to stay in love with her, or with his memory of her.

DAY THREE

SEPTEMBER 29

Kit, Afternoon

Kit and Carlos went to Mary's house to take Arla's dog for a walk, up and down every street in downtown Camargo, eventually stopping on a hill that overlooked the eastern end of Main Street. They sat for a while watching caravans heading west—horse trailers, trucks loaded with bawling cows or sheep and one with turkeys, their white feathers floating from the truck like pollen.

Morgan already knew the way back to Mary's and he loped ahead of them. Mary set out iced tea and a plate of cookies. She told them the whole story of the diary, concluding that Ray hadn't been able to find it at Arla's house. "I'm sure that's why she tried to get back there—to get the diary," Mary concluded.

"I wonder if she made it." Kit remembered the pickup truck, parked pointing toward the river canyon, but also at an angle that made her think it had been heading west. And that meant Arla had been coming *from*, not going *toward*, her house. "How big is it?"

"Well, I didn't see it, but it was inside the cover of a Catholic missal."

"Why is the diary so important?" Carlos asked.

Mary smiled. "Even routine day to day records can be of immense help to historians. But there's something else of great importance. First, you should know that in 1885, two men were hanged for arson. There was a rumor that Hiram Cushing hired those men to commit the arson on property he then acquired. Up until now, I've found only one source that so much as mentions this rumor, and it's far from authoritative: an article was written twenty years after the hanging—an interview with someone who'd watched the hanging as a boy. He remembered the man shouting from the scaffold that Cushing had paid him to do it. No one believed it. Since he waited until the noose was around his neck, it was seen as a desperate attempt to save his skin. It didn't work; he was hung minutes later, according to this article."

"But there was no evidence that what he said was true?" Carlos asked.

"Not until now. Arla told me the diary describes Hiram Cushing paying those two men, two nights after the fire. In history, this is what's called a primary source. Primary sources are the best evidence, but often there are none and historians must resort to conjecture, to adding up the circumstantial evidence. So, this diary is a crucial document."

They left about half an hour later, walking through town toward the fairgrounds. They held hands, but for once Kit wasn't thinking of how his hand felt in hers.

"What if she did save it?" she said. "What if she got back to her house and was on her way down the road again and got trapped by the fire?"

"She might've left the diary in the pickup."

"After she went all that way to get it? I bet she didn't leave it. I bet she took it when she ran to the river."

"It might've fallen into the river, or got burned up."

"I know. I know."

Carlos was frowning. "What?" Kit asked.

"When we rescued her, she said, 'Is it here?' And then she started talking about a bear. I thought she was delirious, but we saw bear scat pretty close to where we found her."

"So you're thinking 'it' might've meant the diary."

"Probably not, but…"

"As soon as it's safe and they let us up there, we have to go look."

Laura, 7:30–9:00 pm

"Were you able to get all the cattle?" Laura asked, gripping the receiver.

"All except for that goddamned old bull," Pete replied. "I'll have to ride out and look for him, but I'm not doing that until this fire's under control. Until then, he's on his own."

"He was in the eastern meadow?"

"Yeah, there's plenty of grass there. He'll be fine. Or else he's already dead. Either way, nothing I can do right now."

"No," Laura agreed.

"How come you aren't staying at the hotel?"

"Both the hotels are full. We're fine here for the time being." She made an effort to keep her voice normal. "Do you and PJ need anything? Clothes, or…"

"I got some stuff for me and him when we went up for the cattle," Pete said.

Laura allowed her silence to make her point.

"If you have to buy anything, keep the receipts," Pete said, gruffly. "We got fire insurance; it ought to cover evacuation expenses."

"All right."

He hung up. He hadn't asked to talk to Kit.

She sat down, surprised to find herself trembling, perhaps from the effort of trying to sound as though nothing had changed. Of trying not to arouse his suspicions. Of not saying that she would be going to court tomorrow, and if things went well, he would never again live at the Double-L.

She was alone in the kitchen. Joe and Stella were in their room with the radio turned low, playing jazz. Kit was reading *Yertle the Turtle* aloud and occasionally, Troy's voice joined in, repeating lines he knew by heart. From the backyard came Trixie's and Carlos's voices, the thud of the soccer ball and occasionally, a bark from Puddles.

She put on a pot of water for the pasta, spooned some of the sauce Joe had made yesterday into a small pan, brought out the salad and opened a bottle of Zinfandel.

Terri looked terribly weary when she finally arrived, but her eyes widened in delight at the scene in the kitchen. "Is this for me?" she exclaimed.

"Of course," Laura replied. "Troy's in bed, and Trixie's with Kit and Carlos in the den. She's had her shower already."

"I could get used to coming home to you." Terri laughed.

"So, is Ray going to stay at the hospital?"

"Yes, at least until Arla's ex gets here. He's on his way up from Marin County."

Laura set down the stirring spoon and reached for Terri's hand. "You're all right?"

"I'm fine." Terri smiled her lovely smile. "Is this the ravioli I heard a rumor about?"

"Yes. Have you ever had Stella's ravioli?"

Terri shook her head. "I've heard about Stella's cooking."

"She learned in her grandma's kitchen," Laura said. "As did I."

"Well, I know she taught *you* well."

Ravioli began to float to the top of the water. Done! She drained them, put them into a serving bowl, spooned on plenty of the sauce, sprinkled Parmesan generously, and heaped a large serving onto Terri's plate.

Terri took one bite and moaned. "Oh, my God. And this sauce!"

Laura smiled. "Joe made this. Stella taught him how. It's what Nonna called Sunday gravy."

"Stella should open a restaurant. She wouldn't even have to serve anything else, just this. People would be lined up outside the door."

Before Terri had finished eating, someone knocked on the front door. Laura opened it to Clay DiMauro. He looked tired and somber. "I wonder if I could talk to Joe and Stella?"

"I'll find out," said Laura. "Come into the kitchen."

"Hi, Terri," he said, and then, "Oh, wow, is that Stella's ravioli?"

Terri jokingly brandished her fork. "Keep away from that dish!"

Laura smiled and got a plate from the cupboard. She went to get Joe and Stella, and by the time they all returned to the kitchen, the serving dish was empty and Clay's and Terri's plates nearly so.

After greetings were exchanged, Clay ate his last ravioli and said he had some news for them. "We made an arrest earlier tonight. Jerry Frye was taken into custody and charged with arson. For burning your ranch."

For a few long moments, no one spoke. Joe and Stella seemed stunned.

Clay continued, "The grasses near the propane tank were only partially burned. That's an indication that it's a point of origin. So, we took soil samples." He paused. "The fire was started with gasoline.

"I asked Jerry and PJ to empty the LNG tank at the Pine Gap store … I saw him taking gas … He was hanging out at Wanda's drinking that Oso Grande beer, the same brand as the bottles I found at the ranch, right where the fire started … Someone laid a line of gasoline from the forest to the cabins and the propane tanks … opened the tanks … another line of gasoline from the stable to the house … book of matches next to a beer bottle with Jerry's fingerprints…"

For now, Clay said, no one could go onto the ranch because investigators were still gathering evidence. If Joe or Stella needed to go there, they should check with Ken Sizemore, the investigator in charge. "I'm not officially involved in this anymore. I brought it to their attention and now I'm out of it, except for being a witness."

"What happens now?" Joe asked. Laura thought his voice sounded thick.

"He'll be formally charged and arraigned sometime next week."

"But why would he do it?" Terri asked. "What's his motive?"

"I don't know, but—" Clay broke off, cleared his throat, then said, "This is off the record, just my personal opinion, but my guess is someone paid him to do it." He looked at Joe and Stella. "And that's the one good thing about you not having insurance on your house—no one could accuse you of doing it for insurance money.

"Jerry might end up naming someone. I've been told the DA's down at the jail right now, trying to convince him to talk. Most guys do, eventually." Clay reached for his hat. "Thanks for the dinner, Terri. I hadn't eaten since this morning."

"Anytime, Clay. I mean that."

He smiled his thanks and stood. "Laura, I wonder if I might have a word with you?"

"Yes, of course." She removed the apron and hung it on the hook behind the pantry door. They went into the den, and Clay closed the door. "Laura, I want you to know that I think PJ was involved." He held up his left hand in a stop gesture. "Right now, he's not officially a suspect. But I'm pretty sure he did it, and I'll tell you why."

She waited.

"Him and Jerry were in the Gap together. They were *both* filling those gas cans. Roxanne and I saw them. We thought they were just stealing it. The arson investigation picked up a small portion of a tire track at Joe and Stella's. But even if it's the same brand as PJ's, that won't prove it was his truck. And if they can prove it was his truck, that doesn't prove he was driving it at the time. It won't even prove when the track was left." Clay paused. "But there's one other thing."

"Go on," Laura said.

"Last summer, Stella called me. Someone had dammed up the creek at the mouth, on national forest property. They'd dug a new creek bed, either with a backhoe or a plow, brought in a load of sand and dumped it.

"The agency wouldn't go to court for warrants to search the construction yards and see if they could get a match on the sand. They didn't even make a mold of the tire tracks. So what I'm telling you now, it's not the kind of evidence that could be used in court. But it told *me* what was going on." Clay flushed. "I kept a sample of the sand. And one night when I was leaving the Tavern, PJ's truck was outside. I saw sand in the bed."

Laura wasn't surprised. Sand was used on the ranches for flood control and patching.

"Well, I took some of it. I had it analyzed by a lab—

unofficially, on my own dime. They were the same, Laura—the sand in the creek and the sand in PJ's truck."

She closed her eyes.

"It wouldn't stand up in court," Clay said. "I took the sand without getting a warrant and I didn't keep a good chain of custody. And maybe a lawyer would find another fifty samples of the same kind of sand within a hundred-mile radius. But I know damn well PJ's the one who blocked that creek.

"The arson squad's going over the Pardini ranch with a fine-toothed comb. They might get evidence against PJ. Or maybe Jerry will implicate him." Clay shrugged. "Or maybe not. Maybe he'll skate."

Laura knew PJ wouldn't have done it without Pete's approval, tacit or otherwise. She didn't know how Pardini Ranch figured in Pete's plans, but the pieces of the puzzle were beginning to fall into a nebulous shape.

DAY FOUR

SEPTEMBER 30

Terri, Afternoon and Evening

When Stella returned from the hospital that afternoon, she reported that the doctors said Arla's operation had been successful. "Which apparently means she didn't die while her leg was amputated," Stella said matter-of-factly, then began to sob. Terri had never seen her cry. She went to the liquor cabinet and poured two generous glasses of whiskey.

They sat in silence for a long time, until the phone rang. It was Laura calling from Sacramento: the restraining order had been issued. It barred Pete and PJ from coming within fifty feet of either Laura or Kit. It also prohibited them from coming to the Mathieson house, and from the Double-L, except on ranch business if they gave Laura twenty-four hours' notice.

Even though Trixie and Troy were now at Aggie's, there were plenty of things Terri had had to deal with, from helping Joe with dinner, to finding a local hotel for Arla's ex, to calling various friends and updating them, to running loads of laundry almost around the clock, to keeping enough food and supplies in the house for eight people. So it was nine o'clock before she and Laura had a chance to talk privately.

They got iced tea and went into the living room.

"Why should he come onto the Double-L at all?"

"He'll have to get his ranch equipment and he'll probably want to get Oscar, the old bull. And at some point, his personal possessions." Laura paused. "I don't think he'll become irrational or violent, since there's a restraining order, but it is a possibility. I'd like for Kit to stay here, if that's all right with you and Ray, but I'm going to stay at the ranch. I don't want him coming here looking for me."

"If he did, he's violating the restraining order and we call the cops. They're five minutes away. And there's more people here, and we're armed. The ranch is isolated. Stay here please, Laura."

"I couldn't forgive myself if he came here and … if anything happened."

"How likely is he to flip out?"

"I think his first reaction might be anger, but it won't take him long to realize that if he does something criminal, he's letting himself in for a lot more trouble and expense."

"When will Pete get the settlement offer?"

"The lawyer's drawing it up now and she'll have it delivered to him Wednesday." Laura set down her glass and faced Terri. "He really can't afford to refuse the settlement because if we end up in court, I'll get considerably more than I'm offering to settle for. To get a favorable judgment, he'd have to pay a lawyer all the money he didn't pay me." She shrugged and added parenthetically, "Of course, he may want to do that out of spite."

"But he may not realize you'll fight him if it goes to court. After the way things have been between you for so many years…" Terri trailed off.

Laura shook her head. "The very fact that I'm divorcing

him, that I know the exact state of our finances, and went to court for a restraining order, and took those photos the last time he hit me—all of that's enough to make him realize I won't back down."

Terri acknowledged with a nod. "But I still think you should stay here, at least until he agrees to the settlement. Or until he refuses it."

"Let's see what Ray thinks."

"Okay."

"Can you dim the lamp?"

Terri reached over and turned it to the lowest wattage. "Is that better? Do you still have a headache?"

"Just a small one."

"Lie down. I'll rub your head a bit."

Laura rested her head in Terri's lap and closed her eyes as Terri kneaded her scalp. "That feels wonderful," Laura sighed. "What hands you have. I've always enjoyed your shampoos, because it's like getting a head massage."

Not much later Terri thought Laura had fallen asleep, when she sat up and said gently, "It's time to talk about Ray and Arla."

Terri nodded. "What's happened has made me see how much he cares about her. He really does love her."

"Yes," Laura said. "I believe he does."

"So it's a pretty bleak situation."

Laura shook her head. "Quite the opposite, now. The fire has changed everything. Instead of spending weeks or months going through the usual, predictable, conventional emotions and arguments, it's as if you both said, 'We'll deal with that later.' Well, maybe by setting it aside, you've come beyond it."

Terri almost laughed. If Laura only knew that she'd been stoking the embers of her anger, keeping it alive until the time came to let it become a bonfire. That she sometimes felt gleeful that the woman who'd taken Ray from her was now mutilated and had lost her house. The shame of feeling that way never completely dowsed the smoldering resentment.

But she respected Laura so much that she confessed. "I haven't come beyond it, Laura. Sometimes I'm glad her house burned down. Sometimes I'm even glad for what happened to her. Other times, I wish she'd died, and the only thing that stops me feeling like that is knowing it wouldn't stop Ray from loving her. I'm still only a thread's width from—never mind, let's just say if it weren't for this fire I probably would've shot Ray by now. But why don't you lay down and let me rub your head some more. I can see in your eyes you've still got a headache."

"It's not bad," Laura said, but she stretched out again with her head in Terri's lap.

"Now. I want to hear all about Stella's grandmother." Terri loved the feel of Laura's thick hair. She ran her fingernails over Laura's scalp, and Laura closed her eyes.

"Octavia was so kind to me." Laura sighed deeply. "It's been thirty years since she died and I still miss her."

DAY FIVE

OCTOBER 1

Ray, 8:00am – 9:00am

"This copy is for you to keep here." Laura set the folder with the restraining order on the coffee table. "I don't want to put any of you in danger, Ray. You or Terri, or anyone staying here. That's why it would be best if I go back to the ranch."

"You can't go back up there right now. It's too remote, too dangerous. And who responds up there when you call 911? Stick Jensen. He's still the sheriff for another two weeks." Ray shook his head. "Terri's right. You should stay here."

He hoped Laura's reluctance was because of concern for her friends' safety, but it could be that she was having second thoughts about leaving Pete. She'd stayed with the guy for thirty-some years, after all.

"This restraining order," he said, and she turned toward him, "it's just paper."

"I know that."

"It won't stop him from coming after you. But if he does, and the cops don't get here in time and someone has to handle him, you or someone else, the restraining order gives whoever it is a pretty good case of self-defense."

"That's why I got it," Laura said.

She kept surprising him. Still, he had to be certain. "The problem is, how do I know whether, if I had to hit him, you'd back me up?"

"Ray," Terri protested, but Laura said, "I thought of that myself. So I wrote this affidavit." She opened the file folder and handed a paper to Ray. "I've sworn that I believe both Kit and myself to be in physical danger from Pete, and possibly from PJ, and that I came to Ray and Terri Mathieson for a safe place to stay. That I have advised you, as well as your other guests, that in the course of divorcing my husband I've obtained a restraining order against him and my son. That I've informed each of you that my husband has beaten me on numerous occasions and that on September 27 he struck my daughter Kit and threatened her. If you think of anything else, let me know. And I've made copies, enough for everyone."

"Good thinking. And thanks." Ray impulsively reached over and shook her hand. "So you'll stay here then, right?"

"All right. I will."

"Good."

"And one other thing," Laura said. "I'm going to apply to Chief Silva for a concealed weapon permit."

"You don't need a permit to carry a gun in your own home," Ray said. "And when you're living here, this is your home."

"I know that." She nodded. "The permit would allow me to carry a gun when I'm out. I hope the chief will issue it. But even if he doesn't, at least there will be one more thing on the record attesting to my fear of Pete."

Ray was amazed. She was covering all the bases. If she, or someone else, did have to use force against Pete, Laura was making sure they wouldn't go to jail for it. Hell, he almost hoped Pete *did* violate the restraining order.

"You think Pete will sign the settlement agreement?" Terri asked.

"The only reason I can think of that he wouldn't sign it, aside from his male pride, is that he wants the Double-L so badly. He's fixated on it."

"I know why," Ray said. "He's got a deal to sell it to Cushing." Both women looked at him with expressions of disbelief. Ray went on, "That's what Cushing told me, and PJ told me the same thing the other night."

"I know Pete *wants* to sell it," Laura said. "But I *own* the Double-L."

"Yeah, Pete told Cushing it's in your name. But he said it was just a formality; it was in your name for tax reasons."

He hesitated, and Laura finished. "And that I'd do whatever he told me to do?"

"That's about the size of it." Ray leaned forward. "I think their deal went a little deeper. I suspect Pete's getting a piece of the action."

"What action?" Terri asked.

"Cushing wants to put a big development on those three properties: the Double-L, Pardini Ranch, and the mill."

"Pardini Ranch!" Terri repeated. "Joe and Stella wouldn't sell their land to a developer. Everyone knows that. Joe's been speaking out against development for *years.*"

"Cushing's been leaning on them, because if he can't get their place, this development he's planning won't come off."

"But Ray," Terri said, "it's completely unrealistic. Joe and Stella don't want to sell their ranch and Pete *can't* sell the Double-L."

"Not only that," Ray said, "but the whole project hinges on the mall. You build that many houses, you have to have a mall. But he's losing his backing. Two big mall tenants already pulled out, and the anchor tenant was on the verge of pulling out, last I heard. So the whole project might be dead. I doubt Cushing could buy your ranch, Laura, even if you wanted to sell it."

"Even if Hiram Cushing is bankrupt, does that mean the project itself is dead?" Laura said. "I would imagine there's someone, some cabal, behind Cushing. The people with the real money. They'll just find another frontman."

Ray stared at her. That had never even occurred to him before, but hearing her say it, it seemed obvious.

"And there's something else," she continued. "Whoever is responsible for that arson knew Joe and Stella had no insurance, and knows that with all the buildings destroyed, Joe and Stella will have no choice but to sell."

All of a sudden, Ray remembered something else. He cursed under his breath, then said, "The other night, the night before the fire, I was at the Tavern. PJ and Jerry Frye were there. They were talking about how everything would be all worked out real soon." He flushed. "I was too drunk and too distracted by, uh, everything on my mind—" He cut himself off. Both women were watching him, expectantly.

"Anyway, PJ said his dad was gonna sell the Double-L to Cushing. I said something like how everything depended on Cushing getting the land. And Jerry said not to worry about Pardini; that would be worked out by next week. Next thing you know, Jerry burns the place down."

"But Ray," Terri said, "that was before the forest fire started. Jerry couldn't have known there would be a forest fire."

"No. But he could've taken advantage of it."

"It was Jerry who told you not to worry about the Pardinis?" Laura asked.

Ray's eyes met hers. "Both of them said it, Laura."

Laura just nodded, as if something had been confirmed for her.

"What it comes down to is, Pete wants title to the ranch

and he'll be plenty pissed off at you for not giving it to him, especially once he sees the settlement offer."

ON HIS WAY to the hospital a little later, Ray was still thinking about the arson. He was jolted by a sudden realization. Maybe that remark about Ray's 'intimate friend' was an offer of a deal: 'I won't tell your wife about your girlfriend. In return, when something happens to Pardini, you turn a blind eye.'

The plan had probably been arson all along. In extremely hot, dry weather, a fire could start from something as ordinary as a reflection. That was all it would take: a small grass fire next to old wood buildings, propane tanks, and a barn full of hay.

If not for the wildfire, Joe and Stella might have been at home when the fire started. They might have been asleep. They might not have got out.

But this was all conjecture, not something substantial enough to take to anyone in authority, especially not when it concerned a guy like Hiram Cushing. Cushing had never said anything incriminating. He'd lied to Ray about Joe Pardini's intentions, but no one else had heard the lie. Even if they had, so what? Cushing could have any number of explanations for lying, and most of them would seem a lot more plausible than that he was diverting Ray's suspicions from a tragic fire that hadn't even occurred at the time of the conversation.

Still, Joe and Stella might want to hear his theory.

When he got to the hospital, Joe was there. Ray leaned over and kissed Arla; she was groggy but kissed him back and put her arms around his neck. "So tired," she murmured.

"Go to sleep, then, baby. I'll be here. How you feeling, does it hurt much?"

"Not now."

"It did before?"

"They gave me something." He had to lean close to hear her say that. Her eyelids fell shut heavily and he brought his lips to her cheek.

It didn't seem good that she'd lost so much weight in just a few days. She was almost emaciated. How could a person go from looking healthily slim to skeletal in that short a time? She was not eating real food yet; just whatever was in the IV. She said she had no appetite. The doctor last night had said it wasn't anything to worry about and she'd probably get her appetite back in a day or two, after the anesthesia was completely out of her system. Ray worried anyway.

As Joe stood up to leave, Ray said, "Before you go, I want to run something by you."

Laura, Late Afternoon

The lawyer wanted Laura to call at the end of every day. Tuesday afternoon, she went into Ray's office to make the call in privacy and quiet.

This was the first time she'd been in the room for more than a few seconds. She could see Ray's presence, from the neat desk and small oak filing cabinet to the sports memorabilia and photographs on the walls and shelves. One picture caught her eye—the famous magazine cover of Bobby DiMauro burning his draft card in front of the Oakland draft office. Laura knew that he'd died in prison. She was surprised to see this picture of him on Ray's wall, though come to think of it, she remembered that they had been friends as boys.

"Oh, hi, Laura." It was Roxanne, hesitating at the door. "I was going to use the phone."

"Yes, go ahead. I can make my call after yours." She stepped back and turned toward the door.

Roxanne's eyes went past Laura slightly, to the photograph. "You're looking at the pictures of Bobby?"

Laura nodded. "Did you know him well?"

"Very well."

"He's the boy who got into a fight with PJ."

"Did PJ ever tell you why they had that fight?"

Laura reached into her memories. "I remember he said Bobby had started it, that Bobby had been taunting him for some time."

"He had been," Roxanne said. "Because of something PJ had done. For years, I hardly ever thought of it. But lately it's been on my mind quite a bit." She sat down heavily in Ray's office chair. "It was the end of summer before my junior year. Labor Day weekend in 1966. You and Pete were out of town and PJ had a party at your house the first afternoon you were gone."

Although it was nearly twenty years ago, Laura had never forgotten that weekend. She was pregnant with Cindy and the summer had been even hotter than usual, so she and Pete had spent three days in San Francisco, basking in the cool fog. They got home to find beer cans in flowerbeds, stacked in pyramids on the front lawn, and floating on the pool.

Roxanne went on, "Almost everyone was outside, in the pool or on the patio. I went inside to use the bathroom. When I came out, PJ was right there. He pushed me back in and shut the door. I tried to get away, but he was so strong." Her voice caught. "The only thing that saved me was another boy came to use the bathroom. That distracted PJ enough for me to get away. I ran out. The other boy stared after me. I could hear them laughing. PJ was talking as if I'd gone in there with him. As if it was mutual. As if we'd just had sex."

Laura closed her eyes briefly.

"You know how it is in this town, and at high school," Roxanne continued. "Word got around. I couldn't deny the rumors by saying PJ tried to force me; that would've been admitting that something had happened. People had backwards ideas back then about what rape was."

"I know," Laura murmured.

"Going to an unchaperoned party, getting high, and running around in a bikini was just asking for it. That was the prevailing attitude. I didn't even think of it as attempted rape myself." Roxanne grimaced. "I was more ashamed and embarrassed with myself than angry with PJ. So I only told two people. Loretta and Bobby. He wanted to beat PJ up, but that would have been like confirming that the rumors were true. Or at least it would have kept the rumors alive. So Bobby picked a fight. For weeks, he insulted PJ and badgered him over petty things, whatever he could think of. Finally, PJ took the bait and they met on the football field one day during lunch hour. Everyone knew about it; a big crowd gathered to watch. PJ was really strong, but Bobby knew how to fight. He got PJ down and that's when he cut him.

"The other kids exaggerated it, later. The more they retold it, the worse it got. They said Bobby hadn't fought fair. But he didn't fight with the knife. He took it out when he already had PJ down. And he didn't mean to stab him, and missed, the way some of the kids said. He knew how to use a knife. He did what he meant to do—draw blood, just enough so PJ would know it was serious. He told PJ why he was doing it. He whispered, so no one else could hear."

"You heard?" Laura asked.

"He told us later, me and Loretta, that he'd nicked PJ with the knife and said, 'If you ever try to force yourself on a girl again, I'll slice your balls off.'"

To think that all this had happened without her even knowing any of it. Thank God it hadn't been even worse.

Thank God Roxanne hadn't ended up in the same position as Laura had, sixteen years earlier.

"So Bobby got suspended and PJ got a scar. And every time he looks in the mirror," Roxanne said, her voice bitter, "he sees that scar and probably blames me."

But Laura thought that perhaps the scar reminded PJ that all men weren't like him, and that there were even men who would stop him.

Roxanne faced her again. "Bobby was never the kind of person to do nothing or say nothing when he saw something wrong. That's what made him so special. Most of us think we're good people if we don't do awful things ourselves. But that's not enough. To do nothing is to cooperate with injustice. And it's what most of us do." She indicated the UPI photograph. "But Bobby always stood up. No matter what it cost him."

While Roxanne used the phone, Laura waited in the living room. How fortuitous that Roxanne had come in just when she did. Because now Laura knew what she had to do. What Roxanne had told her about the past made Laura realize the truth about the present— about what PJ had done to Joe and Stella.

But unless Jerry Frye told the authorities what had happened, PJ would not be charged. PJ's father was wealthy. His second cousin was a Superior Court judge. He was a Jensen.

Even if PJ was charged, she doubted that the DA would prosecute the case vigorously, or search any too hard for evidence. And if, despite all that, PJ got convicted, Laura doubted he would go to jail. Not that she wanted him to go to jail; that was not a fate she wished on anyone, let alone her own son. But a crime had been committed and two people were suffering for it.

Joe and Stella could sue Jerry Frye for their loss, but he had no assets. Without evidence that PJ was involved, they wouldn't be able to sue PJ. So they'd end up with nothing, with no restitution. They might be forced to sell their land just to pay their debts.

She would call the lawyer and instruct her to change the settlement offer to almost double what she'd intended to ask. She wouldn't tell the lawyer why; let her simply assume Laura had come to have second thoughts, that she'd decided the lawyer was right about the cash portion of the settlement offer being too small.

Pete could afford another $75,000. He would have to liquidate the stocks and government bonds, but that would cover it.

PJ was her son. She was no less responsible than Pete for the kind of man he had become. So she and Pete would pay. Justice demanded no less.

Stella, Late afternoon

Under normal circumstances Stella was no proponent of secrecy. But neither she nor Joe wanted to give Arla something else to worry about, so they'd asked that no one mention their financial problems or the arson to Arla.

Joe was in the backyard, pruning shrubs and trees. From the kitchen window, Stella watched him taking the bundles of clippings around to the front. Had he really aged in the past few days, or was it her imagination? Or was it simply that being tired and disheartened showed more in a man of sixty?

She poured two tall glasses of iced tea and joined Joe on the patio.

"This is what I think," he said. "When we get the insurance payment for the outbuildings, $30,000, let's use it to pay the bank loan. That will get it almost entirely paid off; it'll leave a balance of $4,000. And once we sell the stock and gear, we can pay that, too."

"It won't leave us much," she said.

"But the land will be safe. That's what we have to do now, Stella: protect the land."

"Where will we live? And on what?"

"We'll figure that out after the land is safe." He rested his hand on her knee. "Don't worry, *cara*. We'll have enough money to get by for a while. We'll board the horses with George and Maddie. We can rent a place here in town for the winter, and come spring we'll build ourselves a cabin."

Here they were, in the same situation as his great-grandparents had been a century ago: over fifty years old, burned out of their home, and having to start from scratch. She doubted they could build a cabin but maybe they could buy a used house trailer. Whichever, there would be considerable expense involved to make the ranch livable. The water system components had all been ruined and the well water itself was probably contaminated. The propane tanks were destroyed, and the lines probably too damaged to be used. Winter was coming; some kind of shelter would have to be made for Tabasco and Tippy. There was no forage; they'd have to buy feed all winter.

There would be many other expenses, too. Except for two changes of clothing each, they had no personal property at all. No cookware or bath towels. No shampoo or stationery. They would have to buy everything, the accoutrements of day-to-day life that were usually accumulated bit by bit, over years.

But she shared Joe's sense of urgency about protecting the land. Someone wanted it badly enough that they had burned the house down. Not for a moment did she or Joe believe Jerry Frye had acted on his own. He didn't know them and had no motive to destroy them; no motive except being paid to do it.

Nor did she believe Jerry Frye had been the intruder last week. Whoever that was, he'd been confident enough in the layout to come onto the ranch in the dark, leaving his vehicle all the way out on the highway.

PJ had motive and opportunity, but she didn't think he'd have acted on his own, either.

"We'll find out," Joe said. "Eventually, the truth will come out."

"Do you think Jerry Frye will say who paid him?"

Joe shrugged. "Whoever it was, their next move will be to offer to buy the ranch. They'll assume we'll give up, now. Whoever's behind the arson knew we weren't carrying insurance."

Stella thought about that. "Maybe they assumed we had insurance, but figured it would hurt us to lose the house anyway. People never insure the contents of their house, or at least not for the full value."

Joe shook his head. "They knew, Stella. And they burned the cabins and barns so we'd have no place to live, so we'd be more likely to have to sell the ranch. And how did they know? No one knew, except Patrick."

"Oh, Joe. Would Patrick throw away a lifetime of honesty and decency just for money? Or just to get on the good side of someone powerful?"

"If Patrick's like most people, what he thinks of as his principles are just fuzzy guidelines. He follows them when it's convenient, ignores them when it's too much trouble. He might well have persuaded himself that leaking one little piece of information wasn't really a violation of principle. People get used to not standing up for what's right, Stella, even on matters where taking a stand isn't risky. Then, when something important comes along, they're already in the habit."

Laura came out. "Joe, there's a call for you. It's Hiram Cushing."

When Stella looked at Joe, he was smiling. "I'll take it," he told Laura, and went inside. Stella followed a few moments later, but Joe was already hanging up.

"He wants to have a meeting with us tomorrow."

"I hope you told him to take a—"

"Now Stella. Of course not. I told him we'd be glad to meet him."

She stared.

"Let's find out what he has to say."

DAY SIX

OCTOBER 2, 1985

Roxanne, 7:00am–1:30pm

Roxanne poured her first cup of coffee of the day and turned on the radio. The Jackrabbit Fire had consumed over 83,000 acres and was only five percent contained. The smoke was so thick and heavy that flight patterns had been changed at northern California airports. Air quality warnings had been issued as far away as Minnesota.

Carlos came into the kitchen, greeted her, and got a bowl of cereal. Roxanne sat down across from him and said, "I think we'll be able to move back home tonight."

He didn't look up from his bowl, but the set of his shoulders told her he'd been dreading this moment.

She rested her hand on his shoulder and he said, "Baba'll be happy, anyway," and put his arms around her waist and hugged her. Roxanne thought she'd melt with happiness; he so rarely touched her anymore that being hugged by him was an unexpected joy.

She drove to work, pulled her pickup into a space at back,

and went in to start work. About 11am, the Forest Service arson investigator came into Elsie's. He was Ken Sizemore, the same man Roxanne had brought up to Pardini Ranch on Saturday. Everyone wanted to know what happened in court. "He got bail," Ken said. "Hi, Roxanne."

"Morning," she replied, offering the coffee pot. He nodded yes. Someone asked what Jerry Frye was charged with.

"Two counts of arson. He's due back in court next week for a hearing."

Roxanne worked hard all morning. Waiting tables during a fire was like breakfast rush all day long, but the customers were in even more of a hurry, and there were more of them.

She finally got a break around 1pm, and stepped outside for a smoke. Several members of a hotshot crew were hanging around a truck. They'd just gotten off a 36-hour shift and seemed beyond sleep. Clay DiMauro was with them. All the firefighters were covered with ash and soot, mud and dust; their eyes were red and swollen. Clay waved and came over to her, giving her arm a squeeze. "We're evacuating Pine Gap," he said. "Voluntary for now, but…"

Roxanne used the payphone to call the Mathieson house. She told them about the evacuation order. Stella said she'd be right up with her pickup to help Roxanne get some things from her house.

Arla, afternoon

Arla was running.

She laughed as she ran, laughed with the pure joy of her strength and health and speed. One final challenge in the Dipsea remained, and after that it was down all the way to the beach. She accelerated, because it was easier to go up a hill fast rather than slow. Perspiration ran between her breasts and down her neck and forehead, cleansing her pores and cooling her body.

She woke up. Unable to move. Tubes attached to her body. Monitors tracking the beating of her heart. An empty place where her leg was supposed to be.

She looked out the window. The deep blue western sky had vanished and she wondered if it would ever come back.

The door opened and her ex-husband stuck his head in. "I'm awake," she said.

Steve dragged a chair close to the bed and sat down. "How are you?"

"I feel much better. Not as groggy." She looked for the glass of water; he handed it to her.

"Does it hurt much?"

"Not now."

"You still getting something through the IV?"

"No, no more mainlining," Arla said, smiling. "They've switched me to oral painkillers." What the therapist and doctor had mentioned might happen had started happening today: tingling where they'd done the amputation, and strong sensations where her leg used to be. Pain, for one. And when she'd first awakened after the operation, she'd thought her leg was still there. She still felt that way. She could actually feel its weight sometimes.

After Steve left, Ray came in. He must have been waiting nearby, giving her and Steve privacy. He set a small ice chest on the table, came over to the bed and kissed her cheek. His lips felt soft and warm.

"Will you help me sit up?" she asked, putting her arms around his neck. He gently helped her to the edge of the bed. The gown wasn't long enough to cover the clump of bandages over her leg. No, she said to herself, over your stump. It's not a leg anymore. Get used to it.

She ran her hand over her hair. It hadn't been washed for five days. She'd seen herself briefly in the bathroom mirror this morning and shuddered at the memory. "I look awful," she said.

Ray's eyes filled with emotion. "No, you don't. You're beautiful." He went over to the table and took something from the ice chest. "I brought you a milkshake. I made it myself."

"Oh, Ray."

"I used Dreyer's ice cream and real strawberries."

"It's so thick, just the way I like it." She took a big spoonful. The cold felt wonderful on her throat. "It's so good. I'm going to get fat—tapioca pudding this morning and now a milkshake."

He kept urging her to take one more spoonful, one more. She ate as much as she could, knowing it wasn't very much. Eating exhausted her, and she fell asleep with him sitting beside the bed, his hand on hers.

When she woke again, it was dark. He was still there, but he'd fallen asleep sitting up, with his head resting on a pillow propped against the windowsill.

Her heart went out to him. The first few days, she'd found it reassuring to have him there; he was her rock, her love, her joy. But then, more cognizant, she began to think things over. She had pieced together the bits of information each person gave her, and knew how helpful Terri was being, how practical and supportive and generous. Terri had made it possible for Ray to be here. She was keeping in touch with Arla's friends; taking care of a house full of people and animals made homeless by the fire; and when Arla asked about her dog, Mary said, "Oh, Morgan's fine. Terri sends Carlos and Kit over to take him for a nice long walk every day." And now she'd even found a local hotel room for Steve.

All of that, Arla thought, while she thinks her marriage is over and I'm the cause.

She thought of Ray's two children. She thought of her own future, too. She would have to learn to live differently, in ways she couldn't even imagine yet. But that was the least important aspect. After all, she wouldn't suffer the additional horrors that many disabled people did from lack of money.

She'd always considered herself to be a good person, but now she knew the truth: that her life had been easy. It's not hard to maintain a veneer of niceness, she told herself, when you grow up never missing a meal, or a private school payment, for that matter. So I skimmed over life thinking that a certain kind of manners and habits—like being polite to cab drivers or patient with store clerks—proved I was good. That giving dollar bills to subway performers—when dollar bills meant nothing to me—proved I was generous. I can even remember congratulating myself that it was because of my goodness that fate had rewarded me with good fortune: with Steve, with the interesting job that I only had to work at for three years, with our business success, with my money, with being able to live where and how I wanted, and not have to work.

With Ray.

I never even thought of Terri as a real person, with real feelings. Just as 'Ray's wife.' And here she is now, showing me what it really means to be a good person. What it really means to make sacrifices. What it really means to love Ray.

She sighed deeply. When she'd seen him that night, about to go off and fight the fire, she'd told herself that it might work after all.

But that was before all this. Before she'd risked her life and, in a way, his too. Before she found herself in a hospital with her leg gone.

Everyone would be better off if he went back to Terri: Terri, the two kids, Ray, and Arla herself, because how could she stand herself if she ruined all their lives?

So she would have to convince him that she wanted him to leave. She'd have to convince him that she didn't really love him.

Stella, Late afternoon

"Thank you for agreeing to meet with me on such short notice," Hiram Cushing said. He led them into a room overlooking his property and the landscape beyond it. Three chairs sat in a semi-circle before one of the French windows. A pitcher of lemonade and three glasses sat on one end of the table. He filled a glass for each of them, then sat down across from Joe and Stella. "Again, please accept my sympathies for the loss of your home. What a terrible tragedy. I understand they've charged the fellow responsible."

"So we hear," Stella said.

"Let's hope it all comes to a successful resolution."

"We think it probably will," Joe said.

"I didn't ask my lawyer to join us, because I wanted this conversation to be just the three of us. We're all old-timers in Piñon County, lifelong residents, and sometimes these things can be worked out much easier and better without lawyers getting involved. Less expensively, too," he added wryly, as if he had the same money woes as they did.

"There's an outstanding offer for your property which you were told was valid until October 15th. It's now October second. Due to extenuating circumstances, primarily created by the fire, it would be helpful if I could let our investors know sooner than the fifteenth what answer we might expect."

Stella thought it interesting that he was not pretending that the offer had come from anyone other than himself. Nor did he pretend that Joe or Stella might have *thought* it had come from someone else.

"So, I hope you'll both forgive me for presuming upon our long acquaintance to suggest that we discuss some of the particulars of the offer. Perhaps you have questions."

Stella made up her mind, then and there, not to speak. Trading horses was her forte; horse-trading was Joe's. She sat back and sipped the lemonade. It was wonderful, with the flavor of Lisbon lemons and not overly sweet.

"No, we don't have any questions," Joe said in his open way. "Stella?"

She shook her head. She noticed a rivulet of perspiration trickle down Hiram Cushing's face.

"It must be devastating to lose a house you've lived in for so long. So I'm prepared, as a gesture of sympathy, to raise the offer for the property to $600,000."

Neither she nor Joe reacted visibly, though Stella for one, was surprised. She'd been expecting him to offer *less* because of their situation being even more desperate than it had been a few weeks ago. Did this mean Cushing's situation was more desperate too? So desperate that he was showing his hand?

"When your lawyer came by," Joe said, "he told us the offer is for the entire property only."

"Yes." Cushing waited a few moments, but when Joe said nothing, went on, "But I think we could work something out, Joe, if that's the only sticking point. I understand how difficult it would be for you to leave the property. You've lived there all your life."

"Matter of fact, I've lived in that very house most of my life. My grandparents built it. But you probably know that, too."

"Yes," Cushing said. He got up and stood before the east windows, staring out for a few moments, then turned around and faced them. "We have different ideas about what's best for

Piñon County; I know that. You've spoken publicly several times against development. I know the position you've taken; now I'd like to briefly explain my own.

"The kind of preservation you favor just isn't feasible. Like it or not, people pour into California today, just as they did 135 years ago. You seem to think if we don't build houses, people will stop coming here. But they won't. Nothing stops them: not earthquakes, landslides, fires," he gestured expansively at the windows, "bad economic times, drought, skyrocketing home prices, our high tax rate—nothing. They keep coming, and they need places to live. They need places to shop. They need work."

Joe sipped his lemonade, and carefully set it down. "I'd like to tell you a story, Hiram."

Cushing shrugged and lifted one hand, in invitation or perhaps resignation.

"Forty years ago, I got back from the war and bummed around for a while with my cousin. He'd been stationed at Port Chicago in Contra Costa County and that's where he met the girl he married. We looked around together, Creti and I, for a place to buy for them to live. We found one in Walnut Creek. The house wasn't much, a rundown old farmhouse. It was set in the foothills of Mount Diablo. Creti and June bought it and the two acres that came with it.

"This was in the spring; everything was green and lush. The front yard looked out to a big field with poppies so thick, all you could see was orange. The air was saturated with bay laurel and jimbrush. There always seemed to be a breeze coming off Diablo and it brought the sound of cattle lowing and the smell of sage. The farm next door was growing crops that don't grow anywhere else, or not the way they do in California. The apricot trees were in bloom and the flowers on the orange and lemon trees were the first thing you smelled in the morning and the last thing at night. The sky was so blue it almost hurt your eyes to look at it. At night, we could hear the coyotes singing a long way off.

"Well, Hiram, you wouldn't recognize the place today. That field of poppies is now an office building and parking lot. Five thousand people live where once there were twenty or thirty. The lemon and orange groves are gone and so are the apricot trees. Coyotes come down at night and take house cats."

"And the moral of your history lesson is, you don't want the same thing to happen here," Cushing said. "Joe, let me tell you something. If you'd bought land there in 1946, you'd be a millionaire now. And let me tell you something else. It's people just like you who *did* buy that land, and sold it to a developer twenty years later."

Joe nodded. "Some people did. But others got together and managed to preserve some of that land. Otherwise Mount Diablo itself would be covered with houses today."

"That's fine, Joe, but what works one place may not work in another. And besides, twenty percent of the land in California is already preserved. The state's a big patchwork quilt of public lands. As for preserving little pieces, what do those little pieces amount to?"

"You mean in acreage? Not much." Joe smiled. "But look at it this way. Central Park in New York is about 850 acres."

"Eight hundred and fifty acres in the middle of a city of eight million is one thing. But out west, 850 acres is nothing. Preserving random thousand-acre patches means that instead of developers like me being able to build attractive and spacious housing developments, we're forced to squeeze the houses—houses that *must* be built, houses that people need— onto smaller lots in far less attractive surroundings."

"But what you're creating by insisting on building everywhere you possibly can is a future with fifty million people living in California, jammed into a dozen cities and thousands of cookie-cutter suburbs. To get into Point Reyes or Muir Woods, maybe just to go to the beach, will require a reservation made months in advance. And poor people won't ever get there; the time and effort will be beyond their means. More and more animals will lose habitat and go extinct, and so will indigenous plants and trees. As it is, we've only got four percent of the redwoods that were here a hundred years ago."

"You may be right," Hiram Cushing said, shrugging. "Maybe we *are* looking at fifty million Californians in the years to come. Maybe a hundred million. There are a hundred twenty million people in Japan, and it's about the same size as California."

"Is that what you want?"

Cushing waved dismissively. "I asked you here to talk about the current problems both you and I are facing, and how we might be able to help one another. I've invested in Piñon County, and have persuaded others to do so, people who were willing to trust my wisdom in these matters in which I am—and I hope I don't sound immodest—an expert.

"Unfortunately, we must now decide whether to go ahead with the projects we've planned for the county, or to take those projects elsewhere. It would hurt Piñon County to lose these projects; with the lumber mill closing down, and with the devastating effect this fire will have on tourism for years to come, we could use some large-scale projects that would bring employment."

"I wondered how long it would take you to utter the mantra," Joe said. "'Jobs,' the justification for any and all destruction. 'Jobs,' the magic word that gives politicians an excuse to approve any proposed development."

"And your mantra? 'Environment:' the justification for opposing all progress and for giving more importance to a dragonfly than to human beings."

"Actually, environmentalism means figuring out whether

the extinction of that dragonfly might ultimately hurt humanity, and if it's a worse injury than doing without another shopping mall."

"Well, Joe, as it happens, my projects threaten no endangered species and will bring jobs to Piñon County."

Stella thought of the Higuera paintbrush, but didn't want to interrupt.

"Don't pretend that's your motivation, Hiram," Joe said.

Cushing smiled sardonically. "My motive is to make money. And when I make money, jobs are created. Now, in this particular situation, I'm not the only one trying to make money. My partners are anxious to see a quick return on their investments. There's an extent to which that return depends on whether you sell us your land. In practical terms, Joe, I'm hoping to know today what your answer will be to our offer. No lawyers, just us talking, will you tell me whether you intend to accept it?"

Stella and Joe exchanged a brief glance. Joe turned back to Cushing and said gently, "I'm sorry, Hiram, but our answer is no."

"Suppose certain changes were made to the offer? Suppose certain concessions were made? What could I do that would change your mind?"

"There aren't any inducements that will change our minds. We won't sell you the land."

Cushing leaned forward, his eyes intense. "I'll level with you. I'm in a tight spot. A very tight spot. If I can't get this project going, as I have all along assured the investors that I could, they're probably going to pull the rug from under me. I don't expect that to be of any concern to you. But if I end up in Chapter 11, the people of Piñon County will not be well served. My construction company, which employs fifty people even in slow times, will shut down. The mall will be frozen in its present state, providing no construction jobs, and therefore no subsequent service jobs. The developments that I've started will be completed, if at all, by outsiders."

"I'm sorry for all that," Joe said. "But don't lay it at my feet, Hiram. You overextended yourself. That has nothing to do with me."

"From what I hear, you've overextended yourself, too."

"You proposed a project to those investors that included my land, after I'd already refused to sell it three years ago. What made you feel so confident I'd change my mind?"

Cushing stared at Joe unblinkingly. "The same thing that changes everyone's mind: money."

"No, I don't think so. You offered us more money three years ago. That's not it. What is it, Hiram?"

"Just what are you getting at?"

They all three sat in a silence so tense and thick that Stella could feel it physically.

"You're beaten," Cushing said at last. "You know that. This is your only chance. If you don't sell that land to me, you'll be foreclosed on, and I'll get it from the bank."

"If you could wait until then, you wouldn't have asked us up here to talk today."

"I told you I'm in trouble. I am. But I'll come out of it. People like me survive. People like you…"

Joe and Stella stood up to leave. "Thank you for the lemonade. Good luck."

DAY SEVEN

OCTOBER 3, 1985

Arla, Morning

"Ray, I want to talk to you," Arla said.

He was about to take her hand. But there was no way she could go through this with him touching her. She clasped her hands together under the covers.

"I don't know any way to say this except to just say it. It's that I've been thinking about things, thinking quite a bit. And I realized that … I was mistaken. About us."

He very slightly but perceptibly shook his head. "Arla, you know, they've had you on drugs for days."

"It's not the drugs. I'm not confused or in shock, or doped up. I'm thinking clearly, Ray. More clearly than I have for a long time."

"Don't you know I'll take care of you?"

"I don't know if I even want to stay in Piñon County."

"Then if you want to live somewhere else, I'll go with you."

"No, Ray. You wouldn't want to leave Trixie and Troy, and I wouldn't want you to."

471

"If you don't want to live together, okay. We can work something else out. I know it might be hard. But if we're–"

"Please, Ray. I'm trying to tell you something." He fell silent. "What we had was so incredible, so special. Let's just be glad we had it. You saved my life, and you saved my dog, and I'm so grateful to you for that; but I don't want to feel that because of the debt I owe you, I can't tell you the truth."

"You don't owe me anything. Why are you talking like this?"

"I know you don't want me to feel indebted, but I do, not only to you but to Kit, Carlos and Roxanne. And to the men who came and rescued me. But what I mean is, I don't want to stay with you because of it—to mistake gratitude and our physical compatibility for something more."

"'Physical compatibility'?" He shook his head again. "You know what? I don't believe a word you're saying."

Her heart pounded. "What?"

"I know you love me."

"Please, Ray, don't make this harder than it is."

"It ought to be hard when you tell me something this bad and it's not even true."

"I'm sorry, but it is true."

"No. You're only saying it because you think I'm here out of pity or something. That I feel obligated not to leave you because of that." He indicated her leg.

"Ray." She sighed. "Hasn't it occurred to you that I'm just thinking of myself? That it will be harder on *me*?"

Something passed over his face: fear. It was only there for a moment, but that was long enough for her to know that what she'd just told him was believable. She went on, "If I loved you the way I thought I did, I'd want to work through all the obstacles we'd be up against. But … I'm sorry, Ray. I don't *want* to work through them. The very thought makes me tired. And

I don't want to have to deal with that when I'm trying to learn how to walk."

He drew back, looking stunned.

"What happened has made me re-evaluate my life," she continued. "Made me see what matters to me. I don't regret what happened between us; I cherish it. I'll always cherish it. I do regret the mess I'm leaving behind, but I don't know what to do about it."

He reached over, moved the sheet and took both her hands in his. "No," she said.

His shoulders slumped and he stared at the floor. She paused, then said softly, "Go home. Go back to Terri and your children."

"Is that what this is about?"

"No. But it's what you should do. It's what you really want, even if you don't know it yet yourself."

He got up heavily from the chair.

"Ray, I want you to know one thing. Terri has been incredible. In fact, I've come to realize why you love her. Not once has she shown the slightest anger or resentment. So I don't want you to think what I'm telling you is because of some hint she might have made, or anything like that. She didn't. It's nothing to do with you and Terri. It's because of me, of how I feel."

He seemed about to speak, opened his mouth, but said nothing. He walked toward the door.

She squeezed her fingernails into her palms and bit her lip to keep from crying out his name.

He paused at the door, turned and looked at her. "I'll do what you want. But when you get out of this place, I want to talk about this again. I'll take that as payment for the debt you think you owe me."

Then he walked out of her room, and out of her life.

Afternoon

By noon Thursday, the Jackrabbit Fire had burned over 120,000 acres and was less than two miles from Pine Gap. Aerial bombardments of both water and fire retardant had been increased with, as yet, little effect.

At around one o'clock, Roxanne stepped outside Elsie's for a cigarette. If the fire got much closer, Elsie's would have to be evacuated.

Suddenly, a powerful bolt of lightning turned the smoke-filled sky bright red. Two seconds later thunder roared, thunder so loud it rattled the windows of Elsie's and seemed to shake the ground itself. All over Piñon County, dogs began howling.

A few drops of rain sputtered down, widely separated. Then nothing. Was that it? People looked up at the sky, willing more rain to come.

Directly above Elsie's, a small lightning bolt blinked. Most people didn't even notice it. The thunder was a timid little rumble.

It was as if they had finished the job that the huge lightning bolt had started, tearing open the sky that last crucial inch. All at once, sheets of rain poured forth. Roxanne even thought for a moment that one of the helicopters had dumped a load of water on the parking lot. But it was rain!

Rain bounced off pavement and concrete. It hammered into the dry ground, little dust clouds rising at each droplet. In the forest to the south, the fire hissed angrily at every strike.

People poured outside, fire supervisors and Forest Service coordinators and the staff of Elsie's. Even Harry the fry cook rushed outside in his stained apron, waving his spatula at the sky.

At the fire camp, firefighters sleeping in tents, or just in sleeping bags in the open, woke up. Shouts of joy rang out. On the fire lines, firefighters abandoned their bulldozers and Pulaskis. One man took a running dive into the mud and soon, others were sliding alongside him and shouting with joy.

In the streets of downtown Camargo, in shopping centers, on the roads outside town, horns honked and people stopped their cars in the middle of the streets and ran outside. Even in the county hospital, the atmosphere became festive. Nurses opened curtains so patients could watch the rain. Weary doctors smiled with relief.

Stella, Late Afternoon

They rode slowly through the downpour, back to the fairgrounds. Joe went to buy hay; he also planned to stop by Patrick Burnham's office to find out when they could expect the insurance payment for the cabins and outbuildings.

Stella stayed to clean out the stalls.

The past few days, she'd heard people talking about the ability of the forest to regenerate, and they spoke as though that regeneration was fast and thorough. But in Stella's experience, forests didn't come back quickly, and they never came back the same. She often passed areas that had burned ten, twenty, or thirty years ago, and every one of them looked vastly different from the way they had before the fires.

Wildflowers often flourished the spring after a fire, but trees didn't come back so quickly. And since some trees seed by fire and others by the proximity of other trees, the type of trees that grew after a fire might be different. Fire drastically changed the composition of a forest.

With the canopy of trees gone, smaller plant life was altered, too; plants needing shade couldn't grow, while sun-loving ones thrived. Although many animals survived the fire pretty well, their food supply was gone, or greatly diminished. Within a few years, many species died out. Hawks and eagles feasted in the immediate aftermath of a fire, since their prey had nowhere to hide; but when the rodents were gone, the raptors moved on. The entire food chain was affected, and the death toll in the years after the fire was usually very high.

All of that was natural. Other aftereffects were not.

Damage from bulldozers left scars that lasted for years. In especially sensitive areas the damage was permanent. Fragile habitat was destroyed and the creatures living there were wiped out. Delicate plants, that could only live in a precise balance of soil, insects and other plants, never regenerated. Stella didn't doubt that there were aftereffects of fire retardant on plants and animals, although she'd never seen studies on this. She *had* seen dead golden trout floating downstream after retardant drops.

But the most damaging aftereffect was what the Forest Service allowed after a fire: salvage logging. Stella knew she was in the minority on this issue, but she believed the forest should be left undisturbed after a fire. There was no ecological need to remove burned trees. They toppled and decomposed into the soil, meanwhile providing shelter for insects, animals and birds. Their roots held the soil in place.

Sometimes, the weakened trees were invaded by harmful insects. The Forest Service promoted logging as a means of control. But the logging was more harmful than the insects. Besides, some bird species, such as the black-backed woodpecker, actually thrived on a diet of post-fire insects; the woodpeckers moved into burned forests and began the regeneration process.

But salvage logging vehicles and equipment crushed tree

sprouts and everything else in their path. Further damage was made by the construction of roads into the areas where burned trees (salvage timber, they called it) would be removed. Worst of all, vehicle tires brought in seeds of non-native plants. Stella had spent as much time in the Higuera Forest in the past twenty years as any forest ranger. And she had noticed that in areas where salvage logging had been allowed, noxious weeds thrived: yellow star thistle, bull thistle, spotted knapweed, and puncture vine. These weeds, once established, spread quickly, grew thickly, and drove out the natives. They caused far more damage than the fire.

But the common point of view was that salvage logging after a forest fire was beneficial. Lumber companies had been promulgating that idea for decades, of course, under the pretense that it was necessary for the health of the forests.

Profiteers saw disasters as opportunities to exploit. That was the case no matter what the disaster or where it occurred.

She heard the pickup turning into the fairgrounds, and a few minutes later Joe drove up. She saw at once that the news was not good. His eyes were dark and his mouth set in a grim line.

"What did Patrick say? Can they expedite the insurance payment?"

"They not only won't expedite it; they aren't going to issue payment until their own arson investigation is complete, which may take months."

"No!" she cried. "We don't have months! Oh, Joe!"

"I already called the horse broker and told him we've got some horses to sell. We'll drive them to Davis next week. He'll put me in touch with a guy down there who can sell the trailer for a five percent commission. Tomorrow morning maybe you can take out an ad to sell the new pickup."

"All right," she said dully.

"That'll give us a few months' leeway. We might be able to

renegotiate the bank loan based on expecting an insurance payment for the outbuildings."

"Sure," Stella said. But she felt heavy and hopeless. They couldn't fight the bank and Cushing both; they were too rich and too powerful. They wanted the land and would apparently stop at nothing to get it.

DAY EIGHT

OCTOBER 4, 1985

Kit, 8:00am–11:00am

"Will this rain cause mudslides?" Arla asked.

Kit nodded. "But that's only a problem if it happens in places where there are still houses. Like if ten houses on a hill burned, and ten didn't, they might get wiped out by the mudslides."

"No problem at Blackberry Springs, then," Arla said.

She seemed so sad, so defeated. Kit didn't know what to say to her. She didn't know how bad Arla felt about losing her leg and her house. And she didn't know what was going on with Ray and Arla, either. Ray had seemed pretty upset since yesterday. He went back to working on the fire lines instead of coming down to the hospital. They must have argued.

"Right before it rained," Kit said, "I was thinking I could go back to the river and try one more time to find the diary." She sighed. "I'm really glad we got rain, because the fire was probably gonna burn down Pine Gap. But now even if the diary's up there, it's ruined."

"It's not there, Kit. It probably fell into the river."

"I guess so."

"The things I broke can't be fixed." Arla smiled sadly. "Sometimes, learning a lesson comes far too late to do any good."

"If it got buried Friday night in a dirt slide, and then more slides came down before it even rained, the diary might still be okay."

"Especially in that vinyl bag," Arla said.

"Arla, excuse me, did you say it's in a vinyl bag?"

"Yes, a camera bag. About this big," she gestured, "with a zipper. I don't think it's waterproof, but water resistant, anyway."

"So if it's there, maybe it's okay!" Kit jumped up excitedly. "Now I know for sure I'm going to go look." Arla clearly didn't share her enthusiasm, and Kit knew it must be because she didn't want her hopes dashed. She swallowed hard and sat down again. "I mean, it's a one in a thousand chance, but what the heck. But maybe you could tell me … Exactly where were you the last time you remember having it?"

Arla closed her eyes and frowned in concentration. "I could smell the river. I was at least three-quarters of the way down the hill. Something hit my head and knocked me out. When I woke up, I was in the water and I didn't have the bag."

"And was the wind blowing?"

Arla nodded. "Toward the east. Very strongly."

"I'm going up there. The wind might've carried the bag that direction."

"Isn't it too dangerous? There must have been mudslides on that river canyon. Or there will be mudslides."

"I'll talk to Joe and Stella; we'll go in on horseback. They'll know if it's too dangerous or not." Kit tried to quell her excitement. She cautioned herself not to let her own hopes get too high.

"Stella says they'll probably wait to start rebuilding," Arla said.

"Yeah, they have to figure out if they have enough money to build anything."

"Besides the house?"

"Well, they already know they haven't got enough for that."

Arla looked confused, and Kit suddenly remembered she didn't know Joe and Stella didn't have insurance on their house. They hadn't wanted her worrying about other people's problems when she was trying to get well.

"What do you mean, Kit?"

"Uh, nothing. I mean, they'll have to wait until after winter."

Arla raised herself up onto her elbows. "You said they don't have enough money to rebuild their house. What's going on?"

Kit was torn. She didn't want to break the promise she'd made, but she didn't want to lie to Arla, either.

Arla must have seen the hesitation on Kit's face. She added gently, "I can help them."

So she told her. She told her about everything, all the way back to the creek being blocked and the other sabotage on the Pardinis' ranch; about Stella and Joe having canceled the insurance on their house last year because they had to cut costs; how they'd had to fix a lot of things and took out a bank loan to pay for all of it, so now they owed money to the bank. And how on Wednesday, they'd had some kind of meeting with Ray's boss, Mr. Cushing. But Kit didn't know the outcome of that. "I got the idea he wants to buy the land and they told him no." She added confidentially, "Carlos and I think he probably had something to do with the arson."

"Arson? What do you mean?" Arla's voice was trembling a little.

"Clay—he works for the Forest Service—he saw some beer bottles up at Joe and Stella's after the fire. Also, he noticed the grasses weren't burned all the way down, and the fire made a trail from the beer bottles to the propane tanks. So he got an investigator, and they took samples of the soil. It turned out there was gasoline in it. And fingerprints on the beer bottles and on a matchbook."

"Do they know whose fingerprints?"

"This guy Jerry Frye. He used to work at the mill, but got laid off and Ray said he was working for Eagle Construction this summer. He got arrested."

"Just him?"

Kit nodded.

"But he had no motive, did he." Arla wasn't asking; she just said it. "So, he must have been paid or at least encouraged by someone else, someone who did have a motive. My God, the historical parallels…" Arla indicated the door with her eyes. Kit closed it and came back beside the bed.

"Kit, one more favor? Could you bring down my savings passbooks and my checkbook? Ray said he got them from the house, so they'll be in the box, which was in the trunk of my car."

"All your things are at Ray and Terri's," Kit said. "We brought everything over there. There's two boxes and I know just where they are. You want me to get the bank stuff right now?"

"Well, the sooner the better." Arla reached for the telephone. "In fact, if you went to the house now and put those things in a bag, Stella could bring the bag down for me. I'm going to call her."

"You don't want me to tell her any of this, right?"

"If you don't mind."

Kit got up to leave, but impulse grabbed her. She leaned over and hugged Arla, who seemed surprised, but then hugged her back, very tightly and emotionally.

"Thank you so much for telling me this, Kit, and giving me the chance to do something about it."

LATER THAT MORNING, while Stella went to the hospital, Kit, Joe and Carlos loaded Sadie and Tippy and Griz into the horse trailer, and drove up to Blackberry Springs Drive. They parked along the pavement, where the old logging road dead-ended, and offloaded the horses.

Three inches of rain had fallen, but even that much had been absorbed by the thirsty land. The forest was like something from a grotesque fairy tale: all the trees were black, some twisted and shriveled, others decapitated and limbless. After a week of the world smelling of smoke and burnt buildings, there was a new smell today: wet ash. From not far away came the buzzing of chainsaws and an occasional boom as smoldering trees were felled.

The scorched pickup was still there, its tireless rims sinking in the mud. Joe searched the cab for charred remains of a diary, but found only a few loose browned papers in the glove box.

They rode west to where the slope was less steep and carefully picked their way down to the river, then rode alongside it, to the spot where they'd found Arla. From there they proceeded upstream.

Joe tested the ground for five minutes while Kit and Carlos watched anxiously. Finally, he began to dig.

Twenty minutes later, the camera bag came up in his shovel.

Terri, Friday morning and early afternoon

One of Terri's regular customers called at nine o'clock Friday morning and begged for an appointment. "I know the salon isn't open," the woman said, "but I'm desperate! My roots are at least half an inch. Lord have mercy, I didn't realize I'd gotten *this* gray!"

Terri laughed. "I'll meet you there at 11."

"Thank God. You're saving my life! Well, slight exaggeration. You're saving my marriage."

Terri gulped down her third cup of coffee. Speaking of saving a marriage, she thought wryly. She knew something had happened between Ray and Arla. Yesterday, he'd gone to the hospital in the morning, but returned right away. He hadn't gone back all day. Previously he'd spent every moment there that he could. Today he'd left early, before seven, to go to the fire camp to help with the mop up. Not to the hospital.

She couldn't help it; her spirits soared.

She smeared peanut butter on toast. Better not get too excited yet. Obviously something had happened between him and Arla, but what, exactly? Had another of Arla's boyfriends shown up? Had she got back with her ex-husband? Had her ex confronted Ray? Had she and Ray had an argument? Or had she broken up with Ray?

Terri drove to the salon and took care of her customer. When she got back to the house Kit and Carlos were eating sandwiches. As Terri made one for herself, Kit said, "We stopped on the way here to tell Arla we found the diary. After all, she almost died trying to get it."

"She must be pretty happy that you found it."

"Kind of," Kit said, "but she seemed distracted."

"Sad," Carlos said, and Kit nodded.

"Well, she's lost a leg. That has to be pretty demoralizing."

"Yeah, but still, she didn't seem very excited about the diary."

Terri took her lunch to the table and sat down. Kit continued, "She said she'd be starting a new phase in life and it would be with a clean slate."

"I hope she's keeping enough money for herself," Carlos said, looking worried.

He and Kit exchanged a quick glance, then Kit turned to Terri and said, "I don't know if Arla talked to them yet, but she's going to give Joe and Stella the money to pay off their loan."

Terri was stunned. She managed to praise Arla's generosity, then listened to the two teens talk. Soon, they'd finished eating and withdrew to Troy's bedroom.

She pushed away the rest of her lunch and thought things over. So Arla was sad and distracted—more evidence that she and Ray had broken up. And she must have been the one to end it; quite obviously, *he* wasn't the one who'd wanted the affair to end.

Clearly he wasn't the least bit concerned that his sadness over losing Arla drove another stake into Terri, increased her pain. The gall of the man! The appalling, self-centered insensitivity!

Well, Arla was recuperating and the life-and-death crisis had passed, so Terri was no longer bound to remain calm and supportive. She didn't have to hold back anymore. She could let Ray know how pissed off she was.

She admitted to herself she'd been deliberately ramping up her sense of betrayal in order to justify her anger. She didn't want to let go of her hard-earned righteous fury.

But would that be so terrible? Maybe what Laura had said was true, that you could become a better person by acting like one. At the moment, though, the idea of letting go of her anger felt mostly like weakness or cowardice—the easy way out.

Stella, Late Afternoon

When she and Joe walked out of Prospectors Bank, Stella was almost overcome with relief. The ranch was safe.

Cushing would soon learn that Joe and Stella had paid off the loan, and would realize that he could not get the ranch—that Joe and Stella's economic problems wouldn't force them to sell, that his money wouldn't induce them to sell, that their love of the land meant they would not allow it to be harmed.

Finally, Cushing would have to give up.

They walked in silence all the way to the Mathieson house. Just as they arrived there, a car pulled up. "I was hoping to find you here," Mary O'Malley said, leaning out the window. She seemed quite agitated.

"Are you all right?" Stella asked.

"Oh yes, quite all right. I just had to come show this to you." She gestured with a sheaf of papers.

"Well, come in and have some coffee," Joe said, opening her car door and extending his hand to help her out.

Soon, they were all sitting around the kitchen table with cups of coffee.

"As you know, two men were hanged for the Russian Camp fire," Mary said, and Joe nodded. "In the course of my research I found a newspaper article from 1925 that recounted one of the men, just before he was hanged, accusing Judge Cushing of having hired them."

"You told me that," Joe said, "but as I recall, the story

came from someone who'd been a boy when it happened forty years earlier."

"Yes. The story was dubious and never confirmed," Mary said. "This diary proves it was true. Mrs. Cushing saw the two men being paid by her husband the night before the fire."

Joe and Stella could only stare at her.

Mary's voice trembled. "When she confronted him, he had her locked in a sanitarium, and she died a few months later. And there's something else. A document was hidden in the lining of the cover. I don't think Arla found this, or she'd have said. Here."

Stella quickly scanned it: two photocopied pages of a typewritten document signed 'Helen Childress.' Mary added, "Helen Childress was the granddaughter of Rosa, the Cushings' housekeeper. In the Historical Society, we always believed that the Cushings covered up Catherine's suicide, both to avoid scandal and so that she could be buried in the Catholic cemetery. But it turns out to have been something else entirely." She set the cup down, coffee sloshing into the saucer.

"Read it," she said.

```
April 28, 1933


Approximately one month ago I received a
visit from a Mr. Jorge Salvador, a
dignified man of nearly seventy. He told
me that he had been employed at the San
Joaquin Sanitarium some years past. He
was the person Catherine Cushing
entrusted to mail her letters to my
Grandma Rosa. Therefore, he knew of our
apple farm, and arrived hoping to find
Rosa and to relieve himself of a burden
he has carried for nearly five decades.
```

We settled down to coffee and applesauce cake, and Mr. Salvador said he was certain Mrs. Cushing did not kill herself. He explained that she had intimated that she would be escaping the sanitarium that very night. For the first time in her six months there, she had been happy. She'd said cryptically that she'd learned that happiness came not from wealth and comfort, but from freedom; that she would not mind being penniless. She'd said she would have one last letter for him to mail. She died before giving it to him.

And she was a devout Catholic, Mr. Salvador said. She would never have committed that final mortal sin, knowing that to do so would deny her entrance into heaven.

What then, I asked him, do you suppose happened to her?

He hesitated briefly and spoke in a low voice after glancing around as if to make sure he would not be overheard, even all these decades later and so many miles away. "The cemetery of the sanitarium has many graves. Some were of patients who died of old age, or the disease for which they were being treated. But the others were women of good health, not elderly, and considered troublesome. Mrs. Cushing was not the first, and not the last, to die of a drug overdose. And nearly all of

those women were the patients of one
particular doctor." He named the doctor
and I list the name below.

I subsequently visited the grounds of
San Joaquin Sanitarium, which is now an
ordinary hospital. Behind the buildings
there is indeed a cemetery, with a
rather surprising number of graves of
women under forty years of age.

I also learned that the records of the
sanitarium are housed with the San
Joaquin Historical Society, sealed for
fifty years after the bequest — that is,
until 1968. I shall likely not live
until then. It is my hope that in the
future, an historian will be able to
study those records with an eye to
proving, or perhaps disproving, the
suspicions of Mr. Salvador and of my
grandmother Rosa Escovido Childress
regarding the death of Catherine
Cushing.

/s/ Helen Childress

Mary gathered up the papers. "I have an appointment in two
days to review the sanitarium's papers. I will also examine
records at the county courthouse for references to that doctor. I
intend to review the death certificates of the women in the
cemetery. And there are many other sources."

Mary looked at them, and Stella saw tears in her eyes. "I
cannot emphasize enough the importance of the diary and

these additional pages. It is the secret history; the history that's told in whispers and never written down."

Friday night, just before midnight

The people at the Mathieson house were all either asleep or getting ready to go to bed when, just past midnight, brakes squealed, metal crashed against metal, and someone leaned on a car horn.

Laura Jensen reached for the telephone and dialed 911.

Ray Mathieson was half out of bed (or rather, half off the living room sofa) by the time his eyes were open. It took him less than thirty seconds to pull on Levi's and a T-shirt. In the waistband, concealed behind the loose tee, he stuck his pistol. Better to have it and not need it, than vice versa.

All down the street, people began calling out their doors and windows for the horn-blower to shut up.

Ray looked out the window. The pickup had clipped the rear of Laura's car, which now sat at an awkward angle in the driveway. The pickup was partly on the lawn, partly on the driveway. It was PJ's truck.

Christ, Ray said to himself. I thought it was Pete. It's only PJ.

The horn stopped blowing when PJ opened the door of the pickup and half-fell out onto the lawn. "What the fuck?" he called, slurring. "Kicking me outa my own house! Mom!"

Laura came into the room just as Ray was about to open the front door. "No, Ray. Stay inside."

"It's PJ. I can handle him."

"I know you can."

PJ's voice rang through the night. "Trying to take our

ranch! Dad's *never* gonna let you have it! You hear me, Mom? You ain't getting it!"

"He's waking up the whole neighborhood," Ray said.

Laura nodded. "The more public his mistakes, the better."

"Give 'em enough rope?" Ray peered out the window again. "Well, it looks like he's about to hang himself."

Police car lights painted the street and houses alternately red and blue. PJ turned toward the house and screamed, "You called the cops on me, Mom? You bitch!"

THE FIRST OFFICER to arrive was the newest member of the Camargo Police Department and its only female officer. Donna Driscoll was twenty-five years old and had come to Camargo in June from a police department in Ventura County.

One factor in Officer Driscoll's career choice was the desire to do something about what the sociologists called domestic violence. Officer Driscoll called it wife beating. She'd grown up seeing it in her own house, year after year until her older brother got big enough to stop it.

She'd listened to lecturers at the academy making their carefully unbiased statements about domestic abuse going both ways. She was unconvinced, though she kept her opinions to herself.

Officer Driscoll didn't know PJ Jensen. She was acquainted with Sheriff Jensen, whom she had disliked minutes into their first conversation. She didn't know that the suspect was the sheriff's cousin, so she had no idea that some of her fellow officers considered PJ someone to handle with kid gloves for that reason, as well as because he was the heir apparent of the biggest cattle rancher in the county. Officer Driscoll saw a loud, drunk, potentially violent man violating a court order to stay away from his mother and sister.

Officer Driscoll got out of her unit and approached PJ Jensen. He turned his attention to her, berated women thinking they could do men's jobs, and announced that no woman cop was laying a hand on him.

Officer Driscoll kept her voice calm, addressed the suspect as 'sir,' and instructed him to take the position against her patrol car. PJ advised her to commit a physically impossible act upon herself. Officer Driscoll repeated her command. The suspect cursed, made an obscene gesture, then turned away from her and screamed in the direction of the house an extremely crude slang word for female anatomy.

By a move he never saw coming, Officer Driscoll had PJ face-down on the lawn with his hands cuffed behind his back. She conducted a quick but thorough pat-down.

At that moment, two other squad cars arrived, one containing the sergeant on duty that night, Dan O'Grady.

PJ at once began complaining about being handcuffed by 'that bulldagger' and demanded that 'Danny' remove the handcuffs. But times had changed, even in Camargo, and even for someone named Jensen. Sergeant O'Grady cast an irritated look at PJ, and neither answered nor removed the cuffs.

Meanwhile, two people came outside. One was a blond man of about thirty, whom Officer Driscoll had seen around town; he was a construction worker. He and the sergeant greeted each other by first name.

The second person was a woman. She must be the one who'd called the police, although Officer Driscoll thought she didn't look old enough to be the suspect's mother. Tall, slim and elegant, she was stunning, her movie star beauty only slightly faded, beauty so intense that it seemed almost unreal. She spoke quietly to the sergeant.

PJ Jensen focused all his anger and hatred on Officer Driscoll, pausing only to dredge up yet another insult relating to her gender. He announced to the other officers that his own sister was in that house right this moment, probably engaged in sexual activity with a 'spic,' and how would they feel if their sister did it with 'Chief Chief'? Then, casting an eye on Officer Driscoll, the perp loudly announced that she had probably got her job by performing certain sexual acts upon Chief Silva.

One officer grew visibly angry and reached for his billy club. Officer Driscoll touched his arm, warningly. Let the suspect talk himself into more trouble. Neighbors had gathered nearby, close enough to hear every word coming out of PJ Jensen's mouth.

Sergeant O'Grady gestured to her to search the pickup. She went to the open cab door. The rifle rack was empty, but what she saw behind the seat caused a brief fluttering in her heart. "Sergeant," she said, "there's a shotgun in the pickup."

The suspect yelled, "I'm a rancher! It's for coyotes!"

Even after only a few months in Piñon County, Officer Driscoll knew that a shotgun was not the usual means of coyote control. A rifle provided better distance and accuracy.

"Is it loaded, PJ?" Sergeant O'Grady asked.

"Hell yeah, it's loaded!"

"You got a permit to drive around with a loaded firearm in your car?"

"Hey, Danny, fuck you. All right? Fuck you."

"Oh boy, PJ," Sergeant O'Grady said. "You are in trouble. You won't believe how much trouble you're in. Take him in." He gestured to another officer, then turned to the woman and the blond man. "We'll be patrolling here regularly, tonight. And Ray, you'll be here too, right?"

"That's right."

The police began getting into their squad cars to leave, except for one officer who would wait for the tow truck for the suspect's vehicle. Officer Driscoll paused and looked at Mrs. Jensen. "I'm on duty all night, ma'am," she said. "I'll drive by every fifteen minutes."

Mrs. Jensen looked right into her eyes. "Thank you very much, Officer." She held out her hand. "I'm Laura Jensen."

Officer Driscoll shook it. "My name is Donna Driscoll and my star number is 252. In case you need it."

THE NEXT MORNING before going off duty, Officer Driscoll stopped in to see the chief.

"Morning, DD. So you had some excitement on your tour."

"Yes, sir, a little bit."

"Danny called me last night and briefed me." The chief gestured to the police incident report. "You handled it right, DD. He didn't get the chance to pull out that shotgun."

"I'm concerned that the suspect might go back and harass or assault Mrs. Jensen or that boy he was talking about."

"I know PJ. That one's got a mean streak to match his stupid streak. But a night in jail probably gave him something to think about." He corrected himself: "Three nights. Bail won't be set until Monday."

"What's the husband like?"

"Pete's meaner than the kid, but smarter." Chief Silva set aside the police report. "I don't think we have to worry about him violating that court order. Especially not now, with PJ getting arrested. But we'll be keeping an eye on the Mathieson place."

"I hope she follows through with this and files a complaint."

"Me too, but no matter what, we're filing charges. Carrying a loaded firearm along with a DUI, open container, drunk and disorderly, and disturbing the peace."

She stood and as she turned to go, the chief said, "Oh, I almost forgot. This might be of interest to you, DD." He handed her a paper. It was a copy of an application from Laura Jensen for a concealed weapon permit. At the bottom of the paper, in the 'official use only' section, was Chief Silva's signature granting the permit.

So this was one woman serious about leaving the pig. Oh, yeah.

Officer Driscoll kept her expression impassive. "Thank you for letting me know, sir."

DAY NINE

OCTOBER 5, 1985

A House in Camargo, Late Morning & Early Afternoon

When Anna Perez answered the main phone in the Cushing house Saturday morning, the caller interrupted her greeting. "I need to speak with Hiram Cushing. It's urgent; he'll want to talk to me. Tell him it's Les Kohler, from Prospectors Bank."

Anna knew he was the branch manager, so it must indeed be something important for him to be calling Mr. Cushing at home on the weekend. She approached Mr. Cushing's bedroom with trepidation and had to knock twice before he said tersely, "Yes?"

"I'm sorry, Mr. Cushing, but Mr. Kohler from the bank is calling. He says it's urgent."

"I'll take it in my office."

Anna retreated to the foyer, and when he picked up the extension, she hung up. She returned to the dining room and poured a circle of polish on the table. The dining room was almost directly across from his open office door. When he cursed loudly it sounded as though he was right beside her.

She thought he had hurt himself and stepped toward the office. But he seemed fine. He stood with his back to her, wearing a bathrobe and holding the phone. "*All* of it? The entire loan? I thought Pardini wasn't getting that insurance money right away."

There was a long silence, then Mr. Cushing spoke again. His voice was contained and low, and something in it sent a chill up Anna's spine. "Yes, I know who she is."

He hung up the phone and uttered several curse words. Anna tiptoed back to the dining room, and continued polishing. She heard Mr. Cushing going into his bedroom and getting dressed. He emerged about five minutes later and came to the dining room. "Could you get me some coffee? I'll be in my office."

Anna brewed a pot of coffee. But before she even reached the threshold of his office she stopped, because he was talking, and his voice was angry. For a moment, she thought he was speaking to her, then she realized he was on the phone again. "You know damned well what I'm talking about!"

Anna had worked there for three years. Although Mr. Cushing was often impatient and became annoyed rather easily, she had never seen him actually lose his temper—until now.

"Don't tell me you had nothing to do with it, Ray!" he bellowed into the receiver. "It was your girlfriend who gave them that money! Never mind how I found out! It's a small town; nothing's a secret… No, you don't quit! You're fired!" He slammed down the receiver so hard, Anna thought it would break.

She waited two minutes before approaching the door. He waved her in. She set the coffee tray on his desk and left. He didn't tell her to close the door, so she left it open as he began punching numbers into the phone.

"Pete, we've got a situation. Pardini paid off that bank

loan…" Mr. Cushing's voice grew impatient. "I didn't say he got the insurance payout. He got money from someone … Some woman … That's irrelevant. Pete, I don't want to hear any more excuses. Either you can handle her, or you can't."

Anna stiffened. Before getting this job, she'd worked in the hospital administration. Only occasionally had she had contact with patients, usually to straighten out the paperwork. She had never forgotten a day some fifteen years ago when she'd had to speak with an emergency room patient directly, for that reason. The patient was Laura Jensen.

Laura had driven herself to the hospital. When Anna entered the room, a nurse was taking Laura's blood pressure. Anna was stunned by the bruises on the parts of Laura's body not covered by the hospital gown. Laura must have seen the shock on Anna's face. *'I fell from a horse,'* she'd said. Later, the nurse had come into Anna's office and wept.

"You've been telling me for six months you can get her to sign that quitclaim. It's time for you to come through. I'm meeting with the investors Tuesday morning. If you don't get title to that land in your own name within the next two days, this whole project is screwed … You call me before the end of the day Monday, and it better be good news."

The table had never been so gleaming as when Anna finally stopped polishing half an hour later. By that time, Mr. Cushing had closed his office door and made more phone calls. As she gathered up the polishing supplies, Mr. Cushing emerged from his office. "Anna, something's come up and I'm going to fly down to the Bay Area. If any calls come, refer them to the Los Altos number."

"All right," Anna said. "I'll only be here until five today."

He nodded. "I'll call in and listen to the messages. See you next week."

Ever conscientious, Anna completed all her work and even made a quick trip to the store for orange juice and a fresh carton of milk for Mr. Cushing to have on Monday morning. Then she collected her personal possessions and brought them to her car. She left her note of resignation on the kitchen table, propped up against the sugar bowl where he would be sure to see it.

She headed for the only place she could think to go: the Mathieson house. Ray had just been fired by Cushing and, from the brief conversation she'd overheard, it seemed that Ray knew something about the shenanigans going on with Cushing and the Pardinis' ranch. Maybe he or Terri would know how to discreetly contact Laura Jensen.

As Mr. Cushing had said, it was a small town. A small town in which a woman who came to the hospital with ghastly bruises on her body, and a lab test reporting blood in the urine indicating possible kidney damage, was someone Anna saw regularly at the grocery store, the hairdresser, the library. A small town in which that woman's husband was known to Anna (and others of Mexican descent) as a white man to avoid.

DAY TEN

OCTOBER 6, 1985

Terri, Late Saturday night & early Sunday morning

Terri stared in disbelief. "You expect me to forget everything, to act like nothing's happened?"

"No, but—I'm sorry. I shouldn't have asked you." He went into the room and closed the door.

She felt as if she were balancing on a precipice. She could react with anger: let the fury overwhelm her, tell him he had no right to expect her to be forgiving, let alone to act as if things were the same between them.

Or she could step outside herself and see a man torn by right and wrong, overcome by physical passion that he'd let himself turn into something he thought was love, who now realized he'd been wrong on so many levels and was afraid of losing everything that was important in his life.

She went to the bedroom door, knocked softly and entered.

He made love to her and somehow, the things that he did to her seemed more intimate than they ever had. Yet she sensed a distance in him and, unexpectedly, was swept by a strong sense of desolation and aloneness.

"Don't cry, Terri."

"I've been so afraid."

"I wouldn't leave you; not unless you wanted me to."

"If things had worked out with her—"

"Not even then." Her hands were in his hair, and he put his own hands over them. "I'd thought we could try and figure out a way to make it work. I didn't want to leave you. We're part of each other, Terri. We made babies together."

Terri knew then that she'd been wanting to hear him say, 'I've fallen in love with you all over again.' He didn't say it. He hadn't fallen back in love with her.

And she knew, too, that he was making love with her out of compassion, not out of desire. When they were younger, he'd craved her, grown dizzy with desire for her. Their love had changed and she knew it wasn't because of Arla; the change had been there already. That's what had made it possible for him to love Arla as he did.

When he fell asleep, she lay wide wake. She forced herself to look at things realistically and with brutal honesty.

He still loved Arla. The issue wasn't whether she accepted the situation; she had no choice. She had to accept it, because it existed. Her jealousy and anger wouldn't change it. Wishing it weren't so, trying to show Ray he was a selfish jerk, hoping for harm to her rival, making Ray feel guilty—those responses were irrelevant.

She thought about Arla in a way that she never had before. She couldn't blame her for being physically attracted to Ray. Possibly, Arla had not known at the beginning that he was married; she was new to town, didn't know everyone and their ancestors three deep. God only knows what Ray had told her. And if a married man was willing to risk his marriage, why blame the woman for assuming the marriage was on the rocks?

So, the mere fact that Arla had slept with Ray didn't prove she was selfish or uncaring.

The scale tipped the other way, in fact. Arla had given Joe and Stella the money to keep their ranch. She'd probably told Ray their romance was over just to spare him being stuck with her now that she'd been so damaged, or maybe even to spare Terri and the children. Arla was not self-centered, but was so generous that she was making a sacrifice of incredible magnitude at a time when most people would be wrapped in a cocoon of self-pity.

Terri got out of bed at four in the morning. It was well past, or well before, visiting hours, but she got dressed, left a note and quietly left the house. She drove to the hospital and found a bench outside the entrance.

She sat down to wait.

Stella, 6:00–7:30am

They drove to the ranch. Somehow it looked even worse today; in a week, the destruction itself had become dilapidated. Inside the foundation walls was a black soup of rainwater, charred wood, soot and ashes. The propane tanks had melted into the ground; new shoots were already coming up around the metal. Soil and ashes had washed into the pond, and broken branches and pine needles floated in the brackish water. The tops of some trees were scorched; others had burned all the way down. She suspected that the well had been contaminated.

Stella wandered away from the devastation and gazed to the south. Anna had said Cushing was furious upon learning that she and Joe had paid off the loan, but was still intent on his development project. Perhaps he figured that if he built over the Double-L and the lumber mill, squeezing Pardini

Ranch between two commercial developments, the zoning would be changed.

And it probably would be. Their property tax would become astronomical and they'd be forced to sell.

Joe came up behind her. He didn't say anything, and he didn't have to. She looked at him and knew that he had seen enough. Silently, they got into the pickup and headed down the highway to Elsie's.

This early on a Sunday, there were plenty of empty tables. Stella glanced over at the blackboard and laughed at today's wisdom:

> *Democracy* is two wolves and a lamb voting on what to have for dinner. *Liberty* is a well-armed lamb contesting the vote.

Roxanne gestured that the table choice was theirs, and met them with the coffee pot. "What are you doing here on a Sunday?" Joe asked.

"Wanda needed a day off," said Roxanne, filling their cups. "I think it's the first one she's had since the fire started. Just coffee, or are you having breakfast?"

"Breakfast," Stella replied emphatically, "and lots of it."

"You got it!" Roxanne laughed. She took their orders and paused before leaving the table. "Are you planning to visit Arla today?"

"Yes, later this morning," Stella answered.

"Carlos said she complained about the hospital food last night."

"That's a good sign."

"It is. So could I give you some food to bring her?"

Later, as they lingered over coffee, Roxanne brought a takeout bag. "Here you go. Corn chowder, fruit salad, and for dessert, blackberry pie. That's her favorite."

Joe asked, "How do Arla's spirits seem to you?"

Roxanne grimaced. "Good one day, bad the next."

"That's our impression, too."

"I wonder if she'll be able to ride," Stella said.

Roxanne nodded. "The doctor said yes, provided she has the will power, and so long as she rides a gentle horse."

'Consider this a gift,' she had said, handing Stella the check. *'I have way more than I need. Please don't say no; please give me the chance to do something good…'*

And suddenly, Stella knew at least one thing she and Joe could do for Arla, who had always loved Griselda, as gentle a horse as ever was.

She smiled across the table at Joe. His eyes told her he was thinking the same thing.

Arla, 6:30–7:30am

When Arla awoke Sunday morning, the sky was just beginning to lighten. She glanced out the tinted window and was surprised to see Terri standing on the patio, smoking a cigarette. The windows were darkly tinted, so Terri probably didn't know she had awakened.

Terri, Arla realized, was quite pretty. She had a much prettier face than Arla knew herself to have. And more than that: she had a kind and warm face. A face that reflected her character. Remembering all the things she had once thought about Terri, all her snobbish arrogance, she was so ashamed of herself she felt it physically.

She wondered why Terri was here this early in the morning. People were no longer keeping a vigil, not since she'd survived the initial crisis and operation. So it must be that Terri had finally come to talk about Ray.

I will have to simply lie here and take it. And not just

because I'm a captive audience. I have to listen to it, all of it, no matter what she says. I owe her that much.

She glanced down at herself, at her gaunt body, at the abrupt way the sheet dipped down and lay flat against the mattress. She fought to hold back everything she thought she'd already vanquished: horror at what had happened, terror of her future, anger at herself for her mistakes, regret for having taken her beauty and well-being for granted, and, most frightening of all, fear that no one would love her the way she was now.

She squeezed her eyes shut and reminded herself that she could not take back the past; that to regret her reality would make it worse; that she could either be bitter and self-pitying, or could do the right thing from now on.

The nurse came in to take her vitals and change the bag of fluids. Perhaps Terri saw movement inside the room; she dropped her cigarette into the sand ashtray, and a few minutes later stood hesitantly at the door.

"Hi. Is it too early to visit? I could come back later."

"No, it's not too early. Come in."

Terri stood at the end of the bed. "How are you today? Roxanne said you were having cramps in your back yesterday."

"Oh, they gave me something or other for that. When I get out of this place, I'll probably be a drug addict."

Terri smiled back, but tensely. She pulled one of the chairs close to the bed and sat down. "There's something I want to say to you."

"Terri, you don't have to. I've already told him it's over between us."

"That's what I'm here about."

"I've put you through so much. I know you probably can't forgive me, but I hope you'll forgive Ray."

"Arla, I've been waiting here since four-thirty to talk to you."

Arla was taken aback. "Four-thirty!"

"So, please, will you hear me out?"

Arla nodded. But for a few minutes, Terri didn't say anything. Then she said, "You're trying to spare Ray. You don't want him to feel obligated to stay with you because of what's happened to you."

It took Arla a few moments to recover from her confusion. "No, that's not it. I'm ashamed to admit this, but I was concerned only about myself."

Terri watched her closely, almost studied her, then shook her head. "I don't think so. I think you're concerned about everyone else *except* yourself. Like me and the kids. You think it would hurt us if you stayed with Ray."

"Yes, of course I do." Arla pulled her eyes from Terri's and looked down. "But that didn't stop me before, did it?"

"No, and it didn't stop Ray either," Terri said. Then she got up and went to the windows, gesturing grandly. "Will you look at that."

Arla gasped. "Blue sky!"

"For the first time in ten days."

"It's even bluer than I remembered."

For several minutes, they looked at the sky in comfortable silence. Arla felt something like peacefulness settling over her, and this made her realize that she had been tense with worry over the fire, even though it had already done its damage to her.

Terri returned to the chair beside Arla's bed. She started to speak, then stopped, as if collecting herself. Arla waited apprehensively.

Terri stared at her intently for a few moments, and finally spoke. "So, you told Ray you don't love him?"

Arla was shocked. How had Terri found out? Had Ray told her? Or had she simply put two and two together?

To her further surprise, Terri smiled. "I can't understand

how he went for that." Then she shook her head briefly, and said, "I'm handling this badly. I didn't come here to give you a hard time. I came to ask you to do one thing."

"Yes, what's that?"

"Tell Ray the truth."

Arla couldn't speak over the lump that suddenly filled her throat. Terri watched her, silent for a while, then drew the chair closer.

"I'm going to tell you something I never thought I could say to you. But I see now that I have to, so you'll know I really mean what I'm saying." She paused briefly. "Ray and I–" Terri's voice quavered for just a moment. "Ray and I love each other, but it's not the same kind of love we had ten years ago. But that's not your fault."

"But you love him?" Arla managed to say.

Terri nodded. "Yes, I do love him. What I want more than anything is for him to be happy. But he's miserable. This is breaking his heart." She reached over and set her hand on Arla's. "And it's breaking your heart, too. That's not what I want. Not for him, and not for you."

Arla opened her mouth to speak, but to her mortification what came out was a sob.

"Just love him, Arla," Terri said gently. "And let him love you."

Pete, Late Morning

When Pete Jensen drove his pickup down the Double-L Ranch road at half past eleven on Sunday, he was surprised to see Roxanne Tejada's old pickup and two other cars there. No sign of Laura's, but he knew PJ had smashed into it Friday night.

He cursed under his breath. He'd intended on catching her

unaware. And he'd expected her to be alone. He stuck the manila envelope containing the quitclaim deed in his belt. He might need both hands free.

He was halfway out of the pickup when, from behind him, someone blew a whistle. He turned around to see Roxanne Tejada emerging from the stables. The front door of the house opened; Ray Mathieson's wife stuck her head out briefly, then went back inside.

Laura appeared from the side of the house. She had on the apron she wore to work in the vegetable garden, and a straw hat to protect against the sun. She walked with her arms at her side, holding tools.

Pete put his hands on his hips and faced her. "What the hell's going on?"

"The police are being called right now," Laura said. "Get off this property. You're violating the restraining order."

"I've about had it, Laura. What do you think you're doing, having PJ sent to jail? I can't even get him bailed out until tomorrow morning. Now you listen to me. You're gonna get on the phone and call the D.A. and tell him you're not pressing charges. Jesus Christ, Laura, he's your kid!"

"This is your last chance, Pete. Get in your truck and go."

He laughed. "This is *my* ranch. I'm not going anywhere except inside the house. And you're going in with me, and you're going to sign the quitclaim like you should've done two months ago, the first time I told you to sign it." He grinned. "You remember?"

"Yes. I remember."

"Come on. Get in the house." He walked toward her.

Laura raised her right hand and pointed the tool toward him. But it wasn't pruners or a trowel. It was a revolver.

He froze mid-step. "What the hell?"

Laura dropped the spade and brought her left hand up to steady her aim. "Don't come any closer."

"Put down that gun before you hurt someone! It might be loaded!"

"It *is* loaded. I loaded it myself, with hollow point bullets." She cocked the hammer with her thumb.

Jesus Christ. If she accidentally pulled the trigger … Sweat broke out in pinpricks all across his scalp. "You're in no condition to be walking around with a gun."

She just stood there with her feet spread slightly and her shoulders squared, pointing the revolver at him. A target shooter's stance. Okay, but that didn't mean she'd actually shoot. Not Laura, no way. He took a decisive step toward her.

The gun boomed and a bullet whanged against a rock less than ten feet to his left. "God damn it!" he shouted.

"That's the warning shot," Laura said.

"Put down that gun!"

"You only get one, Pete."

She cocked the hammer again. Her finger was on the trigger. She wasn't even trembling; she stood there steady and calm, aiming the revolver at his chest.

You come to know someone so well after thirty-five years. For a moment, Pete thought he'd imagined that slight smile. Then he knew he hadn't. And he knew that no one else had seen it, and that even if anyone had, they wouldn't know what it meant. It meant, 'Go ahead, come closer.'

Slowly, carefully, Pete raised his hands. "Okay. I'm leaving. Roxanne, you still there? You hear me? I'm going to turn around and walk back to my pickup."

"No, Pete," Laura said. "Stay right where you are."

And he stood there in the sun, held at gunpoint by his own wife, until a sheriff's cruiser came skidding down the road in a flurry of dust and flashing lights.

Stella, Late Morning

Griselda closed her eyes as Stella brushed her; she loved nothing so much as a good brushing. The rain had matted her coat, but also cleaned it, and her black coat glistened. As Stella brushed her forelock, Griselda nickered and closed her eyes. Stella buried her face in Griselda's heavy mane and murmured, "How could we even have considered it?"

And just like that, an idea came to her. Her best ideas, she reflected, always seemed to come when she was with a horse.

"Joe," she said, "I have an idea."

"Uh oh. I believe I am hearing alarm bells, Stellaskaya."

"For once, Joe, you are." She brought the stool to him. "And you'd better sit down."

She sat too, on the hay bale, with her back against a stall.

"I've thought of a way we could make sure the land would stay as it is now. We'd still have the same money problems we have now, but we'd keep the land safe. We wouldn't have to worry about losing it to rezoning or some other disaster. We'd keep it from the golf course builders forever."

"I'm all ears."

"Suppose it means we put ourselves out of reach of that $600,000, irrevocably? Suppose it means we could *never* change our minds?" She paused. "What if the only way to protect the land also meant it wouldn't be ours anymore?"

"Tell me your idea," he said patiently.

Stella took a deep breath and plunged. "We could give it away. We could keep ten or twenty acres, but for the rest, we could set up a public land trust and turn the ranch into a nature preserve."

He began to smile. She rushed on. "We'll always be 'land poor.' Ten acres or a thousand, what's the difference? We aren't ranchers, we don't need a thousand acres."

"No, we don't."

"It's the land we care about, not money. It's the land we're fighting for. If what we cared about was money, we would have taken that money for the ranch three years ago."

"Yes, and it was a lot more money then, too." Joe's dark skin crinkled at the corners of his eyes. He rose from the stool and pulled her into his arms. "Stella, you're ten years younger than me. One day you'll be alone. Money makes old age much more endurable. It wouldn't be wise to reject it without careful consideration."

"Why would I want to endure old age if I've sold out everything I've spent my life believing in and loving, and defending from harm?" She spoke passionately. "Joe, I want to share our love for this land with people who look at a tree and see a tree, and don't calculate board feet and envision stacks of two-by-fours."

He tipped her chin up and kissed her gently. "I believe you're referring to the same people who don't look at a meadow and envision a golf course."

"The very ones."

His kiss this time was a long one. And then he held her against him and said, "Thank you, dearest."

"For coming up with a plan to give away half a million dollars?" Stella was half-laughing and half-crying.

"Exactly."

Law Offices of Webster Hastings, Early Afternoon

"You'd better start by telling me why you went up there, Pete."

"She called me up yesterday and told me I could go there between noon and two today to get the equipment. She said she'd leave before noon. She said she was giving me notice, so I wouldn't go there on ranch business while she was there."

Webster Hastings turned his pen around in his hand. "She gave you notice so you wouldn't violate the restraining order inadvertently, and you proceeded to violate it intentionally."

"The bitch is divorcing me! She had PJ arrested the other night! And what's she do, but fire a shot that barely missed me, and *she* calls the cops on *me*! My own cousin—*our* cousin— came out there and told me I had to leave!"

"That's right." Webb nodded. "The sooner you accept the situation, the better."

"I'm not accepting a goddamned thing!" Pete jumped up from the wooden chair, his heels thunking on the floor. He stood leaning over the desk. "You can tell her bitch lawyer I'm not signing any agreement, and she better get her ass off my ranch! She promised me she'd sign it over to me! She said if I didn't—if we didn't have a fight for six months, she'd sign it over."

"That," Webb said drily, "would be the wrong argument to raise in court."

Pete launched into another denunciation of Laura. Webster Hastings listened dispassionately. When Pete stopped, he said, "Are you finished?"

Pete frowned.

"You've had your say, Pete. Now sit down while I have mine."

Pete stood with his hands resting on the back of the chair.

"Fine, stand. But either you listen to what I'm about to say, or walk out right now and get yourself another lawyer."

Pete knew he'd never get another lawyer at the rates he was paying Webb, whose rates were plenty high enough. And being as Webb was family—and on the Jensen side—Pete felt freer to say things than he would have felt with some stranger.

"I'm listening," he said.

"The facts are these. One. Laura's been a housewife for thirty-five years. She dropped out of high school to marry you. She's not a young college-educated career woman who could be expected to earn a living outside the home. In other words, Pete, she's one of the small class of women in California still entitled to alimony."

"Alimony!" Pete sputtered.

"Two. She has photographs and medical records from July of this year, showing substantial physical abuse at your hands, and she alleges that you have abused her for over thirty years."

"Hell, anyone could claim they got beat up ten years ago," Pete scoffed. "Where's the proof?"

"The whole town's gossiped about it for years."

"Gossip's not evidence," Pete said hotly.

"In any event, evidence of the recent abuse was sufficient, regardless of whether it can be proven to have occurred on any prior occasion. It was enough to convince a judge to issue a restraining order against you, which you violated today. You're lucky we aren't talking over a phone with plexiglass between us."

"Stick wouldn't arrest me."

"Oh yes, he would. And if you do it again, he will. Times have changed, Pete. The days are gone when a man could do just about anything to his wife behind closed doors. Stick's set to retire. You think he wants his legacy to be as the sheriff who allowed a wife-beater to violate a court order to keep away from the victim?"

Webster Hastings didn't wait for an answer to the rhetorical question. He rested his arms on his desk and leaned toward Pete. "I'll tell you something else. If you were to go back there and she were to shoot you, she'd have a pretty damned good defense: she had no choice, because the sheriff didn't arrest you the last time you violated that court order. So. Not only will Stick arrest you if you violate that order again, but you damned well better hope he does.

"Three. The ranch was bought with Laura's money. In her papers she included an article from the *Piñon County Register* of April 1959, which quotes you as saying the two of you used Laura's inheritance to buy the land, and that Double-L means 'Laura's Legacy.' Besides which, it's been in her name the entire twenty-six years."

"Christ, Webb, that's for tax reasons."

"So you say."

"You don't believe me?"

"Pete, *I'm* not the one you have to convince." Webster Hastings put his reading glasses on and looked down at the papers spread across his desk. "Four. The combined net worth of you and Laura includes two ranches, each containing living quarters; numerous stocks and certificates, savings accounts and other moneys, totaling approximately $200,000; ranch stock consisting of approximately 250 head of Hereford-Angus cattle and five quarter horses; and a real estate business with an annual income of ten to twenty thousand a year. In addition, there are personal properties, such as vehicles and ranch equipment, worth, according to your tax returns for the year 1984, over $80,000."

"Christ," Pete scoffed. "They wouldn't let us take any more depreciation than that. Hell, I'd be lucky to get twenty-five grand if I sold every—"

"The point is, you are a wealthy man. The settlement Laura's offering is reasonable. In fact, if Laura was my client, we'd be suing for both ranches and all the property, and we'd have a damned good chance of getting it all, given the abuse situation and the long marriage." Webb shook his head. "You're getting off easy. You'll have plenty of property left. Give her what she's asking for, and be damned glad that's all she's asking for."

"I'd have to liquidate all the stocks and savings to come up with a hundred seventy-five thousand bucks," Pete said.

"And you'll still have money left. Enough," Webb grinned, "to pay my fee. You'll still have your real estate business and the west county ranch, and all the stock except Kit's horse."

"And what about custody? I don't even get to share custody of my kid?"

"If you want custody, you'd better mention Kit at the beginning of any conversation about the divorce, not as the last item on a long list." Webb paused. "Pete, her lawyer tells me that one's not negotiable. Did something happen that I should know about?"

"She sneaked out with some Mexican kid behind my back. I slapped her, not hard, and told her if she did it any more I'd get rid of her horse. What's the matter with that? A father can't even tell his own daughter who she can date anymore?"

"Who's the boy?"

"That Tejada kid, from Pine Gap."

"He's still in high school? Under eighteen?"

"I guess, yeah."

"Any juvenile delinquency? He ever been in trouble?"

"Look, I don't give a damn if he's on the honor roll and gets a gold star from his teacher every week. I don't want my daughter getting porked by a goddamned spic."

Webb closed his eyes and rubbed his temples. "Pete—"

"Yeah, yeah, you don't have to tell me: I can't say that in public."

"Let me ask you something. Do you really want joint custody?"

"I gotta pay child support, then I want to say how the kid's raised."

"So the answer is no. And in any event, since Kit's—what, fourteen? fifteen?—her opinion is what counts the most in court. If she doesn't want to see you, you don't even get visitation. Now as to Cindy, she's eighteen, so custody isn't an issue, but part of the settlement would be that you continue to pay for her tuition and living expenses for the next four years. The same thing for Kit, when she turns eighteen. It will be capped at ten thousand a year; you won't have to pay for Stanford. This isn't unreasonable and, given your income and assets, any family court judge would order it."

"If she's getting almost two hundred grand, why shouldn't she pay for that?"

"You're getting the larger portion of the estate under this settlement, plus you'll have income and Laura won't. Pete, she's not even asking for alimony." The lawyer took off his reading glasses. "My advice is that you sign this agreement now, before she has time to reconsider and withdraw the offer, and we have to fight it out in court. Trust me, you do not want to go to court with this case."

"And what about her pulling a gun on me?"

"Pete, you violated that restraining order. PJ violated the restraining order. You both—how can I put this?" Webb paused, looked up at the ceiling, shrugged. "Hell, only one way to say it. You fucked up."

"But—"

"Now I'm going to tell you something, and I'm only going to tell you once." Webster Hastings folded his arms on the top of his desk and leaned toward Pete. "Never again put yourself in a spot where Laura can claim you harmed or tried to harm her. If you see her on Main Street, turn around and go the other way. Never be in a situation where you're alone with her. Same applies to Kit, and even to the Tejada kid. If you ever hear that something happened to Kit or the Tejada kid or Laura, I don't care if all it is is one of them had a car accident 500 miles away, first thing you do is come to me and we'll find witnesses who can place you somewhere else at the time of the accident. And Pete, I don't want to have to find witnesses who don't exist. You get me? Keep off the ranch and stay away from these people."

Pete reached for his hat. "All right. But I still don't think it's right she's walking around with a loaded gun."

"That's one more reason to stay away from her. A long way away. Now," and Webb stood too, "I'll arrange to get that financial report from your tax accountant first thing tomorrow. And once we have that, you'll realize you can afford to sign this agreement." He tapped the folder. "In fact, you'll realize you can't afford not to sign it."

Ray, Afternoon

Ray picked up the kids from his mother's house and drove home, chiding himself for feeling rejected and alone.

He was going to have to get over it. It wasn't right to inflict the kids with what he was feeling. Let alone Terri. You can get used to anything, he told himself. It just takes time. Sometimes a long time, like Terri said. So, you have to keep busy. Not think about it. Not think about her.

Carlos and Kit were in the kitchen when he got home. Ray hung out with them for a while, then went out to the garage. May as well get started cleaning and organizing his tools. If he couldn't start his own business right away, which was a strong possibility, he'd have to get a job. Tomorrow, he'd call the union and sign up for work.

"Ray, are you out here?" It was Kit.

"Yeah, come on in."

"There's a phone call for you."

He started toward the house.

"It's Arla," Kit said. "She said she tried earlier, but I guess no one was here, and–"

But Ray was already running past her, to the phone.

He tried to sound calm and neutral. "Arla?"

"Hello, Ray," she said. "I'm calling because I—" And all at once her voice broke. "I'm sorry, Ray. I'm so sorry. It wasn't true, what I told you the other day."

"Ah, baby. I know it wasn't."

"I was trying to protect you. I thought it would be best for everyone—you and Terri, and your children—if I left you. But I was wrong, and I hurt you."

"So if what you said wasn't true, then what *is* true?"

"Come here and hold me, and I'll say it then, Ray. I'll say it so much you'll beg me to stop."

"No," he said. "I'll beg you to never stop."

THE MOPUP

Nature has given the state many wakeup calls ... Yet the response is always the same: hunker down all the more, to protect the property investments that form the cornerstone of the American dream.

—William Fulton, "Home, Sweet Home: Pursuing Dreams in a Land of Fire", New York Times, Sunday November 2, 2003

It's called the American dream because you have to be asleep to believe it.

—George Carlin

Monday, October 7

On Monday morning Laura hung up the phone in the kitchen and turned to Terri, who waited expectantly. "He signed it. A certified check will be delivered to my lawyer's office before Friday."

Hiram Cushing worked from home on Monday, irritated that Anna Perez had quit without notice. The agency promised to have a woman there by the following morning, but in the meantime he was forced to make his own coffee.

Shortly afterward, the phone rang. It was Pete Jensen and the news he imparted removed any trace of a smile from Cushing's face.

Tuesday, October 8

"I suppose it sounds ridiculous," Laura said.

"On the contrary. It sounds wonderful."

"You could be throwing money away."

"I could lose it." Arla nodded. "But the amount you're talking about, even if I lost it all, it wouldn't break me."

"Would it mean you couldn't live comfortably? It may cost you quite a bit more to be comfortable now."

"Oh, I know it will!" Arla said. "I've already been looking into that. But don't worry, Laura. I'll be fine. My share of the divorce settlement with Steve was more than generous. I could live comfortably on just the dividends. And it's not like I earned that money from working for fifty years. So please," Arla smiled, "let me make myself useful."

When Roxanne got her mail on Tuesday, she had a letter from the corporate office of Slidell-Pacific Lumber and Paper Company in Coos Bay, Oregon. The letter informed her that the previous offer made by the company to purchase her house for $30,000 was hereby withdrawn.

Thursday, October 10

At 9:00am in the Superior Court of Piñon County, the clerk called the matter of The People of the State of California versus Jerry Frye, which was on calendar for entry of the defendant's plea.

The public defender had no choice but to tell the court that his client was not present, and that he had neither seen nor heard from him since the day he'd been released from custody on bail.

Judge Ellis issued a bench warrant and called the next case.

Laura drove to Sacramento Thursday morning to pick up the settlement check at her lawyer's office. She then went directly to a branch of her bank and had a certified check issued in the amount of $100,000.

She arrived back to Camargo just in time for the meeting she had called with Stella and Joe. They met in the kitchen of the Mathieson house. Laura handed an envelope to Stella. "This is for you. Please don't open it until later. And it has nothing to do with the reason I asked to talk with you, which is to make a business proposition."

Friday, October 11

In her room, Arla set down the *Piñon County Register* and sat thinking for a while. She picked up the telephone, called information and got the number of the lawyer that the article said was representing the Piñon County heirs to the Thelen estate. She identified herself and pleasantries were exchanged. "How can I help you?" the lawyer asked.

"I'm calling about the house on Madison Avenue that's about to be demolished."

"Ah, the Thelen property."

"Yes."

"You're interested in buying it?" the lawyer said. He sounded skeptical.

"I might be, but I'd like to have it inspected first. I'm wondering if that's possible."

"Sure, I can arrange that. You got someone who can do it for you?"

"Yes, I think so. How much notice would you need?"

"Heck, just call my office and come get the key. Anytime."

"Thank you. I'll be in touch within a day or so."

"I should warn you, that house isn't in good condition. It's been neglected ever since old Doc Thelen died."

"The paper said he died in 1976."

"That's right. And he hadn't been taking very good care of the place for a good five, ten years before that. So, if you're thinking this is a nice well-preserved house you can just patch up here and there, I wouldn't want you to waste your time and money on an inspection."

"I know it's going to need work. I just want to know how much. I'm primarily concerned about the foundation, the stability of the lot, that sort of thing."

"Well, now." The lawyer sounded relieved. "We had an

inspection done ourselves, about a year back. They built these old houses to last. The first thing they did in 1898, even before they put the foundation in, was build an underground retaining wall around the whole lot. So the ground's not going anywhere and the foundation, when we had it inspected, was almost like new. Heck, they built that house with heart of redwood, so it doesn't even have termites."

Arla sank back in her wheelchair and smiled in relief.

"But you'll want your own guy to tell you that. You just call me up when you want him to go in. Better get to it soon, though. Time's running out."

"Very soon," Arla promised.

Friday afternoon, Joe drove his loaded horse trailer down the road into the Double-L Ranch. Kit and Carlos were in the pickup with him. They began offloading Tabasco, Tippy and Griselda.

In the room upstairs, Stella and Laura arranged furniture. They shoved and pulled at the chairs, the bureau, and the new bed.

Finally, they sat on the sunny ledge to rest. Then Laura said, "Oh, I almost forgot. Wait right here." She went out and returned a few moments later, carrying a flat package. "This is for you."

Stella unwrapped it. Inside, behind protective cellophane, were three index cards, so old they'd yellowed. They were spattered with a bit of flour here, a spot of tomato paste there. One was a recipe for *bugie*; another for *frutta candita*. The third was for 'Sunday gravy' and at the bottom, Nonna had written, 'Stella's favorite.'

"She wrote them for me when I got married," Laura said. Stella looked up, her eyes brimming. She could not speak.

After leaving the hospital late that afternoon, Ray walked to Mary O'Malley's house and asked Mary if she knew anyone who was an expert on old MiWok burial grounds in Piñon County. Mary did: her friend Jessie, who lived at the Rancheria. "Could you ask her if she can meet with me anytime after Monday?" Ray asked. Monday he would be coordinating a building inspection in Camargo.

Mary telephoned Jessie and set up an appointment for Tuesday afternoon. She ended the call and turned to Ray. "How bad is this going to be?"

"It might turn out to be nothing."

"And if it doesn't turn out to be nothing?"

"Then," Ray said, "it's gonna be pretty bad."

Terri felt oddly restless. She walked around the backyard, picking at the few weeds that had sprouted. She sat on one of the folding chairs for a while, then got up and was just about to wipe down the patio furniture when she shook her head, muttered to herself, and went inside.

She picked up the phone and dialed a familiar number. "Could I come see you?"

"Yes," Laura said at once.

"Not just as a friend. What I mean is, the way I feel, it's…" Her courage faltered and the words seemed to stick in her throat.

"Oh, Terri. I've been waiting for you," Laura said.

Epilogue

THE NEXT FIVE YEARS

Buying and selling California, a very old custom, will continue.

—W.W. Robinson, Land in California *(Berkeley: University of California Press, 1948) p. 211*

After the forest fire, Piñon County dropped into an economic slump. Slidell-Pacific Lumber Mill closed permanently. The business failure of Eagle Construction meant that not only were fifty-eight construction workers and office staff out of work, but that High Mountain Mall sat forlorn and half-complete. The frames that had been built for eighty of the planned 100 houses on Gennessee Mine Road had burned down in the Jackrabbit Fire. Throughout 1986 and 1987, no other developers stepped in to finish those projects. The bankruptcy of Hiram Cushing invalidated his agreement with Slidell-Pacific Lumber and Paper Company. The company was in no hurry to sell either the mill property or Pine Gap. The company could well afford to gamble that Piñon County would soon join the real estate boom reverberating from the Silicon Valley through the rest of northern California.

The MiWok Tribal Council, upon hearing from Ray Mathieson about his destruction of human remains at Buckeye Flat, notified the Native American Heritage Commission. The Commission looked into the matter and determined that the bones had probably not been of a MiWok, since the closest ancestral burial ground had been one mile to the north-east. For that reason, and because Ray himself had brought the matter to everyone's attention, he was not prosecuted.

The Tribal Council proposed to excavate and verify that no MiWok remains were buried at the site. Since High Mountain Mall had been abandoned, there were no objections. Ray helped with the excavation. No more bones were discovered.

The mystery remained unsolved.

Pete and PJ moved into the west county ranchhouse and took over the cattle operation.

After negotiations between the district attorney's office and Webb Hastings, PJ Jensen's criminal case was resolved on the morning of the preliminary hearing. His driver's license was suspended until 1988. All the felony charges were dropped and PJ pleaded guilty to several misdemeanors. He was sentenced to community service (which he served by volunteering at the annual rodeo) and one year in the county jail, suspended upon PJ completing three years of probation.

When Arla got out of the hospital, she rented a small house just outside downtown Camargo. Ray made alterations to accommodate her wheelchair.

She went to physical therapy every day and learned to get around adeptly on a prosthetic. What she missed most was not so much the physical act of running, but the mental relaxation of it and the time she had spent outdoors. The physical therapist agreed that she could try riding a horse. She practiced in the corral at the Double-L and was surprised at how comfortable she felt on Griselda's back. Before long she was confident enough to take long rides into the mountains, usually with Kit.

Despite the economic slump in Piñon County, Laura Jensen and the Pardinis forged ahead with their plans. With Arla's financial backing, they bought the Thelen house and contracted with Ray Mathieson to renovate it.

Ray and Terri sold their Donner Lake cabin and boat and used the money to start Ray's business, a partnership with two of his former coworkers from Eagle Construction, Billy and Eddie. What with the renovation of the Thelen house and improvements to the ranch house at the Double-L, the business got off the ground. Within a few years it was specializing in Victorian restorations. That meant that much of their work was outside Piñon County, in other Mother Lode towns where Victorians were being turned into restaurants, bed and breakfasts, or law offices.

When Hiram Cushing sought bankruptcy protection, he and his wife declared their house in Los Altos Hills as their primary residence. His other houses, including the one on the top of the highest hill in Camargo, were put out to bid in late 1986. The winning bid on the Camargo house was submitted by Arla Stinson. She and Ray moved into the house early in 1987.

In January of 1988, during one of the best ski seasons in recent memory, Octavia's Restaurant opened in a beautifully restored Victorian on Madison Avenue in downtown Camargo.

Word of mouth and rave reviews in newspapers throughout northern California had the expected effect, and Octavia's was soon overwhelmed with customers. Stella knew she would have gone crazy with the frantic efforts to handle staff expansion and turnover, unexpected shorting of food and wine orders, equipment breakdowns, all of it, but Laura's serenity in the face of disaster always won the day.

Shortly after Octavia's opened, Roxanne Tejada took over coordination of the wait staff, and Anna Perez was hired to manage inventory and purchasing – everything from flowers to flour, from delivery of clean linen to replacing broken dishes.

That took a huge burden from Stella and Laura, allowing them to concentrate on the part of the business they loved best, the food.

Whenever possible, Octavia's used produce, herbs, eggs, and chicken raised on the Double-L. That was Joe's responsibility: farming.

The bread was made from sourdough starter that had come from Nonna; Stella's starter had burned up in the fire, but Laura's had survived.

In early 1988 a building boom hit Piñon County. Pete Jensen accepted an offer for his west county ranch. Oakwood Estates came into being, 2000 houses on just over 800 acres.

The people who bought houses in Oakwood Estates added their voices to the age-old clamor for a by-pass that would take them around, instead of through, Camargo. For years the by-pass had been strenuously opposed by downtown merchants, but at last the battle was lost. By-pass construction began in 1989.

Burning Desires: The Secret History of a California Town was published late in 1987. Mary lived long enough to see the book nominated for an award for historical writing, but not long enough to see *Burning Desires* spend four weeks on the New York Times bestseller list in spring of 1988.

To the surprise of both Kit and Carlos, Mary's will included a provision that each of them receive a one-eighth share of the proceeds from the book. This was not a huge sum, but it was substantial enough to save Carlos from having to take out a student loan to get through his last two years at U.C. Davis.

After Pete Jensen received six million dollars for the west county ranch, he bought a duplex. He lived in one side, PJ in the other. He then went on a spending spree and bought a condo at Lake Tahoe, a fishing boat, 49ers' seasons tickets, a Winnebago, and new pickups for himself and PJ, whose driver's license had just been restored.

PJ had his new pickup less than four months before he drove it into a utility pole, plunging the northern half of Camargo into a six-hour power outage. The pickup was totaled. PJ was, at the time, in the last month of probation; his lawyer managed to keep him from being sent to county jail to serve out his suspended sentence. He didn't even try to keep PJ from another driver's license suspension.

A week later, Pete went to Webb's office and made out a new will. He left his entire estate to his daughter Cindy except for a stipend for PJ, with instructions that it be administered by the lawyer. He made sure that the will included an express statement that he was intentionally leaving nothing to his daughter Katherine or any issue of hers, or to his ex-wife Laura.

Pete went back to selling real estate. It was a good time to be in the real estate business in Piñon County.

Wanda finally sold her café. Over the objections of preservationists, the building was taken down to make room for a Blockbuster Video and additional High Mountain Mall parking.

By 1990, the population of Piñon County had doubled. Extensive acreage in west county, as well as most of the privately owned land between Camargo and Conifer Falls, was covered with shopping centers, medical office parks, and housing developments. Several new golf courses were constructed in west county.

The winter after the Jackrabbit Fire was an unusually wet one, causing mudslides throughout Higuera National Forest.

In the summer of 1989, during the ongoing clean-up project, Mark Willits, who was operating a bulldozer, struck hard metal. He and his coworkers thought they had simply found an abandoned car. Mark climbed off his bulldozer and helped the other men dig out the mud. As the car came clear, Mark peered inside. His coworkers were astonished when he screamed and backed away so fast that he tripped and tumbled halfway down the hill.

The authorities were notified. Tests established the body to be that of Jerry Frye, who had not been seen for nearly four years, and for whom a bench warrant was still outstanding. At first it was presumed that he had died in a car accident, but the autopsy established that he had been shot in the head. Suicide was ruled out since no gun had been found in the car. The police report listed the probable cause of death as murder, but it was not possible to pin down the date of death. The case was put into the sheriff department's open-but-inactive file.

For the first year after the fire, Joe and Stella lived on the Double-L with Kit and Laura. Their intention was to eventually build a house on their ten-acre ranch. But the living arrangement suited everyone so well that it was made permanent.

Joe and Stella deeded the last ten acres of Pardini Ranch to the public land trust.

Carlos got his bachelor's degree from U.C. Davis in spring of 1990, and planned to return for graduate school in the veterinary program. Kit had spent one year at Davis. One was enough. She moved back to the ranch, where she worked with Joe on the farm, took care of the horses, and helped out at Octavia's as needed. Tuesday and Thursday nights were always busy; fried chicken was served Tuesdays, and Thursday was ravioli night.

She worked hard and rode often. She read voraciously. She analyzed soil composition and experimented with the effects of different minerals on the taste of vegetables. She visited ranches in Marin County to find out what was being done to raise cattle humanely and how to be certified organic, and made plans to start a small herd. She and Joe had begun to explore the idea of growing grapes and making wine.

The way Mom and Terri looked at each other, the way Mom looked forward to Saturday nights, the way they didn't emerge from Mom's room until noon on Sunday, brought tears of happiness to her eyes.

She wished that Mom had not had to wait so long for happiness. But when she said as much, Laura smiled and said that that was why she so deeply treasured it.

By the end of the 1980s, the two fastest growing industries in California were high tech and what was euphemistically referred to as "corrections."

Not so many years earlier, communities had protested loud and long at the suggestion that a prison be located in their midst. But times had changed, and all over California, towns clamored for the privilege of hosting one of the many new prisons being built. Some Californians referred to prisons as "gray gold."

The Piñon County supervisors added their voices to the clamor and were rewarded. Early in 1987, the State of California purchased the old Slidell-Pacific lumber mill site and nearby property, including the town of Pine Gap.

The prison opened for business in mid-1989. Motorists on the Higuera Highway glimpsed gun towers poking up from behind the rise. At night, drivers on the by-pass could see the prison's bright lights from five miles away.

The state finally did replace the sign to Pine Gap with one that stated simply:

Pine Gap State Prison
   1/2 mile

The population and elevation were not listed. A second sign sternly commanded: "Do not pick up hitchhikers."

A few miles farther up the Higuera Highway, another road sign had been put up. This one alerted travelers to Fiddleneck Nature Preserve.

Fiddleneck Preserve had opened to the public in 1986. In the wet spring after the fire, wildflowers proliferated, and word circulated among nature photographers, to whom the preserve became a favorite spring shooting site. The Higuera paintbrush, which development had made extinct everywhere else, flourished in the meadow beside Cougar Creek.

Next door to the Fiddleneck Preserve, at the Double-L, deer were frequent visitors. That necessitated fencing the three-acre garden in which Joe and Kit grew the herbs and produce for Octavia's. At the gate to the garden, a welcome basket overflowed with rosemary. The basket rested inside a curious container: a warped Dutch oven.

Over the arched gate was a hand-painted sign that read: "Pardini Greens."

Author's Note - August 2024

The fictional Jackrabbit Fire reflects the actual situation in 1985, when wildland fires began to explode in size and frequency. In a three-week period that summer, fires throughout California burned more than 453,000 acres (over twice the combined size of all five boroughs of New York City). Five people were killed and hundreds of homes destroyed. Such conflagrations were unusual that early in fire season.

Not anymore. "Fire season" now lasts all year and catastrophic fires are the norm.

Since 1985, California's population has grown by 13 million. Sixty years of misguided Forest Service policies turned forests into tinderboxes of dead trees, thick brush, and non-native flammable trees and shrubs, while the forest floors are deep in combustible debris. Nevertheless, half of the houses built in the state since then abut wildlands. Miles of electric power lines—the cause of many fires—have been erected. Between 1985 and 2023, the number of year-round firefighters employed by Cal Fire (formerly the CDF) more than quadrupled. Nineteen of the twenty largest fires in recorded California history have occurred since 2000, ten of them between 2020 and 2024. Entire communities have burned to the ground, and hundreds of people have died, along with countless animals.

The same dire situation exists throughout the western United States and even in Canada.

Over eons, the natural landscapes of North America's west evolved with fire. Acting from concern for the future rather than the profit motive, native people recognized fire's benefits and learned to work with it in ways that prevented conflagrations. It's essential that planners and politicians do so, too, and quickly. Because we now live in what fire scientist Stephen J. Pyne has named the Pyrocene Era—The Age of Fire.

Acknowledgments

With deepest appreciation to close friends whose encouragement and support—on so many levels—never flagged: Larry Weissman, Annette Caruso, Kern Weissman, Olga Weissman, and Charlene Sawl.

With many thanks to other critical readers: Matthew Freitas, Lisa Roth, Connie Olejniczak, Judy Grant, and the late Anne Williams.

With fervent gratitude to Bloodhound Books, especially Betsy Reavley for appreciating this novel and for her willingness to take risks on me and other first-time authors; Rachel Tyrer, editor extraordinaire; and Tara Lyons and the many others who helped bring the book to fruition.

And finally, I must acknowledge the contributions of my two cats, Swann and Odette, who warmed my lap during rewrites, patiently (and frequently) reminded me that their dinner took precedence over research, and showed a disdain for keyboards that kept me grounded.

About the Author

Shirley Freitas is a sixth-generation Northern Californian descended from gold rush pioneers. She was a political activist in the San Francisco Bay Area for decades, and wrote for community and feminist periodicals and California historical journals. The Fire Bell Strikes at Midnight is her first published novel. In 2015 she moved to upstate New York and created a website, www.necessarystorms.com, that examines episodes in recent U.S. history with the unique insights and unusual perspectives acquired from a lifetime of political struggles. Her author website is www.shirleyfreitas.com.

www.ingramcontent.com/pod-product-compliance
Lightning Source LLC
Chambersburg PA
CBHW050945210726
48287CB00004B/1140